DOCTOR WHO – THE NEW ADVENTURES

Also available:

THE NEW

DOCTOR WHO

ADVENTURES

SANCTUARY

David A. McIntee

First published in Great Britain in 1995 by
Doctor Who Books
an imprint of Virgin Publishing Ltd
332 Ladbroke Grove
London W10 5AH

Cover illustration by Peter Elson

ISBN 0 426 20439 5

Phototypeset by Intype, London
Printed and bound in Great Britain by Cox & Wyman Ltd,
Reading, Berks

Introduction

Like the Spanish Inquisition, I bet none of you expected to see me back this soon – (and that's the only use of that joke you'll see in this book). Before I get going, a word of warning: though I hope this book carries the atmosphere of the period in which it's set, being a work of fiction there is much in the way of detail here which is – to coin a phrase – apocryphal, or at least wildly inaccurate. I mention this so that history students among you will remember to look up a proper textbook before quoting anything in exams or the like... I also mention it so that I can point out that such changes are deliberate – I paid close attention to many reference works, most notably Lacroix's multi-volume *Of the Middle Ages* series – and not made through ignorance.

At least, that's my catch-all story and I'm sticking to it.

Acknowledgements, thanks and so on are due to: all the usual suspects at Virgin; Stirling District Library's reference department (see, I told you you'd get them back); Daniel Blythe; Paul Cornell, for the freedom to mess around with Bernice's past; Peter Elson for the evocative cover; and – for advice on mysteries – not forgetting the noted crime writer J. B. Fletcher ... And you can probably thank Brian Croucher for the haggis line, if you really want to.

Oh, one further thing: you may note that some words used here should be taken a little more seriously than usual. For example, despite the jokey Hollywood-ish use of it, a varlet was originally an undisciplined looter who scavenged the battlefield; while a bourgeois was simply someone who had bought their way up the feudal ladder to become, directly or indirectly, a vassal of the king rather than some local baron (and not just upper classes – if we were to apply this distinction today then the likes of council road-sweepers who happen to live in towns would be accurately classed as such, for example!) There are others, but you'll know them when you find them.

Now, let me tell you of the days of high adventure . . .

> *Haste me to know it; that I, with wings as swift*
> *As meditation, or the thoughts of love,*
> *May sweep to my revenge . . .*
>
> Hamlet

> *Hot blood, hot thoughts, and hot deeds?*
> *Why, they are vipers:*
> *Is love a generation of vipers?*
>
> Troilus and Cressida

Prologue

A primitive world, unblemished by the speckled glow of artificial lighting, seemed to be nothing else but a shadowy hole in the island galaxy that spun silently in the sea of night.

Far below, where the edge of night lay in wait for the Earth, the granite sky seemed to lean over the land as if it were tilted; propped up by leaning on the rim of the world beyond the horizon.

His head bowed over his horse's fluttering mane as if he were ducking under the oppressive sky, a wearied messenger squinted his eyes against the chill wind as he was borne across the rolling countryside.

Ignoring the occasional labouring colon who toiled in the hillside muck, protected from the elements only by one-piece homespun tunics, the rider guided the foam-speckled horse through a small cutting and into a muddy depression that was bounded by shrub-encrusted rock outcrops. As he drew near to the small knot of men waiting therein, he reined in the horse, which almost seemed to be gasping for breath after its mad dash.

One of several knights, their Order unidentifiable – the woollen cloaks which were draped over their mail armour were simple and unadorned – came forward to take the horse's reins as the messenger dismounted. The remaining knights stayed back, their hands unobtrusively on their swords. The messenger, however, ignored them, moving straight towards three men who remained mounted at the edge of the depression. Their cloaks were of sharper colours, with a gold-coloured edging, and they wore fur-

1

trimmed caps. Their swords hung from finely tooled belts stubbed with gold.

The leader of the three leaned forward slightly, peering down at the messenger along his long nose, his silvering hair peeking raggedly out from under the fur edge of his cap. 'Are the tidings as we expected?' he asked.

'They are, my lord,' the messenger said with a respectful nod, the words tumbling out with ill-concealed excitement. 'The formal proclamation of death was made three days since.'

'Is there any suspicion over the death?'

'No more than usual. The poison was completely undetectable.'

'It certainly took long enough to seem natural,' the squarer-looking man on the left agreed sourly, his forked beard curling. 'Is there a successor?'

'None. Our sources say that the Cardinals are falling over themselves to stab each other in the back – not literally, I assume.'

'No,' the leader said, with a hint of a smile. 'That they can leave to us. Has d'Alsace been told of this yet?'

'No, my lord. I thought it best that you should learn the news first.'

'Quite correct.' The iron-haired leader drew out a small pouch from the purse that was attached to the right side of his belt, and tossed it to the messenger, who caught it deftly. The pouch jingled softly. 'You are proving yourself quite useful, young man. You know where to find d'Alsace?'

'I believe he is camped a dozen leagues to the south.'

'Precisely. Deliver your news to him also, then return to me at Beziers. I may well find some work for you.'

'Thank you, my lord,' the messenger stammered, his face flushed.

'Then why are you still here?'

The messenger opened his mouth as if to speak, then closed it again, and remounted his horse, retrieving the reins from the knight. With a final bashful look of thanks,

2

he led the horse up the damp slope and out of the shallow natural bowl.

The bearded man on the left, and a toadish man on the right, both looked quizzically at their leader. 'I thought we planned to kill him,' the toadish one protested finally. 'He knows too much.'

'I never waste opportunities. That young man has proved himself to be capable of following orders while still having initiative – a rare trait, and one not wisely made extinct.' The leader scratched his chin thoughtfully. 'If the Cardinals get into a cycle of mutual distrust and suspicion, it could be months before a successor is named.'

'Those self-serving leeches? With them, it could be a thousand years before they find someone upon whom the survivors can all agree.'

'An amusing thought, but I had a more practical length of time in mind.'

'Practical? For what possible purpose?'

'One that should have been fulfilled years ago,' the leader said, with a faraway look.

The others looked at each other in bewilderment, but before they could ask their compatriot any further questions, his horse was cantering towards the rim of the depression, and they had no alternative but to follow him into the grey murk of falling night.

Chapter 1

The lands ahead of Chretien d'Alsace and his party wore the rich but drab tones of encroaching winter, and Chretien himself could scent a faint sharpness in the air, the tang of it promising snow later.

He was regretting the trip out into the hilly countryside already; going by his companions' grumblings, they too would rather be under shelter of their cloistered seminary. The outriders had not yet returned to the main party, and Chretien thought in a surly way that they had probably found a barn in which to keep themselves warm.

The man who had persuaded them to ride this fool's errand guided his horse alongside Chretien's on the stony path. He was short and thickset, yet had a sallow aura of starvation and undernourishment about him. His gimlet eyes smouldered slightly with a passion Chretien envied as much as it unnerved him, as he pointed along the curve of the hillside they were traversing. 'The path forks here, your grace,' he informed Chretien. 'To the right, downhill, is a village where we may rest for the night. I instructed the outriders to find suitable accommodation for us.'

'My thanks. How far is it?'

'Ten minutes, perhaps. Certainly no more than fifteen.'

'Very well, pass the word along.'

The first light snowflakes were dissolving in the muddy street as the six fur-wrapped clerics dismounted in an ungainly manner, trying to do so without loosening their thick travelling cloaks in the slightest. The porters, who were on foot, leaned against a fence, oblivious to the damp cold. Two of the outriders, mail coifs glistening damply, emerged from a dark wooden building several yards away, inside which Chretien could make out the forms of several horses. Handing his reins to the first soldier, Chretien accompanied his shorter companion into the stone-built inn which was next to the stables.

The innkeeper had several places laid out on a rough table, while a small pig sizzled in the cooking pit before a wide chimney. The smell of the hot fat from the animal mostly drowned out the scent of peat and damp wood. The room was none too warm, but at least there were no rats in sight, and no leaks Chretien could detect. 'Tonight,' Chretien's companion said, 'we will rest here. At day-break, you will see the despair with which the heretics have swamped the countryside – and, of course, the efforts which good Christians are expending to set things right again.'

'And the blood they spill?' Chretien was too tired to argue in detail, and Francisco Guzman was too stubborn to lose, even when he was wrong. Chretien smiled inwardly; *especially* when he was wrong, he corrected himself. 'Even if there are heretics here, they are too remote to injure Rome.' He laid his travelling cloak by the fire, and slumped at the end of the table. 'Just because they choose the path of learning of the world does not mean – '

'They learn only those things which are ungodly, so that they may attempt to falsely condemn the Lord's creations,' Guzman growled, his Iberian accent thickening. Behind him, the others entered, conflicting emotions playing across their faces. The uppermost feeling, Chretien judged, was that they were all too weary to wish to indulge in debate. 'You will see for yourself in the morning. Any remaining doubts' – he choked off a sneer at the word – 'will be assuaged.'

'As you say,' Chretien agreed, hoping that Guzman would fall silent. It seemed to work, though the Spaniard watched him through piercing eyes for a moment.

'I will see that instructions are given as to the care of the horses.' Brushing off a few droplets of melted snow, he went out into the ashen evening. Chretien moved over to a shuttered window, peering out through a gap in the wooden slats. Guzman was talking to one of the soldiers and pointing out of the village, while talking in a voice too low for Chretien to hear over the distance between them. Chretien shrugged, and returned to his seat; Guzman's zeal was certainly admirable, if misplaced, he thought.

Hooves spattering the mud in miniature explosions, a score of horsemen topped the low rise that led down into the village, and drew to a halt. Though they wore *pot de fer* helmets with nosepieces, they wore neither mail nor identifiable surcoats, being wrapped simply in the padded leather jerkins that normally provided a backing for the mail.

Clouds of condensation billowed from the horses' nostrils as they shuffled around and relaxed slightly, the grey haze helping to obscure a finely robed figure as he rode out to the new arrivals.

'You are very punctual,' the robed man said. 'I like that.'

'You get what you pay for,' the leading horseman, a burly man with a bald pate and a forked beard, agreed.

'Pay?'

'My family may have links with yours, but my men have no such ties – they expect to be paid as usual, even by you or Louis.'

'You have posted your other men?'

'They know what to do. How many men-at-arms are with you?'

'Eight, but they are secluded in the village stable, which is the largest building as you enter along this road.' His impatient tone turned to one of puzzlement as the leader dismounted, his men following suit. 'What are you doing?'

'The horses need rest. I would prefer to wait until dawn, but as you seem impatient I will settle for giving your friends an hour or so to get to sleep.' He nodded in the

6

direction of the village. 'Since you want witnesses to tell of this heretic attack upon your rival – '

'My companion,' the hooded man corrected sharply. 'Or, so he is while we travel.'

'Even so. The delay will give you a chance to get back in time for everyone to see you being woken as surprised as anyone. Would it not be just a little suspicious if you were the one man absent the whole time?'

'You are very quick-witted,' the robed man said, not entirely kindly.

'As I said, you get what you pay for.'

Meltwater bubbled in the dented iron form of an old helmet, chunks of rabbit-flesh bobbing to the surface. A rough and scratched hand added a few small dead twigs to the cooking fire, which whipped around in constant danger of being blown out, despite being built in the lee of a fallen tree-trunk in a copse. Draping an old cloak over a branch as an impromptu windbreak, a tall man, hair flapping heavily around his shoulders, walked out to the edge of the small copse and looked downslope, his arms folded and his leg braced against an icy rock.

A few wavery points of yellow torchlight danced in the village below, mostly around the inn he had noticed on his way past. The light was inviting, but Guy de Carnac had no desire to share a room with one of the Church's men, who would probably spend the night trying to find a reason to hang him like a common cutpurse in any case.

Munching on a small oatcake – he was well aware that there was so little actual goodness in rabbit-meat that a man could starve to death on a steady diet of them – he turned back, squatting beside the fire to check on his meal. He had nothing in particular against the Church – if it kept people busy, then good for them, that was his motto – but he had no great love for it either, and these days that was bad enough. Banishing the other travellers from his mind, he turned back to his cooking-fire.

Once the clerics had all divested themselves of their damp

7

cloaks, they had consumed the suckling pig with enthusiasm, though Chretien was more pleased by the fact that
Guzman seemed to be keeping his mouth shut for a
change.

The innkeeper had at first supplied his customers with
some bochet with which to wash down the meat and
simple vegetables, but the scented honey drink had been
kept far too long since its fermentation, and Chretien and
the others settled for godale 'double beer'.

Chretien had decided over the course of the meal that
he had seen enough of the boring countryside which
Guzman had claimed was visibly ruined by the heretics.
So far, he had seen nothing out of the unusual, bar a few
burnt-out hovels – and even that wasn't too unusual.

He would change their itinerary tomorrow, he decided,
and head for home rather than pressing on through a
country which was so uncomfortably gripped in the throes
of winter.

Making his excuses, he retired to the shabby room
which had been set aside for him, his attendant following
like a faithful dog and taking up position behind the door.

The soldiers who had escorted the clerics huddled round
a carefully tended fire in the stable, wrapped in their
cloaks, as the fire was necessarily small and cool to avoid
the risk of an inferno caused by stray sparks.

They squatted in a rough circle and tossed dice, the few
coins they were gambling with scraping around the crowns
of their upturned helmets. Their tired-looking sergeant-
at-arms, his eye-sockets looking more hollow than usual
under the guttering firelight, cursed under his breath as
the roll went against him for the fifth successive time, and
he straightened on protesting legs which had just become
accustomed to their resting position.

'The odds turning against you?' one of the men asked
with a grin.

'For that, you will be on stable duty when we get back,'
the sergeant-at-arms announced with relish. Rank certainly had its privileges. The soldier looked suitably down-

cast, but said nothing that might tempt the sergeant-at-arms to make the assignment more permanent. Cheered a little by this small piece of revenge, the sergeant-at-arms gathered up his empty helmet and belted on his longsword. 'Keep the fire warm, but keep a watch on it. I will check on young Fulk.' The men nodded.

The sergeant-at-arms winced slightly as the chill renewed its grip on him when he went out into the snowy night. The faces of the nobles and clerics he had served over the years were all beginning to blur into one these days, he considered, as he moved away from the stable and out through the filthy streets to where he had left Fulk on watch at the end of the village.

As he walked, he fancied he heard a faint jingling noise, but dismissed it as his mind worrying at his gambling losses. By the distant gleam of the torch he had left with the boy, he could now make out young Fulk leaning against a low trough. If he's fallen asleep, the sergeant promised himself, I'll have him horsewhipped. Better that than he learns to sleep out in this sort of weather and freezes to death, he decided.

Ignoring the renewed jingling in his subconscious, the sergeant-at-arms jogged over to the trough, and gave Fulk a gently rousing kick in the ribs. Instead of groaning into wakefulness, Fulk simply rolled further over into the ground with a slurping sound, the slim length of black wood that protruded from his wet throat snapping with a faint crack.

When the jingling came again, hot on the heels of the sounds of the body's movement, the sergeant finally recognized the truth of the sound. He cursed himself for not recognizing the soft movement of horse barding approaching the village. He glanced around, but could see no one in the snow-obscured pitch-blackness.

Cupping his hand into a funnel over his mouth, he straightened to call out an alarm to his men in the stable. As he started to draw in air, however, a hot impact rocked him forward on his feet, and he found his breath coming heavily, as if the air had thickened. Looking down with a pale and bloodless face, he saw the glistening point of a arrow-shaft protruding from the shattered links of the mail over his chest.

Gasping vainly as his punctured lung grew heavy with blood, he tumbled into the trough under the impact of another shaft entering his kidney, the layer of ice that covered the trough shattering under his weight. His arms flailed ineffectually as the weight of his helmet dragged his head under the icy water, which then began to flood his other lung.

The soldiers didn't bother to look up when the stable door swung open, assuming that it was their sergeant-at-arms returned from checking on young Fulk.

Since their swords were lying to one side, and they were without helmets, they had no resistance to offer to the four men who approached silently and cut them down like ripe corn.

They didn't even have time to shout an alarm.

Chretien came awake to the sound of barking dogs. His attendant crouched at the door, obviously having also just awakened. Shouts and the ring of metal on metal echoed in the sodden yard outside. Heedless of the cold, he tugged the window shutters open.

Outside, several villagers, in makeshift armour and armed with pikestaffs and axes, were scattering up the road ahead. From the darkness beyond, a muted drumming was audible.

Several of the community's militia spread out along the muddy track beyond the stable, glaives and pikestaffs held forth. Though afraid of whatever might be approaching, fear of losing what few pitiful possessions existed in their village overwhelmed their dismay.

They looked at each other as if their neighbours would know more about what was happening than they did. There were no clues for anyone, however, until a feath-

10

ered shaft impaled a pikeman through the right shoulder, spinning him into the snowy mud.

As if that was a signal, a flurry of black arrows hissed from the night, ramming through flesh as effectively as would the horns of a maddened bull. The village militia scattered to the winds, frantically waving the polearms as a score of blue-cloaked horsemen thundered out of the darkness, Saracen bows now draped across their saddle-bows as they drew their swords for a charge.

A few brave souls lunged forward, swinging their long-bladed glaives at the heads of the riders, or setting their pikes ready to impale their horses.

One rider was caught by a blow from a glaive, its blade hacking through his shoulder and all but severing his sword arm. Knocked backwards by the force of the impact, he tumbled from the saddle with a wet crunch. His opponent was no luckier, however, as a sword blow from a neighbouring rider sheared the blade from the glaive's pole before continuing on and through the vil-lager's skull at eye-level.

Other riders pursued the rest of the villagers back towards the barn, leaning low in the saddle to crush skulls and smash through spines with savage blows to the fleeing men.

Without warning, a burning torch hurtled over the stable roof, plunging into an empty wagon before it. Some of the villagers made it back around the side of the barn as screams split the air. Tugging on his travelling cloak over his undershirt, without bothering with his surcoat or vest-ments of office, Chretien dashed out through the common room. The others were also pouring out, in various stages of undress. 'Where are the soldiers?' he shouted.

'I do not know,' someone answered.

Afraid but angered, Chretien lunged out into the chill morning, ignoring the icy mud that seeped between his toes. A small building opposite was burning, and smoke darkened the grey air in patches. Several horsemen – unarmoured save for the Norman helms obscuring their

11

features – rounded the stable and into the small square, one of them sending a severed head flying as Chretien emerged, stunned, from the inn.

Ragged farmers splashed into the white-layered mud, darkening it once more as their warm blood melted its way through the snowy crust. Chretien called for his soldiers, but none came. Instead, three of the horsemen wheeled about, charging straight for him. Chretien and one of his fellows hastily slammed the door, backing fearfully inside. 'These must be heretics indeed, to hunt us like boars.'

With an ear-splitting crash, the door split open, a black forty-pound blade shearing through it by sheer weight and ripping away half his companion's skull. A booted foot kicked the shattered pieces aside as Chretien searched for a weapon with which to defend himself. A mass of men pressed through the blood-spattered door, heavy blades sweeping in huge arcs, smashing clear through the remaining clerics' torsos, through inertia rather than sharpness. The last thing Chretien saw was Guzman, standing untouched in the blood-slicked centre of what was already becoming an abattoir.

Guy de Carnac took the stretched rabbit-gut down from the branch and untied the stone from the end of it. There was the sound of fighting from the village below, and he had no wish to get involved. Let the Church and their heretics kill each other off to their hearts' content, so long as they didn't bother him. He would make a spare bowstring out of the gut later, after moving on a safe distance.

Mounting his softly nickering horse, he patted the side of its neck, and set off along the narrow track which the farmers used to lead their animals to the higher pastures in summer. Now, however, it was covered in a layer of snow, which cloaked any stones or potholes in the path, forcing him to move more slowly.

By the time he guided the chestnut horse on to the more level cart track half a mile beyond the village, the sounds of killing had long since ceased, and the rich aroma of burning wood was falling with the delicate snow-flakes. Tightening his cloak over his waist-length chain-mail haubergeon, he allowed the horse to set a walking pace away from the village.

He soon found, however, that he was not walking away from the trouble that had befallen it. Three mounted soldiers, with unmarked surcoats over their long hauberks, blocked the track ahead. He couldn't see their faces under the blank helmets, but suspected that they were not pleased at his appearance. 'So,' a voice drifted towards him, as one man addressed the others, 'one warrior did get away.'

'I have not come from the village,' de Carnac called out to them. 'I am just passing by – I have not been into it. I suggest you stand aside that I may pass.'

'None pass here unless they also pass from this world. You have seen us here, and that is enough to mark you.' Reaching across, the leader tugged free the sword that was belted at his left hip, and rode forward.

De Carnac had no real desire to harm any of these three, but had even less desire to let them harm him. Besides, he added to himself, they had had their chance to avoid trouble. He let the knight close rapidly, knowing from experience that he would not expect the quick reaction he was going to get. The knight raised his sword high, its crude steel dark against the swirling grey and white of the air. Its weight would be dragging the man's arm backward, de Carnac knew, and slowing his reflexes. He reached for his own sword as the knight's started to fall, ducking as he swung backhanded at the knight's exposed side.

His sword lashed out with whiplash speed, crashing into the knight's hauberk and splintering some of the mail. The knight's sword passed harmlessly overhead, and de Carnac rose in the saddle, bringing his sword back to block the knight's next clumsy attack. The dark blade rang from de Carnac's silver sword, striking sparks. The light of surprise in the knight's shadowed eyes was the

13

last glimmer of life he displayed, as de Carnac spun his sword in his hand into a backwards slash, and clove the knight's helmet almost in two.

The knight fell from his saddle like a sack of grain, scarlet blood oozing from the shattered helmet and spreading across the snow.

The other two knights charged simultaneously, but de Carnac ducked the first's swing while parrying the second's with a clang, before sweeping his sword back to unseat the first knight. The fallen man rolled into a rut and didn't move. De Carnac didn't know whether he was alive or dead, and didn't really care. It was their own business as far he was concerned. The second knight slashed again, but the weight of his sword was so great that de Carnac merely had to lean out of range and allow the momentum of the man's swing to carry his body round into a position that left his kidneys vulnerable. Clapping his left hand over the rounded pommel, to provide extra force to his thrust, he plunged his gleaming blade sideways, shattering the steel links under the knight's surcoat and plunging into the flesh beneath. The knight slid from the blade with a faint sucking sound and hit the ground with a hard thud.

Guy de Carnac looked down at the bodies unemotionally, noting that the one he had simply unseated was groaning slightly. He wasn't interested in cold-blooded killing, however, and decided to leave the man to the elements.

Wiping his silvery sword on a piece of rag, Guy de Carnac urged his horse onward, and vanished into the swirling snow.

Chapter 2

Far from the winter-bound village, so distant that the human mind can scarcely comprehend the measurement, the stars likewise swirled, albeit at a rate vastly slowed by the difference in scale.

Deep in the midst of the stellar maelstrom, too small to be visible even if it were truly a feature of real, physical space, a ship foundered in what were its equivalent of unfriendly seas.

Her head pounding from the onslaught of a chorus of deafening alarms, a lithe woman with short dark hair and almost, but not quite, elegant features, rolled with the fall she took when the floor lurched. Irritated at how rusty her aikido technique was, as it failed to prevent her cracking her elbow painfully when she slid into the grey wall of the tertiary console room, she put one hand on the wall and one on the floor to steady herself. Forcing herself to be practical and take stock of exactly what was going wrong, she braced herself more fully against the weathered stone, and tried to identify which alarms were being triggered.

With a sinking feeling, she realized that all the ones she knew were blaring, along with a few she hadn't heard before. The harsh two-tone life-support failure warning was competing with the high-pitched structural integrity alarm and a dozen other cacophonous sounds, all worryingly backed by the doom-laden tolling of the Cloister Bell, which seemed perfectly clear regardless of whatever other noise was filling the air.

Hanging on to the rims of the circular access panels that were carved into the six granite walls, ersatz archaeology professor – and sometime co-saviour of the universe, as she occasionally felt like adding to her C.V. when she was in a whimsical mood – Bernice Summerfield pulled herself up into a standing position. Brushing some accumulated dust from her white trousers, she straightened her velvet waistcoat and aquamarine blouse as she lurched over to the elaborately carved console, which had the ancient air of some Gothic altar that belonged in the *Lord of the Rings*. 'Shades! What the smeg was that?'

'Nothing good.' His pale linen suit as shabby as ever, the Doctor was carefully balancing his white fedora on the end of his ubiquitous umbrella when Benny almost stumbled into him.

'Has our take-off aborted?'

'This isn't a tramp freighter, you know. We don't drop back to the ground through not making escape velocity. We've left Gadrell Major all right.' For a moment, she wondered why he wasn't at the console trying to stabilize the ship. She bit off her words, however, when she saw the strangely shimmering curtain of distortion that sliced cleanly through the Gothic chamber a couple feet in front of him, moving in towards the interior door at a slow but steady walking pace.

The vision didn't glow or spark, but was clearly discernible by virtue of the fact that the orange emergency lights were pulsing slightly out of phase on the far side of it. Curious, Benny sidled up to the faint barrier, like a sheet of glass, and cautiously stretched out a hand.

'Don't move!' the Doctor snapped in an urgent tone. He laid a hand on her shoulder and tugged her back from the distortion. 'Keep hold of something, in case the TARDIS lurches again. If you come into contact with that barrier it could be disastrous.'

She nodded, not needing to be told twice. 'Is it a dimensional rip of some kind?'

'No.'

Benny looked on with concern; the Doctor only really

16

got terse like this when something was seriously wrong. His pinched face was set in concentration, as he stretched out the hat-tipped umbrella towards the sheet of distortion.

'Some interference from Gadrell Major?'

'Some kind of disturbance in the TARDIS's temporal environment, more likely; though why it should manifest so soon after take-off . . .'

'I'm not an engineer. You mean in the TARDIS's time?'

'More or less.' He trailed off as a pale blur began growing out from the interior surface of the distortion, a few inches ahead of his hat. As the Doctor continued to press forward, the pale blur grew into the recognisable shape of the hat, appearing on the far side of the barrier a few seconds before the Doctor pushed it through. The hat then shrank back towards the distortion an instant before the Doctor started pulling it back. Once it was free of the distortion, he removed it from the tip of the umbrella and examined it closely. Looking back at the distortion, he jammed the hat absently back on his head, and stepped back from the advancing barrier. 'Come on,' he instructed, turning and scurrying off deeper into the TARDIS.

'Shouldn't we try to reach another console room?' she asked, puzzled.

'No good. All three console rooms have direct access to the ship's real-world interface, so they'll all be inaccessible; the ship's time-field is generated from the centre outwards, so it will have come in through the outside first.'

'Where are we going, then?'

He paused at a crossroads, where the tunnel of carved stone ended. Ahead was a wood-panelled corridor, while a normal, clinically white corridor was to the right. He turned down a brick-lined corridor to the left. 'The only section of the TARDIS where I can get a reading from the main computer core and access the main control systems, but which doesn't have a plug-in to the real-world interface.' He strode off purposefully down the brick-walled corridor, eventually pulling aside the cantilever

17

door of a thirties-style lift which was all wire and wrought iron.

'Evening wear, please,' Benny suggested.

'Ancillary control first.' The lift shook, then sank jerkily downwards.

'So what's causing this displacement effect? Has something gone wrong in the TARDIS's engines? Or whatever it's got that passes for engines.'

'I doubt it. This has all the hallmarks of some sort of external influence.'

'What sort of outside force could penetrate the TARDIS's defence shields while it's not even in realspace?'

'Artificial, you mean? With the Monk and Artemis long gone, I don't know. That's what worries me . . . A Guardian could, or possibly the Old Ones; parts of their conscious minds ride the Time Winds through the vortex, and they certainly won't be too happy at our interfering in Haiti and on Ry'leh . . . Someone with extremely detailed knowledge of the TARDIS's design might be able to affect us as well, though not necessarily quite like this.'

'The Master? He should know enough about TARDISes.'

'As much as any other Time Lord; but if he, or anyone else, were trying to get rid of us there are plenty more straightforward ways of going about it. No, if I could think of any precedent I'd be inclined to think this is some sort of natural phenomenon.' The lift crashed to a halt, and the Doctor tugged the latticework gate open, leading the way out into another level of the TARDIS.

Benny had been travelling with the Doctor in the TARDIS for a couple of years now, but was still surprised by some of the areas they passed through on the journey to ancillary control. She hadn't even dreamed that an arboretum, a well-equipped hospital ward, and a complete indoor sports centre lay dustily far beyond the cloisters, wreathed in a dimming orange light as if they were insects trapped in amber. Perhaps they were, in a way, she thought. They were relics of a bygone age when the TARDIS was used for its original, presumably research, purposes. As usual when travelling near the heart of the TARDIS, she gained the distinct impression of moving downwards, deeper into the workings of the ship, even though they had traversed neither stairs nor ramps, nor had they entered any other lifts. 'Is it just my imagination,' she asked, 'or is this TARDIS bigger than it used to be?'

'Yes and no. This is a different TARDIS to the one you first boarded, remember. I had occasion to jettison some of that ship's mass a couple of lifetimes ago, but obviously that never happened to this TARDIS, so it's still entirely complete.'

Strange mechanical hums and wheezes, like huge ancient bellows made from whales' lungs or suchlike, groaned in the distance. But the Doctor ignored them, so Benny didn't bring the subject up. Instead she memorized the route to those interesting new locations as the Doctor turned right and walked into a fair-sized art gallery.

He didn't stop to relax in the presence of the fine statuary and paintings, but Benny could not help but pause to admire some of the pieces. Most of the collection was from Earth, though there were some pieces of very alien statuary, and a painting of a member of some species she didn't recognize – and wouldn't want to. She stopped at a framed WANTED poster of a vaguely familiar subject; a dignified-looking white-haired man in an Edwardian frock coat. The name at the bottom of the poster was Doc Holliday. The Doctor, meanwhile, had draped his hat and umbrella over a Veltrochni tree sculpture which he had picked up somewhere, and had removed a panel from a plinth under a small Greek statuette of the goddess Athena to examine a glowing patch in the space thus revealed. 'The ship's power remains unaffected at least,' he said in a tone that, to Benny's ears, held delight only at the thought that at least something still worked. It wasn't very reassuring.

Replacing the panel, he moved to a small statue of Atlas supporting the world, and pressed the palm of his hand against the plinth on which the small bronze figure stood. The globe of the Earth immediately faded away, the space which replaced it somehow stretching back into infinity. Benny watched curiously as the Doctor rearranged the position of his fingers on the plinth, and stared into the dark hole in the air.

Small flickering lights lapped around the fingers resting against the marble plinth, while, in the dark patch above, a roughly spherical image formed. It had no outer shell, but was an image of dozens or hundreds of capillary lines, resembling an anatomical diagram of the blood vessels in the lungs or brain. In a moment, Benny realized that it was a graphic display of the TARDIS's layout. Indecipherable symbols flashed around, while a red stain slowly but inexorably crept in from the edges. Parts of the stain seemed to appear without direct connection to the rest of it, but Benny suspected that this had more to do with the multi-dimensional nature of the TARDIS than the cancerous nature of whatever was invading it.

'What is that? Some sort of virus?'

'No, it's just the areas which have already gone under the temporal displacement.' Hesitating like a surgeon unsure where to enter a wound – and unsure whether it was still not too late to save the patient rather than just cause more pain – the Doctor moved his hands to another position on the plinth, and pressed inwards, his face a mask of concentration as he played different areas of the plinth like an accordion.

The display didn't change at all, but the TARDIS shuddered violently, sending several pieces of art to the floor, where the more fragile ones exploded into shards. The Doctor snatched his hands back from the plinth as if it had delivered an electric shock.

Perhaps it had, Benny thought, if it was connected to the TARDIS's power and control systems in any way. She noticed the Doctor frown in renewed concentration, then the image suddenly changed, to show a small blue speck caught in a web of pixels by some large red object that vanished out of the viewing space. A broken line curved around it, while more symbols flashed.

He released the frame with a resigned expression, and

the bronze globe reappeared. 'I thought as much. A rare, if not unique, and thoroughly natural occurrence.'

'Is this something I'd be more comfortable not knowing, or am I supposed to be practising my mind-reading today?'

'Both,' the Doctor said, with a trace of his old humour. 'The only external force that could certainly penetrate the ship's plasmic shell – the chaotic turbulence of Time itself. We've entered a probability matrix in which the TARDIS has passed too close to a black star that isn't on any of the charts. Somehow it's exerting a relativistic effect within the space-time vortex itself, and the TARDIS is caught in it.'

'Black star? You mean a black hole?'

'No, a black hole is just the remains of a dense star of normal matter that's collapsed far enough to drill a hole through the fabric of space. A black star, on the other hand, is a star made of quasi-baryonic dark matter. Because it's only partially real it can become more massive than a black hole, without actually collapsing out of real-space. Also, they don't give out any energy signature – which makes them almost impossible to detect – and their semi-tachyonic nature makes them a danger to the temporal vortex as well.'

I wish I'd attended those astrophysics classes, Benny thought, instead of sneaking off to that Tri-V museum. 'Will we be pulled in?' she asked.

'No, the lateral drift compensators have sent us into a slingshot orbit, so the ship will break free in a week or so.'

Benny hadn't accompanied the Doctor for so long without learning how to read inferences from his tone, however. 'I sense a "but" rapidly approaching.'

'But . . .' the Doctor said, with a smile. 'This close to a dark star, we're bound to experience some relativistic effects. That distortion creeping inwards is the wavefront of a field of relative time displacement. Everything on the other side of it is about three and a half seconds further into the future than everything on this side of it. At its

21

current rate of progress, it will envelop every point in the TARDIS within a very few hours, and the time differential will stretch out exponentially as well – in a few minutes, the displacement will be around an hour. You can probably imagine the rest.'

'Is that bad?'

'Well,' the Doctor said slowly, fiddling almost subconsciously with the knots on an Inca quipu that was draped over a pair of disconcertingly familiar-looking disembodied marble arms, 'there's good news, and there's bad news.'

'Wonderful.'

'The good news is that the TARDIS is designed and built to withstand the strains and pressures of an alteration to relative time. The bad news is that our bodies aren't.'

Benny thought for a moment. 'I suppose the shock of suddenly aging a few years or decades might be fatal, but three and a half seconds?'

'It's a cellular matter. Every cell in a living thing is constantly either growing or dying, but to something as small as each single cell, three and a half seconds is the equivalent of several months to us. How much do you move around in three seconds? Try catching a thrown object, and you could conceivably hurl yourself several feet in that length of time, with every muscle in the body shifting from one extreme to the other.' He shook his head. 'The field would creep over each cell, so bits of each cell would be that much further advanced than the rest of it – of course the shock will be fatal. By the time it reaches here ... How much does a single cell move in an hour? Besides, this is only time displacement going into the star's gravity well; there'll be another one when the ship comes out.'

'So what do we do?'

The Doctor straightened, as if steeling himself. 'There's only one thing we *can* do. Abandon ship.'

Benny felt as if a lead weight had just dropped into her stomach. If they left the TARDIS here, they could be stranded anywhere. 'But we can't,' she protested. 'We

22

can't condemn ourselves to being castaways somewhere . . .'

'Only for the week it'll take for the TARDIS to get free of this,' the Doctor reassured her. 'This TARDIS also has a Jade Pagoda; we can get away in that, and I'll pre-program the navigational systems to home in on it when everything returns to normal.' He looked around brightly. 'You go straight to the Pagoda; outside, turn left, then third right, past the ballroom, first left, along the right-hand side of the tennis court, through the groundcar garage, past the water purification plant, and through the green door set into the far wall of the quarantine bay with no glass in the windows – got that?'

Benny considered it. 'I think so,' she said carefully.

'Good. On you go; I'll just program the TARDIS's navigational systems.' He turned back to the statuette, as if she had already left.

'Right,' Benny agreed, leaving with a last glance at the *objets d'art*.

With a last instruction entered into the computer access point hidden in the statuette, the Doctor hurried out of the gallery.

An instant later, he grabbed hold of a cornerpost to aid in his sharp turn back into Ancillary Control. He noted with alarm that the displacement wavefront was already starting to emerge from the far wall, presumably from an entry point in the tertiary console room. Tensing himself to run at an instant's notice, he snatched his hat and umbrella back from the wooden statue of Veltroch's god of hearth and home, and backpedalled furiously out of the room.

Parfait Jeanne jumped a little at the sound of a reverberating crash from somewhere just beyond the east wall. A plume of steam was gently fading as she looked in that direction. She told herself to try harder to remain calm, and not let the deficiencies of her mere physical form – sensitive hearing, not least – overwhelm her. After all, as the Castellan had told her often enough, the Church's

23

new mangonels simply couldn't hurl anything at a steep enough angle to hit any part of the fortress from their positions below.

Their dedication to continually trying, however, was admirable, if misplaced. A movement off to one side caught her eye, and she noticed a couple of the children of the few mercenary defenders who manned the walls. They had dropped the wooden swords with which they had been playing, and were looking around like startled rabbits.

A woman – presumably the mother of one or both – hurried over, and ushered them back into a wooden lean-to that had been hastily built against the wall of the north tower, which held the library and storehouses. She hardly dared wonder what it must be like trying to look after children here in the Roc. It had been difficult enough on a farm.

She tried to dismiss the matter. The two children had been recovered, so it was not going to be her problem. The dozen wounded men who had just been returned from the small gateway tower that guarded the only track twisting its way up to the Roc, however, were very much her problem. Fortunately the track there was too narrow for the Church to spread out enough to overwhelm the tower, but there were some bad arrow wounds and broken bones caused by men having been shot from the parapet by Church archers.

She hadn't been on a farm in over half her forty years, but it seemed she still spent more time trying to heal injured men than anything else – it was just that now she dealt with deliberately inflicted wounds more often than injuries inflicted by carelessness while handling animals or heavy weights.

Ignoring the constant babble of chatter that filled the bailey, she crossed the filthy open area at the heart of the fortress, and went through into the dim and stuffy hospital area which had been set up in what used to be the great hall, on the ground floor of the main hold. A few other blue-robed Parfaits were scattered here and there, tending to some of the people who were huddled on the stone floor, while a cluster of women were gathered round a rough table. She looked closely and saw that the patient was one of the younger girls who had newly become a Parfait; she was due to have her pregnancy ended around now, Jeanne recalled – it would not do to have a spiritual Parfait give birth to new physical life.

Above her, the minstrel gallery was now a sleeping quarters for the Parfaits who worked here. They had hoped it was high enough to be safe from noxious vapours that spread disease, but had soon found that no place was safe from the sickly smells that wreathed the unfortunates who filled the hall. It had been a long time since anyone had sung from that gallery, and Jeanne would have had to reluctantly admit that she missed it. She had never been a jongleur, though visitors to the farm used to compliment her on her singing voice, but she enjoyed listening to the tales they sang.

The sight of the nearest of the newly arrived wounded put all thoughts of such things out of her head. The red-headed Giselle and the others were doing well treating the wounds, Jeanne noticed, but there was little hope of finding enough material for poultices and the like, not after such a long time in the Roc. She looked at two male Parfaits, who were talking animatedly, shaking their heads over the condition of the wounded, and beckoned to Giselle to join her to talk to them. Perhaps there was hope of new supplies after all, if the two men were willing.

'On what authority did you send them out of the Roc?' Parfait Girard's face had grown as pale as his beard at the news Jeanne and Giselle had given him.

'I must save those men from the deficiencies of flesh, but I cannot do so without supplies, and we have insufficient balms and poultices remaining here.'

'If they are taken by the Inquisition – '

'They will not talk. Why should they? They are not fools enough to think that giving our secrets to the Church will save their lives.'

'I sometimes wonder about you two,' Girard sighed. 'You seem to mother your charges, if such a thing were possible.' Both of them seemed so concerned with preserving people in their material prisons. The women's sect believed that the challenge of coping with one's physical nature would make their spirits stronger, but Girard was not so sure. Physical senses distracted the intellect from better pursuits, he felt. 'It would possibly be a mercy to let the wounded slip away rather than linger in torment. Perhaps they would have better fortune in their next cycle of life.'

'And the lack of their efforts would leave us at the mercy of the Inquisition – or it would if they had any mercy.'

Practicality was no respecter of belief, it seemed, but then Girard had always known that. 'Evidently there is nothing I can do, but you had better be correct about their safety and strength. Should we fall, our faith must continue, and I will not allow that to be jeopardized.'

'They will return. They know what is at stake.'

Girard didn't bother to answer. Obviously some of the groups in the Roc still had to be nurtured along the road to realizing that their spiritual selves were their only true being. Doing so was not easy, but he couldn't give up now. Sometimes, though, he wished he'd stayed a fisherman.

Benny had been waiting only a few moments when the Doctor joined her outside the richly textured antique door, which was inscribed with the symbol of a fist and some Chinese script; the markings, however, were too indistinct for Benny to read under the dim and dense-seeming light at the heart of the TARDIS.

The Doctor had a small bag tucked under his arm, which, Benny assumed, contained a few essentials they might need in a potentially hostile environment. She wondered whether there was time to return to her suite for some essentials of her own – a hip flask of something medicinal, perhaps, or a novel.

The Doctor paused as he approached the door, his face

26

freezing as if he had just caught himself in time to avoid grimacing. A spark of brighter life flickered in his eyes again as they moved away from the inscription. He obviously doesn't have many fond memories of this bit of the TARDIS, she surmised.

'Travelling light?' he asked rhetorically, and she shrugged. You couldn't travel much lighter than with just the clothes you stood in. Not without risking arrest, anyway. She smiled to herself.

'I have to leave room for bringing back souvenirs.'

'Very wise. I'll try to aim for a combined brewery and glassworks, then,' he suggested, pushing through the dark door.

'How about going for Callahan's, then? I've still to get one of their beer-glasses . . .' She followed him into the surprisingly cool interior of the Pagoda. After the oppressive heat of the TARDIS's central areas, it was quite a relief.

'Not after what happened last time, thank you very much. Come to think of it, you've never been to my restaurant either, have you?'

'Your restaurant?'

'Yes, a little place called Tempus Fugit. Convivial sort of place, if I remember correctly.' He moved towards the small central console while Benny looked around. The room was shadowy and cool, with small statuettes in wall-niches. All the walls, floor and ceiling were of smooth – almost marbled – jade, while a faint sunlike light filtered through from the ceiling; just enough to see by. The whole room had the air of some ancient oriental temple built into a mountainside, and Benny also noticed that there was no interior door – instead there were several floor-to-ceiling partitions of paper and bamboo.

While she had examined the room, the Doctor had been busying himself at the miniature version of the central console. This only had four sides, with a triple-roofed housing for a smaller time rotor at the centre, and clearly held far fewer instruments than the main TARDIS console. The Doctor glanced up, as she approached with a

27

questioning look. 'The Pagoda's really just an emergency escape pod of sorts, so it only has the most basic of controls,' he said.

'Enough to pick a nice relaxing bolthole?'

'Not really. Most of these are life-support and environmental systems controls.' He made a few small adjustments to one panel, and the triple-roofed column began rising and falling. Watching its progress for a moment, he moved round, and began typing instructions into a small keyboard. 'The Pagoda just homes in on the nearest location within specified survival parameters, so the best I can do comfort-wise is to specify a Class-M planet orbiting a main sequence G-class star.'

'That shouldn't be too difficult,' she commented, as the central column began rotating to and fro. 'There must be a million to choose from.'

'There are closer to six hundred and fifty million in this galaxy, as it happens; or so the statisticians say. There should be one somewhere out of the nearest four hundred and sixty or so stars.'

'Knowing our luck, the nearest one's probably swarming with omnivorous wildlife.'

'The odds are pretty long, and in any case we certainly had to make a time jump to avoid the time displacement field that was affecting the rest of the TARDIS.'

'*Had?* You mean we've already left?'

'Of course!' The Doctor appeared to Benny to be confused that she even asked the question. 'The Pagoda left the TARDIS as soon as the door closed – it *is* for emergency escapes, after all.'

I must be getting old not to have thought of that, she thought wryly. 'And have we also arrived wherever?'

'No, I'd say our ETA's about three hours – subjective time, allowing time for the autosystems to home in on a suitable site.'

28

Chapter 3

The chestnut mare had borne Guy de Carnac under a hazy cloud of thickening smoke for a few hours before he emerged from a woodland of winter-bare trees and began to pass the first of the bands of refugees who were scattered across the clammy earth like autumnal leaves.

The densest collection was stretched along either side of the overgrown Roman road on which de Carnac rode, but there many carts and shoddily wrapped bundles of meagre possessions were also being manhandled across country by their destitute owners.

Half-stripped bodies lay here and there, their clothes removed by others who felt the cold more than the dead did. He felt that, like wormholes in a worn old chair, they were a depressing symptom of a deeper malaise, and one that affected more than a chair. He wondered if the country would ever be the same again, with its people so savage and fearful. It was like suddenly seeing a vision of how oneself had changed over the years.

Though the air was filled with stifled groans and sobs, and the scraping and creaking of cartwheels, there was almost no talking amongst the despairing homeless. Perhaps, de Carnac thought, their plight was beyond mere words, or perhaps they were just conserving their strength for their journey. He didn't know, and he didn't show any interest in them either.

As his eyes swept the churned road ahead, a pair of wire-thin men, clothing held together by roughly knotted straps, wrestled a driver from his cart. One of them swiftly plunged a dagger into the stunned body several times before joining his partner in leaping aboard the sparsely laden cart, which was drawn by a lean-looking ox. De Carnac watched impassively as they passed him, his hand moving almost imperceptibly towards his sword-hilt before relaxing again.

Ordinarily, he knew, he needn't concern himself with the thought that any of these people might attack him. Indeed, they were already giving him a wide berth as soon as they took note of the sword slung across his back and the bow that hung from his saddle. On the other hand, even a cornered rat would fight like a demon, and these people had literally nothing to lose.

Listening out for any sound of approach from behind, de Carnac allowed his gaze to continue beyond the refugees to a large walled town nestled in the hollows of the hills in the distance. Through the dark smudges of rising smoke, he could clearly make out the energetic dancing of gaudy patches of flame, which stood out clearly against the background of drab greys and browns that characterized the buildings.

Absently patting the horse's neck, he continued towards the stricken town.

Louis de Citeaux scratched calmly on a piece of vellum with a carved pen, pausing only to push the damp grey hair out of his eyes. The hour was late, but he was never too tired to lavish a little more time on the running of his city. The Lord knows, he thought to himself, that it's difficult enough to see by the thick candles that put out as much greasy smoke as light, without trying to see through a curtain of hair as well.

Had he received an answer, it would probably have said that his inability to focus on his paperwork was just as much due to the fact that he was allowing himself to be distracted. He was impatient to have word from Guzman or Philippe de Montfort.

Sooner or later, he promised himself, I'm going to have the Holy See brought closer to home, so I can have immediate responses. His elder brother, the Bishop of

Citeaux until his death, would never have had to wait so long for anything. Even his two co-conspirators would have to have acknowledged that.

He laid down the pen and leaned back in the heavy wooden chair, filling his hand instead with a metal flagon of wine. He grimaced at the way the chair's edges dug into his back, wishing he'd thought to bring home some of those large cushions he'd got used to relaxing in in the Holy Land. His reverie was interrupted by the thudding of a fist on the banded oak door to the suite.

'Come.'

'My Lord,' a page said deferentially, 'Captain de Montfort has arrived.'

Louis' mood brightened visibly. 'Send him in.'

The page scurried away, drawing the door closed after him. Louis swept the vellum pages to one side of the heavy desk, and dumped the large wine pitcher and an extra flagon on the space thus cleared.

The door opened once more, and a tall and burly figure swept in, peeling off his stained blue cloak and tossing it over a curved-bottomed chair. The oily light gleamed from his rough pate, while his forked beard made his face seem even more shadowed than it was. A permanent scowl left his brows furrowed at a sharp angle, and his eyes glittered like reflections from the bottom of a well.

Louis cocked an eyebrow at him, ignoring the aggressive stance and the primitive collection of studded leather armour that his visitor preferred over a standard haubergeon. 'I had expected at least a smile from an old friend of my family,' he said with mock disappointment. He indicated the pitcher and flagon. 'Make yourself at home, Philippe.'

Philippe de Montfort looked Louis up and down impassively, his thin lips set in a grim line. Louis looked back implacably, letting Philippe have his fun – whatever it was. After a few seconds, Philippe's face split into a grin, and he laughed raucously. Dropping into a spare seat with a slight rattle, he untidily tipped some wine into his flagon. 'Nothing ever worries you, does it? Who's to say

31

someone hadn't made me a better offer to turn against you?'

'If they could make an offer of something more precious than your family's birthright, I would probably have to capitulate to such a superior force.'

'Very true. Aumury is a weak-willed fool who fancies himself as the King's lapdog,' he grumbled. 'While I do not care that my brother gives up his own birthright, by handing over the countship of Béziers and Toulouse to that parasitic King as a show of fealty, I do object to him giving away mine. If he *had* to abdicate the countship, it should have passed to me. If you can strengthen my claim, of course. . .'

'Do not worry, Philippe.' I will lead you as effectively as my elder brother led your father, he thought. Simon de Montfort was a good general, he recalled, but suggestible by the Bishop.

'If I worry, the rewards will be worth the trouble.' His features lost their scowl and became more thoughtful. 'Not all my men saw it that way, of course; a promise of payment from the family coffers wasn't quite enough to convince some of them.'

Louis looked up sharply. 'I trust none of them have loose tongues.'

'Each of them had fifteen gold florins of accumulated loot.'

'Is that enough to ensure their silence?'

Philippe paused, as if working out how to phrase his reply. 'The more loyal men had another fifteen florins. They each considered thirty to be better than fifteen.'

Louis nodded understandingly. 'Then it was enough indeed. How did your quest go?'

'Just as I planned. Guzman and a number of novices and serfs were – ah – overlooked in the mêlée, and fled to report the attack. Has there been a response from the Cardinals yet?'

'Nothing.' He shrugged. 'It matters little. D'Alsace cannot plead for moderation any longer, at least.' Louis rose from his seat, cupping his flagon in his hands, and moved with a proud bearing over to the narrow window that was set between two faded tapestries depicting pastoral scenes. Setting the flagon on the ledge, he pushed the wooden shutters open, and looked out over the town spread out below. The city was like a mistress to him, demanding and unforgiving, yet he couldn't give it up. The allure of being responsible for the creation and maintenance of a whole society was far too strong for his mere flesh and blood to resist.

Philippe joined him, brushing the lank hair from his shoulders. 'Your late brother found a good position to leave in one piece when he burnt the city.'

'Yes, and it is a good position from which I can nurse it back to health – once it is free from heretic influence. The merchant who originally had this Hôtel de Ville built probably paid a great deal to gain a attractive view from this hillside. Now, if he still lives, he is somewhere beyond the walls with no more than what he can carry on his back.'

'Saddening, is it not?' Philippe grinned.

'For him, yes. His cloud provides my silver lining.' Louis gestured vaguely towards the burning buildings and mobs of tiny people below. The glinting forms of armoured warriors harried knots of commoners like terriers at a tied bull. Even from the hillside, some bodies were visible, nuzzled at by dogs as they lay ignored in the roadside filth. 'Ironic, don't you think?'

'What is?'

'See.' Louis pointed, indicating hurried stragglers trickling through the streets from various directions, though all drifting towards one destination. A sprawling wooden edifice of a century or two's age thrust its spires into the blackened air. 'You would think they might have remembered what our families did thirty-one years ago.'

'Of course,' Philippe nodded slowly. 'Sanctuary.'

'Sanctuary, as it were,' the Doctor said, his demeanour as cheerfully enthusiastic as if they weren't fleeing from a home rendered – albeit temporarily – uninhabitable. 'That's what we're looking for.'

'I wasn't quite looking at it that way,' Benny murmured as she studied the playing cards in her hand.

'You know, I don't think you're taking this situation seriously enough.'

'Well, it's already happened, so there's nothing I can do about it; isn't that the rather convoluted way you saw things on Gadrell Major? What's the point of giving myself an ulcer over it?'

'Ah, true.'

Benny thought for a moment, then decided to follow instinct, and spread her cards out face up. 'Gotcha.'

'I'm afraid not – those two jacks make a sralk; you're bust, I'm afraid.'

'But you said that on a Tuesday – ' She broke off as the central column stopped rotating, and a gentle sound of oriental windchimes rippled through the room.

Beaming, the Doctor glanced over at a monitor. 'I could make a fortune on the horses, you know,' he said. 'Out of six hundred and fifty million possibilities we're coming in for a landing on the closest Class-M planet orbiting a G-class star.'

'And?'

'As luck would have it, it's Earth.'

'Any idea when? I mean, is there any chance we can pay Ace a visit and see how she's getting on with her *liaisons dangereuses*?'

'No, it looks as if we're too far back for that.' The Doctor frowned at the read-outs as if unsure whether he was relieved to be landing safely or not.

'How far back?' Benny asked suspiciously. The Doctor's sense of time seemed completely unrelated to anyone else's; being 'a little early' to him could mean another dinosaur safari in the upper Cretaceous.

'Going by the relative positions of the stars, maybe half a millennium. I can't be more precise until we land in a few minutes.'

* * *

34

Guy de Carnac held his breath for a few moments just outside the city gates as he passed by what resembled the skeletal latticework of some two-storey building, with wooden beams stretching between squared-off brick pillars. Discoloured corpses hung on both levels every few feet around the square, crows gripping on to the fresher ones at all angles. He guided the chestnut horse around the edge of the crumbling square until he passed between the guard towers at either side of the arched gate. He was half-tempted to question whether any purse was worth visiting such a place, but resisted the urge. If it meant he could finally settle in peace, then it was worth any journey, however nauseous.

The bipedal silverfish shapes of the mail-encumbered soldiers of the standing army on gate duty scrutinized this tall new arrival closely as he passed. They were clearly not pleased at the arrival of this grim and untamed-looking warrior. De Carnac ignored them, certain that their lords wouldn't encourage them to turn back mercenaries such as himself. If anything, he thought, the only good thing about this war was that men in his position were always welcomed by necessity, if not with open arms.

He drew to a halt to one side of the gateway, so as not to obstruct the flow of refugees, and looked around for a soldier of rank. A few yards away was a bare-headed sergeant-at-arms who wore a mantle emblazoned with the Citeaux crest over his mail. De Carnac beckoned him over sharply, as if unaware that he had no rank over the soldier.

The soldier looked up at him, his scowl betraying his irritation. 'Well? Speak, man, I have other duties than conversing with passing travellers.'

De Carnac cocked an eyebrow at him, a half-smile twitching one corner of his mouth. 'Where can I find a Captain de Montfort?'

'Why? What business have you with the Captain?'

'I took his coin in Minerve, it has taken me several days to get here.'

'Just a moment,' the sergeant-at-arms growled, tugging

a scroll from the leather purse at his belt. 'I have a list of those men still expected by de Montfort. What name have you?'

'I am of the de Carnacs. Guy de Carnac.'

'De Carnac...' The sergeant looked down his list slowly, mouthing each name to be sure. 'Yes,' he said finally. 'Your name is here. You'll find Captain de Montfort and his free lancers based around The Cockatrice – it lies on the corner of the town square and the Rue des Artisans Astuces.'

'I shall find it.' De Carnac nodded a brief thanks.

Leaving the glowering sergeant-at-arms behind, de Carnac threaded his way through the hunted-looking people, his expression carefully guarded as he headed for the small inner city, whose ramparts divided the rich from the poor. The militia on guard there, bedecked in colourful Citeaux livery, checked his name again, but passed him through without further delay.

The Cockatrice turned out to be a stone-built inn on one corner of the square. Though it had a fairly solid-looking roof over its upper storey, the stable block beside it had a number of patches of thatch over holes in the roof.

De Carnac dismounted as he approached the stable, leading the horse through the populous market square. Serfs and laeti in rough homespun garments crowded round the edge of the square, waiting while the stalls and carts of their superiors plied their trade to the masses under the grey skies. A couple of jugglers and tumblers were performing in an open space to one side, while a small knot of men placed bets on the outcome of a fight between two blind men armed with quarterstaves. Here and there the helmets and pikestaffs of the men at arms of the town's militia were visible, marching from merchant to merchant to collect their aubaine. Further soldiers accompanied by black-habited members of the Inquisition collected the Church's tithes, frequently following literally a step behind the aubaine collectors. De Carnac ignored them all, but did at least give way to the tax-collectors as

36

they passed in front of him. Finally, he led the mare into the stable.

A stable-lad, his ownership of a belt-pouch for personal earnings marking him as one of the bourgeois laeti rather than a serf, came forward deferentially, nodding a sort of abbreviated bow. Digging a silver denier from his own purse, de Carnac tossed it to the youth. 'Give Rosinante a good rub down, and some feed,' he ordered, in a tone that was clearly used to issuing commands.

'Yes, master,' the lad said hurriedly, as de Carnac relinquished the reins to him.

Stepping back out into the damp air, de Carnac rounded the corner, and ducked under the thick wooden beam that topped the inn's low doorway. Inside, a mixture of militia, church soldiers and mercenaries sat in little groups around rectangular trestle tables, joking and cursing among pools of spilled beer and half-eaten chunks of salted meat. A couple of armed men in the finery of the town's minor nobility drank more quietly in a partitioned-off area, while a jongleur sang nervously of the Virgin Mary from the corner of the stairs that led to the upper floor.

The aging floorboards creaking under his boots, de Carnac moved over to the bar-top, a series of long planks laid across the tops of several heavy barrels. 'I was told I could find Captain de Montfort here,' he began.

'Upstairs,' the hawk-faced tapster said, jerking his head in that direction. He looked to de Carnac as if he had been a fighter, but the loss of one hand had obviously ended that career. 'He has taken the whole of the upper floor, just ask the guards to show you to him.'

'My thanks,' de Carnac acknowledged, his attention switching fully to the stairs. Stepping impassively around the jongleur, as if he were but a piece of furniture in the way, he ascended to the upper level.

Philippe de Montfort was just emerging from one of the rooms upstairs, when the two guards on the landing barred de Carnac's way. De Montfort, however, waved the man aside with a conspiratorial grin. 'You took long

37

enough to get here,' he rumbled. 'Did you walk all the way?'

'You know how the world is,' de Carnac answered carefully. 'Our country is not safe these days.'

'No, at least not from us, eh, de Carnac? Still, at least you do not stew in your armour here, as we did in the desert under King Louis a few years ago.'

'Here you rust in it.'

Philippe laughed. 'It is good to have you back with us, Guy. Come downstairs and we will drink to old times before I introduce you to Uncle Louis ...'

'Do you expect there to be some difficulty, or is the increase in guards at the tunnel mouth merely a precaution?'

'A little of both,' Parfait Hugues told the squat Castellan. 'Jeanne and Giselle have sent two of our number into Béziers to seek supplies for their hospital, and I feel it would be prudent to watch closely lest they are captured and tell all to the Inquisition.'

The Castellan made a note in a small ledger with a quill. 'Girard and yourself are not pleased?' That would be typical, he thought; they'd probably like the poor creatures in the hospital chambers to be free spirits – or dead, as he looked at it. Then again, he was but a custodian, and no Parfait. In truth, he was surprised they hadn't sent out someone to fetch the pair back: Girard's leadership had become increasingly eccentric of late ... He was getting old, though, and the Castellan suspected that he might even be over fifty. He wished he had had Jeanne's initiative when Girard had refused yesterday's request to send someone to find more food, only for Girard to halve the rations to make their meagre stocks last twice as long. It didn't seem to have occurred to him that, with more people arriving every day from burnt-out villages, they would be lucky if the food lasted an extra day or two.

'Neither of us are pleased, but there is nothing we can do so late. You will be able to assign the extra guards?'

38

'They will not enjoy it, but I will reduce their sleeping times by an hour to rearrange the shifts.'

'Good. I knew you would know what to do.'

'I know what ought to be done – that is another matter,' the Castellan muttered under his breath as the lean Hugues left his sleeping cell.

Two squires were dragging a man in shadowy blue robes from a ramshackle wooden house when Philippe and de Carnac marched into the street, a dozen pikemen at their backs. Guy had never met Francisco Guzman, but the Inquisitor was unmistakable from the description Philippe had given. Guzman, shaved head glistening palely, turned as the newcomers arrived.

Philippe smiled as de Carnac gave him a questioning look. 'One of their witches,' Philippe explained. 'You will never have seen one on your lands, I suppose. They seem to prefer the climate down here, though I fancy it might soon be too warm for this one.'

'Where is the other pervert?' Guzman asked the squires.

'Dead from the arrow-wound he received running from the militia,' one of them replied in a respectful tone.

'I will not have the earth corrupted with his foulness. He will not be buried. Bring out his carcass and take it to the keep; we'll scatter his ashes to the wind along with those of this one. Where is the traitor who owns this hovel?'

'Here,' a man-at-arms grunted, shoving forward a short man with torn clothes and a cut and bruised face.

'What are these base creatures doing in your home?' Guzman's eyes burnt into the man's skull.

'I am but an apothecary, your grace,' he babbled. 'They came to seek balms and some poultices.'

De Carnac could sense the man's terror from several yards, and looked back to see what Guzman would think of his excuse. Guzman smiled coldly. 'I believe you, apothecary. You know the penalty; you are fined one silver mark.' The apothecary sagged a little, plainly relieved at the thought that Guzman wasn't going to impose the full penalty. De Carnac wondered if he was being a little premature – Guzman's reputation was not merciful. Guzman turned as if to leave, then turned back, gazing impassively at the frozen apothecary. 'Sequester the contents of this residence and shop, and return with it to the keep. Then burn this building to the ground.'

The apothecary blanched, but managed to remain silent. De Carnac felt no tinge of surprise. He had thought Guzman would stick to the standard penalty of the law, though he hadn't expected him to be so teasing about it.

'Ah, de Montfort,' Guzman greeted Philippe, 'and this is . . .?'

'Guy de Carnac. We fought the Turks together, now he is to be my second.'

'Good. Louis is waiting for us at Saint Jean's.' He looked round at de Carnac with cold eyes. 'You will find this an excellent introduction to our effort,' he promised.

The church of Saint Jean was a relatively small and recent affair of imported granite, with statues of various saints in niches on each of the steeple's sides. Groups of squires and men-at-arms swarmed around the open plaza before it, encircling the streets beyond and causing the street's residents and hawkers to press themselves nervously into the walls away from the church. Small clusters of silver-spurred knights huddled opposite the main double door, surrounding a palanquin bearing Louis de Citeaux and his retinue.

As Guzman led Philippe and de Carnac towards Louis, a minor commotion alerted them to a small knot of men hurtling down a filth-strewn side street, more men-at-arms in pursuit. Drawing up in horror as they saw the reception awaiting them in the plaza, they barrelled through the hawkers in an effort to reach the door. The wooden doors opened, and the men tumbled through, several hawkers and laeti dragged along with them in a confused entanglement.

'More fool them,' Louis murmured as de Carnac and the others approached. 'It seems that people do not have memories which are quite as long as they believe.' He waved for a knight with one arm in a sling to join Guzman. 'This is de Carnac, I take it,' he asked Philippe.

'He is.'

'Good. One can never have sufficient loyal men.'

'Your confidence honours me, my Lord,' de Carnac said, with a slight bow. Especially since you have yet to see any work from me, he thought.

'I suppose it does. Oh, I am well aware of your previous ... disputes, but you will find our terms more satisfactory.' Though he seemed uninterested, de Carnac noticed that Louis was actually watching his reactions quite closely, out of the corner of his eye. 'Philippe, I have some spiced wine here that should take away the chill.' He waved de Montfort to a sheltered spot beside him. He returned his gaze to the newly arrived mercenary. 'Very well, de Carnac, we shall see how you like our work here. Go with Guzman to fetch the oil and pitch; I consider it long past time we found some warmth out here.'

'Yes, my Lord.' Without further ado, de Carnac turned to the short Spaniard, and waited for him to lead the way. As he turned, he caught a glimpse of the knight with the wounded arm watching him. The knight hastily looked away when he noticed de Carnac's attention upon him, but de Carnac kept watching. There had been a flicker of recognition in those eyes, he thought, which was odd, since he was certain he had never seen the man before. De Carnac looked away again with a mental shrug; he had met many people, and surely couldn't be expected to recall every face.

Snapping his fingers imperiously, Guzman motioned three soldiers over to him, then marched off down the street, de Carnac at his side. Peasants ducked out of their way as they wound through the wet alleys, but de Carnac kept his hand near his sword-hilt just in case. Everyone knew the heretics had sympathizers willing to kill – that trouble he had near that small village was proof enough – and he wasn't going to take any chances.

Before long, they reached a large barn-like structure

41

attached to the keep of the inner city. Numerous peasants, sweating in spite of the chilly air, were straining to heave barrels into a sagging cart. 'Excellent,' Guzman muttered. 'We can start the fires more quickly.' He turned to the wounded knight, who was already tugging a scroll from his belt. 'Make certain they are loading the amount specified in the inventory.' The knight nodded, and moved over towards the workers.

A squad of soldiers emerged from the keep, taking up position beside the wagon, and Guzman nodded approvingly as their captain came over. 'I presume,' de Carnac said, 'that this is for the burnings once the heretics are dragged out.'

'I doubt they will let us drag them out, so we shall burn them out.'

'Burn the church?' De Carnac felt a wave of horror pass through him. He had thought that those were the sort of actions the heretics were being reviled for.

'Of course. Better that than let them continue to desecrate it with their offensive presence.'

'But there are women and children inside!' De Carnac frowned. He had nothing against a good fight, but setting fire to a church full of people was hardly that; he sought a fighter's purse as payment, not thirty pieces of silver. It wasn't even a decent execution, he thought, as he himself had seen some innocents dragged into the church with the most recent fugitives. Surely they had to be freed first?

'They are heretics,' Guzman barked with finality. 'Or do you have a good reason why we should spare them to spread their dissent?'

'Aren't we supposed to forgive those who trespass against us?'

'Vengeance is mine, sayeth the Lord,' Guzman shot back. 'We are but the instruments of that vengeance, duty-bound to be guided by His hand.'

'But some of those people are innocents, trapped by your heretics. You cannot allow them to be sullied with the same reputation for a quirk of fate!'

'The Lord will tell his flock from the wolves,' Guzman

hissed, his temper clearly shortening. He turned to the captain. 'Fire the church as soon as you have completed preparations upon arrival.' The captain nodded and moved aside to consult his men. The knight with the scroll and his arm in a sling sidled up to Guzman as de Carnac subconsciously checked the positioning of the men around him. By the time he had noted that there were two men flanking him and one just off in front, he also noticed that the injured man was again looking furtively in his direction as he whispered to Guzman.

De Carnac began to have a nasty suspicion as to where the soldier had acquired his shoulder wound, and the suspicion was confirmed as Guzman suddenly spun to look at him, eyes wide. The Spaniard's arm shot out towards Guy, and he opened his mouth for a shout.

Before it came, Guy spun to the right. As he moved, he drew his sword, clapping his left hand over the base of the blade to give extra weight. He slammed the pommel into the man who was on his right, before lunging back to the left, the blade sliding smoothly into the stomach of the man who started in front of him.

As Guzman's call for the guards passed his lips, de Carnac pulled his sword from the slumping body, swinging it back to parry a clumsy swing by the third man, who had finally drawn his sword. Reversing the sword in his hand with a flick of the wrist, de Carnac slashed the man's face across the eyes, then stabbed backwards into the man whom he had winded.

The soldier was wearing a hauberk, however, and the strike was an opportunistic one, so the blow merely knocked him backwards again without penetrating flesh. Before he could recover, de Carnac turned, spinning the sword back to a normal grip, and cut the soldier's right leg from under him.

Guzman was running towards the rapidly approaching guards even as the screaming man crashed to the ground, but the wounded knight – evidently the one he had spared at the village – couldn't keep up. Determined not to make the same mistake twice, and angry at himself for both

43

being merciful then and for not being so now, de Carnac leaped forward and brought him down with a two-handed sweep from right shoulder to left hip. The man's mail was no good against either the savage force of the blow or the uncommon sharpness of the blade, and he crumpled to the ground in a puddle of blood.

The guards were closing, but none had bows, so de Carnac took the risk of pausing to leave his sword in his left hand as he drew a short dagger and hurled it at Guzman's fleeing back.

With unusual bravery, or, de Carnac thought sourly, either greed for a reward or fear of punishment, a soldier thrust his shield in front of the dagger, and it bounced off with a crack. Not wasting his breath on a curse over what was already past, de Carnac turned and ran.

Guzman glanced down at the dagger with a sense of outrage. He had never seen anyone wield a sword so quickly. It was almost as if he were possessed of inhuman strength – or maybe just possessed. Despite his zeal, Guzman had never seen anything even halfway supernatural in his life before – aside from the odd omen in the skies, which didn't count as everyone saw *them* – but the way de Carnac had wielded that sword. . .

If de Carnac had seen any of the men at the village, then he had to die. He frowned in thought. He'd never even seen a sword like that. It had gleamed despite the dull light in the air. No, he corrected himself, it had almost *glowed* with a silver light. Perhaps it was enchanted, given by a demon as part of some bargain. . . Perhaps de Carnac really was a heretic, he thought, or perhaps he was just a fool, but Guzman promised himself that for this assault he would go to the flames, rather than be granted a quick death.

He waved the soldiers on furiously, longing to join the hunt, but both anxious to return to burn the church and shakily afraid that de Carnac might be more successful if he tempted fate that way. The worry angered him further, and he lashed out at the nearest soldier's back in an effort to force him to run faster. 'A gold florin to the man who brings him down,' he roared, 'and a whipping for you all if he escapes!'

Breathing deeply to bring his rage under control, Guzman spun on his heel and stalked back towards the encircled church. The heretics and their helpers inside had enjoyed a long enough stay of execution thanks to the delay, he felt, but it was over now.

He allowed his head to lower in sorrow at the understanding that there were other innocents trapped inside as well, but he controlled the feeling by reminding himself that they would be guaranteed a place by the Lord's side in recognition of their noble sacrifice. In fact, he considered, he might even preach their story as an example to others of how a truly pure soul should behave . . .

Guy de Carnac pounded through the narrow stinking streets, the few grubby citizens who were about hurriedly dived for cover at the sight of the charging warrior with his drawn sword. He wasn't worried about the soldiers catching him – their mail and shields were too heavy to allow them to outpace him – but if word had been carried by a more lightweight runner there could easily be a whole troop of them waiting at the stables.

Almost skidding in a pool of unidentifiable slime, he rounded the corner between two rotting wooden buildings and into a cobbled street leading directly to the square where he had first arrived.

Evidently a runner had indeed been sent, as half a dozen soldiers were just moving into a position to block the end of the street. For a moment, Guy considered charging them in the hope that the surprise would get him through them, but he quickly realized that the street was too narrow for him to force a passage through them by force.

Drawing in a deep and relieved breath of stingingly cold air as he tottered to a halt, he caught a glimpse of a group of people manhandling barrels from a cart into a low-roofed and dingy inn. Returning his sword to its scabbard, Guy dashed back as the soldiers began their advance, and vaulted atop the remaining barrels in the cart. As the innkeeper gaped in astonishment, Guy swiftly clambered up on to the low roof and scuttled across it, ascending another storey when he reached the higher wall of a neighbouring building.

Glancing back, he saw with a faint flush of relief that the soldiers were not following. Keeping his arms outstretched to balance himself on the narrows, Guy jogged along the rooftops towards the square, which was easily visible by the tops of the stakes that had temporarily joined the town gallows.

When he was just two roofs away from the inn and the stables, he realized why the soldiers hadn't followed him. He cursed himself as a fool for not realizing they would know where he was going, as the top of a ladder rattled against the eave of the stable's roof ahead.

He drew his sword with a sense of fatalism; they would be smart enough to have surrounded the adjoining buildings, and the guards from the church would arrive any time as well. If he was going to die, he decided, he may as well take some of the enemy down with him. Besides, what did he have to lose but his fears? They were the ones who would be constrained by careful thoughts of self-preservation.

The first two mail-clad soldiers retrieved their swords as he reached the inn's roof, drawing his own blade in a wide sweep. The first soldier swung with a two-handed grip, one hand wrapped around the other, but Guy didn't even attempt to block the blow. Instead, he ducked down, his shoulder slamming into the soldier, who was carried over Guy's back by the momentum of his own stroke. Guy straightened as the soldier's feet left the ground, and the mail-clad warrior tumbled over the edge of the roof with a startled yell.

Guy's sword struck sparks from that of the second man as they closed on each other. The soldier had his back to the edge, however, and couldn't resist the urge to try and snatch a quick glimpse to make sure he wouldn't share his partner's fate. As soon as his attention was distracted, Guy swept his foot round behind the soldier's leg, tripping him backwards. The soldier thudded heavily into the caulked wooden roof, and Guy rammed his sword straight downwards through the front of his hauberk.

Planting his foot on the corpse's chest to pull his sword free again, Guy turned to see another soldier gain the roof of the stable. Not wishing to give him any chance to get his bearings, Guy bounded down on to the slightly lower stable roof, sword raised high. This soldier had a shield, however, which blocked Guy's swing despite cracking in the process. Circling warily, Guy hopped from beam to to beam, lashing out at the soldier, who seemed to be stalling for time for his comrades to ascend.

Watching his footing with half an eye, a thought struck Guy. Resisting the urge to let a smile break on to his grim features lest it alert his opponent, Guy dodged to the right, them shuffled back slightly, as if tiring. Grinning triumphantly, the soldier lunged forward – and dropped through the thatched part of the roof, which wasn't strong enough to bear the weight of himself and his armour.

Allowing himself a half-smile, Guy moved to the ladder and planted his foot on it, ready to kick it away from the eave before anyone else could come up. Rather than do so, he paused and looked over the edge. The last of the small group was just stepping on to the lowermost rungs; evidently the other two had remained behind to watch the end of the street in case he doubled back.

He frowned, pursing his lips thoughtfully. The stable had only one storey, and the ground below was mud strewn with matted straw rather than hard cobbles. . . Sheathing his sword decisively, Guy straightened, then stepped off the edge of the roof.

His boots hit the unsuspecting soldier's helmet with a clang, and he rolled with the sudden tumble the impact created, landing heavily and painfully, but safely, in the mud. Flexing his shoulder with a wince, Guy pulled himself to his feet, and reached for his sword-hilt as he looked over at the soldier. Guy's unfortunate landing-pad was groaning a few feet away, one arm twisted severely away from the shoulder and blood spreading from under his coif, whose links had shattered and split. Just to be certain that he was no longer a threat, however, Guy grabbed the dazed man by the scruff of the neck, and bounced his forehead off an oaken cornerpost until he heard a wet crack.

Shoving the cowering stable-lad aside, Guy unhitched his horse and mounted up, ducking under the low doorway as the animal cantered out under his guidance. Heavy footfalls sounded from the nearby street as Guy dashed across the square. The guards were too late, however, to do anything other than make futile calls for him to halt.

Approaching the town gate, Guy saw several soldiers reach for swords and pikes, but their route to him was blocked by the swarm of destitutes who were also mournfully leaving the town. Guy was able to slip past and gallop off down the muddy road.

Chapter 4

'You worthless afterbirth of a rutting donkey!' Louis thundered, causing the pikemen at the arched doorways of the hall to surreptitiously attempt to blend into the walls. Philippe seethed, glowering at Louis' guards in the knowledge that if one so much as blinked, he'd have his head. 'I did not summon you to be the sword-arm of my city, just for you to send traitors to my door! Bad enough that he refuses to help cleanse this heresy, but now he knows that it was your men at the village, in the cloaks of the heretics. When he hears that Guzman's rival was slain there . . .'

'He was a valiant fighter against the infidel Turks,' Philippe reminded de Citeaux, 'but I take no responsibility for his actions today.' Philippe paced the room's flagstones with quick, hunting movements, anger driving his muscles restlessly. 'It was I who was betrayed,' he pointed out in a low voice. 'I who has been struck at by his treason. If you had let me ride after him, I would have brought you his head on a lance to adorn the city gates.'

'You could not have defeated him,' Guzman admonished with a trace of reluctance, 'truly. You did not see how quickly he wielded that sword – it was the devil's work, to be sure.'

'Yes, that sword,' Louis said thoughtfully. 'Did he have that weapon when you knew him?'

'No. He may have traded it for booty from that campaign.'

'He is a traitor,' Guzman repeated from his position near the open fireplace, tossing pieces of fruit peel into the fire with short, angry motions which punctuated each syllable.

'Yes, yes, all right,' Louis said more quietly, ignoring the interested zeal of the Spaniard's tone. Philippe wished he hadn't noticed it either; somehow he just couldn't get as excited as usual about the prospect of an entertaining fight while that sort of faith was being displayed. Still, it fired the men's passions at least. Louis rose from his simplistic wooden throne, pulling a dagger from his belt and an imported orange from a platter on the table. He seemed to be calming himself as he sliced the orange apart. Philippe certainly hoped so, anyway. Guzman and Louis needed each other's help too much, but either of them could survive without Philippe's help – Dukes and Cardinals were rare and valuable, but there were always warriors available for hire. 'It happens sometimes; a warrior's sense of chivalry is so strong he cannot bear to execute in cold blood even though he may be a matchless butcher on the field of combat.' He smiled faintly. 'Though I admit, such a stance seems hypocritical for de Carnac, considering his past.'

Philippe shook his head, dismissing the problem reluctantly. 'His loss makes no difference; we can find fighters anywhere.'

'Yes, you speak truly. We must not allow one foolish man to distract us from the important business at hand. Francisco, go back and complete the burning of the church, then return here while we prepare to question that heretic.'

'As you wish,' Guzman said, 'but it must be done as it is instructed in our laws.'

'Do not overly concern yourself. Would I waste good food on him anyway?'

Guy de Carnac wrapped the cloak more tightly about himself as he was borne unseeingly past the other human flotsam and jetsam from Béziers. His stubbled face was set in a sort of grimly blank expression as the chestnut mare carried him off the old Roman road and up a low embankment to one side. One last campaign, he had promised himself, and he would have been able to buy a small plot somewhere and live in peace. Now that hope was gone, and he wondered how long it would be before he would find another opportunity to buy his freedom from his trade.

The day was already wearing on, and he knew he'd have to find a sheltered spot in which to camp, and soon. He should have known that Béziers wouldn't be the place for him, he told himself sourly. He would just have to ride on, searching further afield. Perhaps beyond the lands of the Turks, he thought slightly dreamily. It was said by some of those he'd met on his travels that there was a truly wondrous, magical land beyond the Silk Road, and maybe *that* land was empty and peaceful . . .

Don't be a fool, he reminded himself. Since when has there ever been a carrot at the end of the stick? He focused his mind on more mundane – and pressing – matters, looking around keenly for the right sort of location to make camp for the night.

The already ancient road faded into the fields as it stretched away from the city wall, leaving the travellers to drift off on to trails or across country altogether. On the far side of it, perhaps three or four miles off, a narrow river wound down from the foothills, while the trees loomed ahead of him, their empty branches blending with and disguising the rock of the hills directly ahead.

The mountains that border Moorish Spain, he thought. Though he was now heading west, perhaps he could find a ship bound for one of the ports on the Bosphorus. From Barcelona east to İzmir, perhaps . . . He abandoned his train of thought abruptly as a trio of mounted knights rode from the edge of the trees ahead, their imposing forms wreathed in their horses' smoky breath. For an instant, de Carnac's hand strayed towards his sword-hilt, his mind racing with the idea that de Montfort or his cronies had sent these men after him. Good sense stayed his hand, however, and he realized that no pursuer would have bothered to overtake him, even in the unlikely event that they could.

Also, of course, the red cross patée emblazoned on the knights' surcoats was a reassuring sign. Though devoted to the Church, he was well aware that these men owed allegiance only to the Pope, not Louis de Citeaux, and even then only at their own whim. They were, after all, wearing the mantles of those who liked to call themselves the Poor Knights of Christ and the Temple of Solomon. Everyone else simply saw them as the Knights Templar.

The three Templars had stopped at the top of the rise between the road and the trees, and seemed to be watching the affairs of the city gate. De Carnac considered giving them a wide berth, but then decided against wasting the effort: there was no reason to assume they'd recognize him, and they were generally men of honour, in his experience. Not that that always meant anything, of course . . .

Wary, but unhesitatingly, he rode along the top of the embankment, slowing as they turned to greet his approach. Keeping his hands on the reins, he nodded to the Templars.

'You are well to have left the city,' one of them said. He removed his cylindrical helmet, revealing flashing eyes at the heart of a genial face, whose hair and beard were becoming tinged with grey.

De Carnac blanched, but recovered his poise quickly; so much for hoping he wouldn't be recognized. Now he would just have to hope for courtesy. 'The open country has always been my home. You, of all people, should know that.'

'A fine sentiment in these dark times. The towns are but hunting grounds for the Inquisition, so where else would a fox go to earth?'

'Not just foxes. Where should these rabbits find burrows?'

'Like you, they should go where they will. Flight is their salvation, and there is sanctuary for them in the mountains.'

'Their fortress?' De Carnac snorted. 'Eventually the

52

Church will find its entrances – you must know that.' He looked back down at the road, reluctantly letting anger get the better of him. 'They are travellers just like the ones your Order swore to protect in the Holy Land. Will you abandon them in your own homeland?'

'We are supposed to side with the Church,' the Templar said pointedly. 'You should be grateful we remain neutral in this civil war, else we would be assisting in the hunting-down of these heretics.'

'Astonished is more the word I would use to describe any reaction to your claims of neutrality,' de Carnac whispered softly.

'They will find their way to the fortress, with ... luck. Of course it will fall eventually, but who knows what may happen after that?'

'I do. The Order will go on with its political machinations for another hundred years, as you will no doubt pander to both sides in the hope of telling whichever one eventually triumphs that you were abetting them as much as you could.'

The two helmeted Templars looked round sharply, but the leader stayed them with a gesture. 'Some of our brotherhood could have been offended by such a remark, were they to be here.'

'I am offended by the abandonment of the very people who built your preceptory for you.'

'Your concern is touching, friend, but why then do you not aid them yourself?' The Templar smirked faintly.

'I am not an army.'

'Evidently,' the Templar agreed in a tone which rankled de Carnac. The knight shrugged finally. 'Every man must go his own way.' He glanced up at the patch of cloud that glowed with a watery light which marked the sun's position. 'For now, we must be on our way, if we are to reach our preceptory by nightfall.' The Templar replaced his helmet and nodded to de Carnac once more, before urging the horse forward, his companions following immediately.

De Carnac's anger faded, and he asked himself why he

had even bothered to approach the knights. It wasn't as if he had thought they would do anything, and these people would be far behind him once he gained passage on a ship east from Barcelona to İzmir. Trying to recall the best route across the mountains to Moorish Spain, de Carnac relaxed, glad he would soon be free from the strange and terrible world that his country had become.

The three Templars reined to halt when de Carnac's hoof-beats had faded away into silence. 'He was most insolent for a mercenary,' one of them commented.

'He is that,' the leader agreed. 'But his manner is unimportant.'

'What will he do now?'

The leader remained silent for a moment, fingering the slim cord that was tied round his waist. Worn by his companions as well, it was a symbol of their chosen poverty. 'He will do what he feels is right, I imagine. That is the only certainty.'

Edouard couldn't help but feel a tense disappointment attach itself to him when the hoofbeats slowed as they approached the sheltered canopy of the evergreens. The others who had gathered around the crackling fire sprang up wildly and looked to Edouard with pleading eyes as they backed towards the nearest tree-trunks.

Edouard could feel his legs shift almost involuntarily into a position from which to bolt for the trees. For once he was displeased by his former position as a bourgeois vintner, responsible for those who worked the vineyards, as the former colons and serfs who had joined up with his family's group in the flight from the city all now looked to him to set an example of wisdom and bravery. All he wanted to do, of course, was flee at least as fast as they could.

Reluctantly forcing down his fear before anyone could do anything foolish, Edouard stood, firmly grasping a well-worn axe, and faced the narrow track that led through the trees. The leather-wrapped wood soaked up the sweat from his palms as a horse wandered into the clearing, moving easily through the shadows like a moth drifting on a summer breeze.

Its saddle was empty. Edouard frowned in puzzlement, but then relaxed: if this was the horse of a warrior, then the soldiers at Béziers may have shot him from the saddle with arrows or crossbow bolts to be on the safe side. Slipping the haft of the axe through a loop on his belt, Edouard approached the horse cautiously, making soothing sounds so as not to frighten it into either running away or lashing out with its hooves.

Finally, he took its loose reins in one hand, and patted its neck gently. Perhaps there would be useful materials in the rolled-up pack behind the saddle, he thought. Some salt meat or dry tinder would be worth its weight in gold, if not more so. Continuing to soothe the horse, Edouard moved along towards its haunches. He started to reach up towards the pack, but suddenly paused, as something caught his attention out of the corner of his eye. There was something odd about its tail, he thought; the horse seemed to have made an unusually strong effort to twitch it. Curiosity getting the better of him, Edouard looked along, and saw a leather rim at the base of it. He stepped back, unsure what to make of the fact that the horse seemed to have an artificial tail, its natural one having been docked for some reason.

'Your concern for your people is worthy,' a voice said from the darkness behind him, causing Edouard to start, 'but I think you ought to realize that if I meant you ill, I could have killed you at any time since you first heard the hoofbeats.'

Edouard turned, very slowly. A man stepped from the shadows, what little light there was glittering from the edges of the cuirass, pauldrons and greaves that he wore over a leather jerkin and short haubergeon. At the very least, his odd armour proved to Edouard that he was no hauberk-clad soldier of the Church or the King. On the other hand, the fact that his armour appeared to be pieced together from second-hand – and some very old, even

Roman-looking – oddments suggested that he may have been some kind of bandit.

As if reading his thoughts, the stranger smiled, as much to himself as to Edouard, it seemed, and sheathed his sword, which had seemed to almost glow in the limited moonlight. 'You seem to have found a sheltered camping spot,' the stranger explained. 'All I seek is a place to sleep by the fire.'

'Why should I let you?' Edouard demanded in spite of himself. 'How do I know you are not a spy for the Inquisition?'

'You do not, unless you are a sorcerer who can read minds. However, if we do happen to be discovered by such a person, I assure you they will kill me just as enthusiastically as they will kill you.' He paused in thought for a moment. 'Likely more so, truly. In return, I will share what salt meat I have with you and your people.'

Edouard thought hard. If this man was a spy, then refusing him would be his excuse to return to his masters and give away the location of the night's camp. On the other hand, if he wasn't a spy, then refusing him hospitality when he needed it was unforgivable. Even Solomon himself would have difficulty with such a choice, he suspected. Better to have him where he could be watched, the fugitive vintner decided – and where his axe was close at hand. 'Very well,' he said finally. 'It is this way, stranger.'

'Forgive me,' the stranger apologized in a sincere-sounding tone. 'Guy de Carnac,' he said introducing himself.

All too conscious of the speed and silence of de Carnac's approach, Edouard nervously led him through the trees.

Chapter 5

Nothing moved in the still night air, save, perhaps, an occasional owl circling distantly above. If such a creature was overhead, however, it was invisible in the overcast moonless sky. Crags of lightly tinted limestone loomed jaggedly to the east, while the ground elsewhere fell away to a small river cutting, which separated the rocky promontory from unevenly rolling fields.

A faint greenish light began to shine on the crumbling rock, as if some phosphorescent moss was growing there. The green light pulsed fitfully, however, and a distant chiming sound soon accompanied it, its tinkling notes drifting lightly across the fields.

Gradually, a darker patch of shadow solidified atop a jutting outcrop surrounded by skeletal gorse. The green light pulsed more brightly as the shadow finally condensed into a tall, triple-roofed box, which had the look of some sort of Chinese cabinet or wardrobe. The green light finally faded from the ornate lantern atop the highest peak of the sculpted triple-roof, and was replaced by a faint yellow glow behind its oval windows that spoke in its own way of plush armchairs, rich brandy and a warm fire in the hearth.

Edouard came awake with a start, and looked shakily around to see what had roused him. A chilly drizzle was descending from the starless sky, cold droplets soaking through the rough canopy he'd made from an old cloak propped up on some sticks. Rolling out from under the wet wool, he noticed de Carnac's mare alone to one side, her master conspicuous by his absence.

Kicking himself for being so foolish as to welcome an armed warrior – let alone one who must bear such shame – into the camp, Edouard snatched up his axe, and moved towards the darkness beyond the dying fire, grateful that the rain had mostly destroyed the crisp and noisily brittle surface of the snow. This de Carnac would see how betrayal was repaid.

Slipping through the trees as quietly as he could – albeit well aware that even when he had been fully awake de Carnac had been able to detect and approach him silently – Edouard followed the path back to the road with only a little difficulty.

The small cutting that led up to the rutted cart-road was a pool of inky blackness, but Edouard felt that he owed it to his people to make sure that de Carnac couldn't bring the Inquisition down on them. If he could just reach the edge of the road, and crouch down for a good view along its length . . . he thought.

Something heavy and solid slammed into him from behind and to the left, and Edouard swung wildly to the side with his axe, twisting like an eel. A bony fist pounded the side of his head, making his vision blur long enough for the axe to be twisted out of his grip as a hand forced him down into the mud at the roadside. Shaking his head to clear the fuzziness, Edouard tensed, ready to make a break for freedom.

'Stop your wriggling, you imbecile,' de Carnac's voice whispered in his ear. 'If they did not see you blundering out of the trees they must certainly hear your struggles.' Edouard froze, and, after a moment, the heavy pressure on his shoulders was gone. To the left, he could dimly make out a cloaked de Carnac peering over the edge of the roadside ditch they were lying in.

'Who will hear?' Edouard demanded in angry confusion. 'Why are you skulking around in the shadows like a wolf?'

'I heard something out there, a series of howls the like of which I have never –'

'The sound must be carrying from the Inquisition's chambers in the city,' Edouard suggested uneasily.

'No, we are too far from the walls, and the wind is in the wrong direction to carry cries. Besides, look,' he gestured in the direction of the hills to the west. Edouard raised himself on his elbows, wondering what sort of trick was being played. As his eyes acclimatized to wakefulness in the dark, however, he realized he could make out a tiny yellow point of light in the distance, perhaps in the foothills.

'Another campfire,' Edouard said firmly. He didn't like the way this situation was running away with him, and he almost hoped that de Carnac was betraying them somehow – at least that was something he could understand.

'Not up there. In such an exposed spot it would be extinguished quickly.' De Carnac shook his head invisibly in the darkness. 'It does not dance the way a flame does, the way a campfire would; nor is it torch- or candlelight.'

'Perhaps it is a fallen star?'

This time, de Carnac didn't contradict him. Instead, his voice took on a wondering, fascinated tone. 'Perhaps. But the stars are white, not yellow,' he added in a disappointed tone. 'It could be the work of a demon.'

Edouard genuflected hurriedly. 'Do not speak of demons, not while it is still dark.'

'There are many Albigenses and Waldensians in this area, according to the Church. Who knows what they do in secret?'

'Who cares, so long as they pay their gold like anyone else.'

'That explains why you are fleeing the city,' de Carnac replied, with a hint of humour. 'But you are probably right; I have never seen a priest conjure up an angel, so why should their heretic wizards have any better fortune with demons?' They both remained silent for a moment. 'But that is no light of nature, and neither man nor beast

59

made the sound I heard. Still, it seems to want to remain where it sits; I think it must be harmless, whatever it is.'

Illuminated by the steady yellow light, beyond the intricately carved jade portals, the Doctor fiddled around with some controls on the console as Bernice watched ambivalently. She always relished the chance to see a piece of history, of course, but she hadn't thought to bring any recording equipment with her, bar her ubiquitous diary.

The scanner screen in the Pagoda was the silvered surface of a free-standing Chinese mirror which had images of dragons and rather more ordinary pagodas painted on the back. As Benny watched, the reflections of the Doctor and herself faded away as an image of the outside world appeared. She couldn't see much, as the countryside was pitch-black, with no light pollution from any nearby towns to add any luminescence to the sky whatsoever.

Although the image was one of shadows and invisible features, Benny couldn't help being attracted to it in a way that even the most exciting image on the normal TARDIS scanner had never achieved. It was, she realized after a quick self-inquest, because the tall mirror was so large that one almost felt that it could be stepped through.

The Doctor adjusted a few more controls, and the computer-enhanced view of the outside environment became as visible as if it were a midsummer's day. They seemed to have landed on a natural terrace on the lower slopes of a hilly area in some temperate region. A small walled city lay some distance to the southeast, beyond the opening of the valley below, while a few scattered campfires were enhanced and displayed here and there across the intervening countryside.

'Western Europe,' the Doctor announced after a moment's thought. 'The southern end of the Eastern Pyrenees, going by the geology of those foothills – that's just a guess, of course,' he added modestly. 'Not a million miles from Ace's new home after all.'

Bernice smiled to herself. For once he actually seemed

to have found a restful spot to wait out the week or so until the TARDIS homed in. 'So when the hell are we?'

'Oh, a little early for Ace . . .' He turned to consult a read-out.

A little early? Benny thought, this probably *is* the Cretaceous after all. I'm going to keep an eye on that scanner, and if I see any sign of Doug McClure, I'm hitting the dematerialization switch no matter what.

'Ah, the Middle Ages, it seems.' He thumped the console, waiting to see if this would produce a more specific read-out. It didn't. He sighed, the sound turning into a little growl of displeasure towards the end. 'Not one of the best times or places to be, in any case.'

Benny thought for a moment, trying to recall the relevant information from her memory of dates and places. Her cheeriness sank sourly as a name came to mind. 'Crusades, wars of succession, Mongol hordes. . .' she said grimly.

'Yes. Another of those innumerable times in your ancestors' history when men with longswords sliced to pieces other men – '

'Whose swords weren't quite as long?' Benny suggested.

'Well I wouldn't have put it quite that way myself,' the Doctor chided gently. 'I've never found the zeal with which you humans pursue sectarian or patriotic murder so amusing.'

'If you can't laugh, what can you do?'

The Doctor didn't bother to answer, preferring instead to compare labels on some of the medical supplies he'd brought from the TARDIS infirmary. 'These should do the trick,' he told her happily, as if his previous sentiment had never been expressed.

'What are they?' It wasn't as if they needed anti-radiation treatments so far back in history, after all.

'Broad spectrum antibiotics, a few immunizations, that sort of thing.' Clipping a small ampoule into a hypospray, he motioned to her to roll up her sleeve. 'I don't want to take any chances on you contracting any variants of the plague that are around in this time period, for one thing.

61

Also, and rather less what you'd expect, there are a lot more bacteria and what-have-you in the local ecosystem than your body is acclimatized to.'

'Get on with it then.'

'I just did it a minute ago.'

'In that case, ow!'

'Very droll. Now, let's see what useful items we have to tide us over for our stay. . .' As the Doctor spoke, he slid one of the bamboo and paper panels aside, revealing a floor-to-ceiling stack of drawers that were flush with the wall. 'Survival kit's usually in the bottom one, which would be of more use if they'd fitted a handle,' he finished crossly, trying to get a grip on the top edge with his fingernails.

'Allow me,' Benny said smugly, tugging a couple of delicate metal scrapers from a slim leather pouch she always kept in a pocket. Originally they were for scraping the rock from small fossils, though since joining the Doctor she had more often used them for picking locks. Hooking the ends of two of them over the hairline gap between drawers, she turned them round and pulled the drawer out with them.

Inside were various thermal blankets, emergency rations, torches and everlasting matches, a Swiss Army knife, a very dusty brandy hip-flask, a spare first-aid kit, and half a dozen paperback books – a copy of the *Junior Colour Encyclopedia of Space*, two books in some weird alien script which she couldn't decipher, something on mythology by Gilbert Horner, a Charles Fort collection, and an Agatha Christie with the last couple of pages ripped out. Benny shunted the contents of the drawer around as if she were stirring a stew. 'Are you sure this lot will keep us all right until the TARDIS gets free?'

'Of course I'm sure,' the Doctor snapped indignantly. 'When you've been stranded in hostile environments as much as I have, you come to know exactly what works best.'

'As much as you have?'

'It hasn't always been plain sailing in that old TARDIS, you know. I've had to fend for myself in lots of places:

62

from the glaciers of polar Mars to the jungles of Veltroch, from the plains of Leng to the fire sands of Canopus
III, from the – '

'Halls of Montezuma to the shores of Tripoli? I get the
idea,' she acquiesced hurriedly at his peevish gaze. She
shoved the books aside to get at the brandy. 'Well, you
might be right about this, I suppose.'

'It's Napoleon's brandy.'

'You mean Napoleon brandy, don't you?'

'No,' he replied firmly, 'I don't.'

Francisco Guzman's pallid features quivered with ill-
concealed anticipation as he looked in on the semi-
conscious man who lay in the rat-infested cell beneath the
Hôtel de Ville. His body was corrupted by his heresy, of
course – the Lord alone knew what he and the other blue-
robed man who had been his constant companion had
been doing alone in the countryside – but once freed from
that corruption by the flames, at least his soul would be
saved.

That was the beauty of the Lord's world, he thought
placidly. Even the most severely decayed could be
cleansed and restored, ready to receive forgiveness – if
given the correct sort of help. His uncle, Dominic, had
been so filled with joy at the time of his own realization
of that fact, he recalled. Dominic would be proud of him
now, he was sure; proud as he watched from the kingdom
of heaven.

Guzman smiled to himself as he closed the small shutter
that was set into the door at eye level, and turned back
to Louis de Citeaux; if only there was some way these
poor wretches could thank him for saving them from
themselves. 'He is weakening, but will last long enough
to be questioned.'

'Your delays are a nuisance, but I suppose a few hours
will make no difference,' Louis said with a shrug. 'Just so
long as this one tells us what we want to know.'

'Our techniques are refined further with each subject.
When this poor creature has been starved for ten hours,

he will be co-operative. Chirurgeon,' he called, his voice bringing forth a black-robed friar from one of the shadowy archways set into the dank tunnel. 'Look after him well.'

'As you say, Eminence,' the stick-like figure acknowledged with a slight bow.

'Eminence?' Louis asked in an amused tone. 'Is that not a little pre-emptive?'

'A little, perhaps.'

Girard missed the scent of the sea up here in the clean mountain air, but never allowed himself to succumb to any memories triggered by the sensation; obviously it was but a lure, a temptation to find something worthwhile in the world of matter.

From atop the main hold of the south tower, he could see a goodly distance in all directions along the river, but there was no sign of the blue cloaks or robes that would signal the return of the two young men whom Jeanne had sent out. A pure spirit would triumph over physical dilemmas, he had always said, but Jeanne had acted so quickly to forestall any such proof ... He sometimes caught himself wondering why she had ever become a Parfait at all. Then again, he used to catch fish for people to eat – who knows how many of their antecedents' reincarnated spirits he had killed. That had all stopped now, but it proved that even he was not perfect.

Still, perhaps everything would work out for the best; Jeanne at least knew how to cope with trouble, perhaps because her farm upbringing had shown her much of it. Perhaps, he decided, it was time he found out more about her life before conversion. Maybe there was something there that could ... His train of thought stopped abruptly, as he saw light spill out through the cracks in the shutters of his window below.

It was strange – no one here had any real possessions, so there was nothing to steal. What other reason could there be for someone to enter his cell? Concerned, he turned away from the low crenellations, and hurried back towards the staircase.

Philippe de Montfort reined in his charger, and signalled for the others in his troop to do likewise. The threatening embers of his eyes glowering out from between the forked beard and the rim of his helmet, he surveyed what little remained visible of the Roman road in the cloudy night.

He had known that de Carnac would leave the road and go across country, but the mud was so criss-crossed with tracks that following one single set would have been impossible. He had known from the start he was wasting his time with this sortie, but had embarked upon it anyway, as he felt he had to do something. The betrayal nagged at him like the aftermath of the sting of a summer hornet.

Holding his flambeau away from him to examine the tracks in the ground, he paused, his attention distracted by a very recent set of tracks. Dropping from his horse, he bent to examine the hoofprints more closely. They seemed to have been left by three large horses bearing the weight of heavily armoured men, yet none of his men had been out this far until that moment.

'Of course,' he muttered to himself. 'Those interfering jackals . . .' He swung himself back on to the horse with surprising agility for one both tired from a long day and wearing a hauberk. Digging his heels into the horse's flanks, he spurred it back towards the city, his men following dumbly after him.

The door was barred when Girard arrived, Hugues beside him. Opening it with a large iron key, both men pushed into the room.

It was empty – but a candle, which had been unlit when Girard had left it that evening, was now burning merrily. What could an intruder have been looking for, Girard wondered. Thievery was common enough in the outside world, of course, but unheard of here, and why make it so obvious?

'Perhaps someone sought you,' Hugues suggested.

Ever the practical one, Girard thought. 'Perhaps, but anyone could have told whoever it was where I could be found.'

'Someone from outside the Roc?'

'Impossible; how would they know which room is mine? I suppose it does not really matter – there is nothing to steal here. It may have been one of the soldiers looking for a private place to share with a woman, I imagine. The thought is distasteful, but the power of Rex Mundi is strong, so we must forgive them for not being in control of themselves.' But only because I hope they learn better as they discover more about our people, he thought. 'It matters little.'

Chapter 6

The snapping of deadwood brought de Carnac awake instantly. His sword was half-drawn before he noticed that the noise had been caused by the dozen or so others in the camp packing their belongings. A few of them were already meandering towards the trail back out of the clearing, meagre possessions rattling on their backs as they squelched off through the white-flecked mud.

Rolling into a sitting position, de Carnac stood up rather stiffly, rubbing his hands to get the circulation going again and regretting not being awake long enough to keep an eye on the fire; he had seen more men die of exposure in the last few months than in all his previous years, and had no wish to add himself to their number.

As de Carnac rolled up his blanket, wondering where he was going to find a stream to wash the mud off it, Edouard approached with a wooden bowl – its base blackened by the fire – of souppe despourre in his hand. 'You should eat some of this,' Edouard said. 'I look after all those who pass the night in my camp, and the others have all eaten their fill, so I have no intention of excluding you.'

'My thanks,' de Carnac mumbled thickly, still slightly addled by sleep. His gratitude was genuine enough, however, and he cupped the bowl in both hands to help warm them as he drank it.

'I am told there is a sanctuary in the mountains,' Edouard said slowly as he squatted down beside de Carnac. 'The Parfaits who occasionally visited the town say they will shelter any who require it.'

'And what do they have to gain?'

'Perhaps nothing. I have dealt with many over the years, and they are no different from you or I, except that they honour a different god.'

'I have travelled far, Edouard, and I have encountered many different beliefs, including those of your Albigenses; you are undoubtedly correct. In their daily life they are as we are.'

'Then you too are making for their enclave?'

'I think not. My country has become alien to me and I would like to put that change as far beyond me as possible.'

'Then you make for Moorish Spain?'

'Yes, from Barcelona I can gain ship's passage to İzmir. I have heard of wondrous kingdoms beyond the Silk Road, and perhaps I will see them some day.'

'You will find the mountains impassable at this time of year,' Edouard warned, 'and even should you find an open pass, it will probably be filled by a Moorish raiding party making for Foix or Perpignan.'

De Carnac smiled tiredly. 'I have met Moorish raiding parties before.'

'I believe you.' Edouard sighed resignedly, with an odd look in his eye. 'Most of my people have gone, so I too must move on, but I wish you well on your journey. Fare you well, Guy de Carnac.' He raised his hand in a parting gesture.

'And to you,' de Carnac responded sincerely. Not many people would have accepted him into their camp like that, regardless of how impolite a refusal would have been. For whatever it may be worth, he added silently.

The Doctor stretched as he stepped out on to a jutting finger of rock, its surface dark and slick from overnight rain and meltwater. Tilting his head back to check the wan sun in the colourless sky, he shook his head with a faintly ironic smile before rapping on the smooth stone walls of the small shrine-like pagoda.

'All right,' Benny's voice drifted out, more gravelly than

usual, thanks to the hectic night of fleeing the TARDIS. 'I'm coming.' She emerged from the Pagoda reluctantly, uninspired by the drab surroundings. Noticing the Doctor interestedly poking at some rockbound moss with the tip of his umbrella and muttering something about 'carboniferous limestone', she pointedly velcroed shut the collar on the thin insulating suit she'd found in the next drawer up from the survival kit. Though trimmed with highly reflective strips so as to aid rescuers in locating the wearer, its multi-pocketed form resembled nothing so much as a thinner version of the protective suit worn by racing drivers. It was certainly more useful here than her silk blouse, at any rate. 'Interesting place you've found,' she commented with heavy irony, after a quick look around her. A faint mistiness hung in the air amidst the hills that undulated away into the distance. 'Are you sure this is Earth? It looks more like Nekros to me.'

'Quite fascinating,' the Doctor agreed enthusiastically. 'Of course this is Earth. Do you really think I can't tell one planet from another even once I'm standing on its surface?' He made an expansive gesture encompassing the surrounding white-flecked earthy mountains, which had the alternately rolling and jagged appearance of a field of melted chocolate that had been dropped from a great height and then frozen when it splashed on to the ground. 'Climatologically speaking, this is a marvellously variable area. The altitude gives the possibility of thick snow in winter, while relative proximity to the Mediterranean offers frequent mild spells, and warm summers. This was when the Med was still mostly water, of course.'

'Pity you couldn't have landed us in one of those warm summers.'

'Oh, you'd still get the occasional chilly night then, thanks to our altitude. It can be rather wet then as well.' He strolled back towards the main part of their narrow plateau. A stubby mound of rock a few tens of yards across rose from the opposite side, but there was a ledge several feet wide which completely encircled it, and it was on to this which the Doctor strolled.

Benny followed, looking curiously about her, wondering if she was actually going to get the chance to see anything, well, historical. The evergreen-laden mountainsides were pleasant enough, despite the cold, but they could be in any time from the Neolithic age onwards. She paused to take a deep breath, holding it to run over something in her mind. Satisfied, she exhaled again, reassured that at least there was no danger of them being in a mechanized era: the air was so clean it just had to be pre-industrial.

Scrabbling over a few loose rocks, she followed the Doctor round a curve in the summit of their low hill. He simply strolled on cheerfully, not visibly affected by the cold. He stopped suddenly, looking downwards, and she quickly caught up with him. 'It seems we're not alone on this hill.' It seemed to Benny that he was stating the obvious.

A jagged spine of rock wound between several sparse trees and shrubs to the red-hued roof of a building of relatively simple angular construction and, from the hillside at least, with no windows. A narrow ridge, like a drystone wall, but one natural formation, led out from the rocky spine of the hill to a wooden walkway that encircled the roof of the windowless building. The ridge was only a foot or two wide, with a long drop to either side. Left of the square building, another long building stretched out away from them towards the next edge of the wide terrace on which it was built. This long structure formed one side of an open plaza. The nearest side was taken up by the length of a church, whose square tower rose to the time travellers' left. The far side of the plaza dropped away into a deeply recessed village square, the opposite side of which boasted another red roof, though from the angle at which they stood, neither the Doctor nor Benny could make out what the roof belonged to. Several other squarish and simple buildings along the other edges of the plaza and square formed the remainder of the village. The bony branches of completely bare trees stretched out like dead fingers far below, beyond the mountainside village. A dog barked somewhere in the village, the sound echoing around the square, but no one responded to it.

'Looks about eleventh century,' Benny judged aloud. It seemed likely the Doctor had been correct about their location.

'More or less. Those angular roofs show some leaching of Spanish architectural styles across the Pyrenees.' He peered down at the village interestedly. 'I shouldn't be surprised if elements of culture and language had become transposed as well.'

The thought tripped an alarm somewhere at the back of Benny's mind. '*Whose* language? The people in this era should be a dawn-to-dusk culture, but there's no sign of life down there at all.'

'No. Depending on the precise period, they could have had to flee from Moorish raiding parties coming through the mountain passes to strike north into Norman territory. Of course, we're safe from that sort of thing at this time of year, when the passes are blocked.'

'Or they could have fallen to one of the plague forms.'

'Even in winter we'd smell that many corpses from here. No, they've all gone somewhere for a reason. I wonder why.' Flicking his umbrella slightly into the air so that he could grab it in the middle, he hopped out on to the narrow and uneven ridge of stone that descended to the village.

Not to be outdone, Benny followed, planting her high black boots on the flattest surfaces she could find. They tended to be slippery, so she settled for the roughest horizontal surfaces she could see. 'Are you sure we really want to know? If someone abandons their home, it's usually for a very good reason.' She frowned, recalling exactly what such a reason felt like.

'Have you any other appointments for the next week or so?'

'Well, I had been planning to get my hair restyled, but I suppose I could cancel for something as important as this.'

'That's the spirit,' the Doctor agreed absently, taking a

71

step back before gingerly hopping across a narrow gap and on to the rooftop walkway. As Benny crossed in the same manner, he bent to examine the ends of two lengths of rope, which were tied to stanchions along the length of the walkway, but which had been cut at the crossing-point. 'Local children probably removed this bit so they could get across and play on the hillside with a little more vicarious excitement. Which is lucky for us, or the rope would have bounced us down the cliff.' He straightened, and pointed towards the gap between the long structure and the church, where the walkway turned round the corner of the roof. 'This way, I think.'

Once round the corner, the walkway branched, a narrower portion continuing to encircle the roof, while the outer section descended in the form of a flight of stone steps leading to the plaza. Once on the cobbled plaza, Benny could see that the long structure was like a row of terraced houses. A large arched portal led through to a short stone road on to which the windows of the building they had first reached opened. The Doctor hurried through the arch, raising himself on tiptoe to see through the gaps left by the wide-open tall shutters. Stepping back after a moment, he frowned as he returned to Benny. 'It's the *Marie Celeste* a few centuries too early. Leftovers on the table, and embers still burning in the fireplace.'

Footsteps clattering in the damp morning air, they walked on to the square. More steps led down from a covered walkway on the left, and arches opened out into the square from all sides, hinting at chambers and cloisters under the plaza. On the far side, a roofed cloister was open – bar numerous slim pillars – on either side, the rim of a wall just visible through the gaps. A thick tree trunk stood in the centre of the square, pierced by iron shackles and surrounded by tied bundles of dry wood. The square's cobbles were streaked with ash, and the surrounding walls were clearly smoke-blackened. 'Ah,' the Doctor muttered. 'Someone is around after all, though probably not for long. I think we might just go back to the Pagoda after all . . .'

'I knew you'd take my advice some day.'

'Shh,' the Doctor admonished, tensing visibly. Before Benny could verbalize any expression of her concerned curiosity, he grabbed her shoulder and ushered her back into the shadows behind the buttress on one side of the large arch.

An instant later, the doors of the church opened, and a double line of black-robed friars filed out, most of them carrying burning torches or small wooden effigies of Christ on the cross. Two of them bore a large standard, with a Latin inscription surrounding a cross, a sword and a tree of some kind that Benny couldn't quite make out. A beaten and bruised-looking man followed them, wearing only a yellow tabard adorned with upside-down flames, and a hat like a dunce's cap. He was followed by four figures in black cloaks and masks, and finally another man in some sort of padded leather armour and a black hood.

The grim procession passed in front of the arch, then turned to descend the steps into the square. Benny tried to recall her medieval customs, and felt a chill from more than the cold as the knowledge returned. She cursed herself for not bringing a weapon of some kind, and wished that Ace was still travelling with them – she'd be able to deal with this bunch of maniacs better than Benny or the Doctor could. 'Come on,' she hissed, 'we've got to stop them.'

'We can't,' the Doctor murmured in a dead voice. 'If we're in the period I think we are in, any questioning of their motives would just be signing our own death warrants.'

'But they're going to burn him alive!'

'Not quite. You saw the markings on his tabard; he must have recanted and confessed his sins after sentence was passed.'

'So they'll show mercy, then?'

'By the Inquisition's standards, yes. They'll strangle him before lighting the fire.' The Doctor's voice was cold and disgusted. 'And we cannot interfere.'

She tried to step out to take a stand, but the Doctor's

73

grip on her shoulder was superhumanly strong. Angrily, she looked back at his shadowy face, chilled at the grim determination there. '*S'nith-roch weth do sha*. Look, there may have been about a dozen of them, but they were all unarmed,' she urged. 'You could bluff them while I – '

'No, I couldn't, and don't think I can't understand Ancient Tzun when I hear it. Firstly the four Inquisition members who followed the condemned out of the church wear hauberks and swords under their robes, and even the Dominicans who came out first will have clubs or knives; secondly we can't mess around with history; and thirdly – ' He paused briefly, and she heard a faint rustle as he turned slightly. ' – it's for his own good.' Benny froze in horror. 'Once his soul is purified he'll be allowed back into God's kingdom,' he proclaimed, much to her surprise. 'And,' he added in an urgent undertone, 'only a heretic like you would say anything about rescuing him.'

'Have you lost your crukking marbles?' she snarled in outrage. With considerable effort, she broke away from his grip. 'That's a human being down there, and I'll save him myself if I have to – ' She turned to give him a withering glare, and only then noticed the small knot of hauberk-clad soldiers who were looming behind the Doctor.

Stepping out from the arch with cold eyes as she backed away, the Doctor pointed at her. 'The wench's mind is addled,' he said. 'Arrest her before she spreads her ungodly heresy.' As he spoke, he shoved the nearest soldier towards her, but as the Doctor's urgent shove was off-balance, the soldier tumbled to the ground, slowing up the others and giving Benny a moment to make a run for it. Nice going, Summerfield, she thought, why didn't you realize that he was saying that for someone else's benefit? The square didn't look like a particularly good place to go, so Benny hared along the path in front of the long building, acutely aware of the rattle of her pursuers' armour.

Reaching the end of the path, she jumped off the edge, sliding down the sloping roof of the covered cloister.

'After her, you idiots,' she heard the Doctor bellow. 'If she gets into those trees you'll lose her and she'll make for some heretic shrine!'

Realizing that the words were meant more for her than the soldiers, Benny paused on the eave of the cloister roof, and looked down. A few feet below was the rim of a high wall which both kept the cliff edge stable and provided a defence. The ground was some thirty feet below that; however, a thick mat of tree branches was about even with the lip of the wall. If she could land amongst them for a cushioned fall, then climb down . . .

She glanced back, and saw that one of the soldiers was trying to winch back the string on a crossbow. 'I'm definitely going to regret this,' she muttered, and hurled herself from the roof, clear over the wall.

The Doctor marched straight up to the leader of the soldiers before he could say a word, his eyes flicking imperceptibly over the coat of arms on his mantle. 'Is this how the soldiers of the de Citeaux look after emissaries from other courts of Europe?' he demanded in a practised voice of betrayed authority. 'By allowing ambassadors to be accosted by heretic witches at the very site of the *auto-da-fé?*'

Though confused, and uncertain as to where this strange little man had come from, the sergeant-at-arms somehow couldn't help but see how he had failed in his duty. His colour rising, he bowed deferentially. 'My master did not tell me that an observer would be present – '

'Of course not! How could he have done so before I announced my arrival? Are you suggesting that your master descries the future?' The Doctor's voice took on a distinctly threatening tone.

'Naturally not,' the sergeant-at-arms said hastily.

'I should hope not.' Scowling, the Doctor turned back towards the edge of the square, just in time to see the executioner tighten a knotted cord around the prisoner's neck. With a distinct popping sound, the condemned man slumped against the rough surface of the stake to which he was now chained. 'Have a horse saddled, the air here is foul enough already.'

Misunderstanding him, the sergeant nodded. 'We will escort you to Béziers.' He hoped his tone was suitably placating. 'The perverted traitors who infest these woods might attempt to exact some sort of vengeance, and there would be greater safety in numbers.'

The Doctor paused for a moment, looking round at the soldiers, and glancing surreptitiously back towards the woodlands into which Benny had fled. 'Very well.' The soldiers made no reaction to his audible reluctance. 'You and your men should be adequate escort.' The sergeant bowed, visibly pleased to have the chance to get away from this threatening emissary and order his men around. 'And at least you can't chase Benny,' the Doctor muttered under his breath.

Deadwood cracked and broke under the impact of Bernice's fall, and she was forced to hastily grab at a thick branch as it flashed past her face, the sudden halt it offered almost tearing her arms from their sockets – or so it felt, at least.

Pausing a moment until her ragged breathing steadied somewhat, she took stock of her situation, and was less than pleased to be stuck halfway up a tree in a medieval winter. The ground was relatively close, however, and she needed only a few moments to scramble down the damp wood and stand safely on terra firma. The ground, its long-dead leaves and shattered deadwood cloaked in patches of snow which had yet to be washed away by the drizzle, sloped down away from the wall-topped cliff. Some distance below, a few gaps in the trees seemed to indicate the presence of some kind of winding road.

Brushing some twigs and flakes of bark from her insulated suit, she carefully scrambled down towards the nearest gap. Obviously the Doctor's words about a heretic shrine were meant to refer to the Pagoda, she reasoned, so that was where she had to get to. Climbing back towards the village was definitely out, however, but she hoped that the inhabitants would have built some sort of spiral track or road that would take her round to the Pagoda's side of the hill. Once she'd had a look at the terrain there – and it had certainly been clearer of trees, she reminded herself in an effort to think positively – she could see about climbing back up.

Occasionally grasping a shrub or branch to balance herself on the treacherous slope, Benny descended towards what she fervently hoped was a road.

Guy de Carnac tightened the last knot which secured his rolled-up blanket behind the saddle, and swung himself up on to the horse's back. Patting the back of her neck gently, he urged the chestnut mare to the left, and ducked as he passed under the bare branches that formed a skeletal canopy over the path out of the copse and on to the open field.

To the right, an uneven stony road wound its way along a narrow valley and round a large hill, whose summit-village glistened slightly from clinging damp that would undoubtedly help stain the stone with the greasy smoke that was rising from somewhere amidst the buildings. His erstwhile hosts were meandering around the tracks at the base of the hill, while a few ragged-looking peasants were waiting at the edge of the tree-line to the side of the road. Though he was too far to hear what was said, there was clearly some discussion taking place there.

Though momentarily curious, he shrugged to himself, deciding that it was probably just more refugees from the village wishing to join the group. That being the case, he wasn't interested. He had, he reminded himself, an appointment in Barcelona. Wheeling the mare to the left, he started off across the open countryside that bordered the hill's eastern slopes.

The thought occurred to him that these people were defenceless against the soldiers and mercenaries who roamed the countryside, but he put it out of his mind, reminding himself that those fighters would probably be more interested in hunting him down than them: except

77

for the more cowardly butchers, of course, to whom defenceless refugees were good sport. Better them than me, he told his conscience firmly.

And yet, somehow he found his horse drawing to a halt. He looked back at the entrance to the valley, irritated by the recollection that perhaps he owed them something after their hospitality. After all, he told himself, you could at least try to make up for almost joining the other side.

Indecisive, he fingered the hilt of his sword, and wondered if he'd ever be able to finally lay it aside. At that moment, a distant rumble of hoofbeats from the wider valley which he had intended to enter heralded a flow of armoured horsemen in mail and de Citeaux livery. Several black-robed Dominicans were with them, as well as four of their Inquisition splinter group. In the midst of them, however, was a strange pale-garbed and unarmoured figure, but de Carnac wasn't interested in waiting to find out who he was.

His intended route temporarily blocked, he grunted angrily, and turned back towards the refugees. They had already disappeared round the foot of a looming mountain that bristled with trees. 'What price a bowl of soup and a dry camp?' Guiding the horse for the most direct route through the trees, he urged it onwards.

Having spent the previous few minutes with the uncomfortable sensation of being watched, Benny relaxed slightly as she heard the heavy fall of horses' hooves somewhere off in the distance. 'Alone at last,' she murmured happily, basking in the stillness of the morning.

Leaning against a surprisingly comfortable tree trunk, she rummaged around in her pockets, finally retrieving a chocolate bar, which she unwrapped with stiff fingers. As she raised it to take a bite, she heard the distinctive sound of a twig cracking underfoot, except that it had come from a few yards to the right. Stepping away from the tree in a loose aikido stance, she circled to the side, trying to see who was following her; hoping it was the Doctor, but suspecting that – knowing her luck – it was one of the mail-clad soldiers from the village. Not for the first time did she suspect that the Doctor had made too good a job of one of his bluffs.

'Come on out; I can see you.' As she moved, she became all too aware that it couldn't be the Doctor – she couldn't recall him ever smelling anything like that. A shadow moved among the twisted branches, and Benny tensed, ready to either spring or run, depending on what came out to meet her.

The sounds of movement gradually increased, until a horseman, his face framed by wildly flying hair, rode out from the broken wood to the left. Benny stepped back warily; this wasn't one of the soldiers from the village, that much was obvious from his lack of a mail suit or livery, but she had no reason to assume that he was here by coincidence.

The horseman halted a few feet in front of her. 'You are moving in the wrong direction,' he said. 'The others are this way.' He pointed off to her left, in the direction he was going.

Benny understood; he must think she'd got lost from some refugee group or other; the population of the village perhaps. 'I'm not with them,' she explained, and he gave her a sidelong look. 'I'm trying to get back to meet a friend at . . .' How did the Doctor describe it again? ' . . . a small shrine, on the far side of the hill.'

'Shrine?' the tall horseman echoed. 'You mean that small hut of Mongol design. Only the soldiers of the Church were there, and they would take you for the Inquisition were you to attempt to gain entry to a Mongol shrine.'

'Maybe so, Conan, but I have to meet the Doctor there.'

'If you require a master of the physic, your ills may be treated at the Roc – or so I hope, for there are many sick and injured on their way there already.'

'He's a friend, not my GP,' she replied exasperatedly.

'One moment. This Doctor – describe him.'

'A short man, wearing a – ' She stopped again. How did they describe clothes in this period anyway? I've been

79

out of circulation too long, she thought. 'He wears cream breeches and a cream cotte, with a white . . . hat,' she finished, gesturing vaguely towards her head.

'Yes, the Church soldiers took such a man away with them, under heavy guard. They will return him to Béziers for the Inquisition.' The horseman scowled. 'His couture will doubtless make an excellent prize for Louis de Citeaux. He is as fond of his finery as of anything else, if not more so.'

Bernice slumped slightly. If he was burnt at the stake, she would be trapped in this century even if the TARDIS did re-form. She couldn't leave him alone for a minute, it seemed, without his getting condemned – or worse. Putting her fears aside, she straightened. 'Then I have to get there, too. Which way is it?'

The rider's eyebrows shot up in surprise. 'I think you must be ignorant of the realities of the city, Lady. I cannot allow you to put yourself in such danger.' Walking the horse forward, he reached down suddenly, and pulled her bodily on to the horse behind him. 'You will be safe once you reach the Roc,' he reassured her, spurring the horse back through the trees.

Benny jumped back down to ground, walking beside the horse with a challenging glare. 'Whoever said I wanted to be safe? And don't call me Lady; the last time someone did that I nearly became a vampire's lunch.'

'I cannot stop you if that is what you really want to do, but you seem a little unprepared to fight off the soldiers who are guarding him, even assuming you could get to Béziers on foot in the time it takes to ride there.'

'Got an answer for everything, haven't you?' Benny strode off towards the distant road.

'My Lady?' She looked round to see what it was now. He pointed in the opposite direction. 'Béziers is two to three days' walk in *that* direction.' That seems to match my usual luck, she thought. Still, he was right that a two-day walk with guards at the end of it – who no doubt now thought she was a heretic – as impractical.

Maybe, though, there would be some opportunity to

recruit help from whoever was at this Roc place. 'All right, Conan, lead the way.'

Chapter 7

A stiff breeze was sweeping down across the overgrown
Roman road and on towards the stained and yellowed
walls of Béziers as the Doctor and his escort topped the
embankment and turned on to the worn road. At a mid-
dling gallop, the Church and de Citeaux banners carried
by the two leading riders snapped and curled violently in
the crosswind. The Doctor had long since stuffed his hat
under his jacket to avoid losing it to the wind, and he
now rode in the midst of the company with a neutral
expression.

The walls ahead cut across the countryside in unmistak-
ably man-made angular sections which had none of the
curves or random shapes of which nature was so fond.
Slated pyramidal and conical roofs rose from an area at
the heart of the city, safely distant from the occasional
streamers of smoke that rose from parts nearer the wall,
though the effect was not so much one of Camelot as of
fungi growing in the decaying areas of a sprawling tree.

The guards on duty at the gate presented arms respect-
fully as the troop galloped under the square tower that
formed the outer shell of the main archway. The riders
didn't stop, however, but pushed through the market area
and past an open-air smithy as they rode on into the
churned mass of refuse-smeared cobbles that passed for
a thoroughfare. The people who were massing in the
square and the street pressed into the walls to get out of
the way, with only the Doctor's vague apologies – which
were mostly whipped away by the wind anyway – to make
up for almost being ridden down.

They were also passed without question when they made to enter the inner city, from which the towers and spires stretched upwards. Here, financially supported both by Royal Charter and the taxes levied on the inhabitants of the outer city and its surrounding environs, the buildings were as often of early Gothic architecture as they were fortress-like, each of them built at the very least of dressed, if not carved, stone.

A large rectangular complex, with a fascia of Gothic artwork and very solid-looking and well-placed crenellated towers and walkways overlooking the open spaces on either side, loomed atop a motte ahead like some urban castle, which was essentially what it was. A steep incline beyond a ten-foot wall surrounded it on all sides, with an angled barbican leading across to a large double-towered gatehouse arch at the front of the building. On either side of the barbican was a rocky crevasse, and the drop on all the other sides was vertical. The remaining fine buildings of the bourgeoisie clustered around the Hôtel de Ville like chicks round a mother hen.

'The town hall, I presume?' the Doctor said to the sergeant-at-arms.

'That is correct, my Lord.' The soldier signalled to the others, halting the column just outside the cottage-like gatehouse.

'Good.' As if someone had tossed a bucket of icy water over him, the Doctor suddenly straightened, fully alert and as taut as a drawn bowstring. Without waiting for any further word from the sergeant-at-arms or the Inquisition members, he leaped down from the horse with which he had been provided, re-placed his hat on his head and strode swiftly through the heavy iron gates, the end of his umbrella tapping out a stark rhythm as he walked.

He had barely stepped on to the worn flagstones of the barbican when an officer in a fine fur-trimmed surcoat hurried out from the gatehouse to block his path. 'Halt!' he commanded in a distinctly affronted tone. 'What business have you here?'

The Doctor stared coldly back at him for a moment. 'Go

83

and announce to Master de Citeaux that Jean Forgeron de Gallifrey is here as a Royal observer from the court of Alexander. Well?' he demanded before the officer could so much as draw a breath. 'What are you waiting for? Is this how the de Citeaux treat all visiting emissaries? No wonder the countryside here is swarming with heresies. Be quick with you, before I . . .' He let the words trail away as the officer sprinted across the bridge. ' . . . before I'd have to think of a way out of this if you called my bluff.'

Guy de Carnac had remained silent as he guided his mare through the trees. He eventually emerged into a crescent-shaped clearing through which an arc of the winding road Bernice had glimpsed earlier cut on its way from the village to the valley below.

Benny had been saving up her ire to deliver a crushing insult to him when they reached the others he had spoken of, but her anger faded away to a kind of horrified awe as the people in question came into view.

Most of them were women and children, the majority of the men, she assumed, having either been conscripted by the Church or killed. A few stragglers were approaching from the floor of the valley, clustered round a couple of rickety carts whose creaky frames seemed to be composed as much of moss and rot as of nailed or tied wood. Most of the people who were slumped dejectedly around the roadside, however, were clearly the inhabitants of the village above. Though less malnourished-looking than the stragglers, they busied themselves at their carts or beasts of burden with the dead expressions of those who had lost everything bar the clothes on their backs. Others among them simply huddled against the cold, and looked upwards at the dark haze that spread into the heavy clouds from the village.

She felt a little sick at her earlier complaints to the Doctor. At least she would recover her loss in a couple of days. At any rate, it seemed that for the moment she was stuck with the others, and, as they started to shuffle along the road, she strolled along beside them.

A young herald showed the newcomer into an open lounge on the floor above the main hall. Stained rugs were scattered across the oak floor, but none were particularly close to either of the gaping fireplaces which dominated the two longest walls. A noticeable draught blew in through the open arched shutters in the outside walls, but at least the air was breathable, and not clogged with cloying wood-smoke or thick candle-grease.

Various tapestries adorned the walls, while the rack of swords and knives in one corner was anything but decorative. He tugged aside one corner of the nearest tapestry as he entered, but there was only stone behind it. A decoratively carved door beside the sword-rack opened, and a squarish, iron-haired man swept through, his robes just short enough to avoid trailing across the floor or becoming entangled in the rugs.

'You must forgive my servants,' Louis de Citeaux began at once, making certain not to say 'I must apologize for. . .' Nobody respected those who were constantly making excuses, regardless of cause, and especially not himself. 'News and messages travel but slowly – if at all – in this province. I would have thought, however, that your outriders would have given us some little warning of your impending arrival.'

'My . . . outriders, are stranded some distance off. My assistant and I barely got away, and I have since become separated from her too.'

Got away? Louis thought, then recalled that the sergeant-at-arms had said something about him being found fighting some heretic. When first informed of the man's arrival, Louis had wondered what he was after, and had been concerned that it might prove necessary to take steps to prevent him from interfering in his handling of the situation. If, however, a personal grievance could be played upon, he might prove more useful than the average Royal or Papal emissary – assuming his claimed identity

85

was genuine. Presumably he would have lost any documents of safe convoy with his entourage, but there were other means . . .

'I am afraid the countryside here is most dangerous for the traveller. But a short time ago, a candidate for the papacy was murdered by the heretics on his way here . . . However, I will issue orders for a search; you can give a description to the Captain de Montfort when he reports in.' He gestured to a low table, spread with breads and cheeses. 'Make yourself at home, de Gallifrey.'

De Gallifrey sat, picking up an orange, which he started to peel with a small penknife, though he showed no intention of actually eating it. 'I'm usually referred to as the Doctor,' he corrected.

'You are a master of the physic?'

'I could be,' the Doctor agreed vaguely, 'but mostly I'm a scholar, explorer, that sort of thing.'

'You are a long way from home, and must have been travelling for some time – ' the Doctor smiled wistfully at this ' – but how was the old fox when last you saw him?'

'Which old fox?'

'Alexander, of course.'

'He died five or six years ago; his son has succeeded him. Of course the Bruce family still claim that they have right of succession, but Baliol is keeping them at bay. However, you must forgive me . . .' Sharp-witted, this one is, Louis realized immediately. ' . . . for not realizing that you will need more concrete proof to reassure you as to my origins.' He chewed on his lower lip as he searched through various pockets, and even looked inside the crown of his hat, turning up all manner of wallets, pieces of bizarrely tiny mechanisms, and other oddities. Finally he brandished a tightly wrapped parchment. 'There you are, a writ of safe convoy signed by John Baliol and Alexander II.'

Even more surprised at the production of the document than at the idea that the Doctor had realized why he had tried to lead him astray by asking him about the wrong Alexander, Louis took the scroll of parchment, and examined it closely. In so far as he could tell, it was genuine, and permitted the Doctor to travel freely in any realm in which Alexander's realms were recognized. He handed the document back with a well-rehearsed smile. 'My apologies, er, Doctor. Unpleasant times have made look-outs of us all.'

'Oh, don't mention it.'

'You have yet to tell me what it is you want in the Langue d'Oc.'

'I'm just observing as I pass through; seeing what methods you're employing against your ... difficulties in the region. Trying to decide whether you'll be likely to have to repeat the lessons of Toulouse, or indeed of this very city in 1209. My liege likes to keep abreast of the goings-on in the world.'

'And will you be taking any part?'

'I'm forbidden to interfere,' the Doctor said sharply, and, Louis thought uneasily, a little darkly. 'Besides, I don't intend to remain longer than a few days at most.'

'I understand.' Louis nodded with false sympathy. 'You long to play your part against the evil here, but the restraint placed upon you by your Lords rankles you, is that not so?' He watched carefully to see how his visitor would respond, hoping against hope that he had spoken the truth, albeit mostly unintentionally.

The Doctor looked up with burning eyes. 'Oh yes.' His low but firm tone convinced Louis that the Doctor was genuinely offended by the local heresies. The righteous were so much easier to command than those who could think for themselves. 'In fact I couldn't possibly have put it any better myself.'

Bernice Summerfield paused in mid-step to look back into the woods and listen carefully for the third time in the past hour. She had been walking on autopilot, so to speak, for some time, as much to avoid regretting giving up a seat in one of the carts for some children as to let her mind work on a way to improve her situation. But in the past hour or so she had felt that niggling sensation of being watched again. Little had happened since she joined the convoy; a few other refugees from hovels in the woods had sought them out for safety in numbers, and she had persuaded someone to tell her that the year was 1242. For once no one had been surprised at her ignorance, as many of the locals were too concerned with day-to-day affairs to know what year it was either.

In the absence of any other suitable destination, she had allowed herself to be swept along with the flow, only occasionally catching glimpses of one Templar or another as they scouted out the trail ahead. She hadn't seen much of her benefactor from the woods either, as he seemed to prefer hanging back behind the column, almost paranoid about the possibility of pursuit. He seemed to be under the impression that his presence would bring the Church down on them, but she couldn't tell why. None of the others on the road with her looked like they'd be much good in any attempt to rescue the Doctor, but at least there should be shelter at this Roc they had mentioned. So long as she could still find her way back to the Pagoda once the TARDIS had re-formed, she would be happy enough. From there she could see about the Doctor.

Fortunately she had brought her diary from the TARDIS, and had been sketching in a rough map on the endpapers, adding important features of local topography as she passed them, occasionally adding little notes and illustrations on the various trees or bankside cottages that were scattered here and there. Having passed through the narrow valley that ran from the hill on which the Pagoda had landed, the stream of people was now meandering between low rolling hills whose bulging forms reflected the shapes of the low clouds, through which the sun peeked at scarce intervals.

Benny was certain that the narrow watercourse they followed was just a tributary leading to some larger river. The water sparkled like a silver lifeline through the dead land, strange reeds and the like fringing the mercurial surface despite the season. Never one to pass up an opportunity, Bernice filled a small flask with it, having to rub the circulation back into her hand after its dip in the unheated water. It should be safe enough to drink, she thought – at least after those broad spectrum inoculations – but more enticing was the prospect of having it analysed properly for one of her papers once she was back in the TARDIS. Who else had an accurate breakdown of the medieval water supply? she asked herself. Not even the formally qualified academics.

Occasionally she would catch a glimpse of some red roofs through a gap in the hills, but no one would say why they weren't heading for that village. Still, if it was in a state anything like the hilltop one . . .

Emerging from a narrow cutting lined with trees, which they had entered rather than climb several more hills, they had gained their first view of the Roc. Benny was impressed, though she probably wouldn't have admitted to it. Rising from the very edge of the foothills that rimmed a reasonably sized river valley, its sheer sides stretched over a thousand yards into the sky overlooking a curve in the river. A steep track wound its way up the only area of climbable gradient, to an artificial outgrowth of stone that protruded from the summit like a worn molar from a thick jaw.

Bernice wondered in spite of herself if those who lived below it ever saw the sunlight, as its shadow seemed to darken the whole valley. She was still admiring the incredible view when the attack came.

With a raucous chorus of roars and yells, a dozen or so men in padded leather and woollens swarmed out from the nearest trees, wildly swinging axes and cudgels. The reaction of the other refugees was to run screaming for the nearest rise. Meanwhile, knots of the bandits clustered round the people on the carts, as there was more likely to be something worth stealing there.

Benny fought down an urge to let them run, or even join them. The others might not be willing or able to stand up to men with primitive crushing weapons, but she was fitter than they were, not to mention a long-time prac-titioner of aikido, which hadn't even been invented in this time-zone. More importantly, if she was able, she felt not being willing to help would be like robbing them herself.

Thibaud hooked one wiry arm round the waggoner, and hurled him from the rickety cart, while a couple of his friends clubbed down a farmer who was trying to protect the cart. Ordinarily, he and his fellow varlets would merely loot the battlefields, but with most of the Church army's work being done in the cities for the moment, one had to be enterprising to survive, and he had long since decided that if any band was going to survive it would be his.

He laughed aloud as he saw the villagers flee from his motley band, waved a few of his men on to follow them. He doubted they would have anything worth stealing, but even a loaf or a skin of wine would go far. It amused him how his ragged and underfed group could strike fear into the hearts of larger groups simply by being bold. Nobody so much as stopped to see how strong or weak they really were. His thoughts were derailed by the unexpected sight of a woman, at least as tall as himself and dressed in some sort of peculiarly alluring padded armour of a pale blue colour, walking calmly towards the cart.

Thibaud's interest in the cart faded, and he called to the other two in the cart, pointing out the newcomer. Their expressions mirrored his own feelings, and together they jumped down from the cart, spreading out slightly as they awaited her approach.

She stopped within touching distance, a haughty and impatient look on her face. 'Leave these people alone,' she ordered, 'and get back under whichever stone you crawled out from.'

Thibaud and the others chuckled at her snappiness. 'Orders, eh? We have a Lady in our midst, come to pay tribute for using this road.' He looked sideways at the others. 'We should treat her better than an ordinary peasant wench, eh?' They laughed, but her expression didn't change. Tiring of trying to worry her, he nodded towards Benny and they reached out towards her.

There was a sudden blur, and a jarring pain.

Benny twisted the first man's arm round, forcing him to double up as she hurled him into the man opposite, before booting the third one in the groin and finishing him off with a punch behind the ear. It wasn't strictly aikido, of course, but then none of her favourite bars were what one would call a dojo. The other two recovered quickly; but Benny quickly tripped one and stamped on his chest then delivered a backwards flailing kick to the jaw of the last, his axe spinning off into the trees as it flew from his unconscious hand.

She moved towards the man who been thrown from the cart to see if he needed any help. He seemed to have been unofficially adopted as the group's leader, and as such she knew that the others would believe themselves to be worse off without him – which meant they really would be worse off, since belief in failure often seemed to spark it. As she approached, however, he waved her off with a groan, getting up under his own power.

More of the bandits were already falling upon those who couldn't run fast enough, and Benny made straight for the nearest. She knew that their unfamiliarity with her style of combat was her biggest advantage. Although she was merely adequately skilled by the standards of her own time, she suspected that to those who had never seen such a display she must seem as impressive as Bruce Lee.

She had no further time to consider this, however, as she launched herself at the nearest bandit, who was busily trying to cut a ring – complete with finger – from a former merchant. Her boot connected with the side of his head as she sailed past, before tumbling to the ground and immediately rolling into a fighting crouch from which she could launch a flurry of punches on to the next bandit.

A jingle of barding drew her attention, and she saw her erstwhile chauffeur's chestnut horse charge into the fray, his cloak billowing. He swept his glinting sword down on the nearest group of bandits, cutting the axe from one's hand before cracking his skull with the flat of the blade. He leaped down from the horse almost immediately, using

91

his left arm to ward off cudgel blows from some bandits while his sword danced with blinding speed through their ranks.

Relieved but puzzled, Benny turned back to find a new opponent, only to see that the remaining bandits were vanishing back into the trees. Keeping an eye on the fleeing varlets in case they returned, she jogged back towards the cart, as the newly arrived horseman poked a booted foot into the ribs of one bandit whom Benny had dealt with. The bandit groaned slightly, but didn't wake. The horseman gave Benny a quizzical glance, then went to join the man from the cart, looking over his wounds critically.

Benny took a look as well, seeing several cuts on his face, and started searching her pockets for first-aid supplies. 'That's twice you've offered unneeded help – Aragorn son of Arathorn, or a knight in shining armour?' she enquired in a voice laced with sarcasm, as she indicated the bodies strewn around. 'Do I look like a damsel in distress to you?'

He looked down at her with a faintly cocked eyebrow. 'Yes.' She was a little too out of breath for further banter, and in any case she was getting quite a pain in the right side of her chest from the cold air she was gulping in, as it hit the damaged tissues left over from a punctured lung she'd picked up a year or two back. 'But I am no lo–no knight, and my armour does not shine.' He gave the waggoner a more caring look, or so Benny judged. He was no simple loutish swordsman, it seemed. 'Well, Edouard, it appears my change of heart about joining you was the correct decision.'

Edouard smiled weakly, as the first of the Templars returned for a belated rescue.

'This is Captain de Montfort,' Louis was saying as the Doctor sat down to his left, in the seat reserved for the guest of honour. Other officers and minor bourgeoisie of the town laughed and chatted amongst themselves around the huge U-shaped arrangement of tables in the main hall. 'If you give your, uh, assistant's description to him, he will pass it on to the patrols. Of course you might run into her yourself tomorrow.'

'You think she's coming here?'

Louis shook his head. 'I plan to invite you to accompany me to our garrison headquarters at the Roc. There, you might see something worth observing, as we have the major part of the local heretic population bottled in there: Cathares, Waldensians, some Jews, and even a few Moorish raiders trapped here when the mountain passes became blocked by snow, I gather.'

'I'm sure you're proud of your achievements.' Philippe de Montfort, at Louis' right hand, looked the newcomer up and down. The Doctor presented an amusing picture to him, with his strange pale clothes, and his cloak-pin on the front of his cotte, with no cloak in sight. As Philippe watched, the Doctor glanced across not at the tumblers who spun around the floor of the hall to the tunes of minstrels who were off to one side in a little enclosure of their own, but at the sergeant-at-arms who had found him. 'She is thirty-three years of age, and has dark hair cut short not unlike that of a page. She will probably be wearing a thin jerkin or padded armour over a silken blouse like those worn by the Mongol cavalry.' For some reason that Philippe couldn't figure out, he kept his eyes on the sergeant-at-arms the whole time, but looked away when it became obvious that the man was ignoring him.

'Unusual apparel for a Lady of the Court,' Louis commented, 'but I confess the image is appealing.' His wide mouth split into an oily grin.

'Unusual for any woman,' Philippe agreed. 'She sounds like a fighter.'

The Doctor looked thoughtful. 'Haven't the women of the Britons always been ready to join the fray? Boudicca, Gwen Avur ... And you should have seen Ace.'

'It is a change from the ordinary, I admit. My men will find her, if she still lives.'

The Doctor looked at him sharply, as if restraining himself from saying something he might regret.

'So tell me, where is your kilt?' Philippe chuckled, then thought of a question he found more amusing. 'Did you get your haggis for breakfast?'

'Porridge for breakfast,' the Doctor corrected. 'Haggis run so fast you need the extra energy in the morning to catch them.' Philippe's expression froze.

'You seem unimpressed by the evening's entertainments, Doctor,' Louis commented, with a dry nod towards the oblivious sergeant-at-arms. The Doctor looked back at him inscrutably. 'Perhaps, to such a well-travelled man as yourself, this must seem terribly provincial.'

'Oh it's fine, I was just a little preoccupied about Bernice, that's all.'

'Of course.'

'Though I actually haven't attended a banquet like this since I was at Fitzwilliam Castle on the eve of the signing of the Magna Carta,' he went on, with rather theatrical bashfulness.

'Indeed?' Louis dropped a chunk of fatty meat under the table, where it was quickly snatched away by a waiting dog, which prowled around looking for dropped or spilled morsels. 'Then perhaps you can solve a little mystery for us. Philippe's father had loaned King John one of our knights – a Sir Gilles Estram. He was also a spy for us, naturally – but he disappeared without trace. Was he caught?'

'Sir Gilles. Oh, him. To be honest, I don't think he ever arrived – a renegade of my own people was impersonating him. He was dealt with, however.'

'You must have been a very young guest, then,' Philippe rumbled suspiciously. Estram had always been a personable fellow, as he recalled, and had given Philippe more than one early lesson in swordcraft at his father's behest. For this foreign interloper to come and dismiss his disappearance and presumed murder with a brief word was galling. If only he had given more details . . . 'It was almost thirty years ago. Perhaps you were a page?'

'No, I'm just sprightly for my age.' The Doctor gave him a disarming smile. 'Of course even that event wasn't

94

as lavish as those given by Coeur de Lion in Jaffa. I found those much more cheery – and they did have the advantage of the presence of his sister, Joanna.'

Disbelief tempered Philippe's annoyance into stunned humour, and he laughed uproariously, almost willing to forgive the references to his mentor. 'Why, Louis, the Scots have sent us a court jester!'

Grinning, the Doctor doffed his hat. 'Let's just say I haven't always been a Royal observer.' He pointedly lifted a couple of small fruits from a platter before him, and started to juggle.

Chapter 8

Guy de Carnac looked out across the dark surface of the river, his eyes darting from side to side. He could have sworn he'd heard someone splashing around out there . . . He drew his horse to a halt, listening carefully. There was no further sound, other than that of the refugees' muffled footsteps.

My imagination, he decided finally. It had been a long time since he had been by a riverbank at night. In fact, he'd always tried to avoid such places at night, ever since he had left the farm that last time.

Rosinante moved sluggishly when he started to move off again, and she was obviously tired. Concentrating on the horse's wellbeing – it was a less unpleasant subject, he felt – he dismounted and took the reins in one hand.

With a last look at the dark waters, he led the horse forward.

The Doctor's cream suit blended in quite well with the sandy greyishness of the stone walls under the dancing amber lights of the torches set into the walls of his suite of rooms. Once he had closed the door, however, the draughty and unlit corridor cloaked him effectively. Only a faint carpeting of light leaked out across the floor from under various doors to give any hint of what might lie in his path. Though his features were formed into a mask of calmness, a careful observer might have noticed his fingertips constantly keeping up a nervous-looking tapping on the handle of his umbrella.

A number of wooden doors were recessed into arch-

ways of stone, and the Doctor moved silently along, pausing to listen at the door to each suite, which was the
equivalent of a modern apartment. Like his own quarters,
which he had deserted as soon as the coast was clear, they
would all have a bedroom, study and reception room. So
far they had all contained either silence or perfectly
normal nocturnal sounds of one kind or another.

Before he could exit the latest doorway, a set of footsteps became audible, ringing metallically from the flagstones, and a lonely patch of candlelight turned the corner
into the corridor. The Doctor flattened himself into the
corner of the archway, pulling a tiny dental mirror from
an inside pocket. Angling it for a look at who was
approaching, he saw the Hell's Angel-like figure of
Philippe de Montfort stalk along then push his way into
one suite. The sound of a bolt being secured echoed down
the corridor.

Smiling happily to himself, the Doctor slipped along,
and fished out an old medical ear trumpet from one
pocket, leaning in towards the door.

'Good news I trust,' Philippe's voice demanded gruffly.

'Of course,' Louis' voice replied. 'You did well – my
esteemed Royal namesake has offered me not just
reinforcements, but several new titles and deeds, should I
bring to justice the heretics responsible for the murder of
his clerical party.'

'So arrest me.'

'I hardly think that will be necessary. So long as we can
enter the Roc on the fourteenth, we will each be able to
claim our greatest desires as a reward.'

'The fourteenth? You mean they still have it?'

'Oh yes, our Albigenses are very taken with it. I shall
go out to the garrison tomorrow, and direct the assault
myself. None could question my motives after such an act
of faith.'

'What of this stranger, the Doctor?' Philippe spat. 'A
Royal observer could be in our way – if he even truly is
such a person,' he scoffed.

'His documents were quite genuine, though I share your

97

concerns. The Doctor is but one man, however, and seems more a herald than an ambassador. So long as he keeps out of the way, I see no reason to waste such extra effort on him. Who knows, he may even be useful as an independent witness to our loyalty and heroism.' Louis chuckled.

'If you say so. Do we have the way in yet?'

'No,' Louis responded in a disappointed tone. 'Our cuckoo in the nest has been unable to find it. I fear we may have to punish his incompetence if he does not succeed. All he can tell us is that the interior gateway opens out directly under the keep.'

'How can he possibly not be able to find it? All he need do is follow it back.'

'He claims that those who were inside before the main entrance was sealed are kept away from it. He says no one will tell him where it emerges.'

'They must be paranoid. It was a mistake to send only one man while the main gates were in use before the encirclement was completed. We should have sent in another spy in a refugee party now that only the hidden entrance is used.'

'It has been attempted,' Louis answered dismissively. 'Those Templars whom you say rendezvoused with de Carnac always seem able to send them back to us. Neutrality indeed!'

'There is still Guzman's prisoner.'

'Yet . . . The Inquiry is tonight.' Louis' voice stopped, and there was a sound of pacing. 'Perhaps this Doctor can be of some use. Go and invite him to attend the Inquisition. He can hardly refuse a chance to observe this, and the loss of his companion to the heretics may give him a personal reason to think of some approach to the questioning which Guzman might miss. . .'

The Doctor barely got out of sight round the corner before Philippe emerged.

Bernice watched closely as the tall mercenary who had fought off their assailants threaded his chestnut mare through the footsore human river, walking ahead of the horse as he led it by the reins. Why, she wondered, did he stay with these mostly defenceless people when, with sword skill like that, he could earn his fortune in the crusades?

Pausing to let the river flow past her, she fell into step beside the mercenary's horse, and looked back at him curiously, her attention drawn to the anachronistic silver sword that was strapped to his back. Had he met another time traveller, she wondered, or perhaps even one of the Doctor's other selves? It was possible, she supposed, if unlikely. I'm going to get a good look at that sword, she promised herself silently; if it isn't an anachronism, then it revolutionizes one whole branch of history ...

She stole a glance at his face, doubtful that just asking would do the trick, but admitting to herself that she would never know unless she tried. It seemed she would have to wait, however, as the eyes at the heart of his scratched and weathered face were drooped in a half-doze. She shrugged to herself, and allowed herself one last glance at the sword on his back.

'I dislike crushing your hopes, my Lady, but the horse is tired and needs to be walked without a rider for a time,' he said clearly, with no trace of sleepiness.

Benny stepped away, startled. Smart move, Summerfield, she told herself. Vampires, chronovores and fossilized amoebas the size of planets don't bother you, but a man turning out not to be half-asleep while upright and walking ... Still, she thought, it was his fault for pretending in the first place. 'If I needed a ride that badly, I would just have climbed up. Isn't a mercenary like you a bit out of place with these people?'

The mercenary opened one clear eye to look directly at her. 'Would you rather I had been with those others?' He jerked his head back towards the spot where they had been ambushed.

'No, I'm just surprised that you weren't.'

'Good. I don't like doing what's expected. Besides,' he added, half to himself, 'show me a place where I fit in, and I'll give you as much gold as you can carry.'

Finding a place where he fitted would be a neat trick, she thought ironically. 'Have you got it on you?'

'No, but I am sure I could find a Church encampment which does.'

That's more normal, Benny thought sourly. 'I thought you might. You could steal from them and give to me – Robin of Loxley, I presume?'

'Guy de Carnac.'

She mulled the name over, and it did seem to have a certain ring that fitted him; perhaps it was just that 'Carnac' sounded sufficiently like carnage. 'Maybe I should just stick to Conan. Is that why you came along here? So that you could get the chance for a quick scrap?'

Guy snorted derisively. 'If I liked fighting for its own sake, I *would* have been with those others.'

'Then you must have had one hell of a reason to come this way.'

'I had the best reason in the world.'

'Don't keep me in suspense.'

'It seemed like a good idea at the time.'

'That's it?'

'That is the only reason anyone does anything, if that is what you mean.'

'Shouldn't you be seeking fortune and glory?'

'Fortune and glory?' He smiled mirthlessly. 'I wouldn't know what to do with a fortune. Build a stronghold? The army would besiege it. It would attract thieves, tax collectors, not to mention vassals who are too much responsibility. As for glory . . .' He smiled lopsidedly. 'That is but the perfect empty purse. You cannot eat or spend a reputation.' His expression darkened. 'It can eat you, though. Eat you and spit you out like a gnawed bone.'

'Well now, you won't earn much with an attitude like that.'

'And you haven't been on the road for long. You wear . . .' he paused as if seeking a suitably inoffensive word. It must be a tricky problem for a medieval swordsman, she thought. ' . . . Strange garments, but they are clearly of fine craftsmanship, and are not damaged or torn.

100

You claim to be no lady of high birth, yet you speak to me with sharpness.'

'Well, I'm not exactly local.'

'A nameless traveller?'

'I'm Professor Bernice Summerfield. But yes, I'm temporarily shipwrecked in this area.'

Guy nodded to himself. 'Hence your presence on this trail. The Church and nobility believe you were trading with the Moors, I imagine.'

'The Mongol horde east of the Danube, more likely. Is that what you believe as well?'

Guy shrugged. 'I do not care what brings you, or any of these people, here. I am on this road because it is as good a direction as any other: especially when one intends to make for Barcelona in any case. I could stay in Spain, of course, or travel north and across to England, but I go where the wind takes me.'

'And here, I thought, you're seeking others with the same beliefs as yourself?'

Guy gave Benny what she thought looked suspiciously like a pitying look. She didn't care for that at all. 'Lady Summerfield, I have ridden from one edge of the world to the other, and have encountered people with many different beliefs and ways, but all of them are united in feeling that their way is the only true one and that all others should be converted or butchered. Despite this similarity, they still insist they are each different from the others.' He shook his head as if it were very heavy. 'As a wise man once said: show me someone who believes in anything, and I will show you a fool.'

'An atheist, eh?'

'Oh, I assume that God exists somewhere; but He will exist and go about His business regardless of what you or I believe. Do the ants kill each other over which way to worship us?'

Benny looked around at the tired walkers trudging along the wet slope of the bank, their heads slumped defeatedly, and had to concede that he had a point.

* * *

101

Despite a brief wince of pain, the man who had been dragged from the apothecary's straightened defiantly, glaring out at the guards around the hall. They ignored him, remaining as impassive and unresponsive as the thick black draperies that hung from the cold stone walls all around, or the ivory effigy of Christ who was spread-eagled on an ebony cross at the far end of the room, above a raised dais.

Between the man and the dais was a round table, to one side of which four men in black masks stood with a number of hooded Inquisition spies behind two clerks. On the dais, Francisco Guzman sat upon a raised throne draped and canopied by black velvet. To either side of him were lesser Inquisitors seated on more ordinary chairs, as well as a secretary to his left, and the Doctor – incongruous in his pale linen suit – on his right.

Guzman glanced at the Doctor out of the corner of his eye. He was unsure what this stranger wanted in Béziers, and anything or anyone who couldn't be relied on to act as expected was dangerous. Why, he wondered, had this observer come straight here from the banquet, rather than returning to his room? He didn't look at all tired, despite having apparently had a long and hard day.

Guzman himself, however, was weary of questioning this Cathare, who had refused to answer a single question over the past hour or two. Lack of faith weakened men, Guzman was sure, so it wasn't strength that enabled the heretic to hold out. More likely the man was just too intelligent to believe that confessing would save him. Guzman didn't like it when others could think for themselves: wasn't God's will enough for them? He also didn't particularly like conducting Inquisitions at night, but it had been ten hours since the man had been brought in, and the law stipulated that he must be starved that long before he could be tortured. That is one law that must certainly be changed.

'Very well,' Guzman said aloud, backed by the scratching of the clerks' quills. 'Take him away and shave him, then bring him down to the torture chamber. I want a confession, and the information I need, by midnight.'

The Doctor rested his chin on the heel of his hand, and watched the unfortunate prisoner with a calculating expression.

The icy moonlight gave Guy de Carnac an opportunity to view their destination more carefully. Rising up from the riverbank along which the refugees were scattered for a rest, a looming peak cast a deep shadow across the river and on to the tree-covered slopes far to the right on the opposite bank.

The lower edges of the pale clouds that fringed the moon were neatly cut off by the massive corner of a huge wall that stretched a further seventy feet or more from the top of the peak. An equally high, but longer, wall ran back from the cliff edge above the river, before also vanishing, thanks to a corner. Tiny glow-worm specks of flickering candlelight danced in myriad tiny windows, with larger torches atop the ramparts casting a golden glow over the light stone.

'Camelot?' Bernice whispered.

'It is the Roc of the Cathares,' Guy corrected. He watched the surface of the river sadly as he leaned back against the tree upon which he had hung the weight of his sword. It weighed only about twenty-five pounds, as opposed to the usual forty, but could still be a burden after a long enough day. 'The Parfaits there are apparently willing to shelter anyone whom the Church hunts for any reason.'

'To spite them, I suppose.'

'I believe so.'

'What was that you said about people who believe in anything?'

'I believe that the sun will rise in the east every morning as it always does – does that also make me a fool?' Bernice chose to ignore that. Guy wasn't surprised, as he had always found that being beaten at one's own game was most irritating. Of course, the stake he had lost had been much higher . . .

'We don't have to climb that cliff, do we?'

'How would I know? I have never been here before.'

'From you, that's a straight answer. Have you ever thought of going into politics?'

'I owe fealty to none of the great families.' He turned to fish out an oiled rag from the pouch at his belt. Lifting his sword down from the tree-branch, he drew it from the scabbard and laid the blade across his knees, buffing it with the cloth. It hardly seemed necessary in the case of this blade, but Guy knew that it was only a matter of degree, and intended to take no chances.

The sword almost glowed under the moonlight, and Guy noticed that Bernice was looking at it in a very curious way. After a few moments of effort, Guy stopped polishing the sword, and looked up to meet her inquisitive gaze. 'It is rare enough to find a woman who shows such interest in a sword, but you look at it as if you have never seen a blade before.'

'Not one like this. It looks like stainless steel, or maybe tungsten carbide.' Guy had never heard of these things, but didn't let it bother him. He was no smith, after all. 'May I?' She held out her hands. Guy frowned briefly, but handed the sword over to her.

Drawing out a small stylus, Bernice pointed it at one of numerous tiny nicks in the edge. A small patch of light glowed from the end, illuminating the metal. He snatched the weapon back. 'Witchcraft!' Perhaps he was wrong about the heretics having no demons.

'What, this? It's just a pen torch.' She looked back at the stylus as he watched her suspiciously. 'It uses copper and vinegar to produce a sort of artificial lightning.' She sounded matter-of-fact enough, but Guy noticed that she redistributed her weight for fast movement, just in case.

His eyes narrowed dangerously, but he lowered the sword slightly. There had been that clay jar he had seen once, which used copper and acid to make a dead rat twitch. It was an eerie enough sight, but there had seemed nothing demonic about it, as he had watched all the preparations. Perhaps this was simply a similar wonder from far to the east, as she certainly didn't seem like any cruel sorcerer. Weighing the sword thoughtfully, he handed it back to her, though he kept a hand on the hilt of his dagger all the same. 'I have seen something similar. A fakir in Alexandria claimed to harness lightning, and could also return dead rats to life.' He shuddered at the memory. 'But he used a large clay jar filled with vinegar and pierced with rods of copper and iron.'

'This is just the same thing, but smaller. And it only makes light – nothing else.' Guy nodded darkly as she put a small glass to her eye. 'What happened to this fakir?'

'The crowd in the marketplace, where he was demonstrating his magic jar, stoned him to death as a sorcerer.'

Chains rattled tinnily, and screams echoed from other chambers as the Doctor and Guzman stood illuminated by the infernal light of an open brick furnace. In front of the open door of the furnace, the now hairless body of the prisoner twitched in semi-consciousness. Blisters hissed and oozed at the spots where his flesh touched the surface of the iron chair to which he was chained, the metal conducting and retaining far more heat than the air ever could.

Guzman watched the display with the concerned look of a caring but resolute nursemaid ensuring that a patient imbibed a foul-tasting but effective potion. The Doctor, meanwhile, twisted some spare chains over and over in his hands, as if he could either form them into a garotte or snap them with frustration. 'You need only recant,' Guzman was cajoling. 'One small piece of information is all I require as a sign of fealty and faith.' The prisoner merely groaned.

The Doctor put down the shackles with a clatter, and walked towards the table, his mouth set in a thin grim line. 'He looks too weak,' he said disgustedly. 'He might die before telling you anything.'

Guzman looked over the strained body suspiciously. 'I

must know by the fourteenth how the heretics enter and leave the Roc with impunity. This wretch is all but the last Cathare in the city.'

'Then you won't want to let him die before he talks.' Guzman smiled to himself at the Doctor's snarl. It seemed that this emissary was a good man after all, if lack of co-operation from the prisoner provoked such an outraged reaction from him. Guzman approved. 'Let me check his pulse.' The Doctor placed two fingers on the man's neck, and bent down to listen to the rhythm of his breathing.

The man's eyelids fluttered weakly, and the Doctor bent closer still. 'This might get you a chance for freedom, or it might get you burnt,' he murmured in a voice too low for Guzman to hear. 'A chance is the best I can do for now.' The Doctor's fingers stiffened slightly, pressing inwards almost imperceptibly.

As Guzman watched, the man slumped limply. 'Too late.' The Doctor straightened. 'I warned you this might happen.'

With an incoherent snarl, Guzman kicked the nearest leg out from under a tripod brazier. Glowing coals hissed and spat as they rolled across the floor. 'Torturers, remove the body. Leave it in its cell until it can be burnt in the morning.' He swung back to glare at the Doctor with a gaze as fiery as the scattered coals. Without the heretic's valuable information, he would be deprived – for the moment – of the chance to relieve those at the Roc from their corruption. He now had less than a week to gain the necessary information, and the thought of not being able to save those souls was not a pleasant one.

The Lord would be disappointed, he felt, robbed of the gift of renewed souls. With a last hiss of displeasure, Guzman turned away and swept from the room.

Once Guzman was gone, the Doctor relaxed visibly, and mopped his brow with a paisley handkerchief. Grimacing at the empty torture chamber, he hurried after the two torturers who had carried the body out. They were already disappearing down some narrow steps at the end of the tunnel as he shut the door after him, and he had to scurry forward to catch up. He reached the door that was the gaping maw to the stinking cell just as the torturers slammed it shut. One of them was already reaching for the iron-bound bar that would lock it, when the Doctor hooked his umbrella-handle round his wrist, immobilizing it.

'Why bother?' the Doctor asked, nodding at the bar. 'It's not as if he's likely to walk out now, is it?'

The torturers looked at each other and shrugged. 'I expect not,' one of them agreed. Together, they wandered off along the corridor.

Leaving the door slightly ajar, the Doctor looked in at their hapless victim. 'No,' he said to himself, 'he won't wake up for at least another ten minutes . . .'

'Fascinating,' Bernice muttered as she let the jeweller's eyeglass fall back into her hand. She had seen the pattern of stress lines in the metal of Guy's sword before – but only in Japanese samurai swords of around four hundred years later. 'The metal has been folded over two thousand times during the forging process, and tempered in a much more sophisticated manner than anyone should be able to do these days.' She gave Guy another suspicious look. Could he be another time traveller, whose equipment was equally anachronistic, albeit more subtly so? He had certainly accepted her story about the pen torch rather easily for an inhabitant of such a superstitious age.

The direct approach might startle him into some useful revelations, she thought, and she straightened sharply. 'Where did you get this? And, more to the point, when?'

If he was at all perturbed by her attitude, he hid it well. 'In Damascus, perhaps four years ago. It cost me the booty from a full campaign, but it was a worthwhile investment; there is not a stronger or sharper blade in all of Christendom, and its lightness makes it quicker than any opponent can possibly expect.'

She thought about this carefully. It wouldn't be the first time some alien or chrononaut had tried to sell sophisticated weapons to the peoples of Earth's past. 'You bought it?'

'I encountered a smith who claimed he knew the secret of forging magical weapons, handed down from the ancient days of the world, before the sinking of Atlantis. Damascus steel is the finest in all the world even when not enchanted, so I bade him forge a longsword for me.' He retrieved his sword thoughtfully, and turned it over in his hands. 'This was the result.'

Benny's fears suddenly evaporated, replaced by a more down-to-earth, in a manner of speaking, suspicion. 'This smith, he didn't call himself John Smith, by any chance?'

'No, he called himself Wayland.' Benny couldn't help but sneer slightly, her knowledge of ancient Terran mythology was not going to let that one slip past. He must have noticed her reaction and understood in some way, however, as he laughed softly, but not loud enough to carry into the village. 'I too have have heard the old stories told by mothers to their children, Lady Bernice, and so have those smiths who are blessed with sons. It is a common name in that trade.'

Benny regretted her foolish reaction, of course. After all, she added mentally, look how many people were named Arthur or the like even in the 26th Century. 'It would be, wouldn't it?' She thought of reminding him not to call her Lady, but felt it would be a waste of breath. If he hadn't taken the hint by now, then he probably never would.

He smiled faintly at her comment. 'Even blacksmiths have heroes.'

'Every profession has heroes. Even archaeologists still long to be like –' she trailed off distractedly, her attention drawn to a flicker of movement far above. She squinted up at the top of the thick wall of the Roc. Hadn't there just been – There it was again, she noticed. A scurrying figure in pale blue was peering over the edge every few feet, as if searching for something on the outside surface of the wall itself. Unfortunately, the figure was too distant for Benny to discern whether it was a man or a woman. Perhaps whoever it was had dropped something earlier.

With a sudden whisper of air displaced by his cloak, Guy rose, drawing his sword once more. 'Someone approaches.' He tilted his head to listen out. Benny strained, but heard nothing for a few seconds. A faint rattling and jingling grew louder as she remained listening. 'Soldiers in mail. A dozen, by the sound of it. Get back and tell Edouard – '

'I know,' Edouard interrupted, as he approached from the fireside. 'Put down your sword, de Carnac, these are friends.'

Guy didn't re-sheath the blade, but he did at least lower it to a less threatening position, though Benny knew that he could still launch an attack in less time than it would take her to blink. He tensed visibly as a dozen Church soldiers emerged from the trees. Benny stepped back involuntarily; bare-knuckle fighting wouldn't do her much good against armour.

Edouard and one of the Templars went over to the soldiers, talking animatedly in low voices. Benny sidled back over to Guy. 'Are they selling us out?' He looked round with a baffled expression. 'Betraying us, I mean.'

Guy watched them silently for a few moments before answering. 'Probably not. But I do not know what they *are* doing.'

Before Benny could think of any suggestions, Edouard and the Templar returned, the soldiers moving back to the top of the wooded embankment and spreading out in single file in a column parallel to the refugee convoy. Edouard paused on his way past. 'We are moving on now. The soldiers' armour will mask any sound we make to their fellows, and they will divert any others away from us.'

'You mean they're friends of yours?' Benny was more than a little surprised, considering what she'd seen in the hilltop village.

'The Church has conscripted almost every able-bodied man in the region, but many of them have relatives among

109

the persecuted, so they turn a blind eye.' This explained, Edouard moved along the line of tired walkers to tell them the news.

Bilious snores echoed around the glistening cobbles of the outer bailey, drifting from the guardhouse adjacent to the donjon and drowning out any tiny sound made by the opening of the iron-bound door.

The prisoner, his blue robes long since torn, soiled and stained, slipped out like some ancient ghost. He looked around, but no one was in sight. Realizing that the guards in the gatehouse would be more likely to be awake than their counterparts on the other side of the courtyard, he padded gently towards a flight of steps on to the parapet.

He had picked his spot carefully, finding a point at which the ground outside was no more than ten or twelve feet below. He marshalled all his reserves of strength, looking around one last time as he did so. Few torches burned in the windows of either the donjon or the keep, and hoped that no one was watching from them. Turning, he took a deep breath, and jumped from the wall, rolling as he landed, and picked himself up to scramble off into the darkness.

Above and beyond the walls, deep in the shadows offered by a suite in which neither torch nor candle burnt, the Doctor watched him drop out of sight. Pulling his ubiquitous probe with its telescopic aerial from his pocket, the Doctor pressed a button on its surface.

A steady gentle beeping pulsed softly in the air.

Chapter 9

Benny had to admire the ingenuity of the ancient archi-
tects who had built this place, and she shook her head in
wonder at the sight of the entrance to the Roc. It wasn't
that the entrance was imposing or impressive, but rather
that it was so simple that no one would think to look for it.

She stood in a natural hallway, roughly the size of a
tennis court, a short way up a curving ravine which almost
split the riverside edge of the Roc from the rest of it. She
had laboriously climbed a flight of worn and water-slick
steps wide enough for the horses, the steps rendered invisible from the other side of the river by the slightly separate
edge. From this cul-de-sac, a wide tunnel sank deep into
the rock. This, however, could only have been seen from
the air – or the walls high above – and since there was a
huge overhang a few yards overhead, which blocked out
even the top of the Roc from a viewpoint so close in . . .

Guy had wandered off to keep watch for approaching
patrols, while Edouard supervised the unloading of the
few carts and wagons, their contents transferred on to
the backs of asses and oxen for the ascent before the
rickety vehicles were broken up and tossed into the river.
Benny had been quite surprised at the mercenary's
integration into the column; though he kept himself to
himself even more than the Doctor or Ace did, something
about him seemed to inspire confidence in the others. She
turned back towards the descending slope that led into
the tunnel. Guy's mare and two more malnourished horses
that had been pulling the carts were shuffling and snorting

nervously at the scent of the stale air that drifted up from the tunnel's mouth.

Breaking up a couple of wafer biscuits which she'd been keeping for emergencies, she ate half of one herself, then offered a half each on her open palm to the horses, patting them gently and muttering reassuring sounds. 'You seem to know how to handle yourself around horses, Lady Summerfield,' Edouard said, as he approached.

'They're the cleanest form of transport.' She paused to feed an extra biscuit to one particularly skittish animal.

Edouard looked at her strangely. 'What other kinds of transport are there?'

'I was thinking of ships. You know, cooped up for weeks on end. But much better is the open steppe, a fast horse and the wind in your hair.' She gestured around. 'Aren't the Templars coming in?'

'Apparently not. They said something about maintaining their neutrality.'

'Sitting on the fence until they can side with the winner, you mean. What now?'

'Food and warmth have been prepared in the fortress. If you think the horses are quietened enough for the journey, you can lead them through. The tunnel has no branches in which to get lost, or so I am told.'

His sky-blue mantle spotless despite the grime and scattered mud, Parfait Girard stepped out on to the relatively wide machicolation that was grafted on to the top of the wall of the main holding at the north end of the fortress. Supported by finger-like buttresses that bulged out from the upper wall, it gave Girard an unparalleled view of the main bailey below.

Below and to the left, the smithy gave off a constant haze of metallic-scented smoke, while the stable block stretched out behind, both sections having their foundations cut directly into the domed outgrowths of rock that emerged from the summit of the Roc. Separated from the fires of the smithy by the stables, a long-roofed complex of wooden shelters had been built for the benefit of the refugees who had been filling up the fortress over the past few weeks. At the far end of the oversized farmyard that formed the Roc's bailey was the long rectangular tower of the library, while the straight wall to the right was obscured by temporary buildings constructed before the winter to hold additional stores. Most of them had been filled by yet more newly arriving people as soon as the buildings had been vacated by the food or fuel.

As he watched, a woman in some ghostly padded armour led in three tethered-together horses from the gaping maw in the rock shelf upon which the smithy had been built. Meanwhile, various other people – all looking dead on their feet – slipped past her, bearing bundles of meagre possessions. Several other blue-cloaked figures drifted among the new arrivals, showing them where they would be sheltered during their stay, and offering assistance to those obviously tired or infirm.

Girard watched them with a paternal eye, pleased that the members of the different denominations were working together so well. With so many of the splinter groups having been displaced from their own holdings, he had worried that factions would develop here atop this mountain. So far his fears had seemed unfounded – apart from Jeanne's brand of self-sufficiency, of course.

That he, a former fisherman out of Narbonne, would end his days at the top of a mountain so far from the sea, was an irony he embraced with affection. On occasion, if he wasn't careful, he would feel an urge to take some small boat out on to the river below, and let himself drift back towards the coast.

It was now long since too late for that. His responsibility to the people here chained him to the Roc as effectively as the strongest steel. Though nearing sixty years of age – even more venerable than most suspected, as Hugues kept reminding him – he was still a spry figure, his white hair wispy and wavy like the filaments of a drifting dandelion seed. He certainly needed all the energy he had retained over his lifetime if he were to cleanly usher those who would die here into the better world.

Still, he thought, it was time to go down and join Hugues, so that they could meet their joint responsibilities in welcoming the newcomers. Moving with a firm stride despite his age, Girard hurried to the staircase.

The Castellan, his stocky frame draped in plain earthtoned robes, shook his head to himself as Girard strode past the mounds of burning wastes and fabric, tended by skeletal Parfaits whose pasty faces were masked by perfumed cloths. There was barely enough food left in the Roc to feed half its population for a few more days, and yet still Girard allowed even more newcomers into the fortress, in defiance of all common sense.

When challenged about this, the old man invariably waggled a placating finger and pointed out that the intellect could move mountains even when the body couldn't move itself. Not for the first time did the Castellan wish he'd remained in the Holy Land with Frederick II.

Still, he forced himself to look suitably ascetic as he and Girard approached Hugues and the newcomers. They wouldn't know the real situation in the Roc, for even if they'd been told, they would have considered it mere propaganda from the Church, seeking to make itself look all-powerful.

'Okay, Obi-Wan, I hope you've got one hell of a stable here.'

It took a moment for the Castellan to realize that the strange words were meant for him, and he came out of his introspection to find himself being appraised by a surprisingly fit-looking woman with short hair like a page, and some sort of padded jerkin. She didn't have the haunted look of the others. 'We will find your animals some room somewhere,' he said with heavy irony. 'The grain stores perhaps.'

'That doesn't sound too promising.' The woman looked around thoughtfully. 'These people look as if they haven't eaten in days.'

'They get one pot of stew each day.' The Castellan suddenly felt the need to defend his handling of the situation. 'Though I admit there is little enough meat in it. The parfaits eat only vegetables, grain and cheese, however, so the meat should last for the rest of us.'

'Shades!' she spat. 'If you're that low on food stocks, why do you let these people in at all? They'd be better off foraging outside.'

The Castellan was surprised at this reaction, when he had been expecting some sort of disappointment at the prospect of imminent starvation. 'I wish I knew.' He threw a barbed look at Girard. 'Perhaps because "We cannot deny anyone succour from the evils of this world of matter".'

'Whatever that means.' She turned to the shocked-looking Girard. 'Are you in charge here?'

Girard nodded. 'My counterpart Hugues and myself are looked upon as leaders.'

'Bernice Summerfield. But, as mine host, you can call me Benny. Look, if you don't get these animals to a stable, they're going to be in the way of all your efforts at whatever it is you do here.'

Well, the Castellan thought, at least she was getting down to business, which certainly suited him better than if she had simply fallen apart at the true state of the Roc. He supposed he owed her some courtesy in return. Did you leave all your manners behind when you left court? he asked himself pointedly. 'The stable is here. For the moment we have not had to put people in there, but the horses will be sharing the shelter with other livestock.'

'You don't mind that, do you?' she asked Guy's horse whimsically. It nickered softly. 'I think that was a nay.'

Thudding footfalls marked out a beat to which a soft exertive grunting was added. Philippe stepped around his virtually empty suite in a vaguely formal pattern, carving through the air with his sword, switching it from hand to hand in mid-swing and practising switches from long two-handed sweeps, to short blocks and parries, then back again.

The sword felt good in his hands as it swept through the air, its weight feeling as if it were part of his arm, which was not yet tired. He was well aware that the power of the sword was drawn as much from the waist and careful positioning of the hips as from his arms and broad shoulders.

A woman – he couldn't even recall her name, just that she was some servant from the kitchens – watched from the bed, which was really the only item of furniture in the wide suite. She looked puzzled and bored as he worked through his routine. He didn't care what she thought, since she was only there on a whim anyway.

The exercise relaxed him, and he allowed his mind to wander. He had needed the relaxation, as this strange Doctor unnerved him somehow. His reluctance to share his obvious knowledge of the fate of a boyhood friend was bad enough, but there was something in his manner . . . Louis and Guzman seemed to accept that he was a friend, taking his words at face value, but Philippe felt that the Doctor's words jarred with his actions. He had looked more than anything else like an emissary of truce in an enemy camp.

Perhaps, he thought, it was not his words which belied his actions, but the meanings that Louis and Guzman ascribed to those words. It was an interesting thought, if only there was some way to turn it to his advantage. If he was to regain the heritage which his brother Aumury had ceded to the King as a show of fealty, then he must gain some sort of political leverage of his own, rather than relying simply on Louis – who seemed far too fond of this city himself, and might not be trusted to step aside – or on the skills of combat which he had seen in his past few years as a mercenary.

This stranger was the key, of that he was certain. He re-sheathed his sword with a loud clap, which startled the kitchen-girl into alertness. Seeing that he was no longer practising, she leaned back a little more provocatively, but then her face fell as he belted the sword back around his waist. He looked at her, not unmindful of her attractive-

116

ness, but reminding himself that he must be as single-minded as his enemies if he was to overcome them. Of course, the night was barely started in any case. 'Wait here,' he ordered, allowing himself a leer of anticipation as he cast his eyes over her. 'I will return shortly.'

'You may rest here,' Hugues said quietly to the weary villagers, keeping his voice low, as the rough wooden storehouse was filled not just with the last scattered remnants of the winter food supply, but also with a few dozen people, most of whom were sleeping fitfully. Benny nodded a brief thanks, not trusting herself to speak. This was, after all, hardly an arcology; the air was thick with smoke from the wide central firepit set into the bare rock floor, which also provided the only available light, but little warmth.

Shuffling with the last of their dying strength after the long hike, the villagers found places around the storeroom, most of them choosing to huddle together under thick sacks and piles of other such insulating materials. Benny slumped to the floor near the firepit, leaning gratefully back against a sack of flour. Her soles were tingling with the heat of slowly recovering muscle strains when she took her weight from them. Tugging off her boots, she tried to rub some more normal circulation back into her feet, grimacing at the thought that she was several centuries too early to find a reputable reflexologist.

She told herself that she really ought to go and make sure the others all got in safely: after all, they did need looking after. The sensation of recovering muscles had spread out, however, and the gently flickering pastel flames in the firepit made her view of the room seem as dim and ruddy as if she was trying to see it through closed eyelids.

Before she even realized that this was exactly what was happening, she had drifted off into an exhausted sleep.

His gleaming pate curving above his long and untied hair like a mountain peak above the tree-line, Philippe stalked down the narrow passageways that connected the keep to the donjon. The knee-height hem of his mantle was prevented from billowing only by the weight of his sword.

A pair of unwashed jailers looked up as he ducked under the low door that led into the passage with the guardhouse and a row of cells. 'You,' he snapped, pointing at the nearest man. 'In which cell was the Cathare from the apothecary's shop interned?'

'This one, Captain,' the man answered nervously, leading the short distance to the door of a pitch-black cave. It was empty.

'Where is he now?'

'The Scottish envoy proved he was dead, and his grace Guzman ordered that the body be burnt.' The jailer looked around for any sign of support from his partner, who was trying very hard to appear invisible.

'The Scot – did you burn the Cathare's body?'

The jailer shuffled nervously. 'Well, we were just waiting for the – '

'Never mind. Why was this cell unlocked?'

'There was no point in locking up a corpse. That's what the ambassador said.' The jailer backed away from the punishment he was certain would follow.

'And when did he . . . vanish?'

'Well, when we – that is, it was my turn off watch and – '

'And you both fell asleep, then woke to find him missing.' Philippe clenched his fists, trying not to lash out at these two incompetent fools. If they were out in the field he would simply slit their throats and be done with it. Here, however, a little more thought was called for. If he had them executed, it would be obvious that something had gone wrong. Politics was a more concealed warfare, however, and required less obvious actions. 'Perhaps he was removed for disposal while you slept.'

'Of course! The guards and servants would not want to wake – I mean, disturb us.'

'Quite.' Philippe fell silent for a moment, thinking. Louis considered himself a great thinker and planner, he knew, but Philippe knew better the everyday concerns of men's minds – even foreigners. 'Then that is what happened, if anyone asks – even de Citeaux or Guzman. The body was burnt.' The jailers nodded ecstatically, scarcely able to believe their luck. 'You will also tell no one, *no one*, of this conversation. Otherwise you will be hanged for co-operating in the escape of a heretic under sentence of death. Do you understand?' Not that he needed an answer. The satisfying looks of dread on their faces were more than enough to convey their understanding.

'Yes, Captain,' they whispered together.

Giving them a last threatening glare, Philippe ascended the sloping corridor back to the keep. Ignoring the main staircase that led up to the great hall and beyond to the living suites, he followed the outermost corridor round the inside of the outer wall to the barracks. There, he found his second in a small officer's room above the stable-block, separated from the men's dormitory by a thin wall. 'Joseph,' he whispered softly.

'Captain?' Joseph came awake instantly, as most of Philippe's band could.

'What know you of the two jailers who stand the night watch?'

'Not much. They take ale around noon in The Dancing Bear.'

'Perfect.' Philippe relaxed slightly, a solution to his dilemma over their punishment forming immediately in his mind. 'I fear it is not safe there, Joseph. There will be a brawl there this noon. Perhaps the relatives of someone who was tortured in the keep have come looking for revenge . . .?'

'Upon his jailers?' Joseph grinned nastily. 'The men have been growing angry at the lack of activity here. I will arrange it.'

Philippe nodded thankfully. He had known he could rely on Joseph to understand. He slipped back out and returned to the main staircase of the keep: he had a warm bed to look forward to . . .

* * *

The last of the night's clouds had drifted off eastwards, leaving the sky speckled by the silver points of the stars, and the icy arc of the moon, when Guy de Carnac padded into the store-room after his rearguard lookout, and quietly placed a few more dry logs into the firepit.

He had discarded his armour and spurs, the rattling of which would have awakened everyone in the room, and now tended the fire in simple breeches, boots and a leather jerkin over a cloth blouse. A pair of basilards hung from his belt.

Satisfied that the fire was good for the rest of the night, he turned to observe Bernice, who had half-turned on to her side, her strange padded armour looking grey under the firelight. Her actions against the bandits earlier had surprised him, and he was curious as to what led her to act that way, and where she had learned to do so. She had certainly been in combat before – that much was obvious to him – yet she didn't seem to have the bloodlust he'd expect from an Amazon. She had cared about what happened to these displaced farmers, he realized; he wondered if she'd deny that if he asked. He knew he probably would, if someone asked him.

In sleep, her features had lost their tough and adversarial set, relaxing to a faint smile amidst an elfin face more suited to warmth and compassion. He'd even go so far as to call her beautiful, as her unconscious and innocent smile – he suspected it was her *real* smile – was infectious.

Her foot moved slightly, as if seeking the fire, and he lifted a threadbare blanket from a nearby pile, realizing at once that the cold must be getting at her, as only her upper body was insulated by the thick padding. He knew from her fighting display at the ambush that she was no damsel in distress, as she could look after herself, and that a little coolness wouldn't even wake her.

He laid the blanket across her legs anyway, before stepping back outside. There was too much serious work that he might need to do here. Off to the left was a steep staircase that led up the wall above the wooden shelters to a wide battlement walkway, parts of which were sheltered by wooden hoardings. Although there were similar steps and battlements all around, Guy judged from his memory of their approach that this wall should give an overview of the occupied village below, and he couldn't help feeling an irritating urge to find out what sort of situation he'd let himself get into.

His legs protested tiredly as he ascended, but he fought down the sensation. He had no intention of letting himself sleep quite yet. Not until he was too tired to dream.

He finally stepped gratefully on to the flat surface of the walkway, the frosty breeze which slipped around the walls from the river helping to keep him awake. The dark earthy texture of the vegetable gardens just outside the walls stretched only a scant few yards before dropping away into the night. Beyond that, a ruddy starfield of torches and campfires stretched as far as the eye could see, the densest galaxy of flames lurking just beyond the edge of the cliff. Guy could make out the dull blocks of perhaps more than two-dozen long buildings below.

He hadn't seen so many campfires since his journey to the crusades. It wasn't a reassuring sight.

Pale feet in worn sandals padded stealthily across the roof of the rectangular tower at the south end of the Roc. Equally chilled hands pressed on the raised stone of the battlements as their owner leaned out to look down upon the river, whose surface was speckled with the silver glints of moonlight reflecting from tiny wavelets.

Stepping back, the ghostly figure checked the carefully inked note that was etched on to a piece of vellum, and decided that the words written in flowing script were just as they should be. Rolling it up, one hand stuffed the parchment into a stout and almost spherical earthenware pot. A cork was rammed in, and some candlewax dripped over to seal it.

After one last glance to ensure that no one else was in sight, this unusual messenger swung one arm back, and tossed the clay pot out over the battlements with an easy precision that could only come through repeated practice.

The pot sailed off into the night, dropping accurately past the jutting overhang to splash into the river far below, so distant that the sound was inaudible.

Bernice Summerfield ran, hair plastered into her eyes by blood from a dozen cuts. A blade of pain twisted in her left leg with each step, jarred further by the cracked and uneven ground. A crisp yet choking tang of ozone filled the air as thickly as did the distinctive whines that trailed off into fading pulses of discharged energy.

Gritting her teeth against the pain from her leg, she turned back involuntarily. Something seemed wrong about all this ... Fallen spires of fire-blackened ferrocrete stretched towards her from the depths of a smoke-filled crater, like dead fingers trying to claw their way out of a grave. She tried to run further, but her strained leg would thrash as if trying to shake off a gripping and unwelcome hand. The rubble-strewn ground slammed into her back as she fell, but she fought off the pain, trying to drag herself further away on her hands and one good leg.

Deep in the churning void of smoke and burning embers amidst the crater, shapes moved: dully glinting, dome-topped shapes, spitting harsh blue lightning to the accompaniment of that familiar sound. Her blood ran cold, but she focused her mind all the same. 'It didn't happen this way,' she protested in a whisper. 'They never landed ...'

A shadow rolled over her, and she looked up, her mind giving in to her fears at last. A single eye stared down at her from what her perspective, coloured by terror, painted as a metallic mountain. The muzzle of its neutron radiation projector moved to cover her, ready to inflict far more suffering than would ever emerge from her bad leg. A thunderously rumbling voice roared 'EXTER–'

She woke up with a start, only sweat sticking her hair to her face. Her leg was still uncomfortably painful, and she looked down. A few spots of the blanket over her left leg were smouldering from pieces of still-burning ash which had drifted from the fire and settled there. She

122

snatched the blanket away, beating out the tiny glowing patches, then paused. She didn't recall picking up a blanket ... It didn't really matter, she supposed, tossing it aside. Though, at least it explained why no one else lay so close to the fire, despite the cold, she realized wryly.

The shelter was now full to capacity with refugees, and Benny considered it no wonder that she had dreamed of the last time she had been rendered homeless and deposited amongst those displaced by war, albeit far from Earth. Though she was still tired, she felt that remaining here would just result in her nightmare picking up from where it left off. Pulling her boots back on, she threaded her way quietly to the door, hoping that some fresh air would calm her nerves a bit.

With the dissipation of the clouds, a distinct frost was in the air, though Benny reminded herself that that was a sign it should be more spring-like during the coming day – unless more clouds arrived.

A dull orange glow seeped out from the smithy on the far side of the bailey, and several people – mainly blue-robed Parfaits or armoured guards – were shuffling around on assigned tasks, even at this late hour. Or early hour, she corrected herself. A few hens were wandering around the bare rock floor, and she almost tripped over one as she glanced up at the battlements.

There seemed to be few defenders actually on duty up there, but she recognized one figure easily as he stared out over the wall almost directly above her. She quickly found the steps, and climbed up to join him. Guy wasn't exactly a scholar with whom she could exchange notes, of course, but he was about the only person with whom she'd shared more than a dozen words since arriving in this century. More importantly, he was the only person she knew by name who was still awake, and she certainly didn't want to wake any of her tired companions from the road, who clearly needed all the sleep they could get.

'Be thou a spirit of health, or goblin damn'd?' she asked, with a faint humour. Guy looked startled, as if he had been on the verge of nodding off. Revenge at last, she

123

thought. 'Bring with thee airs from heaven, or blasts from hell? Be thy intents wicked, or charitable, thou com'st in such a questionable shape.'

'Strange words, Lady Bernice.'

'Then let's just say you look a bit over-tired to be standing watch on the walls.'

'I rarely sleep well these days. Even that is no respite.'

'I know what you mean.'

'Was the blanket not warm enough?'

'What? Well, the fire got a little too hot, I'll grant you.'

'My apologies, then. I should have put on less wood . . .' He tailed off as something caught his attention in the crook of the angled wall. A small blocky tower was situated there, with a few pinpoints of candlelight flickering through the windows. 'If you will excuse me, my Lady.' He strode off along the walkway with a look of curiosity on his face.

Benny caught up with him almost immediately. 'Actually, I won't. If I can't sleep, I might as well see what else is going on around here.' Guy looked back at her with a bemused expression, then turned back to push open the door on the little blockhouse. Inside, four guards were playing at tables with extremely dog-eared cards, which, to Benny, didn't really look much different to those she was used to, except that the faces were cruder, and they were still rectangular rather than circular. A helmet with a scant few coins in it lay to one side, and another couple of men, obviously having lost all their money already, were standing as an audience with their backs to the door.

'It is a wonder the Church has not already breached the walls,' Guy announced loudly, and the men turned with a guilty start, their fingers freezing around the cards. 'Certainly they could approach easily enough, if they but knew it. Do you not patrol the walls, or keep lookout?'

'Who are you?' the nearest man demanded.

'I am the man who is telling you to get out and patrol the parapets lest you anger me with your incompetence. Which of you is in command here?' The men looked at each other nervously and indecisively, though Benny noticed that at least two of them were collecting their equipment, ready to go out. 'No one? Varlets,' he spat, 'and farmers. Go now, and report any Church movement to me.' Ingrained obedience to commands from social superiors taking precedence, the gamblers hastily grabbed their weapons and armour and hurried out. Guy relaxed visibly, shaking his head. 'I should have bade you all follow me to Barcelona, rather than follow you all to this undefended crag.'

'You shouted at them so well, though. Very military and correct.'

'I was not always a rootless wanderer.' His face clouded. 'Besides, they do not know whether I am above them in standing or not, but they know better than to risk impertinence to someone who may have rights over them.'

'And what would you have done if they hadn't gone?'

'I do not know,' he admitted in a tired drone, sinking on to a narrow bench.

It was obvious to Benny that the long day was finally getting the better of him. 'Rest, rest, perturbed spirit.' Leaving the little guardhouse, she wondered where she could find any ale barrels.

The net on the end of the lance scooped up the floating earthenware pot on only the second attempt. The gauntletted hand of the Templar knight who had retrieved it passed it over to the careworn Templar who had spoken to Guy on the ridge a couple of days earlier. 'Here it is, Preceptor, precisely on schedule.'

'Good work,' the Preceptor answered quietly, prying the seal apart with a dagger. 'Fetch the scribe here. I will need him to do his usual excellent job of forged handwriting, once I decide how much of this message to alter.'

Chapter 10

With the shutters open to the frosty morning air, crisp sunlight picked out brightly coloured details of flowers, banners and standards that were painted on the white-washed wooden ceiling of the main hall on the first floor of the Hôtel de Ville. Some distance below the simple decorations, the Doctor breezed into the hall, finding Louis and a few others finishing off their usual breakfast of soup and bread.

'Please help yourself, Doctor,' Louis offered, gesturing to a huge tureen in the middle of the table. A few platters of torn loaves surrounded it. 'We have a long journey ahead of us.'

'Well, it broadens the mind, or so I'm told. Are we going anywhere special?'

'My garrison at the foot of the Roc. I spend half the week there, and half here, but it is a full day's journey each way. En route, we will consult with my bannerets at Limoux and Lavelanet. We will see if they have had any greater fortune in discovering the means by which these heretics and their collaborators evade the attentions of the army which surrounds them.'

'You have a horse for me?'

'Why, naturally.' Louis looked shocked, as if affronted that the question need even be voiced.

The swirling rush of water still managed to override the stern words of funereal benediction and the metallic thud of broken pieces of armour tumbling away. Desert heat and cold dampness fought each other madly enough for the scent of blood to fill the air. Guy dismissed all these echoes of senses as being the last remnants of a fading dream. Then he noticed Girard and Hugues, whom he had encountered only briefly when entering the Roc last night, standing silently just inside the door of the small blockhouse.

Seemingly unaffected by the chill, they were watching him with bemused expressions. Guy made to stand, but Girard waved him back into a sitting position. 'I am given to understand you were displeased with our defences last night,' Girard began amicably.

'I would not call them defences. If they were in my –' He broke off. 'Well, they are not, and neither am I.'

'Oh, I will not pry in your past affairs, but it does seem that you may have a gift for leading men.'

Guy nodded reluctantly. 'I did once, but it was a long time ago, and much has happened since then.'

'Yet you helped lead these people here.'

'We happened to be going in the same direction.' Guy's correction was as much to convince himself as Girard.

'Perhaps ... You may, of course, leave any time you wish –'

'Knowing a way in that the Church does not? I do not believe even *you* could be quite so trusting.' Girard didn't answer. 'You did not come here to discuss what I may have done in the past.'

'True, de Carnac, though I know rather more about what you have done than you might suspect.'

'No doubt, and I can tell whence you gained any such information.' Guy recalled his conversation on the ridge sourly, wondering what else the Order had been up to here.

'I do not condemn you for what you did. Rather I wished to ask if you would consider accepting a post to command the fighting men we have here. We ourselves are ill-versed in warcraft, and most of our men are farmers or labourers who are willing to take up arms, but lack the skills ...'

'And if not?'

127

'Then you will be free to remain here with the other refugees.'

Crammed into a stinking storehouse with little to do but await capitulation, no doubt, Guy answered silently to himself. So much for his dreams of being free from conflict, either in the world at large or within himself. If there was one thing he despised, it was the urge to go back over old ground, or to return to broken habits. 'Very well.' They were forcing him into it, he told himself. 'I will do it. There are things I will need to know; how many men we have, their weapons, those sorts of details.'

'I will send the Castellan to you – he holds the responsibility for maintaining the defence. You may use this blockhouse as your quarters and headquarters.'

'My thanks.'

'There is one other thing. We are about to negotiate a truce, so there should be no further assault. However, the outcome of the truce will be undecided. Also, I will require a party made ready to strike out for a cross-country journey in a few days. I trust you can see to that.'

'It will be done.' Guy wondered briefly what sort of journey was going to be required, but dismissed the thought. By that time, it would no longer be his concern.

Parfait Jeanne looked over the smashed mess of blood and tissues over exposed shinbone that was as much soaking into the white sheets of cloth which supported it as it was lying open to examination. Shaking her head, she pressed the bag of dried herbs, which she wore on a thong round her neck, up to her mouth for a moment, to fight off the stench of blood and rotting flesh that hung in the air as permanently and cloyingly as the smoke from the dull lighting.

'Trampled by a warhorse,' her partner, Parfait Giselle, said, before Jeanne could ask. Jeanne nodded, shadows dancing over her angular features as they split into a familiar smile. She and Giselle had been working together for the better part of a decade, and by now the shorter and softer-looking woman could all but read her mind and

128

anticipate what Jeanne would need next. At least, she reflected absently, while poking at the discoloured edges of the pulped muscles, Giselle never tried to convince her that she owed her anything, as did all the men she had met before taking the consolamentum and donning the blue robes.

'Albucasis the Spaniard wrote that iron was best with the fire for external injury.' Jeanne looked down on the mercifully unconscious man-at-arms who was sprawled on the rough hospital table, his mail tugged off to leave him in a stained and pungent undershirt. Was freedom of the spirit worth this? she wondered. To be trapped in the midst of such suffering . . . 'Fetch the axe, and have a brazier heated. It will have to be tonight. If we leave him until the full moon, it will draw the vapours of infection further up into his body.'

'I will see to it.'

'I am not so certain that we should interfere in these matters,' Hugues said, threading his way through the packed chamber of groaning patients, the bloodstained sawdust of the floor clinging to the hem of his robe. 'Surely if his material body is weakening enough to free his true spirit . . .' The strange woman who was following him gave his back a look of disgust, and Jeanne felt a twinge of amusement at that.

'Your Girardine Chapter may be more spiritual, Hugues, but it obviously does not recognize the value of having people to spread the word.'

'We just do not agree with the further imprisonment and suffering of the soul, that is all. However, we do acknowledge that the constant battle against the deficiencies of flesh and its wounds strengthens us.'

'You should write that down and sue Nietzsche for plagiarism,' the strange woman commented. 'I don't know why you bother with a hospital, if that's your attitude.'

'We have it because we are the swords with which Amor combats Rex Mundi. This is more a smithy than a hospital. However, I did not come to discuss Chapter differences. This is Bernice Summerfield, who says she is practised in the ways of tying bandages, tourniquets and other such minor healing arts. I suggested that she might find useful work here, if you have need of another pair of hands.'

'We can never have enough pairs of hands, Hugues. The last attack has almost doubled the number of wounded.'

'You need not concern yourself with further attacks. Girard has agreed to a truce for negotiation.'

Jeanne froze. There was only one subject for negotiation which could require a truce. 'He intends to surrender after the fourteenth?'

'That was the result of the ballot. Unanimously.'

'I felt it was better to end it quickly, rather than fall and die slowly through weakness from starvation.' She perched herself on a cleaner patch at the edge of the table. She hadn't expected any different of course, but she felt as if her efforts of late had all been for nothing. All she could do was hope for some mercy from the victors, since they would want to seem at least slightly humane. 'All right, let me know what else develops.' She turned to the newcomer, Bernice. 'What know you of healing, Bernice?'

'Just call me Benny. I can apply bandages and tourniquets; I know about CMR, and can suture small wounds.'

'Your words are strange, but I believe you know what you are talking about, even if I do not.' Jeanne was rather pleased at the thought of a more professional volunteer joining their workforce than the conscripted labourers who were usually foisted upon her.

'I've had cause.' Benny looked down at the unconscious soldier. 'But this is the first time I've dealt with someone whose normal scent is worse than that of his wounds.'

'Perhaps he simply has not been away from the field for a long time.' Jeanne was rather amused by Benny's unusual priorities. 'Or perhaps he is one of those who believe that bathing weakens the body's resistance to plague. Such belief is becoming increasingly common, but I hope it never takes hold among our people.'

'I don't think you need worry on that score.' Benny

looked around gloomily. 'Wait a minute. Do you mean to say there's a bath-house here?'

'But of course! We at least have to wash the blood off.'

'Relaxation at last,' Benny thought aloud. 'If only bubble bath had been invented . . . Where is it?'

'Above the smithy. The chimneys there direct the heat to the bath-house. Once a tub is filled from the well it takes some time to heat up, but it never cools down again.'

'I think you've just saved my life.'

'I will be happier to save his more threatened one.'

'Yes, of course. If only we had alcohol swabs, that would help protect against infection. There was more grain than anything else in that storehouse last night. Do you know where I can get some pots and any sort of tubes?'

'We could look, but why?'

'Well, for one thing, we can prevent infections in wounds, and maybe even improve morale with the by-products.'

The florid-looking Castellan looked less than happy about being replaced as commander of the defenders by some young upstart who had only arrived the previous night.

Guy didn't mind this attitude as such, but hoped that it stemmed more from a sense of loyalty to his men than from pride at his own sense of importance. He led the Castellan out on to the battlements, strolling along at a leisurely pace while the Castellan glowered beside him.

'How many men do we have?'

'Two hundred and fifteen, all told,' the Castellan responded – gruffly, but quickly and professionally. Guy nodded.

'And how many of these are proper fighters?'

'There are seventeen former knights, thirty-one former squires, and sixty men-at-arms who have fought in previous campaigns.'

'How do they train?'

'The knights spar amongst themselves and the squires, the others practise on wooden dummies as they feel the need.'

131

'As they feel the need? And what of any lazy ones?'

The Castellan merely glowered more deeply.

'Very well. From noon today, all this will change. It will be your duty to draw up suitable duty rosters.'

'As you say. Thirty of them, however, are stationed at a small tower on the north approach, to hold off any Church advance on the trail up here.'

That sounded sensible enough, Guy thought, though he made a mental note to take a look at this outpost as soon as possible in order to check on its status. 'Thirty new men will be assigned there. Have the rest formed into twelve squads of fifteen men. One former knight is to lead each squad, with two squires under him, the rest of the men evenly divided between men-at-arms and untrained men. These squads will work six hours on and six hours off, with a new squad coming on duty every two hours. The remaining men will be assigned to this outpost of yours, so I will want thirty men ready to leave for it this afternoon. I will escort them there, and also explain the new situation to those currently there.

'You count well enough.' The Castellan looked at him for any reaction, as if it were a compliment. Perhaps it was, to him, Guy thought.

'We all could.' The comment had sparked another thought, however, and Guy paused at a turn, thinking how these men would react to having to keep track of squad numbers and the like. 'Do not assign squads by number. Give them inspiring names – Dragon, Leopard, Sword and so forth. Names that may encourage the sort of prideful rivalry that will spur the men to do their best for their own little band as they try to live up to the name.'

'Names?' The Castellan looked doubtful. 'Very well.'

'Now, where is the armoury?'

Escorted by outriders from Philippe's troop, the Church party had kept up a reasonably quick pace, not stopping since leaving Béziers. Two bannerets with chapes over their de Citeaux surcoats were waiting for them by the western bank of the Aude, which they had crossed around midday, via a wooden bridge encrusted with the dried remnants of the past summer's moss and overgrowth.

The party finally halted for a brief rest while Louis consulted with the bannerets, and the Doctor took the opportunity to look around for the Roc. The distance ahead was grey and hazy, but there was some sort of angular protrusion rising amidst the densely wooded foothills.

'He will arrive there safely, have no fear,' a gruff voice said beside him. Philippe was disappointed that the Doctor didn't jump with surprise at his approach, or ask what he was talking about. It didn't matter; Philippe was less interested in those sorts of theatrical effects which he considered more in keeping with Louis' view of intrigue as some sort of game.

'We've already passed him, I suspect. He's tired and on foot, while we have horses.'

'Do you not wonder why I have not reported this to Louis?'

'Not really. Some local intrigue, I presume.'

Philippe glared at him, his forked beard twisting in a grimace. Perhaps this was some sort of test of his loyalty, arranged by Louis and this Doctor. No, he reminded himself. This one seemed more practical than Louis. He was probably no heretic, since he would never have got into the Langue d'Oc if he were, but Philippe wondered if he hadn't decided to give Louis an unseen helping hand by giving them a genuine heretic to follow to the Roc's entrance. 'You are one with your own plans, Doctor, but I see how you may aid mine.'

'I can't aid anyone's plans here.'

'Ah, but you can . . .' He leaned in closer, looming over the Doctor as he lowered his voice. 'Do not tell Louis of the secret entrance to which the Cathare will lead you. Let him run where he will. When he is picked out from the population of the Roc, and I prove that Louis and Guzman let him escape, *I* will be the one to claim support from the Holy See. With that support, I will claim back my family's birthright which that fool Aumury bargained away to the Crown, and turn the Langue d'Oc into an independent principality on the King's flank.'

The Doctor stiffened slightly, gripping the reins with tense fingers.

'With you as envoy, an alliance can be forged between our countries, once I have regained the title of Count of Béziers and Toulouse. My soldiers are the finest north of Malta, so the whole of Europe can be ours.' Philippe knew that telling the Doctor this was a huge gamble, but if he should attempt to betray the confidence, Philippe knew that the Doctor's freeing of the prisoner would provide an excellent excuse for killing him.

'Don't worry,' the Doctor murmured quietly, sounding like he had a lot on his mind. 'I'm not about to tell anyone.'

'On time as usual,' the sergeant-at-arms muttered appreciatively, as he fished the drifting pot out of the river at a point where the fast current was slowed by a natural dam formed by a long finger of rock. This was one day when he wouldn't have to remain out in the damp cold for too long.

Using the butt of his pikestaff as an aid, he clambered back up the steep slope towards the road back to the village.

After a few hours of tending to the remains of the leg which Jeanne had amputated, Benny was glad to get out of the hospital, and soak herself in one of the wooden tubs for half an hour or so. Guy was cinching his saddle when Bernice passed by the narrow postern gate, his bow and sword already slung. She looked much fresher and more alert now, and he assumed that she too had found the warm bath-house. 'So, you're leaving after all,' she said. 'Taking the road that rolls ever onwards?'

'Not exactly, Lady Bernice. There is a small outpost some two miles north of here, where the paths from the village join the approaches to the Roc. I am going to check upon the men there who defend the Roc's approaches from the Church's advances less than an hour down this road.' He swung himself up into the saddle, and took a loose hold of the reins. 'I shall return by nightfall. Unless, of course, you would prefer me to leave . . .'

'Just hold it right there. I didn't say that. It's just that I'm coming with you.' He cocked an eyebrow at her silently, but didn't say anything. He could hardly refuse a Lady's company. 'If they've been fighting skirmishes over the last few weeks, maybe some of them need as much patching up as I can offer.' She beckoned to the nearest stable-boy to fetch a horse.

'Would not Jeanne or Giselle be able to offer further medicine?'

'Never can tell.' She grinned.

'Very well,' Guy went on. He indicated a group of sword-armed soldiers forming up behind her in the bailey. 'I am not sure what the men of Shark squad will make of your accompanying us, but I know that I do not mind.'

The Doctor's horse splashed quickly through the small tributary stream, its iron-shod hooves meeting with relatively little resistance from the thin film of ice that coated the muddy banks. Once free of the mud and ice, the Doctor reined the animal in amidst the frosted bushes beside the treeline, a cloud of condensation rising from it as it regained its breath while he pointed the antenna of his electronic probe downstream. It beeped steadily and strongly, a small red LED flickering on the casing in time to the electronic beat.

'Odd, he must have found a horse somewhere. Or been given a lift, of course.'

To the Time Lord's left, the sheer wall of the riverside corner of the Roc was stark against the sky like some global tombstone, a wide seam in the trees below it betraying the course of the river. Nodding to himself, the Doctor wheeled the horse round, and threaded his way back through the trees towards the main party cantering along the top of the ridge.

* * *

The outpost proved to be built across a narrow pass that opened out on to a ridge whose sides were steep fields of scree. The ridge zigzagged like a switchback between the rolling hills below and the looming promontory of the Roc.

To Guy, however, it looked barely large enough to hold fifty men, and he was relieved that the Castellan had been sensible enough to assign only thirty even before his own arrival. Thirty men would certainly be able to hold the outpost – little more than a hollow wall with living space inside and a stout gateway in the middle – as well as fifty men could have done, and the extra men would have been more a burden on resources and space than a boost.

Almost all the men already there had minor injuries for Bernice to treat, but none more serious than cuts and bruises, as most of the Church's attacks had been by means of ballistae shot from neighbouring peaks, which were just barely within range of this lower construction. Even so, three shots out of four had been falling in the valleys between them, and the fields were now littered with boulders amidst the muddy craters of their impacts.

Despite their fortunate health, Guy noticed that none of the men were slow to avail themselves of Bernice's skill with a poultice. He wasn't sure whether he should be amused or annoyed, but decided to give them the benefit of the doubt, since the rigorous schedule he intended to implement from midnight would distract them from any thoughts of her beauty.

He smiled wryly to himself. He would just have to hope that he too was kept suitably busy, it seemed.

The leader of Shark platoon, a man called Saint-Clair, was a former knight by Royal charter rather than belonging to one of the religious military Orders. However, he had seemed to have a good head for defensive strategy, and so Guy was happy to let him determine the best deployment of the men who were to man the outpost.

After explaining the new state of affairs to the men who would be returning to the Roc proper – to a fairly apathetic reaction – Guy remounted his horse and led the troop back towards the cliff-like walls of the fortress.

'Well, Conan,' Bernice drawled as she drew alongside on her pony. 'You seemed to know what you were doing.'

'That is what Girard said. He did offer the chance to leave freely ...'

'But you had nothing better to do?'

He looked round, and saw that she was watching for his reaction with a more serious expression than her light tone might have suggested. One might almost believe, he thought, that she knows all about me as well. 'What has Girard or Edouard been telling you about me?'

'Nothing, worse luck, but you remind me of a saying: "Inside every cynic there's an idealist trying to get out."'

Almost, perhaps, he thought, but not exactly. 'I fear it is more a case of my idealism, after having got out, failing to quite get back in again, despite its best efforts.'

The dying sunlight darkened the red-tiled roofs of the village buildings to scabs of clotted blood atop the grey fillets that were the long stone walls. Even from the low ridge almost half a mile from the buildings, the distant clangs of a smithy hard at work rolled across the fields, accompanied by shouts and calls, and a hundred other noises made by an army at camp. Although there was a clear field between the village and the looming form of the Roc, all the tents and lean-to shelters put up by the soldiers were scattered over the low hills through which the party had been riding. In the distance, disappearing behind the Roc, further winking campfires were barely visible against a blackening backdrop.

Louis led the troop through the lines unchallenged, leading them into the village proper. The central section was built of stone, and comprised perhaps four or five long streets of single buildings, not unlike long terraced houses. On either side of this core area were smaller buildings of wood, and even some wattle and daub holdings of ancient design.

There was no sign of any children, and the few women

137

around all seemed to be being dragged around by armoured men. Louis sighed, trying not to look upon this pale and insulting echo of his own city. Being out in the country under the stars was preferable to coming into such a travesty of his achievement.

Still, the seneschal he had left in charge always proved equal to the job of looking after Béziers while he was away, and before long the heretics and all their Jewish, Moorish and foreign friends would be gone, leaving him free to expand his city with new buildings. A cathedral first, he decided. Of course, such a work would take longer than his lifetime to complete, but he could at least lay out the ground plan and set aside land, before moving on to other matters.

He slowed his horse as they approached a large stone farmhouse at the end of the street. Banners hung from the walls, and mailed guards patrolled outside. A middle-aged banneret in de Citeaux colours hurried out; a few house servants following, to greet the new arrivals. 'My Lord,' he said breathlessly – due to excitement, going by his face. 'You return to glad tidings.'

'The entrance has been found?' Louis hardly dared hope for such an outcome.

'Better perhaps. We have received a communication from their leader, Girard.'

'Well? Speak, man!'

'They have agreed to yield, through lack of food. They request a truce –'

'Until the fourteenth?' Louis asked.

'Exactly. In order that we see their sincerity, they also offer us twenty hostages, to hold against their promise not to attempt to escape.'

Louis dropped from his horse, looking across at the dark mass of the Roc. This was an unexpected and welcome turn of events. 'When do they wish a reply?'

'I took the liberty of promising a reply at dawn, as I knew you would be here by then.'

'Very good,' Louis agreed distantly. Was he finally going to be free of his obligations, he wondered.

'We have also received word from our agent.' The banneret brandished a piece of vellum, and a damp earthenware pot with a shattered hole where the short neck for the stopper should have been. 'He recommends that Girard will probably accede if we request hostages to secure their co-operation.'

Showing signs of intelligence at last, is he? Louis thought. Still . . . 'We will agree to those terms. Have a scrivener draw up a formal wording for a truce which will include our need for hostages as a show of good faith. And send a messenger on the fastest horse we have to Guzman. Tell him to come here at once, and that, by the time he arrives, we will have a score of new subjects for his . . . ministrations.'

'Yes, my Lord.' The banneret refolded the parchment with a broad grin, and left.

'Isn't that rather breaking the spirit of a truce with hostages?' the Doctor asked pointedly from his mount. 'You're supposed to treat them well unless the other party breaks their part of the agreement.'

'I can only give my word as to *their* safety, Doctor, and that of my vassals. As an emissary of the Church, I have no power over Guzman.'

'Then you could *ask*.'

'I *could*, but that sort of thing often brings suspicion upon oneself, does it not?'

The Doctor didn't answer.

Chapter 11

Girard sat on the reassuringly solid and comfortable wooden platform that had been built atop the main holding, ignoring the sharp frosty bite in the air, but simply concentrating on feeling at one with the air around him here at the very top of the Roc.

He knew that several of his Chapter were also seated around, eyes closed, each hoping to feel some touch of Amor's presence. The secondhand words passed down to their followers by the leaders of other religions were never good enough as far as he and the others were concerned.

He knew, in himself, that someday he would be a part of Amor, for that was promised to all those who accepted the truth of their spiritual heritage, and rejected the chains of this world of matter. Then there would be only love for all sentience . . .

But not tonight, it would appear, he realized eventually, as the cold air finally defeated his meditative efforts via the weaknesses of his fleshy prison. He opened his eyes, and stood rather stiffly, saddened at not having been able to go beyond simple inner peace. Overhead, the stars began to wink coldly in the heatless night, vanishing off into infinity.

Girard had heard it said – by some of those he had encountered in various cosmopolitan ports while he was still a fisherman – that the stars were other suns, far away. Sometimes they seemed to call out to him in singing tones, promising the joys of floating amongst them as an unfettered spirit.

On other nights, they merely illuminated the sky.

Now that it was past sundown, however, Girard felt it was time to attend to more formal duties.

Hugues was waiting at the foot of the main staircase, which spiralled in a square and angular fashion up the hollow inside of the tower keep. 'Louis de Citeaux is here with but a herald, a scribe and a man whom he claims is an impartial Royal observer from Alexander's court. He says he has come to discuss the agreement of the temporary truce which we propose.'

'Where does he wait?' Girard asked.

'I thought it safest to bid him await our pleasure just outside the gates.'

'Has he waited long?'

'A few minutes only.'

Girard considered this. A man like de Citeaux himself would make his guest wait, and Girard did feel that a restful bath to cleanse the dirt – all further ancillary matter created by Rex Mundi, of course – would do the world of good. However, de Citeaux would hardly notice the difference, and Girard had no intention of making himself seem like the prevaricator his opposite number was. After all, the fishermen of his village had always been content to entertain visitors even among the remains of the day's catch, and no one had minded in the slightest. 'Four of them . . .? Fetch Giselle and Jeanne, and the four of us will go and talk to them.'

Guy snapped a last few dry twigs and placed them round the inside of the small moss-lined bowl of stones he had pieced together. He could feel Bernice's eyes on him, but ignored the fact. She was attractive, it was true, but he didn't think he could afford any distractions from his duty to the varied inhabitants of the Roc – truce or no truce – and he knew Philippe de Montfort better than to believe he would abide by the terms of any such deal.

Privately, though, he wasn't even sure why he did feel any obligation towards them. Oh, he had almost convinced himself that he was truthful about repaying their food and shelter, but he was all too aware that he could

141

leave at any time, and not have to repay either. He unhitched the purse from his belt, and reached in for flint and
steel. As he rooted around in the bag, his fingertips
brushed the roughly cut hairs of a piece of woven fibre
which he hadn't consciously thought of, let alone touched,
for longer than he could remember.

Was that it? he wondered. Did this severed tassel still
tether him to values he had left behind so long ago? They
were values he had held dear for a long time before they
had started to seem hollow, empty and worthless – not in
themselves, but in the way they were carried on. It still
bound him to his sword, though. He had always known
that much . . .

'A penny for them?' Bernice asked.

'What?'

'Something's bothering you, Guy; a blind man could
read your body language right now.'

'Body language?'

'Yes, you know. You're a fighter, you can tell by someone's stance whether he's afraid, bold – whatever.'

'Of course.' That was just instinct, he thought, not a
language. If it were, people would use it to lie. Then again,
wasn't that what a feint was?

'Ever since I came to the Langue d'Oc, it seems people
have been reminding me of my past, using it to persuade
me. Edouard was very quick to notice my horse's tail.' He
stuck another twig in sharply, as if to stab an enemy.
He felt used, to be honest, and he didn't like it any more
than he would have liked himself if he had followed his
own course, bearing in mind the course which he had
planned out for himself.

'I know the feeling. There are always things you don't
want to do.'

'I did not say I did not want to do them,' Guy corrected
sharply, feeling that it was important that she should know
that he knew right from wrong. 'I mean that there are
things which I think I should not want to do, but I do.'

'Like help out here, you mean? Get involved in yet
more trouble when you just want to put it all behind you

142

and live in peace; but you can't, because some idealistic part of you tells you it would be wrong?'

She understands, he thought. She didn't *know*, of course, but she understood. Stranger still, she wasn't trying to lead him into any more responsibilities in the way that the others had. It was a pleasant change to find someone who simply understood, and left it at that.

He pulled the tassel of silken rope from his pocket, and passed it over to her. 'Do you know what this is?'

'I've never seen one before, except in holos – pictures – but it looks like the tassel of the cord belt worn by a Templar. Yours?'

Guy nodded, surprised at how simply the memories came back, without disturbing him with either joy or pain. Perhaps that stage was passed, or circumstances were keeping them at bay. 'I was once the deputy of one of the smaller Preceptories: one of the youngest ever to hold such a post. I had joined the Order because at the time I thought that it was a good thing to go and protect travellers on the pilgrimages to Jerusalem and Nazareth from the usurper Saracens. Soon, though, it became obvious that there were other reasons for our battles – to force our views on others. At first even that seemed right, as God was on our side, but many of us soon felt that the Saracens were no different from us. They were just as certain that God was on their side, and who is to say which of us was right? People of other faiths also sometimes appeared, and they were the same. Many of us returned home, and I thought that at last I could perform the duties of a proper Knight – protecting travellers, guarding caravans, and so forth.'

'And did you?' Bernice asked quietly.

'Yes. I saved lives, and sometimes took others, but the ordinary people were protected by myself and the others.'

'So why did you leave? Were you ordered to do something you didn't want to?'

'No, and I did not leave.'

'Kicked out?'

'It was . . . a matter of honour. I did something which I

143

believed – which I believe was right, but which was not in accordance with the Order's code of honour.' He had been wrong, he realized, to think that the memories weren't painful this time. It was just taking longer, until he recalled the anger ...

'Would it be indiscreet to ask what?'

'Since you are sitting here with a disgraced knight – who is clearly a dangerous man,' Guy smiled, attempting a little humour to lighten his own mood, 'your question could not be indiscreet.' It didn't work, and a gloomy pall settled over him. 'But,' he went on sadly, 'the answer might be.'

The corners which led the huge walls back away from the narrow esplanade were soft angles which offered the Roc's visitors an impressive view of the seemingly endless stretch of dressed stone that capped the mountain.

Its builders had most certainly known their craft, Louis de Citeaux reflected admiringly. If only he could enlist the aid of such men for the continued rebuilding of Béziers ... It would be a tragedy if such a structure were to be destroyed.

But then, he could hardly deny his people their right to erase the stain of non-belief from their lands, could he? And, of course, it wasn't in his city anyway. Still, with the place being so far up this mountain, perhaps the people would find it too much bother, and would prefer to leave it as a monument to the folly of heresy.

He suppressed a snort of laughter. Now, he thought, I am beginning to sound as obsessive as Guzman. Better that, though, than burnt as a sympathizer, let alone forced to watch the laeti trade with the Cathares instead of his own agencies and vassals.

The herald to his left looked bored, while the scrivener was busy sorting through his parchments. To the right, however, the Doctor had raised himself up in the saddle, taking a long and visibly fascinated look at the fortress. Louis had suspected that the Doctor might be interested in the last bastion of the hunted on his lands.

The Doctor had been strangely silent all through the previous night, sitting off in a shadowy corner as wrapped in his thoughts as in the fur-trimmed cloak he'd been given. Perhaps, Louis had thought, he is trying to decide whether to disobey his instructions to only observe. If so, it was clear that Louis should do his utmost to ensure that he made the right and worthy decision.

Louis, therefore, had included him in the journey to settle the truce which the Parfaits had offered. It would give the Doctor an opportunity to see what Louis was hoping to protect the citizens under his wing against.

The foreign emissary was now scanning the parapet above, pausing barely perceptibly at each defender's face up there. He has the eye of an Inquisitor, Louis thought, strangely surprised and perturbed at the idea. No one so clearly sharp-witted should hold such a dangerous position. That was for those who trusted in their faith more than their ingenuity.

Louis' motto had always been 'God helps those who help themselves.'

So Louis did, warmed by the fact that by helping himself he helped his citizens, who so clearly needed protection from the evils of the world – whether they liked it or not.

The other odd thing which Louis was noticing about the Doctor was that he was the only one of the quartet who never spared so much as a glance backwards, in the direction of the thirty heavily armed men who were all-too-close at their flank in the guard tower at the bottom of the steep and winding track. Even though he was here to confirm a truce, Louis' mind insisted on plaguing him with memories of news about Inquisitors and landowners slain by – genuinely, his conscience piped up briefly – vengeful Cathare warriors. They always professed non-violence, of course, but he knew from the occasional slaughtered patrol his men found that the tiny number of fighters they had seemed to be distressingly adept at infiltrating garrisons for their murder raids.

Despite his misgivings, he still managed to keep his expression carefully masked with a diplomatic look of blandness as the small door set into one of the large main gates swung open.

No guards emerged, as there were sufficient men on the parapet above, no doubt with bows strung. Instead, four people emerged – a pair of men and a pair of women. Though men and women were reputed to hold equal rank within the Roc, there could only be one leader. The older of the two men stepped forward, not so much insolently or disrespectfully as familiarly, as if he counted himself on even terms with Louis. Louis felt even more offended by this than by insolence or disrespect. Neither subservient nor arrogant, the man couldn't help but cause Louis to admire his straightforwardness. Until, that is, the light caught the messianic gleam in his eye. Louis groaned inwardly: a heretical version of Guzman was all he needed.

The old man approached with a firm step, pulling his robes more tightly around him against the cold. 'You have decided your answer?' he asked simply.

'If you truly intend to bow to the inevitable, the least I can do is grant you some time to ... make your peace with God.' He hoped this would go quickly, as he didn't really want to waste time with another fanatic.

'Not your God,' Girard declined. 'But we will have peace and tranquillity when we become a part of Amor.'

'I have heard many fine words from many people, but a promise of tranquillity is usually short-lived. I shall require security.'

'You mean hostages?' Girard snorted. 'If you insist, but no more than twenty.'

Smiling more vindictively than he had originally intended, Louis motioned to the scrivener.

The truce was signed in silence, but all through the scratching of quill on parchment, Hugues wore the look of someone with a sour taste in his mouth, Jeanne glanced back at the walls with a worried look and Giselle remained stoic.

When the twenty hostages – ten of each sex and all volunteers, Girard had assured – were gathered and ready to move, Louis was unaccountably glad to be leaving the Roc. Perhaps Guzman was right after all, he thought. There was something unnerving about their willingness to give themselves up to the flames; perhaps because, in his experience, such people often attempted to take those around them with them.

As they descended the steep track once more, the hostages following quietly, Louis was presented with another oddity.

Why did the Doctor continue looking back at the walls with such an inscrutable air?

The chestnut mare nodded its head in eager anticipation of some small treat as Guy entered its little enclosure in the stables. He wished he had some small sweetmeat to give it, but had long since ran out. Patting it on the nose, he dug a grooming brush from one saddle-bag and started to brush along the grain of its coat. He may have let himself fall into being this fortress's champion, but he wasn't going to let it cause him to neglect his long-time friend.

He unstrapped the finely woven tail that was cupped over the stump of its own, docked, tail. It was a good match for the original, much more so than his current armour, which bore no relation to the armour which had been broken and thrown to his feet at the same ceremony. Protocol, he thought, had much to answer for. Omit the right words before you set out to kill someone and you're branded 'false to your plighted faith'.

Deciding that it was time to have it cleaned – or perhaps even replaced – Guy left the stable to look for a weaver. Instead, he almost walked straight into Bernice, who was watching with a look of fierce concentration as Hugues and Girard raised a silver stand on which a trepanned skull lay, grinning with enigmatic superiority at the triple row of Parfaits kneeling before them.

'Couldn't get enough of me?' Bernice suggested.

'If I ever reach such a limit, I will let you know.'

147

'Behold the calcified remnants,' Girard intoned. 'The only future of matter.

'What are they doing?' Bernice asked.

'I do not know. Some sort of ceremony to reaffirm their belief in spirit over matter, I suspect.'

'It means that much to them, does it?'

'They think that all the world was made by an evil god, Rex Mundi, while men's spirits were made by a good one, Amor, with the principle of love or some such. To them, all material things are made by evil.' Bernice only nodded silently, and looked back to the ceremony. 'This does not offend you?'

She gave a stifled laugh. 'Look, Conan, I've been around quite a bit, and seen a lot of strange stuff. This is just another hokey religion in a long list. Now keep quiet and let me try and memorize this so I can write it in a history book later.'

'It has spread everywhere in Europe. How could you not have seen it before?'

'Nobody's seen this in over a thousand years . . . Where I come from, I mean.'

Guy fell silent. Girard had placed the skull on a pedestal by now, and turned to address the assembled Parfaits. 'In a few days, our calendar will reach its perihelion, and you will each be able to share in that touch of knowledge without which the spirit cannot live. We shall leave this world then, the Inquisition will see to that, but it will be the beginning of a new existence, in a new world, in a new year.' After a moment, Guy continued on his way. People's religious activities didn't interest him these days, and so long as none of the Parfaits bothered him, he saw no reason to pay any attention to them.

Philippe led half a dozen of his troops down the gentle gradient of the river-bank and turned to follow along the muddy border between land and water. Despite the leather and wool which protected their skin from being chafed by the steel mail, the metal still managed to conduct the cold to them more than Philippe would have liked.

At least this, however, was more bearable than the heat that the various layers of armour and clothing had baked them with in the Holy Land a few years ago. Joseph had waited behind to oversee the others' descending of the treacherously slick slope, but forged ahead to draw level with Philippe once they were all down at the water's edge.

'The jailers?' Philippe asked.

'They will trouble you no further, and a fire has disposed of the bodies.'

'Excellent. Do you wonder why I do this?'

Joseph shook his head. 'You are the Captain of the troop.'

'Yes.' He fixed Joseph with a speculative air. 'How would you like a troop of your own?' Joseph flushed guiltily, but Philippe wasn't in the least surprised. In fact, he would have been disappointed if Joseph hadn't had any ambitions to lead. It was a natural instinct, after all. 'Do not worry, my friend. This Doctor or whatever he calls himself has proven to be the key to the treasure vault. If we can but find the heretic who escaped from Béziers . . .'

Joseph gave him a sideways look. 'All three divisions of the standing army have searched the countryside and found no sign of him.'

'The standing army is mostly made up local peasantry, who may have friends or loved ones at the Roc. Most of the rest are not hunters: they are farmers, or guards who think war is but a larger tavern brawl and cannot read signs. Either way, they are not the best.'

'No. We are.'

'Precisely. This river flows past the Roc, almost directly under its walls. As I must return to continue as Louis' personal bodyguard, I want you to take these men and follow its course. If a wounded man were making for the Roc, this would be his easiest way of keeping to the right path – which means that you might find some sign of where he left it to enter the fortress.'

'And if we find such a trail?'

Philippe thought for a moment, this more military problem being more to his liking than the difficulties of politics. 'Do not enter,' he said finally. 'Just bring me the knowledge. Tell no one else, not even the Archangel Gabriel, if he should descend and ask. Understood?'

'It shall be as you say,' Joseph replied, with a predatory look that mirrored Philippe's own expression. Philippe nodded in satisfaction, and wheeled his horse around to climb back up the bank. It had taken him a long time, but he believed he was finally about to correct his brother Aumury's greatest mistake.

The Castellan hurried though the wet straw, acrid smoke from the smithy stinging his eyes as he passed it on his way to the north tower. As if he should have to run errands while some uncouth – no doubt he would show such true colours eventually – mercenary stole his honourable position . . .

He had to admit, though, as he cast a glance over the various groups looking up expectantly at the tower's parapet, that de Carnac seemed to have grabbed their interest in a way that he had always failed to manage, no matter how hard he had tried. De Carnac and the other former knights were already up there, a squire counting the attendance, but he didn't seem too concerned that the Castellan was a few moments late.

Wheezing slightly as he hauled his bulky frame up the open stone steps to the walkway, the Castellan fervently hoped that, if the Parfaits were right about reincarnation, he would come back as someone fitter.

'Now that we are all present . . .' Guy said dryly, and the Castellan flinched as he felt the eyes of the whole troop on him. 'By now you all know that I am taking charge of your duties. Some of you will wonder why. Others will not care, but I will tell you why. I have fought in several sieges, on both sides. I also know Philippe de Montfort personally, and I would not trust him to honour a drunken gambling bet, let alone a truce in wartime. If any man among you would have another captain rather than myself, then let him come before me and issue a challenge. If he wins, I will step down.'

While the men digested this, Guy rested his hand on his sword-hilt. 'From now on, your duties will be regimented, with set times for rest. Each group will be instructed in the use of the bow and the sword. Some of you will also be taught to wield polearms. You will save all your anger for those times: any brawls, drunkenness or other foolishness will be met with severe punishment. Doubtless you will test me on this, so I pity you now.' He paused briefly, looking over the arrayed warriors. 'I know you will expect me to tell you that you will fight for honour and glory, but we all know that such words are empty. If the truce is breached, you will be fighting for your lives and those of your families. Fight well and you may save them. Cross me, and you must hope your family are skilled chirurgeon-barbers if they are to save you.'

The Castellan had expected an outcry of jeering at this, but was surprised to see that the troops below simply chatted amongst themselves and waited to see what would happen. Guy, meanwhile, had moved over to confer with the other former knights. 'Which of you is in charge of the men who were on guard last night?'

'I am,' one of the knights answered in a surprised tone. The Castellan sidled away from the short, arrogant man quietly, hoping to stay out of the way as he judged where this conversation would lead.

'Where were you while your men were sleeping and gambling on duty?'

'Asleep, of course. We mere mortals need it, you know.'

'Ah, of course . . .' Guy's fist lashed out, snapping the knight's head to the side. Guy hit him again, knocking him to the ground. 'Worthless whoreson! Squad leaders should share the same duty hours as their men. Regular spot-inspections will help maintain discipline, while not being afraid to join in with them will help morale. You will no longer lead . . . which group is it?'

151

'Eagle squad,' the Castellan put in helpfully, glad to be doing something.

'Eagle squad.' Guy stepped back to look over the assembled men, who were watching the display with astonishment. 'Eagle squad, take one step forward.' In response, an uneven group of men moved forward from near the centre of the mass of warriors. Guy pointed at the nearest squire among them. 'You! You are now squad leader. Get up here now for your duties!' He turned back to the groaning man who was spitting out blood on to the damp stone. 'You are a message-runner from now on.' He looked back at the other knights. 'You will all share the same duty hours as your men, and will conduct regular unannounced inspections. I, of course, shall do the same for you.'

The Castellan shuddered in spite of himself. He could never have dared assault one of the knights like that. The thought led him to wonder whether the new leader would be able to read the duty schedule he had painstakingly drawn up. All the knights could read, but a mere squire? He was just about to draw this question to Guy's attention when there was a loud commotion from below; the men surged towards the entrance to the tunnel.

To the best of his knowledge – and he was the man who should know – there were no more refugees within a day's march of the Roc. Who else could it be?

Bernice had just finished bandaging up a sprained wrist when a wry-looking Guy led two men bearing a litter into the dark and sickly room. Since anyone who had to be carried in was clearly worse off than a man-at-arms with a sprained wrist, she shoved the newly treated man aside – not too unkindly, she hoped – and beckoned the bearers to bring their charge over to her table.

As the two soldiers laid down the man they carried, Guy nodded towards his horrifically scarred body. 'I fear he is beyond your field talent,' he said, not bothering to make any other comment. 'Are Jeanne and Giselle here?'

'We are here,' Jeanne acknowledged, as she hurried

through the mass of tightly packed wounded. 'The nego-
tiations took less time than I expected.' She teased away
a part of the man's blanket as soon as she arrived. The
flesh beneath was red and puckered, leaking blisters
inflaming most of his skin. Jeanne's expression was almost
as fierce. 'Trial by fire. He would be better dead.' She
started wrapping one of the fugitive's arms with bandages
over poultices.

Benny grimaced in disgust as she used a cold damp
cloth to wipe away the sticky excrescences of the weeping
blisters which were all over the puffy and swollen burns.
'For once I agree with you there.' The only worse burns
she'd seen were from a breach in the plasma chamber of
a matter–antimatter reactor on a negligently maintained
– to criminal levels – freighter which had crashed on take-
off not far from a dig she was heading up on Keezarn.
She hardly dared imagine how such a primitive culture as
this had produced such an effect, but knew all too well
that it was foolish to underestimate people's ingenuity for
this sort of thing.

'Fire and iron,' Guy said in a low voice, as if he had
read her mind. 'They will have chained him to an iron
chair fixed before the furnace.'

'And the metal heats up like a frying pan,' Benny
finished. 'It's a miracle we ever made it into the
Renaissance.'

'No less a miracle that he could make his way here with
these wounds,' said Jeanne.

'The Templars found him wandering beyond Béziers'
walls, and brought him here. They feared that he had been
released so he could lead the Church to the cavern mouth,
but there was no pursuit,' Guy said.

'Then how did he escape the donjon at Béziers?' Jeanne
asked.

'Doc-tor,' the man groaned painfully, making a weak
attempt to rise.

'Don't worry,' Benny reassured him absently, 'we'll get
you a doc–' She looked down at him in surprise. It was
hardly a common word in this century. In fact she doubted

that more than a hundred people had ever heard it, so soon after the founding of the first medical school in Paris. Hoping against hope, she leaned in closer. 'A small man with a white cotte and breeches, and a Scots accent?'

'Doctor ... tricked Guzman. Told him I was ... dead.'

'Hardly a great trick,' Guy muttered, too low for anyone other than Benny to hear.

'He requires a master of the physic?' Jeanne asked. 'I doubt that much more could be done.'

'He's not asking,' Benny told her, trying to contain her excitement. 'He's telling – He's talking about *the* Doctor, not a doctor. Obviously he's worked his way into the other side and fooled this Guzman into letting him go.' She stopped, a nasty thought occurring to her. 'This Guzman ... Not Dominic, by any chance?'

'No,' Guy answered. 'A bastard nephew, I understand.'

'Bad enough, I suppose.'

'Certainly. He uses the Inquisition his uncle Dominic created just as effectively.'

'That's nothing; just wait a hundred-odd years until Tomas de Torquemada gets started.'

'What?'

She waved the question away. 'Nothing, just speculation. If the Doctor's in Béziers, we'll have to go and get him here.'

'Why? He is clearly in no danger from them if Guzman takes him at his word on anything.'

'For one thing, he might be able to save more of these poor smeggers than you or I could, and secondly because he owns our ship, and without him I'll be stuck here for life. Not that that should be much of a problem,' she added, with a touch of gallows humour. Especially considering what happened – will happen, she reminded herself – to these people.

'There was a man fitting your description with the herald who came to confirm the truce,' Jeanne interrupted. 'He was some kind of observer, apparently. Certainly he was observing the walls, as if looking for something.'

'Probably for me. Or he could have intended to follow

this friend of yours to the tunnel; it's just that he wouldn't tell the other side.'

'Then he must be with the garrison in the village below,' Guy said.

'Yes.' Benny thought about what she knew of the garrison. It wasn't a lot, except that it was large, and some of the men had turned a blind – 'A blind eye,' she said aloud. The other two looked at her blankly. 'Those soldiers who ran interference for us when we came along the river to the Roc,' she reminded Guy.

'Yes, of course. But what of them?'

I'm glad I didn't do all that travelling with a female Mad Mitch for nothing, she thought. 'Fifth columnists, Guy. We can use them to help us get the Doctor out of Church hands.'

'But he is helping them.'

'I doubt that,' Benny grinned. 'But even if he was, would you rather leave him there to continue helping them?'

'No. Rather, I would kill him to permanently remove any threat from him.' He smiled more softly before she could marshal her anger in response. 'But, I will trust your judgement in this. Girard has bade me train some of the best men for a sortie of some kind outside the Roc. Perhaps it is time they were given some manner of practical exercise in this matter?'

Bernice forgot all about Jeanne's presence, surprised and relieved that he took her word on the Doctor's value. 'You must be reading my mind. These sympathizers can tell us where the Doctor is likely to be at any given time, and we can pop in and snatch him.'

'It would work best if the sympathizers were to be the first guards to arrive in pursuit. They could then draw off the more . . . faithful hounds in the wrong direction.' His face took on a more sober expression. 'It would have to be a very fast raid, faster than Saracen cavalry perhaps, and even then the Church forces are so densely packed into the surrounding valleys . . .'

'There's an old saying common to many cultures, which a friend of mine would have been very familiar with. Four

155

thousand throats may be cut in one night by a running man. And you don't have to tell me you love it when I talk that way.'

Guy raised an eyebrow.

Francisco Guzman was waiting for Louis and the Doctor when they finally entered the twenty-foot by ten foot main hall of the Hôtel de Ville. He had been pacing the room like a caged lion for the better part of an hour, irked at Louis' having kept him waiting as if he were a mere vassal. 'I hope,' he said immediately, 'that you are prepared to do penance for bargaining with those who have no moral sense?'

'He would be much quieter,' Louis said to the Doctor, 'had his uncle not created this practice of reciting rosaries.' He tossed his matted cloak aside and turned back to Guzman. The Inquisitor wondered if their antecedents had had these same arguments. 'We were, in fact, bringing you some new heretics to interrogate.'

'And you have brought yourself the stain of their insolence, I see. It would take but one such accusation. . .' Guzman had the right to interrogate anyone of any rank, and he sometimes thought that it would be a suitable reward for Louis' impertinence. He was not so stupid, however, as to overlook the certainty that Louis would have been intelligent enough to arrange some unfortunate fate for him in any such eventuality.

'I think the saying you're looking for,' the Doctor interrupted, 'is "battle not with monsters, lest a monster you become," as someone once said.'

'Never have I heard anything so ridiculous.'

The Doctor nodded, and looked away in the direction of Philippe, who was staring into his goblet with a bored expression. 'That's what *I* used to think.'

Louis clapped his hands loudly. 'Enough of this. With the truce assured, we no longer need to know where their hidden path is – '

'Unless they use it to escape,' Guzman warned.

'If they did so, we would be able to follow such a

large outflow of people back to its source. What is more important is that we know where that little bauble of theirs is.'

'That should be possible. It surprises me that they still accept it.'

'Not at all. They are like animals in this respect. Show a bull a red cloak, and it attacks. We profess to deny and denounce the validity of their treasure, so they naturally accept it. I understand several other enclaves have followed the lead of this one, each claiming it to be the genuine original.' Louis shook his head, suppressing a laugh. 'It may be amusing to reveal the truth to them before we burn them.'

Guzman couldn't help but smile. The idea was an attractive one. 'The shattering of their own illusions before death might help to cleanse their souls and allow them to ascend to heaven after a period of repentance in purgatory. I will make the proclamation.' Guzman sat down, forgetting his irritation at Louis' presumption. Recovering the heretics' souls in addition to cleansing God's Earth would be a great victory, he thought, which the Cardinals could hardly ignore at the next election.

'What is this un-genuine treasure?' the Doctor asked quietly.

'You do not know?' Louis looked surprised. 'Of course, you have seen few enough of them . . . It will be a surprise for you, but I think you will find it amusing.' He looked up as some servants entered with wooden boards heaped with food. The Doctor turned and made for the door. 'Will you not eat? The head of my kitchen here is from Dourlens, and makes fine game pies.'

'Almost as good as Chartres pastry, but I'm not very hungry. One meal a day is quite enough, as I've often said to my friends.'

Chapter 12

The night was mercifully free of incident, now that the truce was in effect, and only the clouds moved through the darkness as Guy de Carnac made his way to the small sleeping quarters adjacent to the hospital. Bernice had been allowed to rest in here after her long day's work, and Guy had taken some minutes to find the shadowed door to it. 'Are you prepa–' Guy began, falling silent as he noticed that Bernice had donned a leather jerkin over her padded armour, and had tucked a dagger into her belt. She was brave enough – you had to grant her that. How much good a dagger was against the sword, of course, was more of a concern, and he was concerned.

'Well, I can't seem to find a parrot or an eyepatch, but I suppose I'm as ready as I'll ever be.'

'Bernice,' he pointed out cautiously, not wanting to offend her by casting doubts on her abilities, 'we will be facing armoured men with swords and polearms. Are you quite certain that you are suitably equipped?'

'Ask those bandits we met the other day.'

'Please, Lady Bernice. I could not countenance being responsible for any harm that may befall you. I would be happier if you remained here.'

She gave him a withering look. 'Don't give me any more of this machismo; it's too early in the morning for me to deal with it. I can look after myself, and – unlike some people I know – I'm not likely to single-handedly charge a whole platoon. Besides, I want to keep an eye on you.'

'Only an eye?' He smiled. 'Very well, the others are waiting at the tunnel entrance.'

Although this end of the tunnel that led up from the riverside was illuminated with the dancing flames of flambeaux, Benny didn't see the small group of men whom Guy had picked out until they stepped from the shadows to greet them, the undulating light briefly turning them into the images of demonic trolls. Guy indicated the nearest man, small and ferret-like, but with a ready smile. 'This is Hubert. He used to be a gamekeeper of the Trencavel lands. This,' he said, pointing to a dark-skinned man in faded greens, 'is Ibrahim, who became separated from the rest of his raiding party, and used to be in cavalry. You already know Edouard, of course.'

He gathered the others round, the gamekeeper and the Moor armed with hunting bows, while Edouard carried an axe. 'The village is close, so we will travel on foot. Hopefully we will be in position before sunrise, and can then recover the Doctor while the night watch are tired and the day watch not yet fully awake. Hubert and Ibrahim, go and scout ahead for us – you know the route I have chosen. Once we are in the village, Edouard, Bernice and I will find and free the Doctor, while you find good hiding places from which to pick off any soldiers who arrive.' The two men nodded with faint smiles, and vanished down the damp stone tunnel. Benny was surprised neither of them had protested at her coming along, but assumed Guy had probably gone over just that argument the previous night. 'Edouard, once we enter the tower you will stand guard at the foot of the stairs, and I will go ahead of Bernice.'

Edouard nodded silently, and Benny judged that he was sincere in his determination, neither boasting of plans nor shying away. The other two, of course, were obviously men very much at home in the wilds. Guy certainly knew the right men for the job, she thought. Thank the gods for simple professionalism. They began to walk down the echoing passage, Guy already moving in an alert, catlike

159

manner. 'I thought you wanted to give up fighting,' she murmured to Guy.

'I do, but I do not want to give up other people's lives, such as this Doctor of yours. In any case, I believed you disapprove of violence.'

'Touché. And I wouldn't say the Doctor is "mine",' she added sarcastically. Don't tell me he's thinking of him as a rival, she thought. All the stories she'd heard of unrequited love in medieval settings usually involved much self-pity and frequent suicides. All the examples she'd encountered on any planet more often involved the sacrifice of others than the self. Last time she had visited her own time – a couple of years later than she had left it, though – she discovered that the condition had been unofficially christened 'Ace's Kiss of Death' by Spacefleet veterans. Sometimes – any time she thought of it, in fact – she wished she couldn't think why.

Guy threw her a wounded look. 'If I believed you were spoken for by him, I would neither court you nor appreciate any betrayal of him on your part.'

'Last honourable man in the world, eh?' she quipped, while something at the back of her mind tried to attract the attention of her consciousness.

'I am *now*.'

The interloper from the back of Benny's mind finally got a foot in the door. 'Did you say court me?' she demanded disbelievingly. Who did he think she was? More to the point, who did he think he was? Yet another gloryhound with an eye for the ladies, who is sick of fighting, uninterested in every other woman in the Roc and who was careful to ensure the Roc's security before approaching her, some part of her reminded the rest. 'Look, Conan, I – ' I don't know, she finished silently. He was a sharp, considerate and caring individual, it was true, but then so was Kyle – at least to start with. 'Shades, I thought life was supposed to have been simpler in the past.' Besides, with the TARDIS due back any day . . . Ace may have been the brief fling type, but *I'm* sure as hell not, no matter *how* cute he is.

'We are now at the entrance. We should remain silent from here onwards.' Guy looked around at the multiple shades of black and dark blue under the stars, keeping a careful eye out for anyone who might see them. Benny envied him that ability to switch to such a complete state of alertness instantaneously, but could only nod mutely and follow closely as he padded down the worn steps of rock.

Noting the ghostly pre-dawn light that painted the village in pastel shades reflected from the low clouds, the bullish form of Bernard, sergeant-at-arms to the garrison, shuffled through into the rough barracks that had been thrown together against the back wall of the small Hôtel de Ville.

For most of his waking hours he was delighted that his aging bones were laden only with light duties around the interior of the garrison itself. However, he would be the first to admit that when he had to go and rouse the morning watch in time to be at their positions by full dawn, he would much rather still be in his damp straw pallet dreaming of those past battles at the start of the crusade, when he had been one of the thousands who fought valiantly to free the Trencavel lands around Carcassonne from the heretics.

He had never actually seen one of the heretics personally, of course: relatively few of them had. He had only dealt with those traitors who abetted them by hiding them, or by resisting the army which needed the use of their lands in the holy work. Still, at least it wasn't as if the guards had to be at their most alert. They were laying the siege, not under it.

Lifting an old shield from its position on the wall beside the door, he advanced into the room, occasionally nudging one of the men with his foot as he hammered the surface of the shield with the hilt of a dagger.

The Doctor slipped silently along the plank-walled corridor with a sour expression, as if there were a bad taste in his mouth. At the end of the corridor was the door to

Louis' suite, but the Doctor was already stopping as he reached a portal set into the left-hand wall. His features draped with hollow shadows, he opened the door quickly. The gap between door and jamb afforded easy access to the narrow metal probe he used to push the locking bar aside.

He stepped in as silently as a ghost, moving with visible reluctance towards the bed, and looking as if he were straining to turn away but was being drawn inwards by some irresistible magnetic force. He stopped at the edge of the bed, looking down on the face which was formed into a wolfish feral expression even in sleep – a face surrounded by wild hair fringing its bald crown, and a forked beard adding shadowy form to the sneering look.

The Time Lord half turned, casting an eye over the sword and dagger lying on the straw-scattered floor beside the pallet-like bed.

He reached out a hand towards the dagger hilt, fingers curling inward as if already gripping it; at which point, a pale, feminine leg emerged from somewhere amidst the mound of furs and blankets, drooping limply towards the floor.

The fingers clenched into a fist, quivering slightly, then drew back, as the Doctor exhaled very slowly and quietly.

He paced out of the room tensely, carefully shutting the door after him.

The view from the midst of a switchback in the sparse hedgerow a couple of hundred yards from the corner of the Hôtel de Ville was a shallow world of blue and grey shadows. Not far off the real thing, Benny thought. The journey from the tunnel had been an almost ghostly trip, with no sign of any other living creature. Despite this, Guy had still insisted they pick their steps carefully to ensure as completely silent a journey as possible. Perhaps it was just the relief of being away from the stench of blood and sweat, but the winter morning seemed so crisp and fresh that it was almost a refreshing drink.

At this time of the morning the soldiers would be much

more interested in a warm campfire than the icy cold of the woods in the wee small hours. She understood how they must feel, as she began to wonder if she would ever feel warm again. The hedgerow offered little protection from the frosty air, and the ground was still coated in a thin veneer of remaining snow, glued into place by the frost.

Guy and the others seemed a little chilly, but not as frozen as she felt. It must be something to do with them having grown up under only the one sun, she thought, since even Ibrahim seemed untroubled.

The two long terrace-like buildings that formed the only street stretched off at an angle a few hundred yards to their right, looking like scars against the pale ground. A cluster of ramshackle huts and cabins surrounded the street and the few other odd stone buildings here and there, but none were any nearer to her hiding place as the Hôtel de Ville itself. Thank the gods for the class system, she thought ironically. The haves were likely to regret their feelings against sharing an area with the have-nots, when the distance meant reinforcements didn't arrive in time.

I hope, she added mentally.

The air was preternaturally silent – so much so that she could hear a faint thudding emanating from one side of the distant street – but she still heard no sound from Hubert as he shinned up an evergreen off to the left, propping himself against the upper trunk with his boots braced against a stout branch so as to leave his hands free to draw his bowstring. Where Ibrahim had gone, she had no idea.

The continued ethereal pounding from the distant street nagged at her, however, and she gave Guy a questioning look, jerking her head towards the buildings. He shook his head almost imperceptibly. 'It is merely the morning watch being roused. They will have to go out to relieve their predecessors, so we still have perhaps half an hour before there is any large amount of movement here.'

'Then now seems as good a time as any to go in there,'

Benny said pointedly, trying to stop her teeth from chattering.

'We had to give Hubert and Ibrahim time to get into position.'

'Where is Ibrahim anyway? I don't see him.'

'Good – hopefully neither will any of the soldiers. He is concealed on the stable roof.' Guy pointed to a low rim running around a single-storey adjunct to the main building. 'We may go as soon as you are ready.'

'No time like the present, assuming I can still move.' A further thought flashed through her chilled brain. 'I hope you've got everything straight with these fifth columnists of yours.'

'I believe so.' Guy drew his sword, and slipped out of the small hollow of the hedgerow. Checking one last time that the coast was clear, he beckoned Benny and Edouard out. They followed with small, quick movements, scampering across the sloping field to the rear wall of the Hôtel de Ville like startled rabbits. Benny couldn't help but windmill her arms a little to avoid slipping and sliding the rest of the way.

'What if there's a guard inside the door?' Guy had assured her that this entrance would be left unguarded for them, but it always paid to expect the worst. That way you occasionally got nice surprises rather than often getting nasty ones.

'Use your magic.'

'My *what?*'

'The lighted stick you carry – it should petrify any guards long enough for me to deal with them.'

'Magic. Right,' she agreed, feeling a little foolish. Some wild psionic talents would have come in useful, she was sure, but unfortunately, such things were rare even in the 26th century. Still, at least it didn't take magic to run stealthily.

Which was when the doorway on to the sloped-roofed hoarding which ran the length of the top of the wall opened, and a figure emerged into the growing light.

* * *

The Doctor stretched out theatrically, taking in deep breaths of the sharp air much as a fitness fanatic might have done, but without commenting on how bracing it was. 'Why couldn't it have been summer?' he wondered aloud.

Leaning both hands on the top of the hoarding's wooden wall, he peered out of the two-foot gap between wall and roof at the lightening countryside with a look of innocent excitement and curiosity, scanning the clean and sharp forms of the winterlands, the pale dawn light glinting from the helmets of the patrol traversing the street of the village. There was a touch of relief there as well, but there were still worry lines around his eyes. He frowned suddenly, his eyes drawn to a furtive movement in the shaded grey hollows of the field beyond the wall.

There were two men down there, he realized, and some-one else, with a lithe figure and a short dark mop of hair he'd recognize anywhere. 'Oh no,' he groaned. 'Why can't she just trust me to be all right for once?'

He leaned out slightly further, trying to attract her attention with an urgent wave.

There was a faint blur in front of his eyes, and a very loud thud at his forehead.

'Stop the stupid crukking fool,' Benny hissed angrily, but Guy had already made a curt gesture to Hubert, who lowered his bow. 'That was the Doctor,' she said slowly and deliberately. 'You know,' she sneered despite herself, 'the one we're here to rescue?'

'Hubert has never seen him before.'

'That's not a good enough reason to try and make sure he never sees him *again*, Conan!'

Edouard, meanwhile, had reached the narrow postern door, which opened into a small antechamber under the lowermost section of the main staircase. A white-shirted black dog, that had been sleeping behind the door, looked up eagerly to see if the new arrivals had any treats for it, but wandered off to a new position in something of a huff when it realized that they hadn't.

Benny paused to pat it for a moment – being rewarded with a severely licked hand – while Edouard took up station in the shadows under the staircase, and Guy padded round to look for anyone who might be coming down.

There was no sign of anyone, nor any sound bar the pounding of her own heartbeat. Somehow, that worried her more than the discovery of a platoon of armoured knights hiding behind the door would have.

The Doctor was frozen for a moment, though not with the cold. When it became clear that no further action was being taken, he stepped back very slowly.

His precious white fedora remained precisely where it was, as if worn by an invisible man. The illusion was spoiled only by the smooth arrow-shaft that pinned it – through the brim and the front end of the crown – to the roof of the hoarding. There was another man perched in a tree off to the right, who seemed to be giving him an apologetic look.

Sighing heavily, the Doctor tugged the arrow free of the wooden roof, and broke off the barbed metal head so that he could gently slide his hat from it. He peered back at the archer through the hole in the brim as if it were a gunsight, then he put the hat back on with a resigned expression.

'Come back Ace, all is forgiven,' he muttered, before ducking back into the building to await his inconsiderate rescuers.

The wood and stone room slipped quietly past in a smooth circle as Benny turned to check every possible approach. Guy was already moving stealthily up the solid wooden staircase, sword held level but drawn back, ready to deliver a thrusting attack in the space which wouldn't allow a full-blooded swing.

Benny followed, straining her ears so much for the slightest creak of a board that it almost threw her off balance. The beating of her own heart was still the only sound, and she wondered idly if it was possible for it to alert anyone else. Guy turned the first corner of the stairs and started briefly, then looked back at Benny while holding his sword out in front of him.

Craning her neck ahead and upwards, she saw the Doctor leaning nonchalantly against a wooden joist on the landing. 'I assume this is your idea of a jailbreak?' he asked in a low whisper.

'You can stay here if you like,' she suggested.

His mouth curled grimly downwards. 'I'd best not – I might be tempted to do something . . . unwise.'

'I know how you feel.'

'I doubt that.' He descended towards her, and left Guy looking rather confused as to what to do next. 'Not unless you've made a very bad error of judgement.' She could have sworn his tone was almost haunted. He looked back up at Guy, whom he had passed by now. 'I assume you're our guide, so you'd better show us how you plan to get us out of here.'

'This way,' Guy murmured disbelievingly, slipping back down the stairs. 'As you are waiting for us, we should not have to kill anyone to free you.'

'There's many a slip twixt the cup and the superglue,' the Doctor warned. 'Or in this case, half a dozen soldiers coming up the street which was hidden from you by that hedgerow.'

'Your fifth columnists?' Benny asked Guy, a nasty suspicion dawning.

'No, they would approach from the eastern side of the village,' he responded, in a wearily disappointed tone. 'Come, we must at least leave this place undetected. If we are trapped here, we die. At least out there, Ibrahim and Hubert can pick off the riders, and the uneven ground beyond the tree-line should hamper their pursuit.' Sweeping downstairs with considerable rapidity despite his careful silent steps, Guy spun out into the hallway, sword at the ready. The Doctor and Benny followed in time for Edouard to part the door slightly from its surroundings.

Guy wasted no time, however, but simply tugged it the

167

rest of the way open and loped out, turning to face the main part of the village. The leading horseman turned out into the open field at the same time, but miraculously didn't look round as Benny ushered the Doctor out and pointed him in the direction of the tree-line beyond the hedgerow. She realized guiltily that if the horsemen were able to follow them, they might well lead them straight to the tunnel – something she couldn't face being responsible for. She just hoped that Hubert was as good against an open target as against one hidden behind hoardings.

Her train of thought was cut off as two bleary-eyed guards suddenly rounded the corner from a side of the building hidden from Hubert and too close in to be visible by Ibrahim, one resting a glaive-guisarme over his shoulder, while the other carried only a belted sword.

They noticed her at the same instant, and froze with comically gape-mouthed expressions. 'Run!' the Doctor squawked, haring off towards the tree-line. The guard with the polearm recovered first, lowering it ready to charge.

Edouard's heavy hand slammed into Benny's back, forcing her out of the guards' way, and jump-starting her run after the Doctor.

With a dark flicker of movement, Guy sliced the blade from the the first guard's glaive-guisarme and quickly twisted his wrists to cut down at his legs. His sword ended up in a backhanded swing which knocked the second man off his feet as the flat of the blade hurtled up to crash into his jaw. He hit the damp ground with considerable force a couple of feet away. Drawn by the screams of the guard whose leg was all but severed, the mounted men suddenly wheeled around, finally noticing the strangers. With a bellowed cry of alarm, they charged up the sloping field, dark swords drawn.

Benny began to think that perhaps she should have trusted the Doctor to make his own escape after all. Further cries and shouts of alarm rose from all around the village, none of which eased her worries in the slightest. Neither did the fact that two of the horsemen were abruptly punched out of their saddles to crash to the earth with arrows rammed through their mail hauberks and deep into the flesh beneath. There were still four horse-men left, already too close for Hubert to get a clear shot.

As a third rider jerked like an impaled fish and tumbled to the ground with one of Ibrahim's shafts through his stomach, the Doctor tossed an irritated glance back towards the approaching horsemen, then threw Benny a critical look as he stopped running. 'Well, it was useful while it lasted, I suppose,' he commented, leaving Benny wondering what he was referring to. Abruptly another pair of riders wheeled round the curve in the stream. The Doctor hastily grabbed Edouard, who was bracing himself ready to receive the soldiers' charge, and shoved the astonished warrior back towards Benny and the approach-ing Hubert and Ibrahim. 'Run!' he yelled, urging them across the churned earth. Benny went all too willingly – and not a little guiltily – not needing to be told twice. There's never a transmat pad around when you need one, is there? she thought.

Guy, meanwhile, swung his sword in a limbering-up sort of way as he strolled towards the middle of the field. The Doctor blocked his movements with his umbrella. 'If you've lived this long as a soldier,' the Doctor chastised firmly, 'you must know that one man on foot against three mounted knights doesn't stand a chance.'

'If it helps you and Lady Bernice escape – '

'And what about foot patrols between here and the Roc?'

Guy looked back at Benny with a worried expression, his tense stance announcing his indecision for all to see. 'But these men will ride you down in moments if I do not hold them.'

'Don't you count your Chelonians before they're hat-ched,' the Doctor responded thoughtfully. 'You and Benny run. I'll put a stop to them.' He brandished a delicate metal rod which Benny would have recognized as his sonic screwdriver.

Grasping his umbrella firmly, so as to be ready to run,

the Doctor waited, sonic screwdriver raised, until the riders were only a few yards away. 'No man challenges the great wizard Quiquaequod!' he bellowed. A couple of the riders took the hint, and reined in in superstitious fear, but the others took no notice, and bore down on him. 'It was worth a try, I suppose.' He triggered the screwdriver then, and a painfully high-pitched squeal slashed through the cold grey air. The horses' reaction was immediate, their riders flailing wildly and tumbling from the saddle as the animals reared and kicked out in startled terror.

Not stopping even to admire his own handiwork, the Doctor ran.

Guy raced to catch up to Bernice, cursing himself for leaving the man they had come to rescue. He had seemed so sure of himself, however, that his attitude had seemed perfectly reasonable. Out of the corner of his eye, he saw Hubert and Ibrahim drop back once they were in the maze of trees, ready to disguise the fugitives' trail.

A quick glance back revealed a surprising view of the horsemen struggling to rise from uncomfortable landing positions, while the Doctor's short legs had somehow already brought him almost level with Guy. 'How did you defeat them so quickly?' Guy asked quietly, not wasting too much breath. Could they be pretending to have fallen, while the Doctor marked out a path to the Roc?

The Doctor waved his little metal rod. 'Magic.'

Of course, I should have realized, Guy thought relievedly. Ahead, Bernice and Edouard were pounding through the desiccated remnants of fallen twigs and branches, and Guy breathed a little easier at the sight. He and the Doctor had just come level with the others when the quick black blur of a rearing horse obscured the woods ahead.

Better to end such a good life by dying fighting, Edouard thought, drawing back his axe. Guy and Bernice had saved his life on the journey to the Roc, so perhaps he could save theirs in return if he was quick enough. It would be a worthwhile last bargain for a vintner with no vineyard.

'Hold,' a vaguely familiar voice snapped, sounding as startled as he was. The horseman held out a placating hand as his men thundered on to the pathway with a jingling and rattling counterpoint. Just as he was about to swing the axe, Edouard's eyes fell on the familiar face of the leader of the group of sympathizers to whom the Templars had introduced him the night before they reached the Roc. He checked himself just in time. 'I see we are barely in time. Antoine here,' he nodded towards a young-looking man whose mail looked about two sizes too big for him, 'will lead you south to the river and keep watch for other soldiers. The rest of us will go and join the guards who have been awakened, and lead them off to the east, towards the road up to the Roc.'

'Shouldn't you try to lead them away from any sign that it was people from the Roc who were involved?' Bernice suggested sharply.

'Who else could it have been? Doing that would only seem more suspicious, and so may betray our position in this matter.' With a nod to Edouard, he spurred his horse onwards, his billowing cloak an easy target for his men to follow. The Doctor and Guy had both caught up, and were enquiring as to Bernice's wellbeing. She didn't look very happy at their mothering of her, though Edouard noticed that Guy seemed to be fighting hard to suppress a smile as she protested that she was still fit to climb Mount Seleya – wherever that was. An oddly independent woman and a strangely philosophical mercenary, he thought, watching them deny being too concerned about each other. They probably didn't even realize what a couple they made.

As soon as the commotion of hoofbeats had reached a peak and turned eastwards, Antoine silently beckoned the small group to follow him. Keeping his axe in his hand just in case, Edouard picked his way through the woodland floor alongside the Doctor, whose mostly colourless garb blended in quite well with the wintry surroundings.

171

The Doctor didn't look relieved or pleased at his escape, however, Edouard noticed uncomprehendingly. Instead, his intense gaze flicked between Guy and Bernice, while his hand fingered the jade brooch on his lapel almost involuntarily. Edouard's heart sank.

Chapter 13

Robert, apothecary and herbman to the Roc, paused in mid-step as he passed the stables. Footfalls and voices, distorted by echoes, were preceding some small group of people out of the tunnel. If anyone had been outside, they might need medical aid, he thought. Should he go for Jeanne or one of her followers, or see if any of the ground herbs he was taking to the hospital would be of use?

Settling on the latter course – he was still just about young enough to harbour mild hero-worship for the mercenary who had been to the crusades – he hurried to the barred gateway, and pulled it open. Guy de Carnac was on the other side of it, hand outstretched to open it himself. Robert grinned: de Carnac was a rarity, staying here though he had no ties to the Roc or its people. Robert admired that, wishing fairly often that he himself possessed such a sense of chivalry. It would certainly offer a more exciting life, he thought. Trying not to look too fawningly impressed, Robert searched the pouches that were looped on to his belt. Jeanne and the others could talk about fire and iron all they liked, but he would put his faith in using oils and herbs for combating the dearth or excess of tension in the body.

Guy looked at him quizzically, then shook his head. 'You would be best to deliver those to Jeanne,' he said. 'None of us are injured.'

'Good,' Robert replied, with genuine relief. He had dreaded to think that the truce would have been broken so soon. 'I was just on my way there.'

'I wouldn't say there were no injuries,' a new arrival

dressed in cream-coloured clothes said indignantly to Guy in a rather tart accent. He poked a finger through the hole in the exceedingly odd hat he wore. 'Your friend with the bow will have broken my tailor's heart, for one thing.' He turned to Bernice, who looked back with a defiant expression. 'And I'd have thought you, of all people, would have known better.'

'Somebody has to keep an eye on you, Doctor. Someday you'll be so busy admiring the scenery that you'll walk off a cliff without noticing.' Robert exchanged a look with Guy. How could he be so annoyed at his rescue? It was inconceivable to Robert that anyone here could be less than ecstatic at being freed from the vicinity of the Church and its leaders.

'I was not admiring the scenery, as you put it. In fact the scenery was something that only de Sade could admire. I was, in fact, trying to get into a position to persuade them not to burn you if they found you. If I'd been sure you were here, I would have come in myself.'

'But none outside know the location of the tunnel mouth,' Robert protested. It was surprising, of course, given the length of time it had been in use, but the fact was undeniable.

'My albatross does.' The Doctor held up a narrow metal cylinder, which beeped quietly. 'And this is the chain that binds his weight to me.' Robert pulled back in alarm, wondering what sort of demon made metal ring without being struck.

'Do not fear,' Guy told him, grabbing his shoulder and thus preventing him from running for help. 'It is but a piece of Moorish artistry with a tiny bell inside.' Robert stopped trying to run, but eyed the metal suspiciously. Still, he thought, Guy had been lucky enough to adventure in the Holy Land, and had probably seen many such devices.

'If you say so, then it must be true.' He remembered the pouches at his belt, and hefted one meaningfully. 'Jeanne will be expecting these. If you will excuse me . . .'

Glad to be away from the man who must surely be a magician, Robert bolted for the hospital doorway.

'Check on the Doctor,' Louis ordered Philippe, before the latter could even ask what had happened. The Lord of the de Citeaux was obviously angered at having been wakened by alarm trumpets, and looked determined to vent his ire on anyone who came close enough.

Though this would normally not bother Philippe, the mercenary captain was very much concerned that he would be on the receiving end this time. 'I already have. He has gone.' Philippe wished, not for the first time, that politics was as simple as swordplay. If it were, he might have been able to judge whether the Doctor's disappearance had anything to do with Philippe's having confided his plans to him. If Louis suspected such a thing even for a moment, the family ties between the de Citeaux and the de Montforts would be forgotten in an instant, and he would never recover his heritage. Indeed, he would be luckly to escape with his life. Damned be that Doctor, he thought, not daring to speak aloud until he discovered what Louis believed had happened.

'Those depraved moral perverts must have taken him, and de Carnac was with them!' Louis paced across the churned field with the jerky speed of extreme nervousness, and kicked the arrow-spitted body of the nearest fallen rider. 'Only the Lord himself must have saved me, because these incompetent whoresons certainly could not. Send patrols to follow every path, goat-track and rabbit-trail that leads up or around the Roc to find their entrance. Tear the entire accursed mountain apart stone by stone if necessary, and bring de Carnac to me, alive and ready for a slow and painful death!'

'And what of the truce you arranged?' Philippe thought hard. So far, he was not being blamed, so perhaps there could still be a way to turn this situation to his advantage. Indeed, it might even be the best thing that could have happened to him.

'A pox on the truce,' Louis spat, visible gobbets of foam

175

exploding through the cloud of his exhalations. 'They have breached it with this affront to my honour. Shall I allow it to be said that that Louis de Citeaux cannot protect his own guests, nor even avenge them?'

Philippe relaxed slightly, relieved that Louis was plainly just concerned with how this would affect his own rank and social standing. 'I had wondered if this could not be a boon for us . . .'

'Since when did you play the game of politics?'

That stung Philippe, but he knew better than to show it. 'It is but a battle, and the enemy have won but a hollow victory. We can now portray them as oath-breakers, and their abduction of a foreign emissary may gain us an alliance and reinforcements.'

'It would portray me as a gullible fool, you mean! Yet we may be able to arrange some sort of explanation that would gain us favour. At the very least, the Cathares are responsible for the "abduction of a foreign emissary" as you put it.'

'King Alexander will want him back. Of that we can be certain.'

'Indeed,' Guzman commented, looking as energetically zealous in this early hour as he ever did. 'But, it may be more useful for the heretics to have killed him even if we have to ensure it ourselves.'

'I think the taste of blood has gone to your head. The Doctor is hardly a rival to your accession to the Holy See like d'Alsace was. For what reason should we kill him?' Louis demanded.

'Who needs one?' Philippe muttered uncaringly.

'The Scots are indecisive in their response to this disease of society. Perhaps the loss of one of their own will encourage them to accede to our wishes and send warriors to join our crusade.'

'That is something you can suggest to the Cardinals at your next meeting. Hordes of clan warriors cutting a swathe through the countryside is not quite what I had envisioned for my demesne once the heretics are gone. All I want is the people of my city to be dependent only

176

on me – not on help from ungodly philanthropes or anyone else. Is that clearly understood?'

'As clearly as you understand that the Church knows what is best for the people.'

Jeanne rolled up the scroll she had been poring over, her eyes too tired after a long night of candlelit operations. At least she had had the chance to be alone for a short rest – most of her patients seemed to sleep through the early hours of the morning until a couple of hours before midday regardless of how they had fared overnight.

Sometimes it seemed that the best she could do was to hope that they would all still be alive by the time she awoke around noon. She would have liked to mother her charges a little more, but somehow there always seemed to be too many of them to spend adequate time with them all, so that part of her soul was left to its own devices. It wouldn't have been such a bad thing if she had just been able to take her mind off it.

Giselle kept telling her that it was only the forms of the world trying to trick her, but Jeanne couldn't agree. Feelings were of the soul and intellect, surely, not the body? Then again, there were certain herbs and fungi that made people happier or morose, so perhaps Giselle was right after all.

There was a faint splashing from somewhere below as someone dropped or leaped into the wide wooden bath, and Jeanne wished that worries could be as easily washed away.

Perhaps they could, though, as the gentle seascape sounds from below did have a calming effect, lulling her to sleep before she even realized what was happening.

The Doctor froze in mid-step as he passed into the small room which Benny had been assigned. 'What,' he asked dangerously, 'is all this? Obviously explosives are hardly your style, but –'

Benny squeezed past him, having to sidle along the wall to avoid bumping into any of the hollow clay and wooden tubes that formed a compressed jungle gym linking several clay pots and metal bowls, some of which were suspended over small fires. Steam escaped from the crude joints and turns with faint bubbling sounds. 'Just my contribution to the Roc's lack of supplies and morale,' she said, putting on what she knew was a very unconvincing expression of innocence.

'If that was your intention, you should have baked a cake, not set up a still.'

'It's for medical purposes – alcohol swabs should help clean up wounds a little better. Of course it's true that it should be drinkable as well, and not true surgical spirit, but that's just a ray of sunshine to brighten up the last days. I mean, we both know these people aren't going to have time to get cirrhosis of the liver. Any who survive this place will die at Montsegur fairly soon. Anyway, look who's talking – you're the one who used to run a speak-easy in Old Chicago.'

'That was – '

'Different? For a higher purpose; isn't that the usual excuse?'

'Where did you learn to make one of these anyway?'

'Sometimes we poor archaeologists can't afford first class, and have to fly with the less scrupulous freighter captains. Anyway, what harm can it do?'

'What harm? Perhaps someone who died of blood poisoning here would have gone on to be a merciless dictator. Any anachronistic item of knowledge risks disruption of the flow of history. If someone duplicated this in this timezone, the next thing you know they'd be developing rocket fuel and flame-throwers based on ethyl alcohol derivatives.' The Time Lord sat down on a depleted sack of mildewed grain. 'Can you imagine the Hundred Years War with rocketry?'

'It'd probably be a lot shorter.' She held up her hands in a gesture of surrender before he could respond to this. 'All right, I'll smash it before we leave. It'll just look like any other pile of old junk in a storeroom.'

'Good. Because, as it is, there's enough work to be done before the TARDIS gets back.'

'What sort of work?'

'Damage limitation. I fear I might just possibly have made a slight error of judgement a little earlier. At all costs, we have to prevent those Church forces from grabbing possession of any sort of physical ephemera from this fortress.'

'But they're going to win anyway. We can't stop them doing some looting, even if we should, going by your own recommendations about not changing things.'

'Well, they're after something very specific, but unfortunately you managed to "rescue" me before I could find out what.'

'So you want to impose a blanket ban. What if we can't stop them?'

'Then we have to take other steps to ensure that de Citeaux and his two friends don't pick a vastly different course for history than the one which we both know happened.'

The Doctor's words had an ominous ring to them, which unsettled Benny somewhat. 'Well, you can play your little games, but I've got hospital duties to attend to. Keep an eye on that, will you? If this hooch vodka isn't delivered as promised, the peasants really will be revolting.'

'All right, go on. A little compassion is no bad thing,' he called after her as she went out. Alone, he took out the probe he carried everywhere. Its beeping was now a steady drone. 'But too much of anything can give you a sour stomach . . .'

Captain Joseph: that would be a good way to be introduced to people, Joseph thought. His ambitions were less bloodthirsty than they might have been, though; he could gain rank much more quickly by arranging the death of Philippe and taking his place, but it wasn't his way. He'd never been part of any knightly Order, but he thought that being the leader of a Royally sanctioned force would

179

be the next best thing, should Philippe succeed in his plans.

Should Philippe fail, of course... Well, no man's patience was infinite, and even loyalty had its limits. There seemed to be limits on travel here as well, even those in the service of the de Citeaux. For just as Joseph started to lead his troop down the embankment to explore this section of the river-bank, a number of knights in de Citeaux house colours had blocked their path, having just come from the opposite direction.

'It would appear we have been searching the same road from opposite ends,' their leader began. Joseph recognized him vaguely from having seen him around the garrison village. His name was Antoine, if he remembered correctly.

'Yes. Have you seen any sign of a path or tunnel?'

'Not yet. And you?'

'Nothing.' Joseph eyed the knight warily. There was something about the way he positioned his men; not threateningly, or even overtly defensively, but very much blocking the path... He wasn't sure whether to trust him or not. Philippe would not want to show his hand yet, however, so it would probably be best to be discreet, and simply report this to the Captain and see what he decided.

As soon as Joseph waved his men back, he noticed the knights forming up to follow behind. There was certainly something strange going on here.

The Castellan dropped a handful of preciously hoarded spices into a second mug of ale while his dagger's blade rested in the fire in the common room, then plunged the blade into it, before handing the steaming brew to Eagle squad's former leader. 'Perhaps this will make things better.'

'I doubt it. Girard's mind must be gone for him to give de Carnac a position of honour.'

'My position, you mean. He must be crazed indeed to take on mercenaries with one hand, while signing truces that mean all our deaths with the other.'

'Not all. We can leave, even if the Parfaits cannot. De Carnac is no valuable mercenary, mind you. Did you not see his horse?'

'It has a false tail; what of it?'

'Its tail has been cut off – it is part of the ceremony to disgrace a knight who has been found guilty of some dishonour and rejected by his Order.'

'You mean he is a coward?' That didn't seem likely, going by his actions.

'Either that or a thief or cutthroat.'

That did not sound promising. 'He is cold-blooded enough, to be sure.'

'I doubt that anyone here will be safe, while he remains in the Roc.'

'Perhaps not,' the Castellan agreed, draining his own mug. He stood up. 'I must return to my duties.' He left the knight glowering into his mug, and wished he'd never started the conversation, since the prospect of de Carnac being a danger was worrisome, to say the least. The knight could, of course, simply be trying to get back at de Carnac for relieving him of his position . . . The Castellan sincerely hoped so. All the same, he would rather be back at the vineyards at Labarre than try to juggle the problems here.

Jeanne awoke with a start, looking around her tiny cell, but couldn't recall why. Some dream, obviously, but if she had already forgotten it then it was not one memorable enough to trouble about, she decided.

The scroll was lying where it had dropped from her hand, and she picked it up and tossed it on to the small desk. It had been sad news – all news was, these days – though she had not known the man to whom it referred. The fact that word had been sent to her was enough to tell her that it was important, though. As if she didn't have enough troubles . . .

She wondered what Girard or Hugues would do if they knew who had sent it. Wring her neck like a chicken's, she suspected. They probably thought she'd been born a

Parfait, considering the assumptions they had made about her.

These things were irrelevant, however. All that mattered was that help was needed, and, as a healer, let alone as . . . Well, as a healer, it was her duty to help as best she could.

Robert watched fascinated as Guy de Carnac oversaw one of the squads – Bear, he thought, but he wasn't certain – drilling with swords and polearms. Only a true knight would have come up with such a scheme, Robert was sure.

Guy looked up as he approached. 'Is something the matter?'

'No,' Robert said, gesturing towards the warriors, 'I just wondered what was going on.'

'Nothing much.'

'Anything a hero of the crusade does is interesting.'

'Hero?' Guy laughed, shaking his head. 'If I were a hero, I would still be a knight.'

Robert had heard of this from the Castellan, but didn't let it bother him. Anyone who challenged the Saracens must be courageous, regardless of what else they may do. 'But you fought the Saracen. What was it like?'

Guy thought for a moment, then gave Robert a plain look. 'Terrifying and corrupting.'

Robert was surprised, and disappointed. 'But was it not good to kill the enemy?'

Guy glared at him. 'Kill or be killed? It is good not to be killed, for that is what all men fear.'

'But, knights are not afraid . . .'

'Of course they are. It is how they deal with fear that makes them brave.'

The Doctor looked down at the recumbent form of the man whom he'd helped to escape the dungeon at Béziers. 'It looks like Philippe de Montfort will be cheated out of his inheritance again,' he whispered to himself, too quietly to wake the injured man. The poultices layered with goose-grease had done little to salve his wounds.

182

The Doctor dug out the hypo from his pocket, and looked at it. 'All preventative medicines, I'm afraid, and too late for you.'

'He's not going to make it, is he?'

The Doctor didn't look round as Benny came out from the well-room with a bucket of water and some pieces of cloth. 'No. First the burns, and then exposure . . . It's more than the human body can take, at least for long. I should either have released him before he went to the torture, or left him there.'

'But you couldn't. He'd be guarded beforehand, so you'd just get yourself toasted instead, and afterwards . . . Leaving him there would be inhuman.'

'But I am. Or at least I ought to be. With the whole universe full of troubles and turmoils, I sometimes wonder: what difference does one man make?'

'All the difference – to that man. It's a perspective thing, I suppose, but perspective can be changed.'

'Aren't I supposed to be the wise teacher?'

'Have you never heard the old Earth saying, "Those who can, do; those who can't, teach"? So you made some mistake? Everybody does, but the smart man learns from his mistakes.'

'The smarter man learns from the mistakes of others. Some people can't afford to make mistakes: shoot a shrew in the Cretaceous and man might never have evolved.'

'We're not that far back. This one has lived a bit longer, but nothing has changed history.' The Doctor remained silent, but Benny could see the shadows flitting across his features in the torchlight, and he looked troubled, tortured even. It was an unnerving sight – the Doctor was never so on edge before as he was here. She wondered why; it had something to do with this Cathare, but she couldn't see what. The truth dawned. 'You came down here to kill him, if he was recovering, didn't you?'

'If he'd been recognized as the man I helped out from Béziers, Philippe could have used the information to disgrace Louis de Citeaux and overthrow him, establishing

183

his own principality. That never happened in this time-line.'

'And you would have killed him for that? You'd be right: you should have left him to the Inquisition. Could you even have *done* it?' She hoped not. She would have liked to think that his conscience would have got the better of him. She was afraid that he very well might.

The Doctor looked back down at him, running his thumb over the edge of the jade brooch he wore. 'I don't know. I really don't know.'

She considered this for a moment, wondering if it meant that he felt the same way about the matter as she did. If so, then she could rest easier – it would prove he had a conscience after all. 'You know, I don't think you would.' She shook off the pall that had settled over her during the conversation, and handed him the bucket. He looked at it as if uncertain what it was, or at least what it was for. 'While you're here, you can take these through to Giselle.'

'I'm not a medical Doctor, you know.'

'Neither am I, but you can mop foreheads, can't you?'

'And where will you be?'

'Getting some air – it's been a long day. Oh, is the hooch ready yet?'

'Not quite, but you'll know more about it than I do. A nice chianti is more my style, but then I don't do a lot of travelling on the Rim freighters.'

'I'll check in on it while I'm busy, then.'

The new moon cast a pastel sheen over the stone of the walls. Benny stepped out of the hospital block to ascend the steps to the battlements for a breath of fresh air free of the long day's taint of rotting flesh and cloying herbs. Guy was watching critically as Bear platoon, swathed in clouds of frosty condensation, dashed up and down various steps and ladders in practice for any possible night attack. He turned as she approached, his features no longer displaying any surprise at her unusual habits. 'You still here, Conan?' she asked. 'Now that these people are

184

as safe as they can be, I'd have expected you to move along home.'

'Home? Sometimes home travels with you.' He looked at her as if recalling something. 'Besides, after what happened this afternoon, can you truly call this a safe haven? I think that my help will soon be needed. And what of you? Have you no desire to return home?'

'My home is the ship I travel in,' Benny smiled. 'And you're right, I can't wait to get back to it.'

'I understand,' Guy nodded, 'but what of your home town, or country? Surely you have a birthplace you call your real home?'

The flash of a missile explosion lit up a Dalek assault craft before Benny's eyes. She blinked it away, irritated at herself for not anticipating such an inevitable question in some form or other. 'Not any more,' she said, more quickly than she might have liked.

Guy held up a hand apologetically. 'These wars, of course. I am sorry, Bernice. I did not mean – '

'Don't worry about it. I just hadn't thought of it in ages, that's all. You're so open and honest, and you don't even know where I'm from.' She needn't fear ridicule, she knew: this fortress was filled with a diversity of widely varying and often outrageous beliefs and opinions already . . . 'The old home town was Vandor Prime, in the Gamma Delphinus system. It was a nice place – lots of trees and parks. When I was a child, a race called the Daleks laid siege to Vandor Prime, bombarding it night and day . . .' A faint scent of smoke drifted past, and Benny shivered, unsure if it was from the fires and torches below or a product of her own memory. Pulling her jacket more tightly about her didn't seem to ease the chill to any noticeable degree. 'They kill anyone who is different from them, anyone who doesn't think the way they do. They killed my mother as I watched,' she whispered. She stopped before her voice could give up entirely.

Guy, his face a mask of horror, spread his hands apologetically. 'I am sorry, Lady Bernice; I did not mean to distress you. I could never – '

'It's all right. It's a bad memory now. After that, I was bounced around a number of refugee camps like this one, before ending up at an Elite boarding school.' He looked at her blankly. 'I suppose you'd call it a seminary.'

Guy nodded understandingly. 'This place must spark such terrible memories: it is little wonder your dreams are haunted.'

'So what's your excuse?' she snapped back, on the defensive at the thought that he'd seen her asleep and vulnerable.

'Why are you afraid of me?'

'What do you mean?' As if I couldn't guess, she thought guiltily.

'You have a notable tendency to become hostile on a regular basis. I have seen such a strategy used for verbal defences in many court intrigues.' He didn't look offended, though, she noticed – just surprised.

'Look, it's not you, Guy. Let's just call it another terrible memory,' she said quietly. 'Betrayal always is.'

'Ah.' He nodded understandingly. 'There are many dishonourable men in this world,' he muttered darkly, with a hint of sadness. 'It seems I must apologize again – '

'Dammit, will you stop saying that!' She shook her head amusedly. His concern for her feelings was surprising considering his profession, she thought. He turned to leave her alone, as she suspected her expression probably suggested he should.

She stopped him with a hand on his shoulder, turning him back towards her. Somehow, Guy reminded her of . . . Of course, she thought, it was only natural that her subconscious would follow on with a memory of how she had felt at the end of that time. 'No. You were right; I didn't even realize I was doing it.' She let herself relax slightly. After all, one didn't often find someone so . . . That was a worrying thought; last time it had taken her six months to get to feel this way about someone. Next you'll be believing in love at first sight or some such nonsense, she scolded herself gently. Lust at first sight, on the other hand – well, what the hell . . .

186

'Now that is your *real* smile,' he commented quietly. His own smile granted his features a warmer, less gritty look.

'So? You want to have your wicked way with me, I suppose?'

'I have never settled in any place long enough to consider wifeing.' He didn't remove her hand from his shoulder, however, though he glanced at it as if wondering why their situations weren't reversed.

'That's not what I meant.' Her other hand joined the first.

'I know what you meant, but that is not how I feel.'

'Now how can a scoundrel like you say a nice thing like that? Haven't you got a reputation to live up to?'

'Scoundrel?' He gave a faint smile, as if amused and flattered by the term. 'As easily as a Lady can make a stand for her strange ways.' He paused briefly. 'You should be inside, where it is warmer.'

'It's just bracing out here, that's all.'

'In that case, I am flattered.'

'What about?'

'That your trembling is not due to the cold.'

'I'm not – I mean, it is the cold.'

He looked at her with eyes that showed concern more than anything else. 'Then you must go where you can be warm, lest you catch pleurisy or . . .' He fell silent as her lips brushed his. He looked shocked at her forwardness, but didn't pull away.

'I think it's –' Both their heads suddenly snapped round, as a distinctly whooping cry of agony sliced sharply through the crisp clear air. She released Guy from her embrace as she turned back towards the main keep. 'It came from this direction, but it was too near to be one of the wounded in the hospital . . .'

Guy snapped at his soldiers to remain where they were, and then hurried off towards the keep beside Benny. 'The upper three levels are the living quarters of the Parfaits themselves. It sounded as if it came from one of them.' They pushed through the wooden door on to the wide

187

landing of the main staircase, immediately noting that footsteps were rushing up from below. Swiftly ascending to the third floor proper, they paused to judge the direction in which the footsteps were all heading. 'The west side,' Guy announced after a moment's thought. They turned into a narrow unlit corridor, boots pounding on the rough wood as a dim glow grew ahead.

They emerged from the passageway into a cul-de-sac in which several people were trying to force a door open. Benny and Guy forced their way through, and Benny tested the door's resilience. It seemed to be giving at the top, but was stuck fast further down. 'Something's blocking it. Just a second . . .' She ushered the mass of people back out of the way, ready to charge it. Guy stepped in front of her.

'If you will allow me . . .?'

'Chauvinist.' She stood aside anyway; she didn't want to risk ending up as one of her own patients.

'There is one thing I would like to ask.' The door creaked open a couple of inches under Guy's weight.

'What's that?'

'This Vandor Prime, in Gamma Delphinus . . .' He slammed into the door again, and it moved slightly further.

'Yes?'

'Is that anywhere near Rhodes?' Something heavy and solid shook the floorboards with a huge crash as the wooden locking bar snapped, and the door swung open wide enough for Benny to squeeze through.

'Not really,' she said in a not unkind tone, as she stepped over the rough seribe's desk which had been propped against the door. On the far side, the shutters of the sole window were firmly closed, and yellow candlelight tinted the whitewashed rock walls in gold. 'In fact it's a bit further away than you can – ' She froze in the middle of the spartan cell, shock and sadness vying for position in her consciousness. She suddenly had to jump back slightly as Guy leaped in, basilards drawn. 'Don't worry, there's no danger in here. We're too late for that.'

Chapter 14

Bernice knelt to feel for a pulse at Girard's throat, but there was none, though his flesh was still warm to the touch. One clawlike hand lay limply to the side, while the other hung against the small crossguard of a plain, but nonetheless effective, dagger of crude steel which was sunk almost up to the hilt just below the old man's sternum. Blood was still congealing throughout the fibres of his white mantle, tiny bubbles occasionally spreading out and bursting as the scent of copper drifted up from it.

Guy shook his head sympathetically, returning the triangular blades to his belt. 'The strain must have been too much for him,' he suggested.

'A suicide?' Benny asked incredulously. 'After all his speech earlier about this Cathare New Year ceremony that's coming up?'

'Though I have no wish to insult the honour of others' beliefs, it is true that the Albigenses and their kin consider all worldly flesh to be sinful. Why should a suicide amongst them be so surprising?'

Footsteps heralded Jeanne's arrival. The petite woman gasped in shock at the sight of the cooling body, and she fought to recover her composure. 'At least he has ascended to a purer plane,' she said uncertainly. Guy threw Benny a 'see what I mean' look.

'Wait,' Benny snapped, cutting off any speeches from anyone else. They were, she thought, overlooking one obvious flaw. 'If it was a suicide, then why did he scream? I suppose he was doubtful about doing it, and so decided

189

to take himself by surprise so he couldn't change his mind?'

Guy shrugged. 'He did not manage such a clean blow to the heart as he hoped, and so the pain that developed before death took him by surprise.' He indicated the bare room, empty but for a poker for the small fire, and the shuttered window and fallen desk. 'No one was in here when we arrived, and the entrances were blocked from the inside. How could a killer leave?'

Benny decided not to try and explain the entire locked-room mystery genre to him, deciding it wouldn't be worth the trouble. 'Magic?' she suggested with heavy irony, and regretted it at once.

'Sorcery?' He frowned. 'A possibility, I suppose.' Benny rolled her eyes at the thought that her most frivolous response had, it seemed, been the correct one to engage his interest.

'But not much of one,' the Doctor said briskly, pushing his way into the cell, which was already crowded with just the presence of the four of them, plus one corpse. Benny smiled in relief: she couldn't really blame Guy for having such strange opinions on the matter, as they were a product of his time, making her the odd one, but it would have been refreshing to hear a reasonably logical and rational appraisal of the situation. He knelt to double-check for a pulse. 'The only real case for this being a suicide is that his own hand is on the hilt. He could just as easily, however, have been trying to pull it back out; or, indeed, it could have been put there by a person or persons unknown – to coin a phrase – once he was dead.'

'How can we tell if this was the case? I could check if there is a seer in the Roc,' Guy offered.

'I don't think that should be necessary, but it's the thought that counts.' He straightened, and looked up at Jeanne. 'Is there any form of graphite dust or chalk dust in the Roc?'

'In the library perhaps, for forming pigments ... Why do you ask?'

'Because if there is any, I'd like you to bring me some

now,' the Doctor snapped impatiently. 'I should've thought that was obvious.'

Jeanne looked as if she was about to speak further, but then simply nodded, and beckoned a younger Parfait over, relaying the instructions to her. Benny, meanwhile, watched doubtfully as the Doctor brought out a Holmesian magnifying glass from one pocket. What a cliché, she thought. He didn't look through it, however, but instead gently grasped Girard's wrist, and carefully lifted his stiffening hand from the dagger's hilt.

One by one, he pressed all the fingers of the hand on to the spotless surface of the glass. Benny shook her head wonderingly, ashamed that she hadn't thought of that. Hoping that making herself useful would help assuage her self-embarrassment, Benny went over to the shuttered window, and opened the wooden panels after undoing the small wooden hook. Outside, a mist gauzily cloaked the river far below, infirm fingers of moisture occasionally clawing at the sheer walls of the Roc. She frowned down at the smooth rock below the window-ledge. 'If someone else was in here, they must have taken the quick way down.'

'That sounds reasonable,' Guy commented. 'As I said – '

'Of course they didn't jump.' The Doctor shook his head irritably. 'Why should they, when there's a perfectly good door here. If they wanted to commit suicide,' he added pointedly to Guy, before the warrior could comment, 'there is also a perfectly good dagger here – with only one not-so-careful owner, presumably.' He looked back over at the door, and then went across to it.

The slim wooden locking bar had broken in its U-shaped brackets when Guy forced the door open, while an iron poker lay amidst the shattered legs of the desk. The Doctor gingerly lifted it out and examined it closely. 'Reverend Green with the lead piping?' Benny suggested.

'No. I was just mentally enquiring into why this poker is by the door instead of by the fireplace.'

'Somebody could have used it to force the door and get in.'

191

'Perhaps, but . . .' He tossed it aside with a shrug. 'It'll come to me.'

Quill scratched hesitantly on paper, forming simple words announcing that Girard was dead. Smooth hands slipped the rolled-up message into a plain clay pot.

The pot safely corked and sealed, it was lifted up, and carried out into the bailey. No one was around, such was the interest in the activity in the main hold, so there was no one to stop the pot being carried up on to the battlement, and thence to the roof of the hold via an outside stairway.

With all the activity and hubbub of murmured speculation, there was no chance that the soft splash far below would be heard.

Below, in the midst of crossing the bailey, the Castellan looked up.

He had always thought there was something suspicious about that one, but had never dreamed it would be something so important. It must be divine intervention that had bade him look up at that point, just in time to see his quarry descend the steps. The Castellan froze, wondering if he'd been seen, but no one approached him.

Instead, a door clacked shut somewhere at the north end of the Roc. He didn't have to look to know which door that was. Should he add this to his notes first, he wondered, or tell someone? The answer was obvious – he should tell Guy, Hugues or the Doctor. Getting to them would be difficult, however, as they would be busy. On the other hand, the Doctor and his friends seemed willing to listen to Jeanne and Giselle, and they would both be working with them tonight in any case, not least when Girard was brought to the mortuary.

That was the answer – tell Jeanne and Giselle of his discovery.

The Doctor had allowed Hugues and Jeanne to remove the body, but had refused to allow anyone else to enter the

192

room. When the younger Parfait returned with some fine chalk dust, the Doctor took it from her with a wordless smile, and closed the door, leaving only Benny and Guy in the room with him.

'You're not going to get a good print with that,' Benny warned.

'So long as it's good enough to tell whether the dagger was touched by more than one person, then it's good enough for our purposes.'

'You are going to cast an augury?' Guy asked.

'It's a long story, Conan,' Benny told him. 'Let's just say that it's a way of telling whether a specific person has held the dagger or not.' Guy nodded at this explanation, and watched the Doctor.

Benny turned back to the Time Lord as he lightly sprinkled the hilt of the dagger with the powdery dust, being careful not to touch the grip. That done, he tugged a roll of Sellotape from one pocket and started tearing off strips with his teeth before laying them smoothly on to the hilt.

Peeling them back off after a moment, he held each strip up to the candlelight, discarding several before settling on one that had a clear print. He smoothed this on to the opposite side of the glass surface from Girard's print, and examined it closely. 'That's all I need,' he grumbled disgustedly after a moment. 'Another added complication.'

'It's not one of Girard's?' Benny asked with a sinking feeling.

'No. There's a murderer in the Roc, as well as whatever it is that Louis de Citeaux and Guzman want to buy the papacy with. It's at times like this I wish I'd taken that job as President of Gallifrey.'

'In other words, you've dropped us in it as usual.'

'You could put it that way, yes.'

Jeanne watched with mixed feelings as Hugues and some of the others laid Girard's corpse on a blanket in the mortuary chamber.

They certainly hadn't always agreed upon everything – upon anything, if she was to be truly honest – but, as a healer, it was painful to see any demise, especially one so untimely. Even on the farm all those years ago, she had been loath to slaughter any of the animals, so she should not be so surprised, she told herself, that a death even in these dark times was upsetting.

There was nothing more that could be done for him, however, and it was time to resign herself to trying to deal with Hugues. Hugues was young enough not be senile, but she despaired of the fact that he was very much a product of Girard's upbringing. They hadn't been father and son, of course, since Girard would have probably had a fit if any woman had suggested indulging in pleasures of the flesh – especially to create new earthly life. However, Hugues had been indoctrinated for so long that he would be just like Girard, only younger and stronger – and therefore probably more stubborn. She doubted she'd get any help out of him, regardless of how good the cause was.

No, Giselle was the only one who would sympathize. The strangers, Guy, Bernice and the Doctor, might, but they were in no position to do any good even if she did confide her troubles to them.

No. With Girard's death already bringing tears to her eyes despite herself, her best hope of having any requests granted was gone. Instead, she'd just have to struggle on on her own. Hadn't she managed the farm as well as her father had once he was gone? She hadn't gone running to her brothers for help then, and she'd be damned if she did any such thing now.

She turned and left the cooling body, leaving the tower altogether, and marching straight towards the library tower. There might be something useful in there, she felt.

Bernice looked at the thin slices of meat bubbling in the pitted iron bowl, and wondered just how long these strips had been packed in the chilled salt. It wasn't that she had anything against eating meat itself, but here they were, still using parts of real complete – at least originally –

194

animals rather than cloned tissues. If she'd thought to bring back a cellular replicator from her usual expeditionary manifest, she could have grown prime steak from a single cell from one of the skeletal cattle here. It would take a few hours to produce enough for one meal, but the effort would have been worth it.

The Doctor sat on his haunches to her left, resting his chin on the handle of his umbrella and staring into the fire with a distant expression. Guy handed Benny a crude mug filled with godale. It was spicier and stronger than she'd expected, but recognizably beer of sorts. 'He scries out the killer?' Guy asked, giving the Doctor a curious look.

'Never can tell,' Benny answered mockingly. 'But I doubt it.'

'I could always cast the I Ching, if you like,' the Doctor suggested.

'I thought you hated all those unscientific primitive fortune-telling systems.'

'The ancients knew what they were doing, you know. By accident or design, fortune-telling systems are a perfect means for testing the general strength of local reality. It should be either accurate or not – fifty-fifty either way – so if you get a more accurate or less accurate series of fortunes, that indicates whether there's any local disruption to the causal nexus. Of course it's not specific enough to pinpoint the problem, but it's still a very useful self-check when you're involved in things that could alter reality, such as time travelling.'

'Then what are you doing? Looking for pictures in the flames?'

'Why was Girard killed?' The Doctor glowered crossly. 'There must be a reason, but what was it?'

'Ask the killer,' Guy suggested.

'Whoever it was,' Benny added. 'Surely we should be asking who did it, not why.'

'Should we? In order to gain a satisfactory answer to our problem, we must first ask the right question. Anyone could have done it. So to find out who, we must know why; and to find out why, we must know why it was made to look like a suicide.'

'So the real killer would not be found,' Guy said dismissively.

'And do you know of any way in which he could be identified?'

'No, but someone always confesses eventually.'

Benny looked at him in despair at his primitive attitude, then caught herself. The Doctor didn't comment on the opinion directly. 'Since there is no method of detection for the killer to fear, the arrangement of the body must be for another purpose. Guy, you said that you'd expect suicides in a culture that believed all solid matter was made by evil?' Guy nodded. 'What if – the killer made his work look like a suicide because he hoped to provoke just such a reaction from the discovery of the body. That it was, in some perverse way, a fairly normal occurrence, or at least one that could be considered relatively acceptable without provoking any awkward questions?'

'For what purpose?'

'Because this murder is just a stepping-stone to some other goal. If he wants things to continue normally, rather than with people being suspicious of each other, the killer is presumably relying on the natural, normal, events following a perfectly ordinary death.'

'Rights of succession. Hugues took over immediately the death was confirmed, and already people look to him as they looked to Girard.'

'Dead man's boots?' Benny mused. It wouldn't be the first time, she thought, and at least it was a simple answer for once; though it probably wouldn't have helped humanity's standing with the Federation that the taking of another's life for personal gain was the simplest event imaginable. 'Well, it's been common since Roman times, if not before; gods know, it's still the preferred method of advancement in the Adjudication Division and in most walks of life in the Sirius sector.'

'Yes,' the Doctor agreed, absently toying with the incriminating dagger. 'Yet Hugues doesn't seem to be the cuckoo-in-the-nest type to me.' He shot to his feet, suddenly alert and brimming with vitality, though he hadn't eaten so much as a single mouthful. 'I believe I'll go and see Hugues; perhaps go over a little philosophical ground. Life, death, life, that sort of thing. When you two are ready, go back to the jobs that you've been given, but keep your eyes and ears open for anything unusual.'

'We're in a castle full of refugees and followers of a whole bunch of minor cults,' Benny replied pointedly, 'what the hell is *usual* that we can tell what's *un*usual?'

'Anyone who looks as if they're in a position to send messages out of the Roc,' the Doctor called back, as he vanished into the night.

'He is very much like the owl, I think,' Guy said, half to himself.

'Wise, you mean?' Benny had heard several people comment on such a likeness. Perhaps it was his eyebrows and keen gaze.

'What has wisdom to do with owls? He is comfortable in the darkness, as they are, and I think he is equally as adept at hunting down prey in cold blood.'

Chapter 15

Hugues was finding trying to run the fortress on his own a little more tiring, and certainly more difficult, than being an ostler had been. It was a challenge to which he felt his intellect was suited, however, as the combat of the human mind and spirit with the realities of the world was rewarding in a way. He wasn't concerned about the supply situation – one or two days without food wasn't fatal, though the reception they could expect from the Inquisition certainly would be – but the task of finding room for the increasing numbers of sick and wounded was tying his brain in knots. And as for the problem of working out which non-Parfaits should leave the Roc in which group . . .

He almost wished that they would all stay, but Girard had made it clear that the non-believers should leave. It was their choice, after all, and someone had to spread the word. Hugues supposed it was for the best, since he would not wish the unclean spirits of unbelievers to join them in the great hereafter before they had learned the lesson that it would be better for them.

An afterlife of complaints and recriminations was not what Mani had had in mind when he founded this belief, Hugues thought.

A goblet of water was resting on the scribe's desk which was the standard furnishing in the Roc, but Hugues had so far ignored it in favour of concentrating on scrolls and parchments.

'The loneliness of command?'

Hugues' head jerked upwards; he hadn't even noticed

that the Doctor was at the door. 'It should not be lonely for a Parfait. There should always be two of us.'

'These things are sent to try us, I suppose. Speaking of which, I wonder where we can find a reliable magistrate around here.'

'Not outside Béziers. Do you mean to say there is some need for one?'

'You tell me. Girard's death was no accident, and it's not uncommon in the outside world for promotion to be gained by assassination.'

Hugues felt a hot flush of anger at the implied suggestion, but resisted. He knew better, and knew that such reactions were just torments sent by Rex Mundi to spite the inhabitants of the world he had usurped from Amor. 'What care I for how others make their plays? We work in pairs, or not at all. I would have cut off my right hand before I would murder my fellow, and anyone who wished to remove the leadership of the Roc would have killed me as well.' Hugues reached for his goblet of water irritably.

The Doctor's wrist twitched slightly, and the dagger he had removed from Girard's corpse buried itself into the table, quivering briefly in the tiny gap between the goblet and Hugues' outstretched hand. 'Before you ask, yes it is a dagger you see before you – and I expect there will be others before long, both air-drawn and in the smiles of men, as it were.'

With exaggerated care, Hugues moved his hand past the dagger and lifted the goblet. He suspected it would be unseemly to look too unnerved – that, after all, was a condition of mortal flesh, and not of the pure intellect. 'I did see you pull it from the body earlier, but it has no tale to tell, unless you are a seer.' He looked askance at the intense stranger to his country. 'Are you a seer?'

The Doctor looked surprised, then smiled tightly. 'There are many kinds of seers.' The Doctor spread his hand before Hugues' face. 'Do you see the patterns on my fingertips?'

'Of course. Everyone has them – what of it?'

'Have you ever examined them closely? If you had,

199

you'd have found that no two patterns are ever the same. Everyone's fingers have a slightly different pattern of spiral lines and whorls, and the print of those patterns can be left behind like a wet footprint on a flagstone.'

Hugues realized the Doctor's point immediately. 'If you know one man's pattern you can tell if he has held an object?'

'Well, recently, yes.'

'Magic indeed.'

'On the contrary, Parfait Hugues. It's just a matter of looking closely enough at the pattern and at the object.'

'Then you must have found the pattern of Girard's fingers on that dagger.'

'Yes, but very faintly, as if they were only resting on it rather than pressing it into flesh. What is considerably more productive is that there is also a second pattern on it. One which is much clearer, and so obviously belongs to someone who held the thing much more firmly.'

Hugues stood angrily. Why had the Doctor been wasting time if he knew this all along? 'Whose is it, then?'

'I'm not sure yet. To find out, we'd have to check the fingerprints – the pattern of lines – of every person in the Roc last night. That could take days, and I don't have that long.'

'Then what is it that you wish of me?'

'What relics do you have here that the Church would be willing to kill for?'

'The Church would kill for any of them ... Are you implying that there is a spy in the Roc?'

'According to Louis de Citeaux there is.'

'He lies as easily as breathes.'

'Undoubtedly true, but as it happens, I believe him, because he was talking to Philippe de Montfort and Guzman at the time. I just happened to overhear; I have something of a knack for these things.'

'Then evidently the spy is the killer.' Hugues stood up impatiently. 'I will instruct the Castellan and de Carnac to – '

'I really wouldn't bother if I were you; they're both terribly busy. Besides, you've no secrets left, have you?'

'One,' Hugues admitted reluctantly. 'Girard could have been killed for it . . .'

'For what?'

'A skull, Doctor: a very special one, unique even. We will require it for the fourteenth, for our New Year rituals, which will cleanse our spirits and charge them ready for the afterlife. That will be the best time for us to die – for we will be prepared for what comes after.'

'Yes, Benny mentioned something about that . . . What's so special about this skull?'

If I told you, it would no longer be a secret, Hugues thought, but then paused. There was something about this Doctor that demanded respect, whether he was a foreign noble or not. And, as a self-acknowledged scholar – dangerous in these times – perhaps he was someone who might understand. Lastly, of course, he couldn't wring the skull's location out of Hugues, for the irony was that he never knew where Girard kept it. 'It is a long story, Doctor.'

'I have plenty of time.'

'Try cleaning the wounds with this,' Benny suggested, handing over a bowl filled with cloudy but colourless liquid. Jeanne and Giselle both sniffed it, noses wrinkling at the sharp and oily bite to the scent.

'What is it?' Giselle asked.

'Alcohol, of sorts. The same as there is in ale, but much more powerful. I can't really explain, and you wouldn't understand it anyway, but cleaning the wounds with it will help prevent any infection getting in.'

'If it is like ale,' Jeanne began slowly, 'will it not make the injured drunk?'

'Do they drown if you clean the wounds with water? Of course not.'

The Parfaits looked at each other. 'I do not see that it will make his condition any worse,' Giselle said pointedly.

'Nor I, I suppose,' Jeanne agreed. 'And they are all but

dead anyway, if they are not well enough to travel on the wagons when they leave.' She looked back to Benny. 'We will try it.'

Benny grinned, and handed the bowl over. Her pleased expression faded, however, as she was acutely aware of the other reason why she was in the hospital chambers now. She wished that classes in first-contact scenarios hadn't been her only introduction to diplomacy, because she wasn't at all sure how to go about this. 'Look, I also wanted to ask you both if you can think of . . . of anyone who might have wanted Girard dead.'

They both gave her shocked looks, and Benny hoped that it was more at the thought of a murderer on the loose than her straightforwardness. To hell with it, diplomacy is for diplomats, not an old-fashioned working-girl. 'Well, any ideas on who'd want to kill him?'

'Surely it was a suicide,' Jeanne protested, paling visibly. Giselle nodded dumbly.

'Unfortunately not. Girard's hand was draped over the hilt, but someone else held it. They left marks, if you know where to look for them.'

'Who?' Giselle asked.

'The killer, of cour– Oh, sorry. I don't know.'

'Well,' Jeanne said, 'you must include myself among your list of possible killers. I did have a confrontation with him over sending out the man the Doctor rescued, along with his counterpart. Girard was not pleased at that.'

At least she's honest about it, Benny thought. Still, she had to ask. 'All right, where were you when we all heard the scream?'

'We might ask you the same,' Giselle said. 'You left here but a few moments beforehand.'

'I was with Guy – '

'It does not matter, Giselle,' Jeanne chided gently. 'I was in the library tower, examining some texts on the healing arts by some of the leading Mohammedan physicians.'

'Did anybody see you?' What good were these ques-

202

tions anyway? With a lie detector they'd be fine, but without . . .

'The Castellan will have seen me enter. When I left, I had to push my way through everyone.' Benny noted that Jeanne didn't avert her eyes, or hide her mouth, or do any of the other things that might be associated with lying. Giselle looked nervous throughout, but Benny wasn't interested in asking her any questions, as she had been with the Doctor at the time, which was about as good an alibi as one could get.

'The Castellan, right.' Benny sighed. With a skeleton dead for centuries she was a wonderful detective, but talking to suspects was another matter altogether. What would Holmes have done at this point? Probably shot some more morphine, she shouldn't wonder.

'The Castellan was also unhappy with Girard,' Giselle said, interrupting her train of thought. 'He did not like being replaced by de Carnac. I overheard he and a knight both being very unkind towards Girard.' Jeanne looked at the red-headed Parfait quizzically.

'Then I know who to chat to next, don't I?'

'No one,' the Doctor said breezily, proving that he wasn't as affected by the long climb as Benny, 'knows a citadel better than its Castellan – or so the theory goes.'

'Even if he knows where the skull is, he still won't tell us.'

'Oh, I'm certain he doesn't know where it's kept any more than we do. However, he does seem intimately familiar with the passageways that positively riddle these walls.'

'So?'

'So, Professor Summerfield, he should be able to supply us with a map of them which will help in our search.'

'If he tells us.' Even if he's not the killer, she thought, he certainly doesn't much like being upstaged.

'If he doesn't, I'll just have to charm him with my good nature.'

'If it wasn't contrary to the terms of the Armageddon

Convention, I'd suggest you'll probably get luckier playing the spoons at him until he can't take any more.'

'Very witty. If I do, you can sing him that song about the goblin.'

'That's a very traditional folk song, at least among tramp-freighter captains.'

'Anyway, I'm fairly sure he's neither the murderer, nor Louis de Citeaux's agent here.'

'You talk as if they're not one and the same person.' It wasn't as if Benny could think of any better reason for the killing than that Girard had caught a spy red-handed, and it was pleasing to think that the situation could be so simple here. It would be a nice change, at any rate. 'Or as if you know who they are . . .?' she continued.

'Very astute of you, at least about them not being one and the same. A spy would hardly have killed Girard just *after* agreeing to surrender to the Church.'

Benny threw him a curious look. She couldn't swear to it, but it seemed as if there was a trace of worry in his voice. What has he been getting up to while out of my sight? she wondered. She had no chance to ask him yet, however, because he stopped at a landing, into the walls of which were set four doors. 'Eeny meeny?'

'Nothing so mundane. According to Hugues' directions, it's this one.' The Doctor rapped sharply on the door in question with the handle of his umbrella. There was no answer. After a few moments, he knocked again, still without response.

'Perhaps he's out.'

'Hmm.' The Doctor tried the sliding bolt that served for a handle, and it moved back easily. 'Well, while the cat's away . . .' He pushed into the room, the door swinging wide open as Benny followed him in. The room was small and bare, with only a bed and desk, an unlit candle atop the latter; while descending from the ceiling was –

'Not again!' Benny tried not to hear the faint but insistent creak of the wooden beam straining under the weight of the Castellan's gently swinging body. He was certainly dead: no one ever lived with a tongue quite so swollen and blackened. The Doctor checked the pulse at his wrist anyway. 'I don't know about mice, but some rat has definitely played in here.' She thought for a moment. 'Unless, of course, a fit of remorse . . .'

'Another suicide? I don't doubt that that's what we're supposed to think. Our killer's imagination is somewhat limited, it would appear.' The Doctor looked around, taking in every detail of the room before moving in. Benny suddenly realized what Guy had meant about the Doctor's owlish look being predatory, and she wondered with a faint chill why she'd never noticed it before. It must be a cultural thing, she decided. 'If he hanged himself, then what did he stand on? That rope is tied on to the beam, so he couldn't use a counterweight to lynch himself, in which case he must have got up on a stool or suchlike to secure the rope before jumping off.'

'If it was a suicide, you're trying to say.'

'Yes . . .' The Doctor sat on the foot of the bed, resting his chin on his umbrella handle again as he scrutinized the hanging corpse. 'Why? What was the point of this?' He jumped to his feet and paced round the body like a caged tiger. 'Were you just the second name on a list, or had you found out something? Humans!' he grumbled finally. He stopped dead in his tracks, peering under the bed. Dropping to his knees suddenly, he stretched out an arm underneath it, and pulled something out.

It was some sort of small leather-bound book. The Doctor opened a page at random, and frowned. 'Most peculiar . . . Benny, go and find Hugues. When you've sent him here, find Guy. He seems to have been working closely with the Castellan on the defences, so he should know what he'd been up to lately.'

'Right.' She turned and exited the room, leaving the Doctor glaring irritably at the body while her comment of 'I should have joined the the Samaritans' hung in the air.

Philippe de Montfort was sparring with a sergeant-at-arms, both wielding wooden swords, when Joseph returned to the Hôtel de Ville. Antoine, of course, was cloistered in the village with the other knights, but being the second in command of Louis de Citeaux's private bodyguard did have certain privileges.

Philippe spared him a quick grin, before renewing his attack. Joseph would enjoy the show, since none of the troop had much respect for the standing army to which the sergeant belonged, and it might also discourage him from conceiving any plans to usurp Philippe. The sergeant was already weakening, relying more and more on the protection offered by his shield, so Philippe pounded at it mercilessly, before finally smashing it aside and laying out his opponent with a crack that probably broke his jaw.

It amused Philippe, if nothing else. He tossed the wooden weapon away as the sergeant rose and staggered off. 'You look like a man in need of ale, Joseph, and I know I do, too.' He beckoned to Joseph to fall into step with him. 'What news? Have you found anything?'

'No, Captain. I wished to speak with you about something that happened by the river.'

'Go on.' This had better be a good explanation, he thought. Surely Joseph wasn't going to become fallible when he needed him most.

'When we were halfway to the Roc, we were stopped by a group of de Citeaux knights. They claimed they were searching the river-bank from the other end, but they refused to let us continue, though I cannot see what harm that it could do.'

'Ah, do not worry. Louis has taken a fit, almost. The heretics have abducted the Doctor from the Hôtel de Ville itself.' Joseph blanched visibly as Philippe told of this audacity. 'Louis has ordered his men to take the Roc apart "stone by stone" to find the tunnel.'

'Then that explains why the knights were there, but why stop us searching again?'

'They enjoy bullying those of us who fight for money instead of God. However, if it pleases you, go back tonight, and search the bank in the direction from which those knights came.'

'Yes, Captain.'

The Castellan's body had been moved to the hospital's mortuary section by the time Benny had found Guy. Entering at a brisk pace, they both moved straight towards the Doctor. 'Lady Bernice tells me you wish to know of the Castellan's recent movements,' Guy began.

'If you know anything about them, yes.'

'He had spent some time drinking with a knight whom I relieved of command. But mostly he has been surveying the walls at my suggestion, to find the strongest and weakest areas.'

'A purely academic pursuit,' Hugues commented. 'The truce expires in a very few days; I would be more concerned about how we can arrange for the non-Parfaits here to escape before we surrender on the fourteenth.' Guy gave him a pitying look at this remark.

'Never mind all that. How far had he got in his survey?'

'I believe he had just finished examining the wall by the small herb garden.'

'That is a part of the apothecary's enclosure,' Hugues added helpfully.

'Interesting,' the Doctor commented. 'In fact, more than interesting . . .' He drew out the small leather-bound book he'd found in the Castellan's room, and flicked through it with a look of fascination. 'I believe I might just have a cosy little chat with that apothecary.'

'Then I will come with you,' Guy put in. 'He seems pleasant enough, but if – '

'I said chat, not accusation.' Before he could say anything else, Jeanne came in with a happy expression. It froze slightly when she saw the body lying on one of the trestles. 'Yes, Parfait Jeanne?' The Doctor gave her a disarming smile.

'Another . . .?'

'Another. Hit on the head then hanged.'

'This would not have happened if you had not bargained

away our lives,' she told Hugues. 'None of the population will feel they have anything to lose by settling old debts.'

'Is that a personal feeling?' Hugues asked mildly.

'It is a suspicion.'

Hugues fixed her with a cold look. 'Is that why you burst in here?'

'No.' At least, Benny thought, she had the good grace to look apologetic after her outburst, even if she didn't sound it. Obviously not all the different Cathare branches and sects had identical views. 'It is the supply situation. There is perhaps one small meal left for everyone. After that ... I do not suppose it makes any difference to us – it will not be the hunger that kills us when we open the gates to the Church – but we owe the other refugees here some provisions, especially if they are to escape across country once more.'

'You have something in mind?'

'Yes.' Her smile returned. 'It was Hubert here,' she indicated a figure standing in the doorway, 'who told me of an aubaine storehouse near here.' Benny recognized the man at the door as the former gamekeeper who had accompanied her and Guy to rescue the Doctor.

'Where exactly is this storehouse?' Hugues asked.

'Perhaps nine leagues upriver,' Hubert replied. 'The reeve there has always extracted the normal rate of aubaine from those of us who live off the land as well as from the travelling merchants.'

'Aubaine?' Benny asked.

'A tribute, demanded for trading on a noble's land,' the Doctor told her. 'Ten per cent of whatever goods he is carrying on the trip. Assuming that merchants still travel the river in winter, there could be a considerable stock lying there.'

'They do,' Hubert confirmed. 'Fruits and grain grown from Alexandria to Constantinople are all traded here in the Langue d'Oc. With a suitable wagon, we could go and collect some of this aubaine as supplies for the Roc.'

'As you say, we will require little more,' Hugues said

slowly, 'but I suppose I cannot allow the people here to die on empty stomachs. And those who are not of the true faith will require sustenance to flee once more . . . Do you have such a wagon?'

'Edouard does.'

'And will the reeve allow you to take any of these supplies?'

'I believe I can persuade him.' Bernice could guess what that meant.

'Very well,' Hugues announced. 'You know the countryside here, so you must go. Guy will drive the wagon, as he is the best able to protect it if need be. You may leave whenever you are ready. I will ensure that the soldiers are otherwise occupied while you leave.' The grey-bearded Parfait turned to leave.

'Now, wait a minute,' Benny protested. 'I'm going, too.' She chose to ignore the surprised look that the Doctor gave her. 'I'm not letting Conan here out of my sight for minute – gods know what he might get up to without me.' The others smiled knowingly as they left.

'I'm relieved that you're retaining your sense of objectivity,' the Doctor muttered drily.

'I'm just returning a favour. On the way here he came along as protection, so I'm just evening the score for womanhood.'

'And I'm Davros' beautician. Still, it's probably not that bad an idea. At least out there you can see your enemy coming, and with this truce in effect you'd probably be at more risk in here.'

'So you do want me to go?'

'You are old enough to make your own choices, Professor: but, whatever you do, I'm still going to have that little chat with the apothecary.'

'I'll go and get ready then.'

'Bernice.' She looked back at him, frozen in mid-step. 'Visiting the past is the trickiest thing anyone can do – it's like being a slug trying to balance on the edge of a straight razor.' His gaze flicked briefly down to the Aztec brooch on his lapel, the eagle and serpent carved into it mirroring the conflicting opinions that she fancied she could discern in his eyes. 'I should know.'

Benny nodded, and continued out of the mortuary.

Chapter 16

Hubert and Ibrahim were waiting on the part of the trail that dipped down towards the small landing, while a thin trail of hazy blue smoke drifted up from the chimney of the aubaine collector's cottage. It had been a surprisingly uneventful journey, and for once Benny thought that the Doctor might have been right. The Church army seemed content to stay in camp for the moment, and they had seen no sign of anyone on their outward trip. Guy gently guided Edouard's wagon to a halt just outside the stout door to the building, while Benny jumped to the ground for a quick look around.

'Isn't that smoke a bit of a giveaway?' she asked the two scouts. 'I mean, even a child would know not to light a fire in enemy territory.'

'The reeve always keeps a fire in the hearth, my Lady,' Hubert explained with a smile. 'It would be unusual, and so more suspicious, if it were put out.'

'Isn't he going to have something to say about us removing stuff from here? Where I come from, that sort of thing can land you in a rehab colony pretty quickly.'

'Not really,' Ibrahim answered with a sad shake of the head. 'We found him inside – he was very old, and this accursed cold must have finally finished him. We buried him a few yards into the woods.'

Benny looked hard at him, wondering if they were covering up for having murdered him. She dismissed the idea quickly, however. Life here seemed to be so cheap that if they had killed him they wouldn't find it worth the bother to try and hide the fact. 'Has there been any sign

211

of Church soldiers? I mean, if he's been dead for more than a few hours, that fire must have been out . . .'

'The most recent tracks are three days old, but they just go straight past.'

Guy returned from leading the horses and the wagon round to the small stables. 'The Church will have little interest in this wide point of the river. They will prefer to concentrate their forces on the narrower points, where crossings may be more easily made.'

'A simple "no" would have sufficed,' Benny muttered, shoving her hands deeper into her jacket pockets as she walked towards the door. Guy got there first, looking around suspiciously as he went in, although he made no move towards his sword.

The interior of the building was split into two sections. The largest part was the one they were entering: a relatively large room filled with dusty sacks of grain and vegetables, casks of ale, and barrels of salted meat. A scruffy ginger cat sleeping atop a comfortable-looking sack opened one eye to see what the commotion was, and then went back to sleep. Guy moved straight over to the nearest sack, and loosened the drawstring around it. 'These fruits must have come upriver very recently; they are not rotted.'

'The cold will have helped preserve them,' Benny pointed out.

'True. We will take as many of these sacks as possible.'

'What about the salt meat?'

'The Cathares believe they can be reincarnated as lower creatures, and may be eating their forebears if they take meat, so two or three barrels should suffice for the others in the Roc. We can leave the ale, if your drink is to be ready by the time we return.'

'It will be. Gods, you worry like a Centauran.'

'I am not worried,' he replied firmly. 'And it is pronounced Centurion, if the Order's teachings were correct. Naturally I wish the best for those under my command.'

Benny sighed, deciding that it wasn't worth correcting him. She pushed though a flimsy inner door into the other part of the building. Here, a low but broad fireplace was set into the outer wall, with a cooking pot and tripod lying beside it. Chinks of light crept in through gaps in the warped shutters, but only at the top. When Benny opened the shutters to find out why, she discovered that chopped logs had been stacked up against the outside of the wall, providing extra insulation as well as removing the need for winter effort which could lead to frostbite. The straw on the floor seemed much fresher than that in the Roc, and a small pallet bed was tucked along one wall, but the rest of the room was completely bare.

She wondered how the reeve had managed to live in a place like this – the lack of mental stimulation would drive her out of her mind a couple of days, she thought. Perhaps he was an outdoor man who hunted or fished a lot. . . She suspected that, overall, the local fish and fauna probably couldn't wait for the invention of home entertainments.

'It is growing too dark to return to the Roc tonight,' Guy said, startling Benny; she hadn't heard him come through from the storeroom. 'We will all stay here. I presume that you personally would not be flattered if I only set three watches?'

'You must be a mind-reader. How long from full dark until dawn?'

'At this time of year, about fourteen and a half hours, but we will have to load the wagon just before leaving. . . Let us say, fourteen hours.'

'Then that's four watches of three and a half hours each. I'll take the first watch, just to make sure you don't – chivalrously or whatever – forget to wake me.'

'Then I will take the next watch. Hubert and Ibrahim will be the most tired of us, so they will need to rest sooner than either of us.'

'Go on and tell them, then. I'll go and find a suitable spot to watch from.'

'When I was stabling the horses, I noticed that there is a parapet on the rear side of this building. The steps go up the outside.'

'You really do know just what a girl wants from her

man, don't you? Don't answer that,' she added hurriedly. 'I'm going to have to stop doing this sort of thing when I'm in primitive cultures.'

Stopping only to stroke the cat, Benny went back out into the cold darkness.

A staccato tapping echoed through the gap between the library and the feed-store, growing faster or slower as the Doctor concentrated the attentions of his umbrella tip on more promising sections of the rugged wall. Occasional loopholes were approached by low stone stiles, and the Doctor tapped especially interestedly at these sections.

The stone was so thick, however, that even if there had been hidden chambers they would be too deeply embedded to sound hollow from a mere tap. Stepping back for a moment, a flicker of motion caught the Doctor's eye, and he turned to see Robert leaving his little room and scurrying off into the gathering darkness. The Doctor smiled a little wistfully at his blatant eagerness to please, then frowned thoughtfully.

Pausing a moment until the young apothecary was out of sight, the Doctor flitted across the intervening space, and slipped into the room. Unlike the other individual cells in the Roc, this room was exceptionally cluttered, with two desks pressed together, and a variety of bowls and mortars and pestles, all streaked and stained with drab colours. The air was scented with herbs, while small bags and pouches hung from every available space. 'It must have been a very good summer last year,' the Doctor murmured to himself.

He picked up the nearest bowl and sniffed it carefully, immediately having to clap a hand over his mouth to muffle the resultant sneeze. 'This is more like a selection of food seasonings than a pharmacy. Aesclepius would laugh his head off.' The Doctor examined several of the little pouches in turn, then hunted around in his pockets, eventually drawing out the small book from the Castellan's cell. Flipping it open, he compared the pouches to some tiny scribblings in the ledger. ' " . . . Never seen any such plant while gardening the vineyards?" Well, that's quite a distance away...' Slamming the book shut, the Doctor dropped both it and the pouch into his pocket, then slipped back out into the bailey.

Hurrying straight to the main door of the library tower, he went in without further ado.

The parapet proved to be a narrow wooden-railed balcony running along the river side of the building. This offered an excellent view both across to the far side, and up- and down-river. To keep an eye on the woods through which they had travelled, however, it was necessary to go back down and walk around the building. For once, this prospect didn't bother Benny; it was probably the only way she'd be able to keep warm.

The river was a dark, iron colour amidst the grey and white of the countryside, and Benny wasn't slow to wonder if she'd been so sensible in coming out here – Vandor Prime, where she'd spent the early years of her life, had had two G-class suns, and no snow. In fact there was no spot on that planet's surface which was as crukking cold as a mountain winter on Earth. She glanced at the LCD sewn into the sleeve of her jacket; she'd only been out ten minutes, and already thought she'd never be warm again.

She clapped her arms around herself, wishing she could have at least brought up a torch from the storehouse. True, it would be a beacon for any patrols wandering past, but right now being burnt at the stake didn't seem such an unattractive proposition. Another thought struck her, however, and she looked around to make sure no one was watching. Satisfied, she unzipped her jacket just enough to get a grip on the hip-flask in its inside pocket. There wasn't much of the brandy left in it, going by the way it swished around inside, but she guessed that it should be enough to warm her just a little.

She only took one sip, not wanting to finish it yet, but it did afford her a brief flush of warmth. Slipping it back into the pocket, she resealed the jacket, tugging its collar up around her ears – better to look stupid for a short time than permanently with no ears, she reminded herself.

She had half-expected Guy to join her out here anyway, but he hadn't. He probably thought he'd get a dressing-down if he tried to come out before his watch, she reflected, and she couldn't really blame him. For once, though, she'd have been glad of the company; at least he cared about some things, even if his knowledge of astrography was – well – non-existent. Was Gamma Delphinus IV near Rhodes, indeed! She smiled at the thought, and looked westwards, upriver.

Delphinus should be above the horizon by now, she thought, though probably not past the treetops, but it didn't really matter tonight, since the clouds hid the stars completely. It was probably just as well as she wouldn't like to think of herself as being so clichéd as to point it out to Guy. And he'd probably just think her crazy – or demonic, of course – anyway.

It was strange how her thoughts of home returned to include Guy. He was certainly attractive enough, but she hadn't let anyone else get so close since she had hypered out to the Rim on that first Corporation-sponsored dig. Then, she'd still been fleeing the sting of betrayal when she'd found out the truth about Kyle, and it seemed she still shielded herself from any feelings that could weaken her resistance to such pain again. The Doctor, of course, didn't count . . .

She briefly felt an icy chill that the last drops of brandy could never ease, though she was tempted all the same, and felt she'd spent enough time standing in the one place. Perhaps walking round to check on the forest side of the storehouse would help keep her warm for the next three and a quarter hours.

Dust hung in the air like a mist, not so much falling back to earth as leaching into surfaces all around, as dampness did from a true mist. There was no sound but for the chirruping of small insects scattered through the orange grove. Even the hoofbeats of Guy's horse were silent, only the gently rocking motion of his vision providing a reminder of his mode of transport.

Although the air was tinted with floating dust kicked up by some great disturbance in the grove, Guy had no difficulty in breathing. Not this time.

Thanks to the information he had brought from Philippe de Montfort, an eminently corruptible Watch captain at Hebron, he had found Godfroi's camp just beyond the bank of the Jordan with little difficulty, the ashes of their fires still warm to the touch. Following their tracks in the sandy earth was child's play for him, and he knew he was now finally catching up with them – they were headed for Es Sair, by the look of things. Something was very wrong, however, and not just the strange silence of his own horse or the faintly dizzying way in which the tiniest movement of his head or even his eye seemed to be exaggerated by his mind.

He should be able to hear speech ahead, and the stamping of hooves. Instead there was only the silence of the orange trees – which surrounded him in seemingly endless lanes in every direction – and the distant hum of buzzing flies.

He drew his sword, the slithering sound of it echoing surreally from somewhere in the diffuse sunlight of the surrounding dust, and dismounted. His horse faded into the dust cloud as soon as his boots crunched into the gritty earth, but he ignored it. If this was some trick by Godfroi to escape him, it was not going to work. Footsteps whispering silkily, Guy moved forward between the slim trees, and glanced upwards to see how much time he had gained upon Godfroi.

The sky was simply a slightly brighter patch of the same yellow colour as the dust. Even if there was a sun up there, it was invisible behind the pearlescent veil. Guy shivered involuntarily – none of this was natural. Perhaps Godfroi had enlisted the aid some Eastern sorcerer . . . He wondered why that thought sparked the image of a man in pale clothes. Steeling himself, as some things could

217

not be left undone, no matter what, Guy took another step. His foot hit something, and he jumped back, startled.

As if it had been waiting for a signal, the dust receded, pulling back from the body at Guy's feet. It was one of Godfroi's troop, half a dozen arrows piercing his flesh and mostly broken when he fell. Looking around this patch in which the dust was thinner, he could make out the dim forms of broken and twisted bodies left behind as the dust rolled back, leaving the flies as the only clouds to surround them.

There was a mixture of Christians and Mohammedans, Guy saw, in fairly equal quantities. Many were sprawled on the ground, the slim shafts of arrows casting long shadows across their blood-stained clothing and armour. A few were propped at bizarre angles, held in position by the spears and polearms which impaled them. Some simply lay like islands amidst a sea of their own spilled blood. The dark mound-like forms of several horses lay among the men, and Guy recognized one dappled grey animal as the favourite of Godfroi. The discovery set Guy searching vigorously, a gnawing worry setting in.

He had come so far that he couldn't allow himself to be cheated. Not when he had paid such a heavy price already – his rank and position in the order. The sight of a plumed helm made his heart plummet. Only Godfroi would have worn such a ridiculous thing in this troop.

The tip of his sword trailing in the dust, Guy forced himself to walk towards the helmet which lay on its side a few yards away, deathly afraid that he already knew what he was about to find there.

The nearest body to the helmet was that of a fairly handsome Templar, shorter than Guy but just as broad, with a neatly trimmed golden beard. At least, Guy recalled, Godfroi had been handsome before. Now that his eye was gone, along with the skullbone from his temple – leaving a few scattered spots of brain tissue between his head and the helmet – the left side of his face was but a black and red banquet of flies. Not handsome at all.

To Guy, it was as if the one-sided grin where his teeth

218

were exposed by his missing cheek was deliberately mocking him. No doubt he had preferred this warrior's death in God's service to that which Guy would offer. He wished it had been himself lying there; at least then he would have had a reason for failing to avenge Iolande.

Guy had seen several knights weep over a fellow knight on the battlefield – with grief, or with righteous anger at the enemy – but he had never seen one weep because he had not been the one who'd killed the fallen man. He knew that if anyone was watching him now, they would be seeing just such an occurrence, and that they would never realize it.

Rage and burning shame stung him, while he could practically hear Iolande's soul scream in torment. Yes, he would rather have died than failed. Through the anger and the wail of shame that he barely recognized as emanating from himself, Guy suddenly realized that he could hear laughter, strident and mocking.

The remaining corner of Godfroi's mouth creased upwards sneeringly, his eye opening and gazing unblinkingly upwards. 'I like this justice,' Godfroi's voice hissed without the benefit of breath. 'I died with honour, while you will be disgraced as a cowardly deserter.'

One of the corpse's clawlike hands grabbed the blade of Guy's sword, no blood issuing from the parted flesh. Slowly, while Guy stood paralysed with horror, it pulled the blade down into its chest. 'Now, do you see how it would have felt? Good, no?' The dead hand released the blade. 'Perhaps it was all God's will,' the corpse suggested. 'It may be that Iolande was meant for him . . . and for me!'

'NO!' Guy screamed, tugging his sword free. He rammed it down again, repeating the actions over and over as if he were trying to dig a well with his sword, punctuating each downward stab with a scream of denial of his failure and Godfroi's escape.

In spite of his own yells, he could still only hear Godfroi's mocking laughter as his arms flailed down furiously.

'It's all right,' someone's voice said tightly, echoing

through the reddening haze. 'It's all right, godsdammit, Guy!'

He found that he couldn't move his arms any longer, and suddenly realized that someone had a grip on his wrists. For a terrified instant, he thought it was the reanimated corpse of Godfroi, but he suddenly saw a woman's pale face before him, and realized that it was she who had spoken. 'What?' He froze, drinking in the woodsmoke-scented air of the dimly lit room. His heart stopped pounding, and he felt his fists unclench themselves as he took a deep shuddery breath. 'Benny, it is you . . . Is it my watch already? I had not intended to fall aslee–' He started to get up, reaching for his sword-belt, but Bernice shoved him back down again.

'It's Hubert's watch – I didn't have the heart to wake you, so I stayed out for your watch as well.' He felt vaguely embarrassed at the way she was worrying over him, but was glad of the surety of her concern all the same. He propped himself up in a sitting position against the wall, wrapping his arms around himself to ward against the chill. He wasn't really sure whether the cold was due to the weather outside – the fire could did seem a little low – or something in himself left over from the dream. 'Whatever it was, it's over now.'

'It is but my . . .' What was that phrase she had used before? 'Bad memories. It was my bad memories.' He looked back at her, flattered by the worry he saw in her eyes, but just as determined to ease it lest it trouble her too much. 'I am all right now, Bernice. It only happens sometimes. It is not seemly that my weakness should be witnessed by anyone . . .' He smiled faintly, knowing what she would say to this latest example of his attempts to appear strong before her. No doubt she would see it as a foolish notion, unworthy of a man of her own people. She was probably right: what can be stronger than facing weakness on even terms? It was a strange concept, and he envied her and her people their simple acceptance of it.

'It's not unseemly where I come from,' was all Bernice

220

said, however. 'I assume it has something to do with this indiscreet answer of yours?'

Guy rocked back on his heels slightly, watching the fire as if its flame was a light behind some shadowplay from his memory. 'I set out to kill someone who deserved it, but without appeals and petitions.'

'I didn't think bureaucracy had been invented yet. Don't you just go around chopping up whoever you like?'

'Not when you have been ordered by your Preceptor to command the Palace Watch.'

'What did he do to you?'

'It was not a question of what he had done to me, but of what he had done to Iolande.'

'Who is this Iolande?'

'She was my sister.' He fell silent for a moment, and Bernice nodded slowly with a calculating expression. 'Another knight, named Godfroi, had raped her, but she hid the fact from the family, until she discovered she was with child.'

'His?'

'Yes. Once she realized this, she told all, and then . . .' He closed his eyes, hoping that no tears could escape the lids that way. 'She drowned herself in the river that ran through our farm. I had crossed the Mediterranean in pursuit of this piece of filth, so I could not stand idly by in the palace while he ran and found new places upon which to inflict his brand of dishonour.'

'You deserted?' Benny asked incredulously.

Guy nodded with a downcast look, not proud of either his actions back then or their results. 'I left Jaffa in the middle of the night. I had heard he was with a troop somewhere in the Hebron hills. I found out that my information was correct, so I pursued him and his troop across half the Holy Land, and yes, I would have fought my way through all of them to reach him, had it proved necessary.' He shook his head, wondering how he could have allowed himself to get into such a situation, when he could simply have denounced the man and challenged him to a fair trial by combat which could not be refused. 'I was more

221

foolhardy in those days,' he admitted with a trace of humour. 'I narrowly missed them in Hebron itself, but I followed them back north. Three days later, I caught up with them just outside Es Sair, on the eastern bank of the Jordan. . .'

'And killed him in revenge?'

Guy looked up from the fire, and shook his head again. 'They had attacked a Mohammedan force three times as great as themselves, and were cut to pieces. All I could do to my enemy was bury him. When I returned to Jaffa, I was stripped of my rank, accused of the cowardly act of deserting my post – and, of course, Iolande was never avenged. Now, when I dream, Godfroi mocks me by making me live though that discovery over and over.' He clenched his fists, angry at the urge to shudder which swept over him. 'All I can do now is search for some other way to fulfil her faith in me, without killing anyone. Or, at least, hope to die well and not as a cowardly deserter.'

'Well, I hope you get them in the right order.' Guy smiled at this; how typical of Bernice to make light of it! 'In fact, I definitely think you should concentrate on the first one – there's no such thing as a good way to die. Those people at the Roc. . . What you're doing there seems as good a way to honour Iolande as any. It's human nature overall that leads to tragedies like that, and though the soldiers around here haven't had anything to do with your story, they're still shattering lives.'

It was true enough, Guy knew. 'One man cannot fight an army, and I would not expect you to advocate such a course.'

'I'm not, Conan. I'm just saying I wouldn't like you to go and get yourself killed when you should just be making a stand for what you believe in. Or do you still say that a man who believes in anything is a fool?'

'No.' He fell silent, unsure how to compliment her as she deserved. She was, after all, no tavern wench to be taken for granted, or courtesan bound by protocol and formality to respond to the prescribed forms of courtship. She was a free spirit like himself, who clearly depended

222

on no one, and whose wit, wisdom and compassion –
though sometimes distant and sharp, but at least always
refreshingly honest – seemed as beautiful as her features.
It was simply a case of either she felt the same way about
him, or else she didn't. 'I believe in you.'

The interior of the library was as thick with the rich scent
of leather and old wood as with that of vellum or paper.
The Doctor looked up into the darkness of the central
space, and turned on his heels. Books, scrolls and parchments lined the walls in an almost solid layer, broken
only by the cobwebbed undersides of the balconies which
encircled the walls at regular intervals. Torches fastened
to a central pillar, a safe distance from the texts, provided
the earthy illumination by which scribes would have
copied out the texts at the numerous desks scattered
around, had these been better times.

Instead, the main chamber was empty, with only the
faint breath of flame from the torches audible. The Doctor
hadn't been in such a place for a long time, and took a
moment to admire its simple power before moving
around. There were smaller chambers adjoining the hall,
serried desks empty and lifeless without the scratch of
quill upon paper. Each room opened on to the next via a
doorless archway, and the whole thing was only one level
of the tower.

Girard had been an old man, though, so it was most
likely that the skull would be on the ground level. A large
reliquary cabinet faced the door from the base of the
central pillar. 'A little obvious,' the Doctor said to himself.
He looked anyway, picking the crude lock with ease. There
were several pieces of cloth and bone inside, but no skull.
The Doctor sealed it up again. 'Thought not. . . There
should be secret passages in a place like this though.' He
looked around, as if suddenly self-conscious about talking
to himself. An old statue returned his gaze unblinkingly.
'You can't have a castle without secret passages,' he told
the statue.

Lifting his umbrella with a purposeful flourish, the

223

Doctor strolled over to the nearest wall, and started tapping again.

No lights marked the position of the landing and storehouse, but Joseph could smell the woodsmoke as it drifted up from the shore of the river below.

The faintly sweet and earthy scent of it seemed appropriate to him. Philippe would be most pleased with this discovery.

Chapter 17

The Doctor had just become complacently accustomed to hearing sharp raps, when a sudden dull thud made him jump. He hit the same section of wall, directly under the first stage of the wooden stairs, again. It still sounded hollow. Hooking the umbrella back on to his breast pocket, the Doctor ran his fingers over a wide area of the wall. Though built of stone, shelves driven into it at some point after its construction had concealed any lines that might give away the presence of an opening.

Tugging on the various books and texts had no effect, but it took the Doctor only moments to discover a trigger on the underside of one waist-height shelf. Silent despite its bulk and crudity, a section of the wall swung outward, leaving an uninviting blackness behind. He tutted softly, shook his head and turned to fetch a torch. As soon as his hand left the trigger lever, the door began to slide shut once more, and he had to leap back to the wall, shoving one foot in the gap to keep it open. The stone door thudded into his foot, provoking a sharp yell, but he held his ground long enough to grab a couple of leather-bound handwritten tomes and to shove them into the gap. With the door safely propped open, he was free to hop theatrically across to the central pillar, but soon gave it up, since there was no one to witness the performance anyway.

He lifted a torch down from the pillar, and returned to the door. Holding it open with one hand, he stepped over the books and waved the torch around. The tunnel was terribly ordinary – by the standards of some he had explored – with wooden beams slashing across the ceiling

here and there and cobwebs festooning the corners. Something squeaked in alarm and scrabbled off away from the
torchlight as he stepped in.

'I wonder if there are any lost works by Aristotle at the
end of this tunnel?'

Thibaud awoke with as much of a start as his beaten
muscles could manage. Even after several days, his jaw
was still swollen and his body ached everywhere from the
beating that harridan had given him. He was sure he
hadn't awoken in the cold and dark just to remember
that, however, and looked around himself cautiously.

Everyone was still asleep in the abandoned church,
which came as something of a relief to him. His first
natural thought had been that someone was about to try
to kill him for his share of the booty they had found in
this village. All was silent and unmoving, however, in the
fitful green – green moonlight? His blood draining from
his face and, by the feel of it, rushing straight to his
bowels, Thibaud rolled to his feet and stumbled over to
the nearest window.

Throwing open the shutters, he saw a distinct greenish
aura being cast against the ridge above the village, and
then fading. The glow resumed soon, then faded again.
Thibaud watched and listened anxiously, but the pattern
kept repeating itself, and only the wind made any sound.
He told himself to hide by the altar and wait till dawn,
then get off this hill as quickly as he could. He didn't
listen.

That light was magic, obviously, and therefore dangerous. He had heard tales, however, of fortune and glory
accrued by those who faced and tamed such sorcery. No
one ever gained anything by hiding from it. Greed over-
coming his fear, he slipped stealthily towards the door,
and crept out of the church.

The flames from the torch suddenly flicked back towards
the Doctor's face for an instant before being drawn back
again, causing him to drop it with a yell. Something small

226

but unseen skittered away from the burning wood and pitch with a frantic scraping of tiny claws. 'I know how you feel,' the Doctor muttered. Bending to retrieve the torch, he felt a faint breath of air on his face, and noticed that a thin line of amber light showed up a few feet away, betraying the location of a door.

The Doctor grinned in the darkness, and picked up the torch, then felt around one cobwebbed surface of the stone for some sort of catch or handle. After a few moments' diligent searching, he found an iron pin that slid to the side, freeing the door from its closed position. Keeping a careful hold on the door, ready to stop its movement if it started to squeak, the Doctor swung it gently open and stepped through.

Before him, tiers of shelves and supports bordered the high walls of the long and narrow gallery. 'Incredible,' he murmured happily, picking up a delicate scroll and glancing at it. 'The *Odyssey*, and in her own handwriting, too.' He set it back down. Though narrow, the gallery was so high that as the Doctor advanced into it, the roof hardly changed position. Narrow vent-holes far above allowed the greasy smoke from the carefully placed candles and torches to escape rather than settle on the things stored here, though it would obviously require regular and careful maintenance as well. He shook his head as if to clear his mind of the stunning nature of the statues, books, scrolls and relics that were crammed into every available square inch of space.

Hugues paused in his stitching at a leather binding, certain he had heard a noise. In the stillness, he could make out a faint voice, talking to itself. Only one person in the Roc had a voice with such an accent, though . . .

'Everyone feels the same way when they first see this collection,' Hugues said amicably, stepping round a large wooden rack crammed with scrolls. He held a needle and thread in his hands, and some primitive bookbinder's tools lay on a bench beyond him, next to a large tome bound in leather. 'Of course, they are all formed of matter, but all these things are the products of humanity's true nature.' He tapped his chest. 'The inner spirit. Pure and unfettered intellect, fit to form its own designs on all this – ' he gestured in a world-encompassing manner ' – residue of sullied evil.'

The Doctor lifted a small porcelain fragment from the bench, and held it near the torch, causing the crystalline structure of the potsherd to glow gold with reflected light. 'Sometimes even the forms of darkness can be turned to light, if you're willing to expend a little effort.'

Hugues nodded graciously with a warm smile. 'Some say it is so, others not. Who am I to tell?'

'This is really a most impressive collection,' the Doctor commended enthusiastically. 'It's a pity you have them locked away.'

'Not all the refugees from the villages nearby are as studious as are we, Doctor. Of course, possession of any of these things would be considered heresy, but under the circumstances . . .'

'You'd be as well to be hanged for a sheep as for a lamb.' The Doctor leaned over to examine a small bronze Buddha. 'Though these works of art – '

'Are considered threats by Guzman and his cronies. Mostly they are artworks and relics produced by philosophies other than Christianity. That is their only . . . taint.' He laid down the bookbinding tools, and grabbed the Doctor's arm, ushering him between items of stock. It was so rare that he met another who would – or, indeed, could – appreciate the beauty and value of the collection, in artistic, philosophical and historical terms. 'Look,' he urged. 'These scrolls you noticed: the only original written copy of the Greek *Odyssey*, proving that Homer was a woman!'

'If you're in the market for a correction,' the Doctor interrupted, 'Homer was a man, who composed the *Iliad*. The *Odyssey* was written as a sequel by a noblewoman who admired his earlier work.'

'Fascinating. I had always thought the styles to be dissimilar . . .' He broke off as a gold torc caught his eye,

228

and he lifted it from its hook and handed it to the Doctor. It was a torc of finely graven Celtic design. 'Arthur Pendragon's crown.'

'Leave it there, I'll see it later . . .' He wandered over to inspect a dusty collection of scrolls that lay silk-wrapped in one corner.

'There will be no later, we both know that. Not for me or the other Parfaits, at least.'

'No, that's true. It's a funny thing, human belief: one moment it produces some tremendous masterwork – the Pyramids, the Sistine Chapel, a million schools and hospitals throughout history – and the next it begets the wholesale genocide of South American culture, Auschwitz, Jonestown, the Roc . . .'

'You speak as if we were already dead.'

The Doctor gave him a haunted look that made Hugues wonder what horrors had driven him to seek sanctuary from the world and its sins here in the Roc. 'Yes, I do, don't I?' He paced for a moment. 'Imagine if someone you knew died suddenly, in some unpreventable way – a seizure, perhaps. Also imagine that you could travel backwards in time to a week before this happened, and went to see your friend then . . . He can't be saved, and to you he's already dead: would you try and warn him? Knowing that even if you could prove the truth of what you say, it would just make things worse, by worrying or depressing him . . .?'

'Such situations are the preserve of Greek fancies, Doctor, not scholars such as ourselves.' Hugues smiled hopefully. This conversation was taking a morbid turn that somehow unnerved him far more than such a ridiculous idea should. 'I would be heartened that he would soon be free of his pain, and would try to make his last few days cheering.'

'Some days can't be cheered, any more than time can be fought.'

'I don't understand.'

'Pray that you never do.'

* * *

Thibaud rounded the ridge just as a powerful green light faded. A small structure sat on the edge of a small plateau there. It was difficult to tell in the darkness, but he judged from its greyness that it was green and large enough for three or four men to enter.

Approaching cautiously, he saw that its roof had different stages, as if it were some Mongol shrine. More important, however, was the realization that the lined and cracked stone surface seemed to be pure jade, like that which the Templar ships sometimes brought into Narbonne. Even a handful-sized piece would make him fairly rich, he thought, at least to start with. Drawing a dagger from his belt, he found a piece on one edge which looked as if it was all but broken off already, and slid the blade into the gap, forcing down on it heavily.

The blade snapped, just as the green glow brightened angrily. Thibaud jumped back in terror, convinced that the light's brightness was in response to his action. The green glow was flaring out from some sort of lamp on the roof, however, which was relatively normal, and he relaxed slightly. Perhaps it was Greek Fire: was that not supposed to be green?

As he watched, the glow flared much more quickly this time, with a sound accompanying it. It was the sound of war elephants, he thought, horror-struck, trumpeting some demonic alarm. Worse yet, the light was turning from an eerie green to a blazing, fiery yellow which flickered and flashed hungrily.

By the light of this new yellow fire, Thibaud saw that his dagger's blade was no longer trapped in a crack of jade, but embedded in a cornerpost of old wood, which was painted in faded blue.

Thibaud didn't stop running until he crashed headlong into a tree at the foot of the hill, and knocked himself cold.

The clouds were lightening with a slight lucent glow when the Doctor emerged from the library. Glancing back towards Robert's enclosure, he noticed a flicker of candle-light within, and so passed by the door.

'The residential area should be emptying about now, I thi–' A muffled electronic chirping cut him off, and he pulled out the ubiquitous probe from his pocket. It tweeted brightly, until the Doctor switched it off. 'Free of the black star at last, old girl? Benny should be glad to hear that.'

Dropping the now-silent probe back into his pocket, he wandered off in search of the spot from which Guy and Benny, who had been first on the scene, had heard Girard's scream.

The winter landscape was turned to a vista of silver and gold by the ruddy tint of the rising sun. Bernice, however, didn't particularly feel the cold as she checked that none of the sacks they had loaded were likely to topple over the edge of the wagon's wooden sides.

Guy strapped on his sword as he exited the cottage, and squinted up at the slate sky. 'It will begin to snow again soon.'

'There's a cheering thought,' Benny answered brightly.

'Actually, it is. The fresh fall will cover our tracks.'

'Just so long as you can find the way back. Have Hubert and Ibrahim moved on already?'

'Yes. I pray that the truce has held, so that the Church men will still be surrounding the Roc to prevent escapees and not out looking for those trying to get in.' He bounded up on to the board seat, and reached down to grasp Benny's forearm and help her up beside him.

'That wasn't necessary.'

'No, but I did not see you refusing my aid.'

'Shades, don't tell me you're developing a sense of humour. I mean, yes, a lot of women like men to make them laugh, but ...'

'In that case I will stop. One look at this face should be enough to cause mirth.'

The Doctor leaned out of the open shutters, holding on

231

to his hat as he stared down at the dizzying drop below. He shook his head at the sight, and pulled himself back into Girard's cell. He closed the shutters with an irritable frown, then turned on his heel to survey the room.

The desk had been replaced in the corner, while the poker now hung by the fire, and a new locking bar had been dropped into the brackets that held the one Guy had broken. Dropped ... The Doctor leaped across the room, eyes widening, and lifted the bar out of the U-shaped brackets. There were four brackets altogether – two on the door and two on the wall – so that the bar could be held by two of them at all times, even when the door was open, as it was now.

Putting one end of the bar in the wall-bracket farthest from the door, and holding the other end high, the Doctor let go of the bar. It dropped straight down and fell into the next bracket, now being held by both.

Grinning eagerly, the Doctor retrieved the poker from the fireside, and carefully balanced it in one bracket, propping up one end of the locking bar. Moving the door until it was almost closed, he grabbed the desk in both hands, and dragged it across to the door. Flexing his fingers briefly, he grasped hold of the edge of the door, and held it tightly as he tipped the desk over until it was supported by only two legs, leaning against the door's brackets from the locking bar.

Gritting his teeth against the weight, he carefully squeezed through the narrow gap between door-edge and door-jamb, until he was holding the door open with both hands while standing in the corridor. 'Of course ...'

Keeping up the same pressure on the door, he slipped back into the gap, grimacing at the point where he had to hold the complete weight of door and desk in one hand again. Once inside, he let go of the door's edge.

The desk's weight shoved it forward, slamming closed loudly, while the edge of it hit the poker. The poker bounced back from the wall, clattering to the floor as the end of the locking bar dropped into the open-topped bracket on the now-closed door.

'If only they were all this easy,' the Doctor muttered, gripping the desk again.

Ibrahim rode with a smile he didn't even realize he was wearing. It had been too long since he had witnessed the beginnings of a new love instead of the endings of them at the point of a sword. Even the dim woodland morning, not yet fully lit by the sun, seemed brighter and more cheerful than it had yesterday.

None of this, however, interfered with his quick but thorough examination of the ground over which he was travelling. There was no sign of hoofprints other than those of Hubert and himself, and he could see no recently broken branches among those slim twigs that stretched out at all heights between the trunks of the trees. If anyone had been here recently they had been very stealthy about it. Wheeling about to return to the road, Ibrahim wondered what Hubert would have to say about it. Probably not much, as usual, he thought.

It took only a few minutes to reach the cart track that led through the forest, and Ibrahim wasn't surprised to see Hubert returning just as quickly through the trees on the far side. 'Did you see any sign of soldiers?'

'None less than a few days old,' Hubert replied quietly. 'You?'

'The same. I think we can tell Guy that this stretch of the track is safe.'

Hubert nodded in silent agreement, and they galloped off back along the uneven track. The horses were well used to this sort of terrain, however, and the journey went quickly enough. Ibrahim had just begun to think that it would be a worthwhile day when Hubert, who was slightly ahead, suddenly jerked upwards and somersaulted back off his saddle. Ibrahim's horse tried to shy away from the body that crashed into the ground before it, but Ibrahim steadied it.

The delay, however, granted him enough time to spot the taut rope that was stretched between two trees. He ducked under the rope disbelievingly, not comprehending

233

how they could have missed the tracks of whoever set this up, be it the Church or some group of varlets or bandits preying upon the displaced.

Either way, Guy and the Lady Bernice had to be warned, so Ibrahim spurred his horse as fast as it would go. Hardly had he passed the rope, however, than a group of armoured soldiers in the same de Citeaux livery they had seen at the village, rushed out into his path. One of them raised a crossbow, and Ibrahim suddenly felt a bone-crushing impact punch him from the saddle.

He smashed into the ground, his body feeling as if it were on fire, and what little breath he managed to take tasted strongly of blood. The hoofbeats of his horse were quickly halted, he noticed, presumably by one of the warriors there capturing it. With a flash of insight, he realized how stupid he had been in only looking for ambushers in the woods. It had never occurred to any of them that someone would simply ride straight down the open track to set a trap.

'This wretch is dead,' someone said distantly. 'The rope must have broken his neck.'

'Good,' a rougher, deeper voice commented. 'We will waste no more time on him, then.' Ibrahim tried to prop himself up to see what was happening, but his arms simply refused to move, and his chest screamed silent pain as the muscles scraped around the intruding crossbow quarrel.

Booted feet carefully stepped over the sticky patches of red around the desperately wheezing body of Ibrahim, but the black cloak hem that trailed behind them could not avoid being dragged across the blood and snow, both of which adhered in tiny patches.

Philippe de Montfort squatted down with a cosy grin, and tutted softly. 'You choose bad hunting partners, my Moorish friend.' He softly caressed the short fletching that swept back from the crossbow quarrel embedded in Ibrahim's stomach. Even this tiny disturbance of the quarrel's position brought forth an agonized gasp. Ibrahim's body felt quivery, as if he were teetering dizzily on the brink of some abyss – perhaps literally so, he feared.

234

'Hurts, does it not? If you had simply ridden away from the Roc then I could not have cared less, even for a Moorish raider. But helping that backstabbing jackal, de Carnac. . . That is another matter.'

Ibrahim strained to move his clenched jaws far enough to allow him to curse de Citeaux's bones, or at least spit in his face, but holding back the hollow pain took too much effort to waste it. Evidently he had been too quick to see Guy and the Lady Bernice as having a future, and the lack of any means to warn them so that they might escape to continue their relationship was as painful as the physical wounds. 'Still, you are but an enemy soldier, so I see no need to waste time on you. Smile. You will have a quick death.' Grinning amidst his forked beard, Philippe wrapped one gauntletted hand around the quarrel, and wrenched downwards, twisting the tip and driving it up through Ibrahim's vital organs in a mercifully brief blaze of white heat.

Philippe released the quarrel with the sense of a job well done, as soon as the last spark of life faded from the dark-skinned hunter's eyes. He straightened instantly. 'Joseph?'

'Yes, my Lord?'

'Take the men. The presence of these scouts shows that the heretics have something of interest to hide in this area. Ride to the river-bank track and search it closely – it is hidden from the main cart trail by that ridge, and so may be used by them.'

Joseph nodded in a deferential half-bow, and jogged back towards his horse. Philippe turned to a group of his men, and beckoned to the nearest two. 'You two follow me. The rest of you go with Joseph.' Leaving the bodies where they lay, he moved back to his horse and remounted.

Guy had been foolish to dally in this area after his treason, and Philippe would ensure that he didn't live to learn from that mistake.

235

Chapter 18

The Doctor sighted along his umbrella to the arched door-way below that led into the hold and, in particular, the hospital room. He shuffled his feet slightly on the damp stone of the parapet, which, being partially sheltered from snowfalls by the ramshackle wooden hoardings, was just wet enough to be slippery. 'This looks about the right spot. . .'

Taking out his pocket watch, he gripped it tightly, and took a few deep breaths as he put his thumb over the button for the stopwatch function. Pressing it suddenly, he bolted along the parapet, slipping and sliding dangerously close to the inside edge, which had no protective barrier.

Pinwheeling his arms in a wild attempt to keep his balance, he yanked open the door of the mid-level entrance to the hold, and leaped into the dark space beyond. Puffing furiously, he hooked his umbrella round a post on the staircase, so as to take the corners more quickly, and bounded up them two at a time.

Reaching the third landing, he spun dizzily away from the stairs, charging down a narrow passageway, which finally opened out into a cul-de-sac. Staggering to a halt at one of the doors there, the Doctor pressed his stop-watch stud once more, and then looked at the display, which was now frozen. 'Let's see. Guy and Benny would have taken a little longer than this, but heard no sounds of flight. . . Right, we'll call this the upper limit for the killer to get to wherever.' He tapped out a tattoo on his umbrella handle as he regained his breath. 'Now, which places in the Roc can be reached in this length of time? Only one way to find out, I suppose.'

Grasping his umbrella firmly, and restarting his stop-watch, the Doctor dashed off down the passageway directly ahead.

Guzman was awakened by a knock at the door. Irritation flooded his mind: didn't whoever it was realize that daylight was the time for men to be awake, which was why God gave light then? Hastily donning his black Dominican robe, he unlatched the door. A quaking herald waited beyond. 'Well, boy? What is it?'

'This message was sent for you. It is from the spy we have in the Roc.'

'For me?' Why not Louis, Guzman wondered. The answer was obvious – Louis would not want to be disturbed so early. 'Very well. Give it to me.' The herald handed over the sealed parchment, and turned to leave as Guzman unrolled it.

Guzman couldn't believe his eyes. The heretic leader dead? No matter, but the Doctor one of them: was his kidnap really a rescue? He might even have been a spy for them, and Louis had welcomed him with open arms. 'Herald,' Guzman called. 'Call out the guard. We have a traitor to arrest.'

Edouard found Hugues in the cavernous kitchen. With the main hall transformed into a hospital, the kitchens were now the place where meals were eaten as well as prepared, and Edouard recognized several faces, the Doctor, Giselle and Jeanne among them. The kitchen was wide but low-ceilinged, with squat pillars dotted around. The airiness of the chamber made it quite chilly, despite the banks of fires burning in the hearths and firepits.

'Hugues,' Edouard began, 'may I speak with you for a moment?'

'Of course. Communication is a pursuit of the intellect, and so valuable. What is it that concerns you?' Hugues

237

dipped some bread in what was left of a mug of broth, and gestured to the vintner to sit across from him.

'Guy and the others could have made their journey twice by now. I fear that they may have fallen foul of the Church.'

Hugues shook his head gently. 'Even the uninitiated among us know that the world can be hostile at this time of year. It is more likely that they have decided to shelter in the reeve's storehouse overnight, and return this morning.'

That thought had also occurred to Edouard, but Guy and Bernice had helped him on the road when the varlets had attacked, and he didn't like the idea of simply hoping that they were all right. 'I would like to take some of the men and go out to keep a watch for Guy and the others.'

'I will not stop you, if that is your decision. It may not be the wisest course – '

Edouard nodded. 'I know, but they are my friends, and I would like to help if they need it. If they do not, at least the handing out of the supplies will be quicker.'

'Wise it may not be,' the Doctor echoed, looking up from a small platter of bread and cheese, 'but human it is. Might I offer one little suggestion, though?'

'Of course.' If Guy and Bernice valued the Doctor's advice, then Edouard was sure it would be worth taking. 'Find a spot for yourself and your men at least half a mile from the Roc. That way, if anything goes wrong, your position won't attract attention to the tunnel.' The Doctor suddenly thumped his fist upon the tabletop, making the wooden bowls and mugs shake. 'Tunnel! Of course! How could I have been so blind?' He leaped to his feet, jamming his hat on his head, and brandishing his umbrella dangerously. 'I'll have to excuse myself,' he said urgently, 'I have a murderer's escape route to follow.'

Leaving the others gape-mouthed in astonishment, the Doctor hurried away, stuffing the last chunk of cheese into his mouth as he went.

Jeanne watched from a neighbouring table, having

finished her meal, but staying to wait for Giselle. The Doctor seemed excited about something. Had he made some progress on Girard's and the Castellan's murders? Doubtless she would hear about it in due course.

'I sometimes wonder what it would be like.'

'What?' Jeanne looked back to find Giselle trying to suppress a smile, while a blush as red as her hair coloured her cheeks. Giselle pointed with a small motion, and Jeanne realized that the younger Parfait had thought she was watching a pregnant woman who was spooning broth to her two children.

You can never find out, she answered mentally, not after receiving the consolamentum. Why did Giselle think that they were constantly kept in same-sex pairs? So that they weren't tempted to bring yet more life into the world. She knew the Church had its own ideas, of course, and they sometimes made her laugh. She wondered what they would think if they had seen Girard hurl two sodomites from the north wall into the river, only a few months ago. The worst form of being led by physical concerns, he had called it. The people, of course, were happy to hear the Inquisition's stories of 'unnatural sexual practices' among the Parfaits, but didn't think twice of asking one to induce an abortion.

She felt more than a little guilty about that, though her faith conflicted with childbearing. She should have seen it as a blessing when she ended someone's pregnancy.

But then, some sights like the young mother there sparked other memories. She didn't really know what was right any more, she realized. Her mind drifted back to Giselle's question of what motherhood was like.

'Unforgettable,' she whispered absently.

There had been no sign of tracks left by the wagon Guy had taken, when Edouard decided that the clearing through which they were travelling was as good a place as any from which to watch for Guy and Bernice's safe return.

The morning was cold, of course, but Edouard was used

239

to that by now, and he was willing to endure it for the sake of his friends. Besides, a little suffering was good for the soul, or so he'd been taught. They had been waiting only a few minutes, when one of the men – a former squire – ran to report that he heard hooves.

Edouard didn't relax yet; the time for that would come when he heard the cart's wheels. Signalling to his men to spread out, he squinted through the white morning in the direction from which the sound came. Sure enough, there were hoofbeats, but they sounded as if there were too many, and his carthorses didn't have barding ...

Joseph scanned the countryside around him, making sure that Antoine's troops were not around. Philippe had promised that they would still be asleep at this hour, though Joseph didn't really care. So long as he was being well paid, he didn't care who he had to fight – heretics or Church knights.

The road was clear ahead, however, and there appeared to be a clearing of sorts ahead, which would be a good place from which to start their search of the river-bank trail.

Waving to the men to follow him, he spurred his horse onwards.

Flurries of displaced snow exploded from battered branches as the troop of horses galloped through the woods, their riders no more than shadowy wraiths wrapped in the gauzy haze of falling snow and cloudy exhalations. The sharp rattle of their equipment carried easily in the cold air, however, and Edouard could already hear the metallic slither of swords being drawn.

The vanguard of the attack were menacing patches of darkness that rushed out of the surrounding white with almost supernatural speed, the thunder of their hooves marking them as elements of the storm.

Bowstrings loosened, arrows singing through gaps in the trees to merge with the dark figures. Only one rider crashed to the ground, though bitten-off yells indicated several woundings. A responding crossbow-bolt flashed past Edouard and rammed home into one of the archers, who almost somersaulted backwards under the force of the impact.

All around the clearing, yells and metallic clangs were rising with uncanny clarity as Edouard gripped his axe with hands white-knuckled from the fear of pain and death, and swung hard at the knight bearing down on him. The axe-head crashed into the horse's shoulder, and the animal gave an almost human screech of agony as it fell forward, shucking its rider. Edouard was knocked aside as it rolled into him, but the knight was left trying to rise with one arm left hanging limply. Edouard recovered first, and slammed the axe into the knight's exposed face, knowing that it was too light and broad a blade to pierce mail with any great effectiveness.

To one side, two men-at-arms moved in to slash at three of Edouard's spearmen, while a knight charged past the falling bodies on his way to crush another's skull with a mace. Enraged and guilty at having led them into such a hopeless battle, Edouard stumbled through the snow, his axe-head taking the first of the unarmoured men-at-arms in the small of the back. The other man turned, slashing instinctively, but only succeeded in trepanning his fellow before a stray arrow spitted him.

The battle was obviously going the Church's way, however, as many more of Edouard's ill-equipped troops were being trampled underhoof as they cooled in the snow than were the Church men. Edouard could only hope that they whittled down the Church force enough to prevent them from moving on this day. If they wasted their time searching for tunnels in this defended clearing, then so much the better for the others at the Roc.

No longer concerned about winning, as it was so clearly impossible, Edouard looked around for someone to take with him. A pounding of hooves behind him made him turn, only to see a knight with a lowered wooden lance wheeling in his direction.

There was a sudden black blur, as if he had been briefly

concussed, and the knight was gone, leaving him with the hollow feeling of a dizzying nausea and weakness in the legs. So was all sound of the battle, leaving only the silence of the empty winter woods, though he could see the snow-shrouded motion of continued fighting all around. He must have been fighting on the right side, he thought, if he was being granted a peaceful death. That knight had been so close ... His knees suddenly gave way, but Edouard found to his surprise that he was still standing.

When he looked down to see why, he heard only the thud of his axe hitting the ground after falling from nerveless fingers.

Guy had been giving Bernice strange looks all morning, as she had consistently refused to identify the song she was humming, and it wasn't one he'd heard on his travels. She wasn't surprised, since the Deadwood Stage had never been dreamed of in any form yet.

At least it had been a peaceful journey in good company, she thought, though the cold was beginning to seep through her insulated jacket again. It was a fine morning for one so cold, with only the echoing of the horses' hooves to interrupt their conversation. She frowned: echoes on a woodland track? Surely not. There was definitely, however, an additional sound of hoofbeats following those of their own horses, and the inference was obvious. Looking back, she saw three armed and armoured men catching up rapidly, their cloaks flying in the wind.

Guy had evidently noted her alarm, as he looked round before she said anything. 'De Montfort's mercenaries,' he spat, as the middle rider waved the other two ahead. Already, one was drawing level with the board seat at the front of the wagon. The mercenary cut down with an axe, but couldn't quite reach Guy, as his horse was dodging back and forth on the uneven road. Guy handed the reins to Benny and started to rise from the seat, but the mercenary had already swung his leg over the saddle and flung himself on to the side of the wagon, hanging on to the wooden side as his feet bumped along through the churned mud and snow.

Getting a foothold on a basket slung from the side, he tugged the axe from his belt and hacked downwards at Guy's midriff.

Guy rolled backwards into the bed of the wagon, leaving the axe-head to bite into the plank that he and Benny sat on. Before the mercenary could work the blade free, Guy's boot lashed out and snapped his head around, jerking him off the wagon with a crushing impact. Another mercenary had ridden in on Bernice's side by now, and swung a spiked flail at her head. She flung herself prone along the seat, barely having time to hope that she wouldn't roll off under the wagon. The flail flew past her head and caught fast, its chain wrapped around one of the posts which could anchor a cover to the wagon. Letting go before he was pulled off the horse, the mercenary rider reached across his body to get at his sword. Seizing her chance, Benny levered up the axe that was embedded in the seat beside her and lashed out, hoping that she wouldn't harm the horse. The blade sheared into his thigh, and he doubled over in the saddle with a tormented screech, instinctively jerking downwards towards the wound. Benny immediately swung the axe the other way, the blunt side of it pounding into his lowered helmet with a crash. Unconscious, he dropped from the saddle into the mud, and the wagon bumped alarmingly as one of the iron-bounded wheels trundled over his chest.

A resounding thud behind her drew Benny's attention back to where Guy was. She hadn't even noticed that he hadn't rejoined her. Another riderless horse peeling away from the road as she turned was the first clue she had as to what was happening. The second was the sight of Guy whipping his sword into a defensive posture as he stumbled and dropped into the pile of sacks. A third mercenary was balancing precariously towards the rear of the wagon, sword raised high.

'You are dead, de Carnac,' he snarled through his

forked beard as he delivered a ringing blow against Guy's blade. 'You simply have not laid down yet.' A second blow was deflected more easily, as Guy had pulled himself back up by means of one of the cornerposts.

'What have I done to offend you?' Both men stumbled a moment, then crossed blades again, the motion of the wagon making it impossible for either of them to easily gain an advantage.

Benny looked around desperately for inspiration, knowing that she should be able to help Guy, but was unable to let go of the reins. What I wouldn't give for a disruptor, she thought. A rattling at her ear drew a quick glance to the flail that was firmly looped around the cornerpost next to her head. 'What the hell; you never know until you try . . .'

Turning sideways so she could try to keep one eye on the rutted track directly ahead and one on the duel directly behind, she held on to the reins with one hand, while gingerly tugging at the flail's tangled chain with the other. It was quite a trick, she grumbled inwardly, for someone who couldn't even smegging well juggle three balls.

'Throwing daggers at a Bishop does not praise my choice of friends,' the mercenary was saying. 'Who will trust my honour now?'

'You never had any, Philippe. You are but the runt of a family whose position was bargained away by the first-born. We are both wandering mercenaries, but you see yourself as a deposed noble forced into homelessness, while I consider myself a free spirit.' Guy made a quick feint and lunge as Benny managed to get her fingers between the chain and the wood.

Philippe rolled into the sacks as the wagon lurched over a large stone Benny had overlooked, and Guy toppled past him. 'You are no one! You are but a dishonoured knight for whom destitution is a rise in rank. You cannot understand humiliation as I do.'

'Watch your mouth,' Benny rapped irritably, getting sick of insults to the most human person she'd met in this godsforsaken century. Guy bounded forward as Philippe spun to see who had spoken, his attack forcing Philippe back against the front wall of the wagon.

Braced against the shuddering wood, Philippe was able to kick out at the nearest sacks as he parried Guy's attack. The jouncing of the wagon caused the sacks, so disturbed, to topple inwards from the wooden side, knocking Guy's legs from under him. Guy pitched into the scattered sacks as if poleaxed.

'No one embarrasses me!' Philippe raised his sword over the spread-eagled Guy, just as the flail came loose in Benny's hand. Drawing it back without being able to fully turn, she swung it almost blindly at Philippe de Citeaux's looming back on the other side of the wooden wall. The rocking of the wagon meant that the spiked ball missed Philippe's head by an inch.

The chain, however, caught in his wildly flying hair with a snap, jerking his head back painfully and arresting his downward hack. He started to turn towards the source of the interruption, his face a demonic mask of rage. But with the speed of a striking cobra, Guy snatched up his sword and rammed forward.

Still watching as best she could with her neck twisted almost as far as it would go, Benny drew back in shock as the silver tip of Guy's sword burst from the sweaty crown of Philippe's bald head like the beak of a chick hatching from its egg. Pinky grey flecks left trails of blood lightened with cephalic fluid as they started to slide back down the steel towards the potsherd-like splinters of bone that were raised jaggedly around the wound. Philippe's last breath bubbled away as thick blood ran down towards Guy's gauntlet from the entry wound under the chin.

Benny tried, with dubious success, to choke down rising bile as Guy withdrew his sword, leaving the briefly twitching body to tumble from the wagon. Guy climbed stiffly over on to the seat beside Benny, and took the reins from her. 'Was that really necessary?'

'It was going to happen to one of us – which would you

245

have preferred? You can relax now. It should be a quiet journey back to the Roc.'

'Not inside my head, it won't be.'

The Doctor stood in front of the open window that looked out over the river from the south face of the Roc. It had been strange that this cul-de-sac was just the right distance away, but it was unlikely that anyone could have climbed out. The escape route could have been taken directly from Girard's cell window.

All the other points reachable within the time allowed would have been occupied, however, so this must be the one. Rapping on the walls this time, he soon found a hollow spot. The passage was less well concealed than that in the library, but he had missed it at first glance. He felt around, eventually coming across a small catch which released the door.

'Eureka, the game's afoot.'

He looked around for a flambeau, then gingerly touched both eyebrows and his hat brim. 'No, once bitten, I think.'

Switching on a pen-torch, which he retrieved from his pocket, he stepped into this new tunnel.

This time Benny couldn't keep herself from being sick against a tree, while Guy looked around, his expression cooling by degrees. Shattered branches hung from the trees where riders had pushed through them, while the gradually freezing limbs of perhaps forty or fifty snow-encrusted corpses – he wasn't about to go and count them – ghoulishly mirrored the dead wood.

Most of them wore thickly layered rags and little armour, indicating that they were from the Roc, while there were a few armoured Church men in de Citeaux livery here and there. Most of the bodies were lying in the twigs and snow, black crusts of blood capping sword wounds and forming Gothic shells around crushed limbs and skulls, occasional pieces of viscera standing out stark against the carpeting of snow. Others lay slumped against fallen logs, still clutching at the arrow-shafts that had killed them. On the far side of the clearing, at least one man was pinned to a tree by a lance of some kind, a scarlet icicle weighing down the corner of his gaping mouth. She realized with another spasm of her voided gullet that the impaled man was one she knew – Edouard – his ever-present axe lying in a pink patch of snow at his feet.

'What has happened here?' Guy hissed, almost slipping in the hoof-churned pink snow.

Benny threw him a despairing look, her revulsion at the situation sparking the rebellious sarcastic streak that she just couldn't seem to control. 'Well, Conan, I may be jumping to conclusions, but it wouldn't surprise me at all if there hadn't been a spot of foul play here.'

'If you consider yourself no fool, then do not treat others like one!' Guy kicked out at the body of a de Citeaux man, eyes blazing. 'This place is not close enough to the tunnel for the Church men to have found it. Nor has this been an affray with Shark platoon from the gate tower. So, what purpose has this served?'

'Does this sort of thing ever serve a purpose?'

Guy looked at her, then his shoulders slumped slightly. 'De Citeaux obviously thinks it does, if he thinks at all.'

Benny looked around thoughtfully. The terrain here seemed familiar somehow . . . 'Can you tell from the tracks which way the soldiers were travelling when they arrived?'

Guy knelt to examine the hard-packed imprints of the hooves, moving on to repeat the examination at a few other spots before shaking his head. 'It has been trampled too many times in too many directions, and the new snow masks it further. Hubert may have been able to tell, but not I. They left to the north, however. What thoughts have you about it?'

'If they were heading that way,' Benny said, pointing southwest, 'they would have reached the tunnel entrance in less than an hour.'

'And Edouard and the others set out to prevent them getting so close? It would be a sound strategy. An engagement at the foot of the cliff would have proved that there was something worth defending there, while from here there is still much ground to search.' Guy walked back to the wagon, and brushed away some of the snow that had fallen while they had been exploring. He took the reins once more. 'We must go, if we are to be within the Roc before sunset.'

Benny stayed where she was, feeling that it would be wrong to leave the bodies where they were like joints of meat in a freezer. 'Shouldn't we bury them, or something?'

Guy nodded, then beckoned her to return to the wagon. 'We should, before the wolves and foxes scent the blood. Fifty of them, and in this ground, would take a week or more. I think we can leave the Church army to deal with them, as reinforcements will certainly be on their way to divine why this site is so important.' He looked around with a look of contained fire, and then joined her back at the wagon. 'This is no country for you. We must return these supplies to the Roc. You take the reins, while I follow and attempt to hide our tracks as best I can.'

The light from the pen-torch had been much less than that from the flambeaux earlier, but still enabled the Doctor to make his way through the warren of tunnels. Many were very narrow, and he wouldn't have got through them if he'd been much larger, but, by persevering, he had slipped through.

Judging by the distances and few turns he had made, the tunnel encircled the outer wall of the Roc. He had seen only one other exit so far, which was in what he judged to be the west wall, and it refused to open, indicating that it was probably blocked by something. That being the case, it had probably been forgotten about. This was some fifty yards along the wall, which would place it in the stables, if his calculations were correct.

His hands had brushed against strange sensations as he felt his way along, but so far he had resisted the urge to turn the torchlight on his fingers to see what it was. Something suddenly gave way under his fingertips, and he stopped to investigate more closely. He hadn't long since turned left, and this was another latch already.

Pushing open the door, he blinked in the yellow torchlight.

He was in one of the scribes' annexes off the library, the desks dusty and untouched, but the walls thickly padded with scrolls and handwritten books. Turning, he saw that he had emerged from a bas-relief pillar set into the wall. Stepping away from it, he lifted the nearest couple of texts from their shelves. 'Albucasis, St Antony . . .'

With raised eyebrows, he pulled the magnifying glass from his pocket and looked closely at the slightly distorted images of the fingerprints he had taken from the dagger. 'About three per cent longer and thinner than Girard's print. Yes, that would be fairly average.' He dropped the glass back into his pocket. 'I wonder which of the two it was, and why . . .'

Chapter 19

'I don't know about you,' Benny said gloomily, filling a small bowl with the first batch of her home-made vodka, 'but I sure as hell need some of this.'

'You say it was Philippe de Citeaux?' the Doctor was asking Guy, as the sat on a couple of barrels next to the smithy, which was where Benny's still had been moved to for the benefit of forthcoming customers.

'I knew him well, once,' Guy said. 'He ambushed us, and I believe it was his men who killed Edouard and the others, but he will not do so again unless it is as a revenant.'

The Doctor relaxed, seeming quite relieved. 'You've no idea how much of a burden that takes off my shoulders. There's still work to do, though. We have to get that skull from its hiding place. Fortunately, I believe I know where it is.'

The hooch felt as if it was about to strip the flesh from Benny's gullet, but she wasn't complaining. 'RomuluS Hiq it isn't,' she croaked as best she could, 'but it'll do. Why are we still wasting our time looking for this skull? Surely we can just leave as soon as the TARDIS arrives?'

'No, we can't, for three reasons. One: there's still a murderer loose, and finding the skull should be a perfect lure. Two: no matter what happens, we have to prevent it from falling into de Citeaux and Guzman's grubby little protruberances, because it's destined for other things, if my theory is correct. Three: Hugues will need it for tonight's New Year ceremony, and its non-appearance could shatter so many people's faiths in here that history might also be at risk.'

'They might be saved, you mean. The Parfaits could disguise themselves and make a quick getaway with everybody else.'

The Doctor gave her a stem look through hooded eyes. 'I doubt it.'

Benny gaped at him. 'We can't help them escape?'

'All the Parfaits and those who converted on the last night here died – you know that from the fact that the Inquisition kept detailed records which are invaluable history texts for centuries to come. There are ten thousand soldiers out there ready to do their bit for their god by killing anyone they can get their hands on, so I'm rather afraid they'll die anyway. At least after their New Year ritual – I gather it's supposed to energize their spirits, or some such thing – they'll be a little more ... sanguine about it. It'll also reduce the risk of innocent non-believers getting cut to pieces in the middle if the Parfaits should decide to resist.'

'You mean, better to go with a smile?'

'If you put it like that. . . Yes.'

Jeanne straightened from examining the wheels of the first haywain, shaking her head as she did so. It was a very rough and basic construction, and she was determined that no patient of hers would travel in it. She wanted those in her care to recover, not get yet more broken bones from bumping around in a shoddy cart.

Giselle looked at her understandingly. 'Either they go in these, or they stay for the flames.'

'If Girard and Hugues had been better prepared as I suggested ... Very well.' She turned to a mound of empty sacks and torn blankets that had been brought out to the carts in the open section of the stable. If they laid down enough of these, Jeanne thought, it should make a suitable cushion for those travelling in it. So she hoped, anyway. She bent to lift a double armful of the sacks, tossing them into the cart and spreading them around.

251

'Surely that is not the Doctor going into the library?' Giselle asked suddenly.

Concerned at her partner's comment, Jeanne came round the side of the cart, peering across the bailey at the north tower. Some of the refugees were in the way for a moment, but their movement took them out of the way quickly enough for Jeanne to make out the short pale figure vanish in through the door. 'It is the Doctor . . . and de Carnac and Bernice, I think.' She wondered what they could possibly want in there at this hour. Had not the Doctor mentioned something about leaving today? She took a few steps away from the cart, then thought better of it, and returned to tossing sacks into the cart. Perhaps the Doctor was just interested in his scholarly activities.

'Jeanne, will you excuse me a moment?' Giselle asked absently. 'There is something I must see to.'

'Of course. I will continue here.'

Giselle nodded gratefully, and walked back towards the hospital in the south tower's ground floor. Jeanne watched her go, wondering what could be both so urgent and so sudden.

'What makes you think we'll find it this time? You said you've searched in here already.' Benny looked around the library, which was currently illuminated only by their own torches.

'Because I was looking at the problem from the wrong angle.' The Doctor handed his torch to Guy, and stretched his arms out around the reliquary cabinet. 'We all assumed that the skull was a valuable relic, hidden from jealous eyes. However, why would a culture that sees all physical matter as being the domain of an evil deity place any value in a physical object?'

'Then why hide it?'

'You keep medicinal supplies away from prying children, don't you? Bury reactor wastes in hidden caverns. Out of sight, out of mind?'

'Well, yes, but a skull could hardly be a danger to them.'

'That depends on whose skull you think it is.' The cabinet slid aside easily – as it would have to for an old man like Girard to move it – revealing an opening from which grinned the skull she had seen earlier, still sitting on its silken cushion.

'Jesus Christ,' she muttered.

'Exactly.'

'No, I didn't mea – What?!' Benny thought about this. The obvious assumption – which would explain why the Church felt the heretics to be so dangerous – was numbing. 'You're not serious?'

'Of course I'm serious. Girard believed that it was Jesus' skull, and his belief convinced his followers. They think it proves the Crucifixion was irrelevant, which it would have to be, in order to fit their world-view.'

'And is it genuine?'

'No. Look at the lower jaw – that's not even a male skull. Louis de Citeaux and Guzman manoeuvred the heretics into acquiring it, so that when this place falls, they can prove that heretics were fakers trying to destroy Church power. Naturally, the grateful Cardinals would heap rewards upon them for this discovery. Guzman expects to become Pope now that his only rival was murdered, while Louis probably hopes to have his city become an independent principality.'

'And the killer is the Church spy, who wants it to hand over to them?' Guy deduced.

'Not exactly. The Church spy is Robert, the apothecary.'

'You knew?' Benny hissed, then caught herself. Of course he knew; he always did. 'Then let's go and get him.'

'Not yet. You see – '

'You see, I am already here,' the vaguely quivery young voice announced from behind them. The trio turned to find a rather nervous Robert stepping out from hiding behind the door. He gently pushed it shut. 'Though I am not sure why the Church forces are not here, since I have told them of the tunnel many times.'

'Really?' the Doctor asked. 'I'm afraid that part of those messages doesn't seem to have got through.'

253

'But I have killed no one. I am but a messenger.'

'You expect us to believe that?' Guy demanded.

'As much as you believe that skull is genuine. The Doctor is quite corre–' Guy's arm shot out, grabbing Robert by the neck and hurling him back into one corner.

Before Robert could rise, Guy planted a foot on his chest with a grim smile, and levelled the point of his sword to the younger man's throat. 'Now we need only find a rope long enough for you.'

'No, Guy,' the Doctor squawked urgently. Benny began to get the sinking feeling that he had once again neglected to tell them something they ought to know.

Guy half-turned. 'What –' He broke off as Robert squirmed free and pulled a dagger from beneath his baggy surcoat. The young apothecary lunged for the tall warrior, but his inexperience counted against him, and Guy simply dodged aside, slashing into Robert's abdomen as he slid past. Robert's bowels were following their squealing owner into the straw-covered floor before Benny even completed her first step towards Guy in the hope of avoiding further bloodshed.

Accompanied by the clacking of the door slamming open against the dressed stone, a fuzzy blur whirred past Bernice's cheek as she reached out to prevent Guy from administering a *coup de grâce* to the writhing spy. Her heart missed a beat as something black flickered in the midst of a splash of blood on Guy's shoulder, flipping him into the wall with a crunch and a muffled groan.

Dropping beside him, she felt as ashen as he looked, as she noticed the thick quarrel that had buried itself up to the fletching in his right shoulder.

'Now, I feel somewhat safer,' Jeanne said, lowering the crossbow. She tossed the weapon to the floor, and drew out a long dagger. 'But I will defend myself if I have to. Give me the skull, Doctor. I have no quarrel with you or the Lady Bernice.'

'Are you a spy for the Church, too?' Benny asked disgustedly, torn between the urge to tend to Guy and to throw herself at Jeanne.

254

Jeanne looked at her as if she were insane. 'Why would I help those butchers?'

'You've already helped them twice,' the Doctor said pointedly. 'I imagine you killed the Castellan because he let slip that he had evidence as to the identity of someone with a secret here. And you assumed he meant that he had found out that you killed Girard. You murdered him to keep him silent, but in doing so, prevented him from laying evidence against Robert.' The Doctor held up the small book he had found under the Castellan's bed, it appearing from nowhere as if it were a card in a conjuring trick. 'The Castellan used to be a gardener in a vineyard, and had noted down the herbs and plants which Robert claimed to be collecting from the north side of the Roc. They didn't tally with Robert's claims, because Robert was really going there to send messages to the Church by dropping them in sealed pots into the river, where they could be fished out later.'

Jeanne paled. 'If he had simply said that at first . . .'

'Well, he didn't. Do you really think that skull is worth the price you're paying for it? It isn't even the genuine article.'

'It matters not whether it is Christ's skull or not. The value of the legend that is already growing around it will make it worth a king's ransom. Even were you to denounce it as a peasant skull, the people would not believe it.'

'A king's ransom?' Benny echoed. She wanted to be sick at the thought. 'You mean, you just want this for the money?' She could hardly believe it. 'Grief! What happened to all material phenomena being evil?'

'The way those poor unfortunates in the hospital cling to life shows to me that we are made to live in this world, for good or for ill. I did not intend to kill Girard. I had hoped only to extract the hiding place of the skull from him, but he threw himself on to my dagger rather than tell me.' She smiled wistfully. 'It is ironic that we would not be confronting each other like this if I had left his suicide looking like a murder.'

255

'But why did you do this?' the Doctor asked reproachfully. 'There's a wagon-load of valuables and treasures in the storehouse that you could have taken with you.'

'I have three sons in Perpignan, Doctor. At the moment, they are serfs with no master. I recently received word that their master died when his farm was looted. With the profit from this, however, they will be able to become villeins, buying leases in a Royal borough. Next year, they will be free men, bourgeois who can trade freely as merchants and try to make something for themselves.'

'Then why didn't you just ask for help? I'm sure you would have been given some aid for your sons.'

'Not by Girard. A Parfait having given birth to new life in this world would have offended him more than anything, even were it before she became a Parfait. More likely he would have cast me out from the Roc.' She weighed the dagger thoughtfully, though it looked very heavy in her slim hand. 'I will do anything to ensure that life for them.' She looked at the time travellers almost pleadingly. Benny might ordinarily have been tempted to sympathize with her – at least her desires were not selfish – but the presence of Guy's sprawled and gasping form precluded that.

'You're not leaving here with that skull,' Benny said coldly. 'Not in a million years.'

'I am sorry you feel that way.' With a speed belying her years, Jeanne lunged for Benny. It was almost as if this was what the Doctor had been waiting for, Benny thought, as he hooked Jeanne's wrist with the handle of his umbrella, and tossed the contents of a small pouch into her face.

Jeanne's thrust was disrupted by a fit of sneezing, long enough for Benny, with considerable relish, to deliver a long, arcing kick to her midriff, before punching her out cold. Her knuckles felt as if someone had split them apart like clam-shells. 'How come this never happened to Ace when she hit somebody?'

Guy managed a weak smile through short sharp breaths. 'I have never seen a woman fight for me before,' he

256

grunted, in visible pain. 'It is supposed to be the other way around.'

'Don't get too used to it, Conan,' she whispered. The wound looked serious, with a lot of blood darkening his mantle. 'Just take what you can get.'

There was a chorus of in-drawn breath from the door as Giselle and Hugues entered. Giselle froze at the sight of the three prone bodies, not least because Jeanne was one of them. 'Jeanne?'

Hugues looked around in disgust. 'This life's only legacy. Robert was the killer?'

'Worse than that, I'm afraid,' the Doctor answered gloomily. 'Jeanne was the killer. Robert, for his sins, was only a spy for the Church.' He lifted the skull gently out from its hiding place. 'The stuff that dreams are made of . . . Yours, I believe.'

Hugues gently took the skull, and ran the palm of his hand over its yellowing crown. 'Yes. This is the one.'

Chapter 20

Louis de Citeaux prowled his room at the Hôtel de Ville irritably. The fact that, as a noble, he did not have to submit to torture until after conviction didn't ease his pained anger. Guzman and his ambition to become Pope be damned, he thought. When they eventually took him for questioning, he would have some very interesting tales to spin about just what had happened to Guzman's predecessor and his chief rival. If the headsman was to have him, he'd have Guzman for company.

He grew bored with the idea, however, having thought of little else for the past day or so. He wished he could believe in it as much as he desired it, but he knew that Guzman was his equal in slyness as well as rank. He wondered if his brother had had this problem with Guzman's uncle Dominic. Probably not, since they were both Church men, while Louis was not. Philippe's father, Simon, had run the war well for those two. Their three families had started the war well enough, but it seemed that they simply couldn't continue it together, even if Philippe had not gone and got himself killed.

That thought reminded him of Joseph, Philippe's replacement. Why had he yet to respond to Louis' summons? Under house arrest, he might be, but he was still the ruler of Béziers, and the King's man.

As if drawn by the force of Louis' will – and Louis would certainly have liked to believe that this was the case – Joseph chose that moment to throw the door open and enter. The new mercenary captain was neither as tall or broad as Philippe, but he shared his predecessor's flair for showmanship, as evidenced by his proud entry. 'You wish to confess?' he asked mockingly.

Louis let that go; this was too dangerous a situation for him to risk upsetting his guest. 'Not yet,' he answered smoothly. 'I simply wished to enquire as to the terms of your army's employment.'

'Guzman has offered my troop a fair price.' Louis didn't miss Joseph's careful use of the word 'my'.

'Philippe once told me that your men preferred thirty florins to fifteen.'

'But not thirty pieces of silver. I have been expecting an additional offer from you, but, you know, the pity of it is that, once I have been paid, I always follow the job through.'

'I have the treasury of a city at my disposal, Joseph, for those who are loyal.'

'The Church has many such, not just one. I did not come here to solicit for employment, however.' He stepped over to the window, and opened the shutters. The Roc loomed above the village roofs. 'I thought you might enjoy watching our victory at dawn. Come, see what a fine view we have for you.'

Amused by the similarity to his own greeting to Philippe back in Béziers, Louis drifted towards the window. The dark side of the Roc was like a blight in the countryside, he thought.

He didn't even feel the arrow which slid through him with rapid deceleration.

'I really shouldn't be doing this, you know.'

'What harm can it do? Nobody's going to analyse his bloodstream in this century.'

Despite his protestation, the Doctor checked the charge remaining in the hypo from his pocket. 'This will deaden the pain, prevent infection from the wound, and bolster his immune system to counteract any weakness through shock or blood loss. But it won't stop the bleeding or repair tissues.' The Doctor pressed the hypo to Guy's arm and triggered it.

'What is that – a wand?' Hugues looked at the hypo with almost palpable curiosity.

'Just a method of applying herbs more efficiently, Hugues.'

Benny paced around the table on which they had deposited Guy, clenching and unclenching her fists in rapid succession. She felt as if she might fall apart if she stopped moving, and didn't dare risk even slowing down. 'Tourniquets and stitching, I can do – it's amazing what you can learn in a resettlement camp after a Dalek assault. It should heal if he lives.'

'Not necessarily.' The Doctor peered at the wound. 'But, in this case you're probably right. His wound's quite high, so it shouldn't be life-threatening now that I've given him this, and much of this blood doesn't seem to be his.'

'Robert's, presumably.'

'Yes.' He straightened with a sigh. 'Your hands look a bit shaky to be thinking of suturing.'

'You should feel them from this end.'

'I'll do it, if you can tell me where what laughingly passes for medical equipment in this century is stored here.'

'I will fetch it,' Giselle said, her face almost as white as Guy's. It couldn't be easy discovering that a life-long partner is a murderer, Benny realized, and she felt a little pang of sorrow for Giselle as well.

Benny moved round to the end of the table on which Guy's head rested. She thought that if he didn't come round soon, she'd probably hit him, in case that would wake him. Guy's eyes opened slowly, blinking in the bright candlelight. He looked straight up at her. 'Bernice . . .' he gave a small, pained smile. 'I must be in Heaven, but I am glad you are not Saint Peter.'

'I thought you weren't going to try to be funny any more. I thought Jeanne had killed you . . .'

'Perhaps she has – I cannot feel anything, but I should be in agony.'

'I'm rather afraid that was me,' the Doctor admitted. 'A little magic to dull the pain while we piece you together.

So long as you get yourself a good long holiday after this, I don't see why you couldn't tell your grandchildren this story.'

'What of Jeanne?'

'She's locked up somewhere in the cellars. I imagine she will die with the others after all. You, of course, will leave with the other fighters and displaced refugees. Giselle should be able to find a space in one of the carts for you.'

Benny bent towards Guy's ear as the Doctor turned away to receive the suturing materials from Giselle. She could scarcely believe the difference in Guy in the space of only a few minutes – from energetic knight to shattered near-corpse. And to think that the woman responsible would be effectively unpunished, since she would have died with the others even if she hadn't been caught . . . A glint of edged steel caught Benny's eye, and she unhooked the basilard from Guy's belt. 'I'll go and see Jeanne. I think we have a lot to discuss,' she said shakily.

Guzman examined the arrow carefully, making sure that his simple Dominican robes didn't brush against the unclean body of the traitor. Sometimes one had to be cruel to be kind, he reflected sadly. It was such a shame that their family ties should end this way, but if such was the Lord's will, then so be it . . .

'Your man used an arrow retrieved from the body of a heretic?'

'It was brought back from the clearing where we fought their rabble, eminence,' Joseph agreed. 'It is definitely one of theirs.'

'You have done well then. Have word given that the vengeful heretics have slain our . . . beloved leader,' he said, with a commendably straight face and severe voice.

'Yes, eminence.'

Guzman nodded wordlessly, and left the room. All that remained was to take the heretics' surrender.

Giselle left the Doctor to carry on his work, and went

261

down into the tunnel as the air outside grew dim with the onset of evening. Antoine was waiting at the tunnel mouth, easily blending into the shadows in his grey mail. 'My little sister looks ill at ease,' he commented concernedly.

'It is Jeanne,' she said stiffly, holding back the confusion that still reigned within her. She wanted to tell him, but the words just wouldn't come. Perhaps she was not ready to face them. She could face asking questions, however. 'Is the trail safe?'

'Yes. The Church is not interested in anyone but yourself and the others. So long as everyone remains out of sight for a few days, they will be able to return home.'

'Those who have homes.'

'You still have a home,' Antoine reminded her.

'This is my home now. I will not leave it. The first few people will be down with their wagon in a few minutes. Look after them, Antoine.'

'I will. I will see that they get away.'

Chapter 21

Bernice Summerfield didn't feel particularly professorial at the moment as she stood watching Jeanne from the shadows. The disgraced Parfait's dark blue robe swallowed up what little light had crept into the cellar storeroom in which she had been incarcerated. Benny had at first been surprised that the fortress had no dungeon, but Hugues had reminded her with a rather shaken gentleness that this was a religious building built as a refuge, and so had no need of prisons. In any case, it was, he had suggested, more merciful to simply put miscreants to death, as their weak spirits were obviously at the mercy of the evil forces of the world.

Benny's spirit didn't feel much better, having been somewhat battered of late.

For a long time, she had professed to despair at the vengeful attitude of Ace, her former travelling companion. Her aggressive, in-your-face brand of independence had seemed rather unsophisticated to Benny. Then again, Ace had been a product of a less-developed era. Benny had wondered on occasion what it would take to drive her to be like Ace.

Standing there in the dank passageway into which Jeanne's cell door was set, her fingers tracing a pattern on the chill flat of the blade of one of Guy's basilards, she wished – would have given her soul, in fact – that she had never found out.

Even though she had chosen her time carefully, so as to ensure that no one was around, she still couldn't help looking around just in case, before unsealing the door and going in.

'Died, has he?' Jeanne asked. Her voice, emanating from the shadows, was flat and lifeless. It seemed to Benny that the disgraced Parfait already considered herself dead. Was revenge such an obvious and inevitable step? Benny had hoped she wasn't so ordinary.

'Not yet. I just came to tell you what's going to happen now.' It occurred to her that killing Jeanne would most likely be an act of mercy, all things considered. She told herself she didn't feel particularly merciful either, but she wondered if was more a case of killing in cold blood just not being her style. It was just too . . . Daleky, really.

Instead, Benny kept her distance, with the basilard in one sweaty palm – the chance to kill Jeanne in self-defence would be an entirely different matter – and quietly told her of the massacre to come, of the fire that would sweep through the fortress, of the fall of the last remaining Cathar stronghold, of persecution and war for decades – centuries – to come . . . By the time she finished, Jeanne's only contribution to the conversation was a series of quaking sobs alone in the darkness.

Benny left her then. A little knowledge is a dangerous thing; she knew that someone in Earth's past had said that once. A lot of knowledge should have been shattering, she thought. She wondered if Jeanne would still be crying by the time the fire reached her. All the tears in history wouldn't douse the fires of her hell.

Guy awoke gasping for breath, and looked around to see where he was. From the stench, he could tell that he was in the hospital room, but a curtain separated the small alcove in which he lay from the main part of the room.

Would Bernice have used the basilard on the imprisoned Jeanne? Probably not, he decided finally. Her disapproval of his dispatching Philippe in such a manner, even though it was in defence of his own life – and hers – in mortal combat, counted against the likelihood of her being willing to kill in cold blood, regardless of the provocation.

It occurred to him that he might feel better if he knew that Jeanne was suffering at least the same level of pain and disability as she had seen fit to inflict upon him, but somehow he doubted it. It hadn't worked that way last time, and he didn't expect it to now: pursuing Godfroi hadn't dulled the pain of Iolande's loss. Of course, he hadn't actually managed to kill her abuser, but even the chase had seemed worthless and empty. It wasn't something he could change, however – only try to live with.

His chest and shoulder were painful enough to draw the strength away from him, but he felt as if they would heal eventually. Much of the blood which had so worried Bernice had in fact been Robert's, and his was a clean wound. Guy rose painfully, but was glad of the fact that he could get out of bed at all. His head swam for a moment, but he resisted the feeling, and sat up.

What must Bernice be feeling even to lift the basilard? He lowered his head into his hands: he should never have allowed her to get so close to him, for whatever hurt she felt was surely his fault for involving her. Perhaps if they were somewhere else, far from here ... The thought faded. He couldn't think of any place that didn't have its own troubles.

Despite his avowed intention to make for Barcelona and gain passage east to find some place to settle down, he knew in his heart that there was no such place. The best he could hope for was to salvage and renew his honour by finding others who needed help as the people here had done. That was, after all, what the Order had originally been founded for. He certainly had no plans to die along with them. The surrender to the flames was their choice, and they didn't need help for that. He would leave the following day, he decided, in the wake of the other mercenaries and families who were even now being led out to embark on new, Templar-led, journeys to who-knows-where.

Regardless of where he went, there was nowhere that

his presence – or the hunters it would drawn – would not put Bernice in more danger than he was willing to allow. The attack by Philippe was proof enough of that; and Guzman would not rest, not after having a dagger hurled at him, until Guy was just another bad memory. This whole country was no better, and women could expect worse tortures from the Church's army of glory hounds and cut-throats than a warrior ... She was such a rarity that he would do anything rather than see harm come to her, he thought.

He almost laughed at the irony of it. To continue the relationship clearly risked exposing Bernice to dangers and despair that only a hated enemy should be shown. The only way to avoid this happening was for them to stay apart. He was glad of the solitude, as he could already feel tears welling up inside – something that had not happened since that day he found Godfroi's body fallen in combat.

'She is but one woman,' he murmured to himself. 'There will be others, to be sure.' He didn't believe a word of it. But the sacrifice had to be made: he knew that. Better to live without her, but know she is safe, than to live with her injury or death – indirectly – at his hands. He only hoped that she didn't believe that he had stopped caring about her. That would hurt her in just the sort of manner he was doing this to avoid.

For once, the dull ache from his wound seemed like a good thing, inspiring a simple ploy within him. At a loss for any alternative, he reached for his jerkin, and wondered when he would see one of the chirurgeon-barbers.

The Doctor was watching Hugues' conducting of the Parfaits' last ceremony with half an eye, when Benny climbed up the steep steps to join him on the parapet. The blue-robed faithfuls each stepped forward in turn, reverently placing their palms atop the skull. Once they had felt it for a moment, they seemed joyous, and ready for anything. Usually they would be now be ready for the rigours of their forthcoming year, but this time they were already to pass on to another plane. Maybe, she thought, they were deliberately repudiating it as an act of faith in the next life.

Perhaps they were rejecting the concept of death, to reaffirm their belief in reincarnation? Truth was, Benny thought, that even by the 25th century, there hadn't been enough detail left on these people's beliefs to really know them. The Inquisition had certainly done as thorough a job as any memory purge she'd ever seen on a second-hand ship's mainframe. For once, however, she decided that she would really rather forget this place as soon as the opportunity arose, rather than take notes.

Depressed by the apparent rejection of their efforts in recovering the skull, Benny turned to face the shelter that crouched beneath the wall of the library tower. There, a group of tired men oiled their swords to ward against rust. 'Interesting?' the Doctor asked. At least he wasn't trying to cheer her up by being his usual overenthusiastic self.

'We see yonder the beginning of the day, but, I think, we shall never see the end of it.' She laughed mirthlessly, a little embarrassed at having recalled so vividly something from her Academy days.

'*Henry V*, act four, scene one. This is going to be what I believe they call a strategic withdrawal, not a battle.'

'That's what they said about Dunkirk. I was just thinking of things that get started, but never reach their conclusion. Dogma, I mean.'

The Doctor shifted slightly, like a hermaphroditic Centauran at the patriarchal Draconian court, unsure whether speaking out was a good idea or not. 'Isn't there something you want to ask me?'

'You said we can't save anyone.'

'I said we can't save any Parfaits. Guy doesn't seem the type to become a vegetarian pacifist. The TARDIS does seem a little empty these days.' The Doctor didn't quite meet her eyes. 'A family home with all the children grown up and gone . . .'

'I thought we were leaving pretty much immediately?'

'We can come back, if you like. The TARDIS is several hours away, but it'll only take instants to get back.'

'He does seem too nice to be left here, doesn't he?'

'Who does?' Hugues asked, ascending the steps softly, as the assembled Parfaits drifted back to their duties.

'We were just discussing Guy,' the Doctor explained, 'and the fact that it's time for us to leave.'

'I was under the impression that you travelled on some ship.'

'Well, yes, but first we have to get to it, of course. There's a small hilltop village between here and Béziers. Reaching that will be the first stage of our journey.'

'Then I would like to make a request of you.' Hugues looked a little sheepish, Benny thought, and she wondered if he was going to ask to be rescued. 'I would like you to take the skull to a safe hiding place, Doctor. I know it is but a physical object, but the Church could find a way to discredit it, and in so doing discredit us.'

'Who's to say they have the right skull?' Benny asked.

'Phrenology,' the Doctor answered. 'The bumps on a skull have significance to the personality as some people have believed, but they are as unique as fingerprints.'

'Every Parfait knows the touch of the skull as well as they know their own faces.'

'I'm sure I can think of a few places where the Church won't come across it,' the Doctor reassured him.

'I will accompany you as far as the village, before going on to Montségur. Our people there must know what has happened here.'

'I doubt the circumstances will be exactly the same there,' Benny pointed out.

'All knowledge is invaluable,' Hugues reminded her. She felt as if he used that tone to teach children in a seminary.

'It's all right, Hugues. I'm sure we can both use a rest anyway.'

'I will see you at first light, then.' Hugues walked off towards the Parfait's quarters.

'Isn't that interfering a little?' Benny asked.

'No. History is still on its proper course.'

Chapter 22

The right pauldron didn't sit quite properly over the extensive poultice that had been applied to him, but, as far as Guy was concerned, it was good enough if it went on at all. Once his armour was comfortably settled, he rather stiffly gathered up his cloak and sword, then paused, hearing footsteps approaching.

Giselle stepped through the curtain, looking on disapprovingly as he fastened his sword belt. 'The Doctor said you should rest for at least several days. A place has been prepared for you in one of the wagons.'

'The last time I was carried anywhere on a litter, my rank was stripped from me,' he growled. 'I will not be placed in any such position again.'

'The Doctor also said that the spell he cast on you – anti-boat-ticks, I believe he called it – would last less than a day, after which the pain would return. We all owe you so much that – '

'If you owe me so much, then I will reclaim it now.' Dammit, he thought, can the wench not see that I dare not tarry lest I succumb to temptation and change my mind? Of course not.

Giselle looked at him blandly. 'Your wound will probably open and eventually kill you, if you strain it too much.'

'Would it ease your fears if I promised to find an inn and rest there for several days?'

'A little, perhaps.'

'Also . . .' He faltered. Why could this not be easier? It was only words after all, not a hundred Saracen cavalry-

269

men. He'd rather have faced the Saracens than leave like this. 'Also tell the Lady Bernice that my last thoughts were of her.' And they will be, he promised himself.

Water pooled on the dark rock here and there, where drifting snow had settled just inside the tunnel opening and had been melted by the torches that were now set there. The flambeaux would be left where they were from now on. Once the Roc had capitulated, there would be no point in hiding the tunnel, since the soldiers could simply follow it down from the bailey.

Outside, a few yards ahead of the handful of people who were gathered in the wide entranceway, the previous night's snowfall was glistening like a thickly spread coating of diamond under the morning sun. None of this light reached the three people in the tunnel who were struggling with unfamiliar arrangements of straps and buckles for their journey. 'Grief,' Benny grumbled. 'This is worse than those Victorian corsets.'

'I sometimes think,' the Doctor said, putting his hat on over a mail coif, 'that you're as addicted to haute couture evening wear as any drug abuser.' He removed the hat, presumably realizing how silly it looked when worn on top of a suit of mail, and tugged on a surcoat embroidered with the de Citeaux crest. 'Failure to experiment with the latest fashion accessories for either sex at least once a week seems to give you withdrawal symptoms.'

Benny looked daggers at him, grabbing a handful of heavy steel links from the hem of her hauberk by way of effect. 'I thought we were supposed to make a fast getaway. In this knitted Cyber-suit I'll be lucky to get up on the horse in the first place.'

'Stealth and secrecy, Benny. We don't want to be apprehended and turned into human marshmallows over an Inquisition campfire, do we?'

'Then why didn't we just get some monks' habits?'

'Because no monks have come up to fight us directly,' Hugues interrupted placidly, pulling his coif over his head with a look of distaste. 'The Church did not donate this armour to us willingly.'

'Look on the bright side,' the Doctor suggested, 'we're still a few decades shy of the invention of plate armour.'

Benny refused to rise to the bait. Plate armour wasn't as heavy as people believed anyway, and – more importantly – the weight was far more evenly distributed, not just hanging down on the shoulders as mail did. Deciding that she'd just try and wistfully imagine she'd brought along a Veltrochni holosuit in the hope that she could fool her muscles into ignoring the weight, Benny lifted the sword that had been supplied with it.

Unlike Guy's sword, this was a perfectly ordinary European blade – crude, blunt and half as heavy again. Benny slung it across her back instead of belting it at her waist. The weight was easier to bear that way, so she didn't care how unusual the locals might think it was.

The Doctor looked at the sword offered to him by Hugues as if it was a grenade with the pin pulled out. He took it with a visible air of reluctance, and weighed it in his hands. Noticing Benny's attention, he drew the blade with the smile of a child about to show off a party trick, and launched into a brief but startlingly agile display of practice strokes. He stopped after the sword had danced around his wrists and carved up the air around him with at least as much ease and grace as Guy could have mustered. 'It's just another weapon,' the Doctor explained with a superior look. 'Any fool can use one of those.'

With a weary shake of her head – a gods-knew-how-old scientist should have more sense, she thought – Benny mounted the horse that had been saddled for her. This time, with both the Doctor and Hugues pointing out to the ostler that speed was essential, she had been supplied with a proper steed, rather than a pony that would be left staggering under the weight of an armoured Bernice Summerfield. She tried to look suitably surprised that she'd managed to get up on it at all.

Hugues had already settled into his saddle, and the stable-hand handed him a hatbox-sized casket whose lid

271

was firmly fastened with leather straps. Benny didn't need to be told what was in it.

'It is time,' Hugues announced. 'Let us go.'

Giselle watched the horses shrink into the distance until the stiff breeze carried away even the sound of their hoofbeats. From the hoarding at the top of the gateway tower, she could see both the three riders and the spreading mass of the besieging army. She was relieved to see, however, that a copse on a low foothill hid the trio from the crowds of soldiers gathering around the foot of the winding road that led up to the Roc. By the time they came out into view of the army, however, there would be no sign that they had come from the Roc, and the disguises would hopefully allay any suspicions.

If not, well, she would probably never even know about it. Although she knew that Hugues would consider the possibility of their failure without concern, as they would be freed from their physical bonds, something about the way the Doctor and Bernice had taken everything in their stride made her glad that she had stayed true to the principle of bettering oneself through challenging the chains of matter rather than seeking to escape them. Certainly the two of them had seemed to thrive on it without becoming servants of evil.

Still, it seemed that the sun was setting setting on Amor, its mirror image, Roma, finally completing its ascendancy. Giselle did not look forward to her own death the way some of Girard and Hugues' followers did, but she didn't fear it – there was simply nothing she could do about it, other than briefly delay it, and that didn't seem worth the bother.

She was just about to call to the Castellan's replacement to have the gates opened, when another horse burst forth from the tunnel, little explosions of snow being kicked up by its hooves as it set off after Hugues, Bernice and the Doctor. For a moment she was confused, wondering who it could possibly be. There had only been a few horses taking up the valuable room in the stables . . . The chestnut mare, however, could only belong to one person – and she had left him in the hospital with a barely wrapped crossbow wound. She shook her head, saddened that he was taking the dangerous step of throwing himself back into his normal lifestyle rather than accompanying the others downstream to rest and recuperate.

Still, she thought, it proves that Guy de Carnac cares if nothing else.

Walking along the parapet, she finally stood at the base of the few steps that led up to the raised portion over the main gate. The new Castellan, and a handful of Parfaits who were scattered across the bailey like desert oases, all looked up at her with the expectant and peaceful look of those who were resigned to their fates. She wondered if Girard, Hugues or even Jeanne would have felt as weak-kneed as she did right at this moment. Girard, of course, would have had some poetic and wise speech prepared for the inevitable, but Giselle was too straightforward to have much feeling for such things.

She nodded her head as slowly (but inexorably) as if her hair weighed as much as the copper whose colour it shared. 'Wedge the gates open, and let them come in when they will. It is over.'

She turned away to look out to the west. She didn't think she could bear to watch the hordes of undisciplined Church soldiers come for them, secure in the the knowledge that they could commit any atrocity without reproach because they were engaged in holy work.

Instead, her attention followed the mismatched foursome westward, hoping despite her professed faith that they would reach some form of safety and live to tell the tale. She didn't know how long it might take them to get a safe distance from the Roc, because she didn't know what distance was safe. All she knew was that they were now out of sight, with only the spindly trees as witness to whichever route they took.

Chapter 23

Francisco Guzman and his masked Inquisitors were moving amongst the blue-robed heretics, scribes following to take notes on the Cathares' confessions. There seemed to Guzman to be no difficulty whatsoever in obtaining confessions from them. It was unnatural the way they were so willing to co-operate without even mere words of resistance, when only a day before they would have fought to the last drop of their blood.

He didn't pretend to understand it, and he didn't care. All that mattered was that it was over, and he could get back to build his beloved cathedral. Perhaps he could even persuade King Louis to grant him the title of Count of Béziers, now that Philippe and Louis de Citeaux were but a fast-fading memory. People never stayed long in Guzman's memory, at least not after their deaths.

Simple robes sweeping past, an inch from the floor, Guzman ignored the irrelevant details of the footsoldiers packing the self-confessed heretics into the crowded stable, his ears deaf to the pleas and screams that mingled with curses and threats. Instead, his squat head turned about, searching for any sign of the young messenger whose eagerness to serve had so caught Louis' roving eye a couple of years earlier.

He saw no sign of the apothecary, either among his own men or the prisoners. 'Sergeant-at arms!'

'Yes, Eminence?'

'Which of these creatures is the leader here?'

'This one. Giselle,' the soldier replied, indicating a young woman who stood proudly, radiating calmness.

Guzman moved across to her, while the sergeant pulled her out from the prisoners in the stable, his men keeping the others from resisting the separation. 'Well, my Lady,' he began, mocking her with an ironic tone in deference to her position as leader. 'You had an apothecary here – a young fellow – yet these soldiers seem unable to locate him among you. Can you tell us where he is?' He knew he could simply torture the information out of her, of course, but he suspected that the simple courtesies would be more damning – proving his position to be so strong that he needn't bother trying to demonstrate it by force.

'Certainly,' the redhead said frostily, with what Louis suspected to be an air of relish. 'He is in the library – or, at least, such parts of him that have yet to be eaten by the crows are there.'

Guzman recoiled with a barely human snarl. That young man had shown such promise, such eagerness to please. 'You did this?'

'No. The Doctor and his friends.'

Guzman snarled. The Doctor had made a laughing stock of them all. He almost regretted having had Louis killed, as it would have been so much more satisfying to do it now. 'What of the skull? Where is it kept?'

'I do not know. Parfait Hugues and the Doctor have taken it to safety.'

'And Guy de Carnac?'

'Free, long since. Your treachery in murdering your rival will soon bring about your own downfall.'

Guzman felt the blood drain from his face. He could kill them, but he couldn't erase his own errors, or counter their claims as to the skull's origin with his own. His scheme had fallen flat, and the culprit, upon whom he should vent his ire, was long gone. 'Pervert bitch,' he spat, punching her to the ground in the absence of any better target. 'Sergeant! Burn this one firs– ' He paused, the thought of a more demeaning fate presenting itself. 'No! Burn her last – after the soldiers have tired of her.' He waved for him to take her away – which the sergeant did – a lewd grin on his face.

Joseph appeared silently at his side, a sly look on his grizzled face that suggested to Guzman that he knew exactly where Guzman's plan had gone awry. 'You are certain these are all the heretics?' he demanded, taking the initiative.

'The Roc has been thoroughly searched, and guards posted at all passages. These are all the Cathares, though some of their relatives and few mercenaries left during the night. A common failing, I understand.'

Guzman looked sharply at him. 'And how are you going to prevent these from escaping when you try to fire the Roc?'

'They are confessing willingly to your Inquisitors – that earns them the right to be burnt after death, does it not? Your people have brought insufficient scapularies, so they must die in their own robes, but I expect it does not matter to you, so long as they do die.'

Guzman spared a glance for the squirming mass of humanity pressed into the stables, and the soldiers who were carrying bundles of wood and barrels of pitch and tar across the bailey. 'Put them to the sword. We will fire the Roc once the soldiers have retreated to the valley below, where I can give a mass and benediction to give thanks for this holy victory. See to it personally, Captain; I expect the best for Church coin.'

'You get what you pay for, Eminence,' Joseph grinned.

The twig-strewn ground blurred as it disappeared under the horses' hooves and was left behind. Benny hadn't ridden a horse in some time, but it was, after all, the original version of riding a monoskid – once you learned, you never forgot. The Doctor, of course, somehow managed to appear on the verge of incompetence while still outdoing the rest of the group.

They had been following almost exactly the reverse of the course which Benny had walked to the Roc originally, but had covered the distance in far less time. Even though it had been only a couple of hours since they had galloped from the Roc, they were already clattering up the winding stretch of the stone-paved road that led to the hilltop village where she had originally separated from the Doctor. She was more than a little relieved at the prospect of getting out of the cumbersome hauberk and surcoat. Despite the climate, it was perversely sweltering her, and she had been wondering for some time how long it would be before she sweated her way into a case of frostbite.

Ahead of her, Hugues kept a firm grip on the box that was slung around his neck. He held it like a baby, she thought, and she wondered how he could possibly have failed to hear Robert's confession about its true nature. Perhaps he was simply aware of the power that the legends about it would hold, true or not. More likely, the cynical part of herself argued, he simply refused to believe what had been revealed.

It didn't matter to her, really. All that did matter was that they would be safely back at the TARDIS in minutes, and could pop back for Guy. A few minutes' treatment with the best surgical nanotechnology and he would be right as rain.

Guy de Carnac winced as what felt like the whole right side of his torso protested at his tugging of the reins. The momentary weakness allowed a wave of nausea to assail him, and he fought it down with mumbled recriminations about his own foolishness.

The Doctor knows what he is doing, he reminded himself, and will not allow Bernice to come to harm. Certainly he is fitter and better able to protect her than myself, he added mentally. Nevertheless, he was dragged along as if he were a piece of iron drawn by a lodestone, rushing after her. It was the least he could do and would at least ensure that he could be secure in the knowledge that she was safe from any acts of vengeance the Church may perpetrate.

He knew he should have made it a clean break, simply never seeing her again, but that was a coward's way out, and he could live with regret better than he could live with grief or anguish. Besides, he tried to convince himself, the route he was currently following would, within less than a day, lead him to the very passage through to Spain that he had intended to traverse originally. Once he had seen Bernice safely free and gone, he could continue on his way and make for Barcelona.

Of course, his standing watch over her was one thing, but he daren't allow her to observe him. That might cause her further distress, and, he thought ruefully, it would be his fault. To this end, he threaded his way through the trees near the top of the hills, hidden by the shadows. The pain from his wounds flared each time he pulled one way or the other to guide the horse round a tree, but it was a worthwhile price.

For this assurance, he felt, any price would be worthwhile.

The ringing of iron-shod hooves on cobblestones echoed around the split-level square as the trio of disguised riders charged under the stone archway cut into one of the village's terraced walls and slowed their mounts at the Doctor's signal.

'Should we not continue on the horses?' Hugues asked. 'They are faster than we are.'

'The footbridge across to the ridge is neither wide nor sturdy enough to support their weight,' the Doctor explained. 'Shanks' pony is the best one for us from here onwards.'

'All is smooth and sweatless,' Benny said, feeling neither. 'The bridge runs from just past the top of these steps, and the TARDIS is just around the corner on the hillside.'

'TARDIS?'

'Our safe haven. Sanctuary from our sanctuary.'

Benny's unease grew by the moment, as they looked around the village. The last time she had been here, there were Church soldiers present, and she'd seen no sign to indicate that they were definitely gone now. She walked over to the edge of the upper part of the square, looking down into the shaded lower area. The stake and its associated burning materials had been removed, but more worrying was the sight of footprints already impressed into the fresh snow.

She turned back to bring this fact to the Doctor and Hugues' attention, but they were already trudging towards the steps built into the wall of the long building that stretched out towards the peak of the hill. She hurried after them, wondering if she would be able to hold her own with the sword that had been supplied with her 'borrowed' mail. By the time she reached them, however, the Doctor was already looking round as if listening to something.

Benny paused to see if she could hear whatever it was, and was chilled, if unsurprised, to hear the clatter and jingle of rapidly approaching movement. As the noise grew to a crescendo and echoed from the sooty walls all around, three horses cantered in through the wide archway under which the soldiers had first found her and the Doctor.

These three mounts, however, were ridden by helmeted knights whose surcoats were tied with silken cords and emblazoned with a scarlet cross patée. Though they blocked the fugitives' path, they didn't draw their swords. Benny thought that their lack of overt hostility was practically a warm greeting for around here.

'Parfait Hugues,' the middle Templar greeted, inclining his head stiffly. 'We are most gratified at your escape from the Roc.' The steel cylinder of his helmet made his voice somehow both muffled and echoingly booming. It reminded Benny of the villain in an old 2-D movie she'd seen while the Doctor had once left her stuck in Oxford. 'I had begun to think that the Church would take the Roc before the relic could be delivered to us. It was beginning to worry their leaders that their spy had never reported the location of the tunnel entrance, and I had feared that our censorship of his messages may be discovered if we had to continue much longer.'

'I had hoped you may have escorted us when we left,' Hugues replied, puzzlement mingling with the relief evident in his tone. Benny relaxed a bit, but not much. 'You

279

have come for this?' Hugues tapped the box with the skull.

'That is correct. The Church will be unable to use it for their own ends while it is protected by our Order.'

'It may have escaped your notice, Darth,' Benny interrupted, 'but there are three of you and ten thousand of them . . .'

'They would not dare. Our preceptories are many, and answerable to no one.'

'Except the Pope,' Benny reminded him.

'When one is elected, yes. Until then . . . We will give you safe passage to Montségur – it is the only large fortress remaining for your people.'

'That's very kind of you,' the Doctor said, 'but my friend and I have our own way out of here. Hugues, you seem to have a choice . . .'

'I will go with the knights, Doctor. The other branches of our sect have a right to know wha– ' He fell silent, his mouth opening and closing like that of a fish. A few bubbles of frothy blood seeped down his face, and he slowly dropped to his knees. The Doctor turned and rushed into Benny with superhuman speed, shoving her through the archway as a second arrow slipped through the mail links of Hugues' armour and sent him face-first into the snowy cobbles. The leading Templar dropped low in the saddle to scoop the box with the skull out of the air before it could smash into the ground, while the knight on the left nocked an arrow of his own and loosed it.

Slapping a hand into the side of the arch to avoid crashing her face into it, Benny caught a glimpse of a de Citeaux man flipping backwards off the top of the far wall that separated the square from the tree-line. 'Run,' the Doctor snapped. Not waiting around to count the reinforcements that she could already hear running heavily in through the smaller arched gates on the other side of the church, she crouched low and bolted for the stairway.

No more arrows cut through the air, but the three Templars wheeled around and clattered out through the arch which the time travellers had just vacated. Risking a quick glance to see what was happening, Benny saw a number of de Citeaux men running into the square, trampling uncaringly over Hugues' body and converging on the base of the steps.

The disguise was no longer necessary, so Benny tugged the hauberk over her head, while still stumbling upwards, hoping that the freedom from the weight would give her an advantage over the soldiers in a straight dash to the TARDIS. Ahead, the Doctor was doing likewise, exposing a now rather rust-stained linen suit as he clambered up the steps.

'The TARDIS had better be there, or we're dead,' Benny gasped breathlessly.

'It's there, all right.'

Almost slipping several times, the Doctor and Benny continued up towards the walkway.

Fear – fear for Bernice's safety and fear of the guilt that failure would bring, should anything happen to her – fuelled Guy's urgent anger and overtook the ache from his crossbow-wound as he swept his sword free from its sheath, swinging it low as he charged into the square.

A spray of blood scythed through the air as the first soldier spun into the snow. The other stragglers who had yet to start up the steps turned towards Guy. He tugged on the reins, rearing his horse so that its waving hooves kept the men in front at bay while he hacked downwards into the heads and shoulders of those too close on either side.

A further five men had been smashed into the ground with shattered bones and torn flesh by the time Guy dropped from the saddle, landing on his feet with ease. Determination to keep this threat away from Bernice drove him on in a strangely nervous red haze. Wielding the sword in wide two-handed sweeps, its unusually keen edge sheared through the splintering links of their mail with ease under the force of his furious blows.

Visceral slime and thickening blood escaped the shattered steel to melt the snow with their fading heat. Meanwhile, Guy stalked in a dead-straight line towards the stone steps up which the soldiers were laboriously clambering only a few steps behind the Doctor and Bernice. Guy started up the steps without breaking his determined stride, even though a fire was starting to burn once more in the right side of his body.

He could already hear the delicate tinkling of the barding on distantly approaching horses, but all that concerned him was to prevent these soldiers from catching up with Bernice. It was true that she seemed able to look after herself, of course, but the odds were against her, since the soldiers were both more numerous and more used to fighting in armour. So, he would do his best to lower those odds. Besides, he thought, what is love, if it is not being more concerned for one's lover than for oneself?

By now Guy had ascended some two-thirds of the stairs, and was but a few steps from the rearmost of the de Citeaux men. The soldiers could hardly have missed the commotion below, as the buildings that surrounded the square would have caused the ring of steel upon steel and the hoarse cries of the fallen to echo upwards, and three of them had stopped to try to hold back this madman who was engaging them single-handedly.

Rather than allow the first man the chance to take advantage of having the higher ground, Guy lashed out before he was within what they would ever have called striking distance, shattering the soldier's ankle. The soldier fell forward with a scream, and Guy hunched forward to catch him on his shoulder, straightening to leave the man to roll over his shoulder and sideways off the steps altogether. There was a crash of steel on stone from below, which easily blotted out the simultaneous wet crack of skull on stone.

Guy flung himself full-length along the steps as the next man chopped downwards, overbalancing as he did so. There was a second crash from the square below, and an accompanying whinny of startled horses. Looking back down, Guy saw that more de Citeaux soldiers were riding in through the large arch, and were shouting curses as they saw the carnage that had been wrought in the square. Angry yells rose as the newcomers noticed Guy approaching the top of the step – where the last of the trio had stopped – his sword drawn.

Terrified that he might have wasted too much time on the rearguards already, despite the speed with which he had dispatched them, Guy slipped his dagger from its sheath, and swung it underhand so that it would have greater uphill momentum. True to his judgement, it speared into the last man's eye at an almost sheer upward angle. The soldier went down with a howl, and Guy didn't even spare him a glance as he passed him and dashed for the top of the steps. Only one person was in his mind, and he cared about nothing and no one else.

Benny had to consciously force herself not to pause to rejoice in the comforting sight of the familiar battered wooden police box that had replaced the Jade Pagoda on the rocky promontory overlooking the foothills to the west.

The Doctor was already digging into his pocket as he turned on to the walkway with surprising speed in spite of his short legs. Benny was less than twenty feet behind him when something slammed into her back, and she went down. Rolling free, she picked herself up as the soldier who had rammed her with his kite-shaped shield drew his sword now that she was cornered.

Recalling how she had practised aikido with the aid of a bokken wooden sword, Benny swept up the sword from her disguise with an agility born of desperation, and swung it as best she could.

The crude steel cracked the soldier's shield from the edge to the boss, and sent him reeling, the weight of his armour dragging him down. His partner reacted before the sparks from Benny's blow had hit the ground, delivering a long sweep that forced her to leap back. The handicap of his mail suit matched Benny's inexperience, so she was able to parry as he swung again, sparks exploding from the resounding crash of blades. Benny hadn't expected such a forceful impact, however, and the sword was jerked from her grip, while her palms stung. Gripping the pommel with his free hand, the soldier dragged his sword back for a final blow.

Chapter 24

The breeze that rolled through the cutting between the building and the hillside hit Guy's face like a wall as he rounded the corner on to the walkway at the top of the steps. A few yards away, a sword was spinning to the rocky earth from Bernice's hand, while a soldier in de Montfort livery was recovering from the momentum of a failed attack. He feared that there was no way Bernice could avoid her fate on her own, and the prospect was like an icy blade sliding through his chest.

He hurled himself forward. A cry of pain from the burning of his strained upper body and his fear for Bernice transformed itself into a howling war cry which caused the soldier to jerk round like a startled rabbit.

Ignoring his own mere physical pain, which was more bearable than any harm befalling Bernice could be, Guy swept up the slope towards the opening on to the narrow bridge like a dervish. The weight of the soldier's sword was such that he couldn't change the direction of his swing in time, and Guy's razor-sharp blade was able to slip inside his turn and slice through one wrist. The dark sword twisted away at an angle as the hand that guided it sailed through the air with a trail of raining blood.

The soldier's eyes widened in shock, his mouth opening to scream, but Guy knew only that this man was ready to kill Bernice, and reversed his grip on his sword to plunge it down and ram it up to the hilt in the soldier's chest before the scream could escape his lips. Guy followed the soldier down to the ground until he felt the tip of his sword hit the wooden planks under the man's back. Only then did he twist the blade in the writhing body and tug it free.

Guy finally steadied his breathing as he looked down at the still-quivering unshaven face which stared up in silent agony from the cold and wet earth. The Doctor was watching from the middle of the narrow spine of rock that led across to the hillside like a natural bridge. A strange blue hut now stood where the Mongol shrine had been, but Benny was watching him shakily with a mixture of relief and shock on her face. 'Now you see what I have become.'

'It's this place, Guy. In better circumstances you wouldn't have to – '

'Everywhere I have been is like this, Bernice. All of it.'

Bernice looked across at the Doctor, who jerked his head towards the wooden hut. Her face was anguished in its pleading. The Doctor nodded almost imperceptibly. 'It can be different,' she said hurriedly. 'Come with us, Guy. I could take you to a million wondrous places: places where you could be free of this.'

'Come in what? I see no horses or wagons, only a hut. We will not be safe in that wooden box: they will simply pile wood around and burn us together.'

'That's been tried,' the Doctor muttered in a scornful tone.

'I can't explain,' Bernice said, 'but if you have ever felt anything for me, then trust me on this. We will be safe in there.' She held out a hand to beckon him.

Guy quivered with indecision. The whole idea of seeking safety in a wooden box was ridiculous, but he couldn't refuse her appeal to his feelings. Perhaps they had some magic that would save them. I owe her my trust at least, he decided. Besides, it would be better to die together than to flee like a coward to live without her. He let slip a brief smile. 'How could I dare refuse my Lady's wishes? I will – ' He broke off as a mail-clad figure slammed into him from the roof of the building.

Guy's chest and arm exploded with pain, his sword clattering across the wooden walkway as the armoured soldier rolled aside and drew his sword. Reacting with blind instinct, Guy snatched one of the basilards from his belt, and punched under the soldier's slash with it. The triangular blade hammered through the shattered links and into the sternum below. Guy kicked him aside and dived for his sword as a dozen men swarmed up the steps, their cries the bloodthirsty baying of a pack of hunting dogs.

Keeping the basilard in his left hand while recovering his sword with the right, Guy positioned himself between the soldiers and the rock bridge. He felled the nearest man with a basilard in the face while maintaining a wide figure-of-eight sweep with the sword that forced the others to hold back for a few moments. It didn't last, however, and he had to start taking small steps back to avoid them encircling him.

'No!' Bernice shouted, lifting the nearest fallen sword. She started towards the group of men, but the Doctor grabbed her shoulder. She had been too late in any case, he reflected. Three more men had climbed over the roof, and were already in a position to cut them off from him. He risked a quick glance round, seeing that the rocky promontory on which the Doctor and Bernice stood ended only a scant yard or two to his left. It didn't take Alexander the Great to work out that they were herding Guy towards it.

'Doctor! Get her away from here!' Feinting to one side, Guy briefly broke the rhythm of his defensive pattern to smash the flat of his blade into the back of the head of the man who was closing in on the right. Arms cartwheeling wildly, he toppled off the edge of the walkway with a terrified howl. Another man appeared on the roof above, this one wielding a bow and already drawing back the string.

Guy watched with mounting rage as the archer sighted on the Doctor and Bernice; he was too far off to stop the bowman from doing whatever he liked. 'Go while you can!'

Bernice had frozen like a mouse faced by a hungry cat. 'But I –'

Guy risked taking his eyes off the soldiers for an instant to meet hers. 'I know. Go, my love. Save yourself.' There was only one way he could think of to buy her time to escape, and he could only hope she would use it wisely. Ending his defensive figure-of-eight slashes with the sword upraised in a forehand position ready for an overhead swing, he tossed the basilard aside.

Then, grasping his sword with both hands, he bolted forward into the knot of men, hammering furiously at their armour to get at the vulnerable flesh beneath. Momentarily startled, the soldiers stepped back slightly, giving him the chance to cut and slash to far deadlier effect. Several of them tumbled down the steps, and he moved on to the topmost stone slab, lifting one of the oil-lamps from its hook on the corner of the building. Luckily it was still alight, and he hurled it towards the part of the walkway that met the ridge. It burst, a sheet of flame spreading out across the walkway. Smiling emptily at the thought that the men on the roof couldn't follow the Doctor and Bernice through the flames, he descended the steps, the fiery barrier scorching his soul.

Several barrels of oil and pitch were stored at the side of the square, ready for the next executions. Lifting a small barrel, he hurled it back up the steps. It splintered, the oil within splashing down the steps. He could already hear more men running towards the square as he struck flint and steel.

A ball of fire rushed up the lower part of the steps, the flames eating away at the building's wall. Pieces of glowing ash were already starting to settle on thatched roof here and there, as Guy tried to judge from what direction the new arrivals were coming. It seemed to be from all of them, and a full dozen men were already running in through the wide archway, while horses were galloping in from the other side.

He no longer thought of them as individual opponents, because then he would have to consider numbers, but instead saw himself hacking apart a dark wall that surrounded him. All he had to do was try to break free by shattering the tightening bonds of blood and steel that were trying to crush him.

It would be no distasteful chore, however, Guy felt. The pain of his wounds was all but forgotten, but his fear had not faded. He had something to live for now, and regretted it, for having nothing to lose had always been to his advantage. His arms guiding the blade almost without conscious thought, Guy knew that he could, however, wait for her in the next life. His blood sang a resonant tonal hymn of sheer joy as he cut through the muscle and bone of those who would harm Bernice.

The cold world disappeared in a cacophony of the ring of steel upon steel, and the hot salty taste of blood and sweat in the clear mountain air. Love, fear and joy burnt together as a red haze of inner strength that banished all tiredness and pain into the darkness, where he would join them at his own leisure, either to heal or in death.

It didn't matter to him either way.

Benny broke free from the Doctor's grip, taking a few steps forward. Guy was already enmeshed in a field of mail and swords, and the troop of men blurred and shifted wildly in a haze of smoke and gut-wrenching screams and yells. She lifted the heavy sword, ready to rush to Guy's aid: it never occurred to her that it would be impossible for someone as inexperienced and outnumbered as herself to get through to him.

Abruptly, however, a firm hand spun her round and shoved her across the natural bridge. It sent her reeling through a narrow portal of darkness, an arrow clattering off the stone wall opposite, after passing through the space where her head had been. A second shaft rattled from the closing double doors as they slammed together, sealing the Doctor and Benny up in the TARDIS's tertiary console room.

Pulling herself upright, Benny dashed back for the doors, the image of Guy's battle so strong in her mind that she didn't even register the fact that the doors had closed. Bumping up against them, she looked around desperately for the door control, spurred on by that last image of Guy's silver sword flashing and dancing amidst the press of liveried soldiers. She found it in seconds, and rattled it urgently, but with no effect. Then she froze in dread as the realization crept upon her as inexorably as the newly changing tone of the TARDIS's background hum.

The tiny LEDs in their shadowed Gothic arches were winking and glimmering, while the central spire ground slowly but steadily up and down. The Doctor stood by the console, as if daring her to accuse him of dragging her off, his fingers tracing a talismanic path round the circular jade brooch he wore. 'Fighting unbeatable foes . . .'

Forcing herself to be calm and rational, she knew that she had to get back to the battlefield. 'Take us back,' she snapped, her agitation getting the better of her manners.

'I'm doing the best I can.' His fingers blurred over the controls as he entered instructions rapidly. 'There'll be an automatic time-jump to recalibrate the ship's autosystems, but I'm trying to keep it down to as short a hop as possible.'

Benny joined him, looking over the console with little understanding of what the displays there were indicating. 'We have to get back. I can't let him die!'

Joseph split the cover of the last barrel of oil with a small hatchet, and tipped the wooden cask over, sending a thick spray down the steps that led from the library down to the cellars. Rather than remove the barrel once it was empty, he kicked it down the steps after the oil. It was wood, and would burn just as well.

Outside, some squires tossed further buckets of flammables over the bodies that were scattered around the bailey and stables, before placing some of the tightly wrapped bundles of wood in positions where they would burn quickly. Occasionally, an arm would flap weakly, clutching at a passing man as its owner tried to gather the strength to cry out at the pain of his or her wounds.

The soldiers would invariably just kick the hand away, leaving it to twitch amidst the oil and blood on the wet ground.

A haze of condensation rose from beyond the gates, as several thousand men jogged back and forth through the snow, setting up cooking-fires and chopping and carrying wood here and there. The gentlest face of the Roc swarmed with a flow of humanity that matched any summer anthill Joseph had ever seen.

All the sounds that carried through the morning, however, came from outside the Roc. Inside, there was no longer any speech or sounds of work or cooking. Inside, even the dying faded silently.

A brazier had been set up out in the bailey, and already men were dipping pitch-coated torches into it. Joseph did likewise, carrying a flaming club back to the doorway, and tossing it down into the darkness. Immediately, with a rushing of displaced air, orange fire swept back towards him, and he had to jump back quickly. All over the Roc, torches were being thrust into bundles of dry wood, tossed into slicks and pools of oil, or touched to patches of pitch and tar smeared across the walls.

Joseph was an old hand at sieges, and knew that even stone could burn, eventually shattering, until the walls would topple. Then the heresy would be truly ended. Personally, he wasn't concerned whether it was ended or not, so long as there was plenty of booty for him and his inherited troop.

As the fires burst into life, spreading their grip throughout the stone warren, the air in the cellars thickened. Acrid smoke roiled and swelled with the earthy tang of scorched wood counterpointing the choking greasy stench of bubbling flesh from the dead or dying in the bailey and stables above. Wisps chased each other along the ceiling like playing children before the full churning cloud rolled through the stone passages in an almost solid and ethereally thrashing mass.

Smouldering sparks carried by the air current started secondary flames in patches of straw, the damp proving surprisingly little obstacle.

Whether the playful motion of the smoke was due to it comprising the freed spirits of the others, or the sooty remnants of burnt fat, Jeanne didn't know. All she did know was that she would soon be a part of it. She had heard the screams of those burnt alive in towns throughout the countryside, and would have given anything to avoid it – she would have preferred to die in any other fashion.

She knew she deserved to die for what she had done, but was equally certain that she had had to do those things. She knew Bernice and Guy wouldn't have understood, but they were not parents. They had not had to watch their children leave to become slaves with the prospect of dying a beggar and outlaw the only alternative. She couldn't let that happen to them, could she? Perhaps Girard and Hugues were right, and bringing new life into the world *was* just increasing the pain and darkness. She hoped that that wasn't true. She also hoped she would suffocate in the smoke before the fire began to cause her flesh to blister and run. The terror of the alternative was overpowering, tormenting her with screams from other fires, while Girard's features smiled beatifically in the darkness.

Between the thick stone and the crackling of the fires amidst the obscuring smoke, no one would ever hear her screams.

Francisco Guzman spread his arms wide in a theatrical beseechment to the Lord, silhouetted by the spears of dawn sunlight which lanced through a cutting in a neighbouring mountainside to illuminate his carefully chosen spot. He was also not unaware of the fact that his stance would make him appear to be summoning the smoke that rose from the Roc before him, and darkening the sky.

It was a worthwhile image, he thought, if it helped

reassure the people of their faith. A few feet down the rocky path, watching over the field of glinting mail and grubby livery that was hooked on Guzman's every movement, was Joseph, with a thin smile on his face. Guzman paid him no heed, however, knowing that he was only going through the motions. All he would be thinking about inside was how to get more money. Guzman didn't mind this, feeling that honourable payments were a fitting tribute to those who bravely fought this heresy. De Carnac was still a problem, but he was but one man, and a failed knight at that, so who would believe him? His first act as Pope would be to build a new cathedral in Béziers: a place of joy at his having cleansed the souls of the heretics of their filth so that they could be accepted into God's kingdom.

He wondered when would be the best moment to announce his ascension to the Holy See. After this victory, and the fact that his only rival had given his life against the heretics, albeit unwittingly, it was only a matter of time.

Guzman nodded to the Dominicans gathered on the ledge below, and they started to sing. Raggedly, in fits and starts, the soldiers in the valley below started to sing as well, their rough voices adding an earthy power to the eerie chant. Guzman couldn't help but join in, swept away by the emotions that the singing unleashed.

On the hilltop opposite, three Templars watched impassively. 'The Cardinals have been told of his treason?'

'Yes, preceptor. We even have the archer who killed de Citeaux in our dungeon.'

'Excellent. I knew we could not expect a challenge from such amateurs to politics. Did they really think we would allow either of them to gain power here? No, our censorship of any mention of the tunnel from their agent's messages has kept the Roc safe long enough for our rivals to finish each other off, rather than cement their alliance with a victory. And, of course, we have this holy relic. . .'

He patted the box with the skull. 'Let us return to the preceptory, and choose our candidate for the Holy See.'

'And de Carnac?'

'Will be remembered with honour, whatever happens to him.'

Smoke stung Benny's eyes as soon as she stumbled out of the TARDIS's door, and waves of heat rolled over her despite the snow. She had been standing in the square just a few steps from the TARDIS for several seconds before she realized that her legs weren't working and that she was no longer moving.

Scattered timbers and chunks of masonry were spread all around the square, the flames that wrapped them obscuring the vague shapes of the various bodies that were slumped between the burning skeletons of the buildings. The village square was as hot as the centre of an oven, but Benny still felt cold, her thoughts and emotions churning as darkly as the thick smoke.

He had cared after all, she knew. Somehow, she was used to that from him. Some part of her mind told her that his loss was sad, but that there would be others. Until now, she had believed it.

'He might have got out,' the Doctor said quietly. 'His horse isn't here: he could be anywhere within a dozen square miles by now.'

'And if he didn't? The soldiers' horses are gone, too. Perhaps they captured it or it ran from the flames.' There had been so many men opposing him. Too many. The Doctor didn't answer, which didn't surprise her – what *could* he have said? Some speech about noble self-sacrifice, no doubt.

She didn't want to hear it.

The smoke had faded into a grey blur, and she couldn't really have said whether it was through tears, detachment or even whether her eyes were still closed, though the gentle hum that pervaded the air indicated that she had returned to the TARDIS. She didn't even remember doing so. The normally atmospheric stone had never seemed such a cold and hollow shell, and neither had she.

The cynical part of her mind that had so often held her in good stead against the wonders she'd seen in her time in the TARDIS. She knew Guy would have been cut to pieces in seconds, and it numbed her to the core. She hadn't realized it was possible to feel so cold and lonely, with no other emotions intruding, and she longed not to be realizing it now. *If there's an awkward way of doing things, I'll find it.* How typical to be able to recognize, well, love, only in hindsight. Only when the pain showed it up for what it was. The Doctor had seen it, of course, she realized, even though she hadn't.

She was wide awake, but could already feel the memories weaving themselves into nightmares around her. More bad memories and bad dreams for her collection, as if Vandor Prime, Kyle, and all the suffering and deaths she'd seen on her travels hadn't left her enough of those already.

Its mathematically generated environment poised, and spread across all the possibilities of the universe, the TARDIS was at rest. The Doctor had wrapped Benny in a thermal blanket with visible concern, as shock took hold of her. She shook as if all the energy in her body was being drawn from maintaining temperature and circulation and was being rerouted into trying to prop up her emotions.

'We could go back after the fires have burnt themselves out,' the Doctor offered. 'At least you would know, one way or the other. . .'

Intellectually, of course, she knew that even if he survived the battle he would have died twelve hundred years before she was even born. At least, however, she wouldn't have to see his torn and scorched flesh cooling in the mud. Perhaps, she thought sadly, he might even have found the life of peace he had wanted.

At least, she could believe that he had – if she didn't know better. She knew she didn't want to know any better.

He had challenged the soldiers with such energy and vitality that she could easily imagine him sweeping

through them and making a daring escape, perhaps jumping from the wall as she had about a thousand years ago,
or so it felt. That was a better image to risk seeing every
time she closed her eyes than one of a corpse.

The thought hurt with each breath, as if her lungs were
wounded. She shook her head, needing to free herself
from the ties to the battlefield. If she didn't find a way to
face up to never seeing him again, she would go mad. The
decision was painful, but she had to at least prevent him
from having given himself for nothing. A phrase flashed
through her mind – until I see a body, he's not dead.
Perhaps, she hoped, she could convince herself that this
was a truism. She opened her eyes, to find the Doctor
watching her worriedly. 'He's still alive, as far as we know.
I couldn't face knowing any further, not so soon. Do you
understand how it feels?' She knew she was anything but
the only person ever to feel such enforced and sudden
emptiness, but it was a lonely feeling and she needed
understanding more than anything. She wished Ace was
still here – she would have understood.

'Perhaps,' he said neutrally, his expression never
wavering.

'Then set the controls for somewhere far away from
here. Somewhere I can take my mind off it all.' She knew
that if she was left to her own devices she would brood
for weeks on end, and she knew that that road led to
trauma and depression. She'd be damned if she'd let herself slip into that. Guy wouldn't have wanted that – he'd
have wanted her to sing songs about him.

'Take your mind off it? Exciting diversions, of course!
How about Blackpool – I meant to go once before, but
never quite got there.'

His usually infectious enthusiasm washed over her like
water from a duck's back, perhaps because it was so obviously intended to try bringing her out of her shell. She
half-expected him to try crushing a lager can against his
forehead to convince her to smile again. She wondered
just how diverting something would have to be to dull the
pain. It was worse this time that it had been with Kyle.

At least with betrayal you had someone to blame, and pass the bad feelings on to.

She felt that she'd never really leave this place behind, not inside. 'Whatever. Let's just get the hell out of here.'